Nigel Farndale is a features writer for the *Sunday Telegraph Magazine* and was named 'Interviewer of the Year' at the British Press Awards 2000.
He has worked as a tractor driver, a ballet critic and for *Country Life*, as an environment correspondent.
He is married and lives in London.

NIGEL FARNDALE

A SYMPATHETIC HANGING

Quartet Books

First published by Quartet Books Limited in 2000
A member of the Namara Group
27 Goodge Street
London W1P 2LD

A catalogue record for this book is available from the British Library

ISBN 0 7043 8141 9

Phototypeset by FiSH Books, London
Printed and bound in Great Britain by CPD (Wales) Ltd, Ebbw Vale

For Mary and Alfie

A SYMPATHETIC HANGING

One

Such a flat and sunless month, November. It's barely gone four and already I've had to flick my headlights to full. They don't help much. The drizzle that has been my companion all afternoon has turned to sleet. And the car is raked with mud. Even in a summer drought the roads in rural North Devon contrive to be muddy. In winter they are like Passchendaele – whiz-bangs, barbed wire, mustard gas.

My editor has sent me down here to interview a faith healer who specializes in treating racehorses. As I try to see through the brown smears on the windscreen, I think how much I'd like to bury an ice-pick in the cranium of this editor. I wouldn't mind embedding one in the faith healer's skull, too. But I can't find her village. I can't even see a sign that tells me the narrow road I'm on is the same one referred to in the hand-written directions on the fax. And already I'm an hour and a half late.

The rain eases and the wipers, stuck on the intermittent setting, squeak against the glass. I know the washer is empty – it's one of the reasons I've asked Mark, some child on work experience, to put his double first to good use and book my car in for a service – but I press the button anyway. When it makes a plaintive rasp I slap the steering wheel and shout: '*Useless tosser!*'

Steering with my wrists and forearms, I peel the wrapper off a smoked salmon sandwich and curse myself for leaving the faith healer's number on my desk in London. Distracted in this way, I don't pay much attention to the coverage of the State Opening of Parliament being broadcast live on the radio. As the reception is poor, I even turn it down a touch and concentrate on holding the top slice of bread open so that I can squeeze some lemon juice onto the salmon.

I take in, though, the commentator's regrets about the absence of the First Lady – she is in Sydney, he says, opening a new hospital. I smile to myself as he points out that the broadcast of the State Opening of Parliament is being sponsored this year by Nescafé, and make gagging noises when he notes how many of 'the people' have braved the rain in order to line the route of the PM's familiar walk from Number 10 to the House of Commons. He adds something about the crowd being supplied with little laminated flags to wave: the cross of St George on one side, the circle of twenty-six gold stars on the other.

The first indication that something is wrong comes when the commentator says that the Premier has dropped his umbrella. When he adds that our leader has collapsed to the ground and is surrounded by policemen, I jab a finger at what I think is the volume control. It's the frequency search and, as I prod again, I take my eyes off the road.

For about ten seconds after my car lurches to a halt, I gape at the body in the rear-view mirror. It, she, is lying on a grassy verge a few metres away from where her bike has come to rest in the middle of the road. Her skirt is rucked up over her midriff.

I guess I hold my breath in those few seconds because only when my lungs force me to gasp do I become aware of a tinny sound in the distance. Looking down, I see two palms pressed against the horn pad on my steering wheel. When my arms unlock, the noise stops. And when the card is slipped out of the ignition, and the scraping of the wipers also ceases, the rhythmic patter of icy raindrops on glass can be appreciated.

In front of me there is a sign which reads: 'Caution – mud!' and mentally I change it to: 'Caution – statement of the blindingly obvious'. I check the time on the car digital clock – a habit acquired after years of wishing I could contribute something useful to *Crimewatch England* – just as the numbers 16:16 click up. This would make a good pivotal moment in someone's life, I think. It's symmetrical. It feels auspicious.

My arms are tingly, I feel nauseous. My heart is palpitating, going so fast I'm sure I'm going to have a cardiac arrest – a common fear, I believe, among those of us about to turn forty. Otherwise, I'm uninjured. I catch sight of my reflection in the mirror and contemplate in an abstract way the dark, puffy bags under my eyes. I have the sort of features usually described as lupine: long face, wide mouth, ashen pallor and, when they are not shot with blood, eyes of hazel-grey. With one finger I pull down the bag under my right eye and stick out my furred tongue.

Hysterical displacement, it's called.

My knitted linen jacket has been pitched forward off the passenger seat. As I duck my head to get out of the car – having been six foot five since I was about three, I always duck, even when I don't need to – I grab the jacket by its collar and, in the same sweep, hold it open above my head. I hesitate. The urge to impose order, to think clearly, must begin with the trivial. I must look for something else to use as an umbrella. The jacket is Nicole Farhi. But this is an emergency and, anyway, it is made of intelligent microfibres. I take a step forward and stop again. I must check my car for damage. I drive a hand-built Aston Martin Volante – a present from my wife, Amanda – and it means a lot to me. More than Amanda herself, actually. I walk round to the front and drop to my knees. There is a dent just above the radiator grille, but nothing that can't be beaten back into shape.

My thoughts catch up with the young woman. She is lying on her back. When I reach her, all I can do is stare in unfocused panic. A thousand tiny fists are pummelling me in the solar plexus.

It's often the case that witnesses to a crime are unable to remember quite basic characteristics of a suspect – whether he was wearing glasses, what colour his hair was, even whether he had a beard. I'd never understood how the faculties of observation could be so impaired – until this moment. If I looked away from my cyclist now I wouldn't even be able to say with confidence if she had a Groucho Marx mask on or not. I would, however, be able to tell you the colour of her knickers. Black.

As delicately as I can, with thumb and forefinger, I take hold of the hem of her skirt – a kilt, green and blue tartan, my mind now latching on to the odd detail – and tug it down as far as it will go, which is a couple of inches shy of her knees. Her 16-hole DMs come half-way up her calves. Inside them are thick woollen socks pulled up almost high enough to meet the kilt – but not high enough to prevent the gravel burns on her skin.

Although under her leather jacket she's wearing a fleecy waistcoat, this is unbuttoned all the way down to reveal nothing more than a white vest which barely covers her ribcage. I can now see that she has a silver ring in her belly button and the skin through which it has been forced looks bruised and sore, as though it's been pierced recently and hasn't had time to heal. The vest, now soaked, is clinging to her slender breasts, revealing that her nipples are also pierced with rings – and that she isn't wearing a bra.

I spin round, paranoid that someone might be watching me staring at her. The cyclist could be dead for all I know – and I might be responsible for her death – and I'm worrying that a passer-by might think me a pervert. I turn back to her and continue staring, trying to control my excitement and anxiety. Should I put her in the recovery position? What *is* the recovery position? The only unscrambled thought I can manage is that I probably shouldn't attempt to move her in case she has a spinal injury.

I feel sick with guilt and shock. My eyes are watering, my hands shaking. I have a tingling sensation in my groin, an urge to urinate. And I've started talking to myself: '*I've killed her. I've killed her. I've killed her.*'

The pager attached to my waistband goes off, prompting me to lope back to my car. On the new PowerBook G21 – which, after much lobbying, I have managed to persuade my office to invest in on my behalf – there's a satellite phone attachment, no bigger than a pen. But I have left the laptop on my desk, with a yellow Post-it carrying the faith healer's phone number stuck to its screen. Fortunately, I keep one of those old WAP mobiles in the glove compartment. It's only as I pull the aerial out with my teeth and tap the memory button for the newsroom – that's the message on the pager, 'phone the newsroom' – that I realize I could be using the mobile to call for an ambulance instead.

When the operator asks me where the paramedics should drive to I remember I don't know where I am. 'In Devon,' I say, panting heavily. 'In the countryside.' I picture my beloved laptop again and think of the Global Positioning System installed on it – which I haven't yet got round to learning how to use.

I look for inspiration at the bulging, inky-black clouds – and I shield my eyes against the vertical billiard cues raining down from them. For some reason, perhaps so that I can be specific about one thing at least, I look at my watch. 'It's 4.22,' I say, adding unnecessarily, 'in the afternoon.'

The mobile bleeps at me to indicate that its batteries are nearly dead and so, with unsteady hands, I rummage around the litter on the back seat – food-wrappers, newspapers, a collection of toy dinosaurs that used to belong to my daughter – looking for the portable charger. I hear in my head the voice of my wife asking if she can borrow it for her car.

There is a village about four kilometres behind me. Recalling this, I place the Aston Martin's two portable hazard signs in the middle of the road, equidistant either side of the bicycle, tear a page out of my Filofax, write on it, 'Have gone for help. Time: 4.24', run back to the young woman, tuck the note into the breast pocket of her leather jacket, nod to myself as I appreciate for the first time what a handsome face she has, pull her bike off the road on to the verge, and drive back to the village which, it turns out, is called Mowbray. 'About four kilometres west of Mowbray', I think, should be enough for the ambulance driver to go on.

On the village green stands one of those red, listed phoneboxes, surprisingly little vandalized and almost entirely free of the smell of urine. I dial 99911 again and am told that, because the nearest hospital is in Exeter, twenty-five kilometres away, they will be sending an air-ambulance and that I should wait by the car with my hazard lights on and not attempt to move the injured woman. When they ask me to cover her up with a blanket, if I have one, the image of pale, goosepimpled thighs and a delta of black material melts its way into my thoughts.

I pat my pockets for some Nurofen, find none and open the door to take a deep gulp of air. My head clears. I then phone the Freefone number for the *English People* and ask to be put through

5

to Alan Cameron, the dysfunctional Glaswegian who runs the newsdesk.

It takes about three minutes before Miss Monotone – as his hundred-year-old secretary is known – answers.

'I've been involved in an accident,' I say. 'Can I have a word with Alan?'

'I think he's a bit tied up at the moment.' She holds out the phone so that I can hear him screaming that he doesn't care whether the First Lady is in fucking Australia which is ten fucking hours ahead, he wants a fucking quote from her right this fucking minute.

The secretary retains her usual eerie calm. 'I think he was paging you to ask if you can get on the next flight out to Bucharest,' she says.

'What's going on? I was listening to the State Opening of Parliament. Has something happened to the Prime Minister?'

'We're supposed to call him Premier.'

'Premier, then.'

'He's been shot.'

'*Fuck!*'

Silence.

'Shot?'

'Shot.'

'*Fuck!*... By who?'

'Whom.'

'By whom?'

'That is the question.' Miss Monotone lowers her voice. 'I'd better get off the line. I'm being frowned at here. Shall I tell Alan you can go to Bucharest?'

'*Jesus!* The Prime Minister of England gets shot and I get sent to Hungary?'

'I think you'll find it's in Romania.'

'He wants me to cover the UN summit out there, right?'

'Must do.'

'What about this faith healer I'm supposed to be interviewing down here?'

'Have to ask Alan.'

'Do I need a visa for Romania?'

'Have to ask the foreign desk.'

Five minutes later I park my car at the spot where I'd run into the cyclist. The rubber marks are there on the wet road, the hazard signs have been cleared away to the verge, but she and the bike have disappeared.

Two

Even though time warps and slows down during an accident –
something to do with a delay in the electrical impulses that
transmit information from the retina to the brain – it isn't slow
enough for me to prevent the car from slewing from one side of
the road to the other. I have my foot hard down on the brake and
my hands are pulling the steering wheel from left to right to avoid
running over the woman a second time. She is lying in the middle
of the road again – she must have recovered temporarily, got back
on her bike and cycled on a hundred metres or so around the next
bend before collapsing.

Now my car is in a hedge. I turn the engine off, flick my hazard
lights on and collect a brown-and-red-striped blanket, covered in
dog hairs, from the boot. This time she is lying in the middle of
the road and, as I drape the blanket over her and check she's still
breathing, I notice that, with creepy symmetry, it's the bike's turn
to come to rest on the grass verge. As its back wheel is still
spinning, I walk over and place the sole of my loafer flat against its
spokes. I begin to shiver – partly from delayed shock, partly
because I'm in my shirtsleeves and I've just stepped out of a warm
car into the freezing rain. I feel as if I'm having an out-of-body
experience and, disconnected in this way, I consider taking the
blanket back – but instead I become distracted by a metallic

buzzing coming from the young woman's long, matted hair.

Realizing that she's listening to a Walkman through earphones, I tease the wires from her, slip the plugs into my own ears, and become entranced by the sound of classical music. It is vaguely familiar – a moment where the strings well up and then melt away – but I have to look through the Perspex front of the personal stereo to find out that it's Elgar's Cello Concerto. For several minutes I straddle the woman, studying her face, listening to the strings soar and subside.

It may be the fading light but her complexion looks sallow and the smoothness of her skin is exaggerated in contrast to the violence inflicted on it by the one ring in her nose and the three in her right eyebrow. I haven't noticed until now that she's wearing glasses: wire-rimmed, flecked with rain. I kneel down beside her and peel them off. Though her eyes are closed, I can see they are large and almond-shaped. She has long, feathery lashes. And though she seems not to wear make-up, nor care about keeping her faint moustache in check, her plump lips are parted enough to reveal a smear of lipstick on her teeth.

With the back of my hand, I brush a strand of sodden hair away from her brow. It is braided with tiny red, yellow and green beads and from this close an oily smell can be detected rising from it. I begin to stroke her hair, slowly, in time to the strings undulating through the earphones. After a few minutes, I stop, sniff my fingers, lean forward and kiss her softly on the lips. It's a protective kiss, the sort I placed on my daughter's forehead when she was leaving for school. 'I'm sorry,' I whisper. 'I am so so sorry.'

From this close I can see some freckles dotted around her raised cheekbones. Cupping her cold face in my hands I brush my thumbs up and over them. I don't know whether it's the affecting music, or the sudden thought that she might actually die, here, with her angel face framed by my fingers, but my vision becomes blurred with tears. A hot trickle on my cheek mingling with the cooling drops of rain. 'It was an accident. I didn't see you. What were you doing out here, in the middle of nowhere, when it's almost dark?' I kiss her again, on her brow this time. 'I'm sorry, I'm sorry, I'm sorry,' I repeat. Another kiss, lingering, on her lips. Her eyes blink wide open for a second. I withdraw my hands and jump to my feet in one fluid movement.

I now hear the throaty rattle of a tractor approaching from the other side of the hedge and take out the earphones to listen properly. I barely have time to straighten out the young woman's skirt before a large, ruddy face appears over the tendrils of blackthorn. The man, who must be standing on the front tyre of his tractor, takes off his flat cap, wipes his brow with a hairy forearm, replaces the cap and shouts above the noise of the engine: 'She all right?' He nods towards the woman.

'There's a helicopter coming to take her to the hospital.'

'Exeter?'

'Yeah.'

The farmer gets back in his cab, reverses along the hedge for about fifty metres and gets out again to let himself through a gate. As the tractor comes toward me scattering bullets of mud with its tyres, I try to work out whether its driver could have seen me with my lips pressed against the woman's. I'm sure he hasn't — it's dark now — but, as he hooks my towbar up with a chain, I think I catch him darting a suspicious glance in my direction. Perhaps farmers dart suspicious glances as a matter of course.

'I already seen her,' he says, revealing himself, at close quarters, to be armed with a broad Devonshire accent. 'I was driving along this road and when I sees her sitting on the grass, in the rain and that, I asks if she were all right. She nods at me and gets back on her bike. But I could see she isn't, right, so I cuts back across the fields and phones for the police from my house.'

'Very public spirited of you,' I say. I don't mean it to sound as sarcastic as it comes out.

'That's a fancy machine you got there,' he says looking across at where my Aston Martin has mounted the hedge, its racing green paintwork almost camouflaging it.

I shrug and smile back at him.

'You from London?'

I nod distractedly.

'Need a pull?'

'Thanks. That would be kind.'

'No problem. It'll cost you, mind.'

I look in my wallet. 'I've only got a two-hundred-euro note.'

'Any dollars?'

'A fifty.'

'That'll do.'

When I unroll it and hand it over, the farmer jumps back on his tractor, drives up to my car and begins hooking a chain carelessly on to the rear bumper. I cringe at the sound of scraping metal. Car headlights approach from the opposite direction and, as the driver of the car sees the body in the middle of the road, he stops and switches on his hazard lights in what strikes me, perhaps uncharitably, as a smug manner: 'Only doing my bit' is how the hazard-light-flasher will surely relate events later in the pub, or the brothel, or wherever it is these bucolic types take their pleasure. Mr Hazard Lights is followed by a dirty white van and, soon after, a police Mercedes, a discreet Tesco logo on its door. Its blue light is flashing but its siren is off.

Soon after, the helicopter arrives, circles the site of the accident with its search light casting a long beam, and lands in the field from which the tractor has just emerged. The farmer sits down on the wet verge, pulls a bar of chocolate from his top pocket, breaks off a piece and eats it as he watches the ambulance crew follow his route back up the mud-spattered road with their stretcher. He continues staring until the paramedics attach a neck brace to the cyclist; then he seems to lose interest and ambles back to his tractor.

I'm joined by two policemen, one middle-aged, red-nosed and jowly, the other sensitive-looking and still in his teens. 'You knock her over, then?' asks the older of the two, a sergeant, as he turns his collar up against the rain.

'Twice,' I say. 'Well, nearly.'

'How'd it happen, then?'

'Skidded. Mud on the road. Think I must have been distracted by the news.'

'Both times?'

'No. Second time, I thought that the woman had been abducted.'

The sergeant raises an insouciant eyebrow, reads me my rights, tells me to repeat what I've just told him, by way of a statement, and asks me if I'm the owner of the vehicle, which he pronounces 've-hicle'. As I'm explaining, for some reason, that it was a present from my wife, the younger policeman reads off the numberplate into a radio mike attached to his cap by a concave wire. The sergeant rips a tube from a clear plastic packet, screws it on to a breathalyser pack and hands it to me.

'There was mud on the road,' I repeat after I've blown into it. We both stare at the tube for thirty seconds until a green light shows that I haven't been drinking.

'We'll be needing a full statement later,' the sergeant says. He surveys the road. 'There *is* a lot of mud. Usually accidents around here are caused by people forgetting to drive on the right. It takes us longer to get used to these things out in the country. Not like you city people. I am right in thinking you are from London? Fancy car like that.'

I pull my wallet out of my back pocket, flip it open and hand him a business card. He holds it at arm's length, pretending to focus, and then purses his lips in mock admiration. 'Michael Yates. Senior Executive Editor. *The English People*,' he reads out loud.

I smile at him tightly and blink, trying to disguise a frisson of embarrassment I'm feeling at having insisted, during my last pay review, on the word 'Senior' being included in my job title.

'I presume we can contact you on this number, can we?'

'Sure.'

'Well, Michael Yates, Senior Executive Editor of *The English People*, you may as well bugger off.'

'The car is registered to him, sarge,' blurts out the young constable with unnecessary gravitas.

I sniff. 'I'll be off then.' I turn to leave.

The sergeant grabs my arm. 'Personally I don't read them posh broadsheets,' he says, obliging me to turn round again. 'I'm an *Evening Mirror* man myself.'

'Owned by the same company.'

'Y'know, Mr Yates, I didn't know that.'

'Well...' I can't think of anything else to add to the discussion. 'It is.'

The helicopter blades throb back to life and the machine hovers for a moment, its nose dipped, before moving off and scattering a herd of Friesians that have gathered in the next field but one. As it is swallowed up by the bruised clouds, I think, rather portentously: '*God forgive me.*'

Which is odd because, although I'd say I have a religious temperament, I have no belief whatsoever. Indeed, if I weren't so cowardly and superstitious I'd say I was an atheist.

'Think she'll be all right?' I say, chewing my lip.

'Hope so. More than can be said for the PM, eh?'

I frown and nod my head gravely.

'Poor bastard. And him with that big family. Who'd you reckon done it?'

'*That* is the question,' I say, repeating the line Miss Monotone had used on me.

'Reckon it might have been the Micks.'

'Possibly.'

'Or that fox-hunting lot. Been having no end of bother with them down here.'

I am eager to get back to my radio to hear some opinions that are better informed. But as I walk back to my car, I notice a mirrored shoulder bag lying in the ditch. I look back to check the policeman isn't still watching me – he is wheeling, as best he can, the mangled bike to his Mercedes – before I pick it up and rummage inside.

There's a box of tampons, an embroidered silk pouch in the shape of a kidney, a tube of lipstick, a pocket diary made from rice paper and covered in doodles and a cot rabbit which has been chewed and stroked until it's gone greasy and bald. I hold it to my nose. Her scent.

There is nothing in the bag with her name on it.

When I hear someone running up behind me, I open my car door, toss the bag on the floor behind the seat and begin flicking stray thorn branches off the roof. The airbag on my steering wheel chooses this moment to belatedly inflate.

'One last thing, Mr Yates,' the sergeant says, resting his hand on his holster and eyeing the airbag thoughtfully. 'Can you tell me what time you knocked her over?'

'Yes, I can. I can. It was 4.15. *Exactly.*'

I derive an indecent measure of satisfaction from watching him make a note of this in his book. And circle it – twice – just as a large bead of rainwater drips off the peak of his cap and on to the page, causing the ink to run.

Three

Beyond the high railings of St Thomas' Hospital on the south side of Westminster Bridge, the PM is still in intensive care. But as far as the presenters on the BBC Breakfast News are concerned, the process of deification has already begun. They are broadcasting images of 'the people' building shrines of photographs, candles and crucifixes. It is still raining in London and the floral tributes that normally look mawkish on these occasions actually present an affecting spectacle.

As a young man I had a mental image of myself: raffish, Byronic, alone with my melancholic thoughts on a wind-ravaged moor. But over the years I've been told that I'm shallow often enough to accept now that I probably am. This isn't just the vanity of self-deprecation. Like being told you can't dance, or you have no taste or no sense of humour, it's a tough one to swing with. And there's one literary quote which, ever since I had to write an essay about it as a student at Bristol, I've always rather resented being too insensitive to get: 'Yet each man kills the thing he loves'. What does it actually mean? As I switch off the television and call up the front page of the *English People* on my home computer, I realize I still don't know the answer.

All the other heavies – *Guardian*, *FT*, *London Times* – show the same fuzzy image of the PM falling to the ground, surrounded by security guards. We have run with a crisp, half-page close-up of the First Lady, looking like a wide-mouthed frog as she tries to smile bravely for the cameras. She is wearing a pashmina and a photo-opportunity bush hat trimmed with corks on strings. A single tear trickles down her cheek. The opening paragraph begins: 'When asked why she thought anyone would want to try and kill her husband, the First Lady replied simply: "I don't know. I suppose every man kills the thing he loves."'

The headline says: 'We never got a chance to say goodbye.' The caption below says: 'Devastated: the First Lady, moments after she heard the news yesterday.' God, no wonder we have the highest circulation of any paper in the US of E.

I call up the front page of our sister paper, the *American People*, and see that they have run with the same image. As I read the story under the photograph I finish off a Chinese takeaway from the fridge.

Before she left on her early-morning flight to Australia, the First Lady adds, she had crept out of bed without waking her husband up to say goodbye. She had thought he looked tired and needed his rest.

I put down untouched the forkful of cold sweet and sour pork, the lump in my throat too big for me to even think about swallowing. I feel depressed and flat, a condition not helped by lack of sleep. Most of the night I lay awake thinking about the cyclist.

Having been told by the foreign desk that I can't pick up my visa from the Romanian embassy until 5.30 in the afternoon, I drive into the daycare centre, as our office is known, to catch up on the gossip and to watch the news as it's being relayed across the six widescreen television sets that line one wall of our open-plan newsroom. These are permanently tuned to six different channels – the only six, out of the fifteen hundred or so available, worth watching.

When the *English People* was launched five years ago, it took over the offices vacated by the *Independent* – a paper it had bought, only to close down – as well as those of the *Telegraph*, after its publication was suspended under New Labour's Hate Crimes Bill. These offices are now located on the thirty-third to the thirty-ninth floors of Canary Wharf. From them you can look down on the Millennium Dome Shopping Experience. And on the other side of the tower you have a panoramic view of the Thames as it meanders towards Tower Bridge.

It's customary for people who work in Docklands to spend about five minutes – certainly no longer than it takes them to hang up their coats, check their voice-mail, e-mail and video-mail and turn on their telecomps – complaining about their journey in. However, since the Northern Line extension opened alongside the existing Jubilee Line, journey times have become much shorter and workers have had to resort to moaning about how pleasantly mild and boring the climate is these days. One reason I still drive in, I suppose, is I'm a traditionalist. I like to complain.

The first person I have a chance to moan to is Miss Monotone. She seems not to be listening as I tell her about the appalling traffic and, when the lift doors open, she looks up and says 'Hello, Michael' to me with an air of distraction that would cut a deeper man to the quick. She almost breaks into a brisk walk as she crosses reception and arrives at the frosted-glass entrance doors to our floor.

'Here, use mine,' I say, as she rummages around in her handbag for her Multicard.

'What? Oh thanks.'

I wave my Multicard in front of the black box by the door but the red light declines to turn to green. Miss Monotone finds hers and presses it flat against the box, but this has the same effect.

'Fucking thing.' Miss M says it under her breath. I have never heard her swear before. Indeed I have never heard her have any reaction to anything before and I am rather impressed by the way she crisply enunciates the 'g' in fucking. Perhaps she is warm blooded after all.

As we wait for a security man to let us in, we stare dumbly at the framed advert on the wall. It is one of the original ones run at the time the Multicard was first introduced. 'Other cards are smart,' the slogan goes. '*This one is a genius.*' The blurb underneath describes how this new wonder card is the only one you will ever need: it is your passport, credit card, security card, driving licence, car key, house key. Anything from your membership of the library to the AA can be added to it. It will even store your vital statistics, it adds, so that when you visit a clothes shop, the models in your holographic fashion show can be built to your proportions.

The advert neglects to mention that your every transaction, movement and misdemeanour will be stored away on some computer disk somewhere and that owning one of these cards will mean sacrificing your privacy for ever and making your whole life history available to anyone who wants to know about it: from policemen to insurance salesmen and burglars. It also fails to point out that, since the Government made owning a Multicard compulsory, you can neither function properly nor officially exist without one. And that the bastard thing rarely works.

A queue has built up by the time the security guard arrives and once he's overridden the door lock there's almost a charge to join the thirty or so reporters and section editors huddled around the six TV sets. Normally when there's a rolling news story which everyone on the paper has gathered around to watch, it's accompanied by cynical banter. Today everyone watches in silence. Most, having worked through the night, look tired and pale. Some shake their heads and loosen their ties. Others hold their hands to their mouths.

Because the screens are set ten feet apart and angled slightly towards the editor's office, it is possible to watch six different viewpoints of the shooting simultaneously. The head of the assassin, his face hidden by the hood of his dufflecoat, has been circled to show where he is standing in the crowd. As the PM comes up to shake his hand, the Dufflecoat raises his pistol and lets off three rounds in quick succession. They make the PM's body dance about like a puppet.

It is clear, too, that the bullets fired are high-calibre because, with the impact of each, the body staggers backwards a good two metres, coming to rest on the steps of the Cenotaph – at which, in just five days' time, the PM was due to lay a wreath on behalf of a grateful nation in remembrance of the glorious dead.

The assassin drops his gun, somehow wrestles free of the security men who try to grab him, and runs about ten metres down Whitehall before throwing up his arms and buckling at the knees as he himself is shot, in the back, several times, by a police marksman positioned on the roof of the Foreign Office. Footage from a TV helicopter overhead gives a clearer indication of just how short the distance is that the Dufflecoat has run.

I pull up a chair in front of the second screen. A clip taken by an amateur video cameraman is being preceded by a warning that 'some viewers may find the following scenes distressing'. The cameraman has been standing so close to the action his lens has been sprayed with a fine red mist. It is just up near the top left-hand corner of the screen, next to the numbers flashing the time – 16:15 – and the date – 5:11. The numbers are the only things that remain in focus as the cameraman is knocked down in the crush of security men, his lens momentarily censored by a falling umbrella. The pictures have become a poignantly confusing blur of movement.

Another clip, taken this time by a professional cameraman from CNN, shows the rooftops of Whitehall – the cameraman has had the presence of mind to work out the direction from which the marksman's bullets must have travelled and has trained his lens on one particular roof where a man wearing a beret can be seen ducking out of sight just seconds after the shots are fired. They play the clip again in slow motion.

'So far,' the CNN anchorman drawls gravely, 'the forces of law and order here in London, Europe, have been unable to name the assassin in what is already being dubbed "The crime of the new millennium". I'm Bob Stiburski. As I speak, no official explanation has been given, either, as to why the unnamed police marksman shot the assassin dead, even though it was obvious he was, by then, unarmed. I predict that, in the weeks and months ahead, this footage, shot by award-winning CNN cameraman Mike Neilland, will prove to be the most vital piece of evidence they have.' He pauses and stares straight at the camera. 'This is Bob Stiburski for CNN International, broadcasting live from London, in the United States of Europe. Back to you in the CNN Center in Atlanta. Peter.'

'Thanks, Bob,' says Peter. 'I'm joined in the studio by Kevin O'Brien, Professor of Criminology at the University of Florida.' The camera cuts to a man with a beard and then cuts back to Peter. 'Professor, what do you think was going through the gunman's mind when he pulled the trigger?'

The next screen down is tuned to the BBC. In its summary of the news it reports jitters on the stock market; the hastily arranged visit to the King by the Chancellor; and the tributes that have been flooding in from world leaders. The American President walks forward to her podium – an impromptu press conference from her holiday home on Martha's Vineyard – and dabs her eyes with a tissue. She flicks back her hair, spun gold in the sunlight, and says how she and her husband had always had a particularly close and special friendship with the New Labour Premier and his wife. Even the Anglophobic new President of the People's Republic of China, General Jiang Cheung, has issued a statement of condolence.

Inevitably, comparisons are being made with the shooting in November 1963 of the PM's spiritual and political mentor, John F. Kennedy. Some wag has even pretended to open a book on which of the many conspiracy theories already doing the rounds will turn out to be true. Scrawled in blue marker pen on the planning board above the lightbox in the newsroom is:

1. Loyalist paramilitaries (not happy about idea of Ulster being part of United Republic of Ireland) 20/1
2. Diehard Old Labour rump (not happy generally) 100/1
3. MI5 3/1
4. Field sports lobby (have own guns, after all) 50/1
5. Chinese intel./People's Liberation Army (because scary enough to do it) 8/1
6. Diehard old Eurosceptics 100/1
7. Other usual suspects: CIA, Mossad, etc, etc 10/1
8. Serbians/Iraqis/Osama bin Laden 15/1
9. Forces of conservatism 20/1

Gallows humour, of course, has its place in helping a traumatized nation come to terms with the shock it mistakes for grief. Like the televised opinions of experts or the pictures of people laying down their bunches of flowers wrapped in cellophane, there is comfort to be had from ritual. Everyone must say where they were and what they were doing when they heard the news. It helps distract us from the sight of the crowds of mourners gathered in the Mall outside the Palace of the People and in front of St Thomas' Hospital, a few hundred metres from where the assassination took place.

The news the crowds have been dreading comes at 2.30 p.m. It's delivered by a doctor in a white coat who reads from a card as he is jostled by the microphones and cameras of the press. 'The Premier never regained consciousness after he was admitted to the hospital yesterday. Earlier this afternoon, he suffered a massive cardiac arrest from which he did not recover. At 14.11,' he adds, 'a decision was made to switch off his life-support machine. Death was caused by internal haemorrhaging resulting from multiple injury to the chest and stomach. I have no further comments at this time.'

I start crying.

How embarrassing.

Four

I may know the difference between Theo Fennell and Bulgari; and I may be able to point with unerring accuracy to the exact shelf in our kitchen upon which the saffron can be found (and yet fumble around hopelessly under my car bonnet if asked to identify the transmission oil stick). But I'm not normally given to spontaneous outbursts of crying.

I return from the lavatory – where I disappeared before anyone noticed my tears – with my eyes puffy and red. I see that, since the news has come through that the PM has actually died, someone has tactfully wiped the betting odds off the planning board. I go to the window and stare down at the whited sepulchre of Greenwich.

'It really does look like a giant mushroom, doesn't it?'

The throaty yet fey voice – a dowager duchess on sixty a day – is unmistakable. So are the fingers I feel kneading my shoulders. Over the past two years – ever since Gavin Sennett left the arts pages of *King and Country* to become our books editor – the office banter has become theatrical in tone. Gavin – always clear-skinned, pleasant-smelling, immaculately groomed and colour co-ordinated – is straight, as far as we know. But he dances suspiciously well, has beautiful handwriting and is as camp as the Eurovision Song Contest in that way only heterogays can be. From the day he first sidled into the office, gave a flick of his foppish hair and started calling everyone 'dear' and 'darling' it caught on. I dare say his tantrums and his habit of addressing men by women's names annoys some of the high-testosterone types on the sports desk, but I find it endearing.

Without turning round I say: 'Yes, Gabby. It does. "All your shopping needs under one roof", though, eh?'

We stand in silent contemplation for a moment and then stroll back to our desks. 'Isn't it too awful about Her Majesty the Prime Minister?' Gavin says. 'I can't bear it. How could they just shoot her like that in cold blood?' He starts fanning himself with a copy of *World of Interiors*.

'I tell you, Gabby,' I say. 'I was in floods just now. Had to rush to the loo. I don't know what the girls thought.' I nod in the direction of the sports desk.

We walk over to my office, Gavin sits on the corner of my desk and I put my feet up next to him. 'How's it going?' He tilts his hand in the drinking sign. That was how he and I met. At the Priory, a last resort for both of us after the AA meetings had failed. On the strength of the friendship we forged in there, I pulled some strings to land him the job on the *English People*. Now we act as a mutual support network.

'Fine. They say the first thirty years are the worst.'

'I came close the other day. Met up with an old friend who was insistent we visit bar after bar. But I should count myself lucky I don't have one of these to drive me to drink.' He holds a photograph of Amanda at arm's length and cocks his head. 'You know from a certain angle she can look almost real.'

'How dare you,' I say. 'You're talking about the woman whose inherited fortune I love.'

'It must be terrifying sharing a bed with those breasts. So tightly disciplined.'

'You're just jealous ... Let me have that.' I snatch the photograph from his hands and study it. It is a portrait by Demarchelier taken when Amanda was thirty-five and she looks her usual immaculate, pneumatic self: tall, slim, head tilted flirtatiously, Valentino dress with plunging neckline to reveal that expensively sculpted cleavage, teeth straightened and bleached, surgically modified lips, nose and cheeks, auburn tresses cascading over shoulders. Beautiful, of course. Everyone thinks so. But I'm afraid, these days, she leaves me cold.

'Do you sleep in separate beds?' Gavin asks.

'Fuck you.'

'Oh, go on. I won't tell anyone.'

I lay the picture face down in my in-tray. Gavin stands up and scrutinizes the three frames I have hung on my wall: one contains an Investigative Reporter of the Year award I won eight years ago; another shows a photograph of me shaking hands with Yeltsin; the third is of me with the Pope.

'You were quite the little star in those days, weren't you?' Gavin says. 'I can see why Tenant was so desperate to poach you.'

'*Fuck you!*'

Everyone in the office thinks it, but only Gavin has the balls to say it to my face. Bruce Tenant is the American publishing tycoon who owns the *English People*. He is also the father of my second wife. When I married Amanda I *was* quite the star, actually. Guest appearances on *Start the Week* and *Any Questions?*, my appointment as political correspondent for the *London Times*, my stint as a presenter on *Talking Politics* and *Newsnight*, two critically acclaimed biographies – one of the Lord Chancellor, the other of the PM's press secretary – all this before my thirtieth birthday.

Then I lost it. Or rather Amanda locked on to me like a laser-guided missile and I lost it. In retrospect I suppose it was pathetic of me to be seduced by the life she introduced me to: private jets, cocaine, weekends at the Cipriani, summers at the beach house in Long Island, winters in Gstaad. But she was relentless. A force of nature. We became an alpha couple. A-list. Hot.

Before he retired to write books, my father was an unreconstructed left-wing academic at a northern university. My childhood was grey, powder dry, so much the opposite of glamorous. I was an easy target. My first mistake was to take Amanda's advice and resign from a regular job in order to write a screenplay. Our daughter Emily was born. Six months later I had written ten pages.

When I tried to get back into journalism I found the inspiration fairy had had her silken wings clipped. Unable to write, I took a job as lifestyle editor of the *London Times on Sunday* for a couple of years. I began drinking heavily and, at my wife's insistence, ended up seeing a counsellor. It got me off the loud mouth soup and, for a while, the cocaine – but it just made me more dependent on Prozac. Which, in turn, left me pretty much impotent.

It was at this point, five years ago, that Tenant took me to one side. In just ten years, he said, Multi-Media International had grown from a medium-sized company based in Providence, Rhode Island, to one of the most profitable listed on the global stock market. It was all thanks to him, he explained gently, and he didn't want me to fuck it up.

No one is sure how many billions Tenant is worth and, for tax reasons, he is happy to keep it that way. But his empire now includes hundreds of newspapers, publishing houses and cable, satellite and digital channels, as well as a large slice of the Net. MMI has also overtaken Reuters and Dow Jones to become the largest provider of real-time pricing, data and analysis to Wall Street and the City of London.

The real money spinner for the company, though, has been the invention and development of the Multicard. And, according to rumour, Tenant is hoping he can now pull off the same trick by investing heavily in Information Warfare – developing sophisticated viruses which can paralyse whole countries when deliberately planted in computers. InfoWar is a highly controversial area of defence, of course. An illegal one, in fact, according to the UN Security Council. But Tenant likes a challenge.

Now, for some reason, Tenant has a soft spot for me. I would even go so far as to say I think he actually rates me highly as a journalist. When we had our little chat five years ago, he said that if I can stay off the sauce and hold down a job until my fortieth birthday he will not only pay off my sizeable loans but also make me a partner in MMI. He offered me a job on the paper he was launching. My *English People* column didn't last long and I soon slid over into the sleepy backwater of features writing and editing. But I have, more or less, kept out of trouble.

'You were quite good-looking then, too,' Gavin says, tapping a photograph on my desk of me walking across the White House lawn with Clinton. 'What happened?'

'I saw something of life. That's what happened. Unlike you with your miserable little existence of singles bars, bedsits and masturbation.'

'Ah, yes. Michael Yates. The Missing Years. *Such a waste.*'

'Watch it,' I laugh. 'I could have you fired, you know.'

'Oh, we all know that, darling.'

'I could arrange to have you shot and dumped in a canal. And no one would even notice you had disappeared.'

'We know. We know. It's the only reason we stay friendly with you.'

'That's friendliness as in "barely disguised contempt", is it?'

'Not me, dear heart. You know I love you. But I can't vouch for the other girls.'

'You mean I can't even trade off what happened to Emily for sympathy any more?'

Gavin lowers his gaze.

'Sorry, Gabby, I didn't mean to make you feel uncomfortable. Hey,' I pat his shoulder, 'look at me.' I change the subject. 'Can you believe they're sending me to Bucharest? The biggest story of the century breaks in London and I get sent to Bucharest.'

'You should be flattered. Didn't Tenant request you personally to cover the summit?'

'Only because he knows I'll write whatever he wants me to write.'

'Now you know that's not true.'

There is a knock on the open door. It is Peter Hardcastle, one of the lobby correspondents. 'Gabby. I'm going to have to steal Michelle from you. The old girl wants us in for a news conference.'

The old girl is the editor, Hugh Johnson. At sixty-seven he is past retirement age and many of his right-wing critics on the staff feel it shows in his eccentrically liberal opinions. He is a quiet, cerebral man who, though slightly cold and snobby, is essentially decent and honourable, I think. With his collar-length silvering hair, his aquiline nose and the salmon-and-cucumber-striped Garrick Club bow tie he always wears, he is donnish and genial in appearance, too. Which always helps.

As we cross the office, negotiating a mountain bike which someone has parked by a desk, I listen to the snatches of conversation you can only ever hear in a newsroom: 'Anyone know a tame bishop? We need a bishop...', 'Who's buggered off with *Hello!*, I was reading it...', 'Three or four s's in assassinate...?'

A dozen of us file into Johnson's office and sit down on the sofas arranged along three walls. I am facing his desk and the large painting of the King's coronation which hangs above it. I know every centimetre of this scene, having stared at it for at least one hour a week for the past five years as I try to stay awake in these interminable meetings. Peter always resorts to doodling and can sometimes fill several whole pages of A4. On the wall behind me are twelve clocks telling the times in capitals around the world. Johnson sits down, stares short-sightedly at the one above my head, taps his watch and holds it to his ear.

There are the usual good-natured jeers as Jamie Williams, the incredibly mild and polite political editor, arrives late looking flustered. 'Williams!' we all chant in unison. 'What have you done now?' It is the office joke that whenever there is an atrocity – rape, murder, terrorist bombing – it is always assumed Williams is behind it. The editor isn't much of a one for frivolity, though, and he brings the news conference to order by turning to the picture editor. 'Lead?'

'We're calling in the CNN shot of the marksman's head on the roof. They haven't named him yet. It looks grainy because of the rain and you can't make out his features, but he is silhouetted against the sky and we can crop in and circle it. Maybe an arrow as well.'

'Good. Now I want a piece from Prof. Robert Sutton on the constitutional implications as well as the historical context. First Prime Minister to be assassinated and so on.'

'Second,' interrupts The Boy Fielding – Edward Fielding, our 22-year-old current affairs editor: starred first from Cambridge at 16, published first book at 18, King's College fellowship at 19. Speaks six languages. Translates Aeschylus from Athenian into French just for the fun of it. A freak in other words. Hard eyes. Weak chin. Virgin. Everyone looks at him. 'Spencer Perceval,' he adds. '1812.'

'Thank you, Four,' Johnson says. That's his nickname for

Fielding, Four Brains. Gavin, being a literary sort, calls him Lord Lackbeard. The rest of us call him The Boy, though not to his face.

'Emma,' Johnson continues, 'can you sort that out with Sutton?'

I hand The Boy a fifty-euro note and whisper: 'Thanks for lending me it.'

He looks puzzled and whispers back: 'I didn't.'

Johnson hears him and says: 'What is it, Four?'

Everyone turns to Fielding. I lean back and look at him through a thin, cold smile.

'Nothing.' He is blushing now. And feeling paranoid, too, I hope.

'Well,' Johnson says with a frown, 'can we get on with this then, please . . .'

Result! The old man sounds pissed off.

'. . . Peter, you look into the succession. Are New Labour a one-man party and so on? Tom, I want you to find someone in Washington to write a piece about how it has brought back memories of JFK and Camelot for the Americans.'

'They'll still be in bed,' says Tom.

'Wake them up. Mary, I want 800 words from you on what the grieving process will be like for the First Lady. Talk to some counsellors. Comparisons with Diana and the Boys. Michael,' he turns to me, 'I wasn't happy with the obit in this morning's editions. I want you to write a more personal one. What it was like on the campaign trail covering his election victories. No more than a thousand words. The cult of the personality. The Messianic demagogue compared with the inner man. The loathing of history. The love of surveillance. His stealthy *coup d'état* against the traditional institutions. That sort of thing. The warmth. The humour. The childhood. Anecdotes. Style of Government.'

'But I've got to go and pick up my visa,' I say feebly, my heart sinking at the prospect of having to dredge through my old cuts.

'What time?'

Bollocks, hadn't thought of that. 'Five.' A lie.

'Write it before you go.'

I look at my watch with discreet theatricality. It is 3.30.

'Now. I want the whole of the news features spread devoted to an assessment of the New Labour years. I think we should do it as a sort of *1066 and All That* pastiche. Thoughts?'

'Well, I think scrapping the voting rights of hereditary peers was A Good Thing,' Peter Hardcastle says tentatively.

'Agreed,' says the editor. 'All agreed?' We all murmur our agreement.

'And devolving power to Scotland, Wales and Ireland – expected to be A Bad Thing,' Hardcastle adds, 'encouraging worst excesses of English nationalism, but turned out to be quite A Good Thing? Especially for economy of Autonomous Region of England.' Everyone nods their assent.

Fatty Robertson, one of the paper's more rabid leader writers, sighs loudly. 'Yes, but we have to mention the ugly emotionalism, narcissism and television-addicted cretinism of the New Labour generation. The contempt for parliament. The thought control. They've made the rest of us feel like strangers in our own land.'

'And we have to say something about his having brought us into the Trivial Age,' I offer. 'I mean, his "Cappuccino List" of ennoblements for entertainers. And having a former film star as Premier of Scotland. A former pop star as Taoiseach of the United Republic of Ireland. And don't forget all the pancetta, extra virgin olive oil and sun-dried tomatoes. Not to mention – '

'Christopher Evans as director general of the BBC,' The Boy says.

I was about to say that. I take my revenge. The Boy had been the most fanatical advocate of the single currency. 'What do you think we should say about your euro, Ed? Do we still think it a good thing?'

'It's improved exports,' he counters, his cheeks flushing.

'And imports . . .' I pause. 'Of the dollar.'

Everyone titters. Emma jumps in to save The Boy. 'European Army. Bad Thing?'

'Obviously,' the editor says. 'Pathetically indecisive over Pakistan's use of that short-range tactical nuclear weapon. No good without single European foreign policy.'

'Yes, but putting us at heart of expanded Federal Europe expected to be Bad Thing but proving to be Good Thing, sort of, er, in terms of political clout on world stage,' Tom adds, taking up the style of talking in clipped sentences.

'What do we think about his plans to offer an e–referendum on downsizing the role of the monarchy?' Hugh asks. 'Good?' Five hands go up. 'Bad?' Four hands. 'Indifferent?' Two (mine and Tom's). All eyes turn to Alan Cameron.

'I thought he was a fucking Tory *wanker*,' Cameron growls darkly, his Glaswegian accent giving sinister almost preternatural emphasis to the word 'wanker'.

Five

By 4.30 p.m. I have put across 1,200 words for the subs to start
fine-tuning and checking. I have to say, I am pleased with it.
There's nothing quite like a proper deadline for concentrating the
mind. It's the reason journalists become deadline junkies. If you
have five days to write an article you will take five days – but only
really knuckle down to it as the deadline approaches on the fifth.
My essay on the PM is as fine a piece of charlatanism as any I have
written. Beautifully crafted and heartfelt. Journalism as prostitu-
tion. Faking it on a grand scale.

Although I've been a political correspondent and written two
political biographies, I think I was born without the political gene,
the one that makes politicians embarrassing yet unembarrassable. I
have voted only once in an election – the first time I was allowed
to. Since then I haven't bothered because, try as I might, I can
never really summon up much in the way of ideological
conviction. Unless, of course, I'm being paid to summon. And
then I can sound so convincing and authoritative I scare myself.
And I always know when it is expedient to toe the paper's far-
right-wing line – which I suppose is as good a definition of a
political mind as any.

I have taken as my theme 'The Premier as Saint' and, as I reread
my magnanimous prose, I find myself blinking back crocodile

tears. At first New Labour seemed serious, sober and priggish, I write. The PM, the most attractive Tory on offer, appeared to be nothing more than an opportunistic cipher whose prime ministerial fingertips were never allowed near anything ungildable. The only thing he seemed destined to be remembered for was the introduction of government by opinion poll. But then he became the guardian of international ethics. Showed moral courage as a wartime leader and, because we wanted to believe England really could be dynamic, modern and successful under him, it became so. Sort of. He inspired us and made us feel proud and confident once more. Of course there were schemes that backfired: his poster campaign in which right-wing professors were depicted wearing dunce's caps, his claim that the giant crystal pyramid he wanted to build in Horse Guards Parade wouldn't replace 10 Downing Street altogether, that it should just be seen as an extension of it. But his England underwent a velvet revolution and, freed from Scotland, Ireland and Wales, it soared to become the natural leader in the new federal Euroland.

I'm in such a good mood afterwards that I celebrate by adjusting the height on The Boy Fielding's chair – and the angle of his computer screen. I try to do this whenever I'm in the office, to unnerve him. As I light up a post-deadline cigar I'm interrupted by a young freelance on the picture desk. She has taken a call from the *Evening Mirror* picture desk, she says. They are asking for a photo of me. They haven't said what they want it for. I ask her not to send one and then, with mounting unease, I try to work out what those bastards might be up to. Presumably it is for something unpleasant. You just can't help making enemies in this business.

The thought of them running a story anyway – with a grainy, unflattering photograph they could easily take with a long lens – makes me toy with the idea of letting them have my byline picture. It was taken three years ago with a 'skinny' lens. It shows my greying hair as I like to think it still is: dusty brown. It makes my gaunt, elongated face look younger and softer. And even my natural, woolfish leer passes for a pleasant smile in the photograph. It makes me look warm and sensitive. Ironic and thoughtful. My wife hates it.

I decide against sending them the byline pic because without a photograph it will be much harder to run a story. As I know how easily they can find out my home address, I ring Amanda – she's in town – to warn her that if she suspects there's a snapper lurking outside our house she should just walk past the door when she gets home. They might not know what she looks like. She asks me what I have been up to. I tell her about the young woman on the bike.

By the end of the phonecall I'm feeling agitated. What if the cyclist is still in a coma? I realize I still don't even know her name.

To lift my spirits, I stub the cigar out and leave it in an ashtray on The Boy Fielding's desk. He'll think Tenant has paid him a visit, with any luck. I shuffle the cards in his alphabetically arranged Rolodex and then go off to find an empty office from which to phone Exeter Hospital. I'm told that the cyclist has been transferred to the Cromwell Hospital in West London – not far from the Romanian embassy in Kensington. I check my watch, close down my telecomp, and make it to the visa department just as it is closing.

There is the predictable denial from the Romanian embassy officials that they ever received the visa form and the cash I had to bike round because they wouldn't accept a cheque. After fifteen minutes of having to sit opposite an evil-smelling, mad-eyed old Romanian who is trying to outstare me, they find my visa and hand it over with a look of contempt that, were I not in such a hurry, would infuriate me.

A pungent smell of disinfectant hangs over the reception area of the Cromwell. Combined with the unbearable heat, it has overcome a wilting rubber plant – just as it was making a bid to wrap its fronds around a Diet Fanta machine. The only relief from the tropical temperature comes from the electric doors which let in blasts of cold air whenever a stretcher is sent to collect a patient from an ambulance. As I wait for the receptionist to help me, I take in the signs warning that mobile phones cannot be used because they interfere with the machines in the building.

The receptionist doesn't look up when it comes to my turn. 'I've come to visit a friend,' I say. 'A young woman. She was admitted this morning. From Exeter.' I pause long enough for her to fill in the gap of the name that I clearly don't know. She doesn't look up from the book she is reading.

'Name?'

'Michael Yates.'

'No,' she says patiently, dealing with an idiot child. 'The young woman's name.'

I hesitate and come clean. 'Not sure.'

She looks up slowly with eyebrows raised. She could be Miss Monotone's ninety-year-old younger sister.

'I was the one who ran into her,' I mumble, averting my gaze in order to study a patch of carpet that has become interesting.

'There. That wasn't so difficult. Your friend's name is Jennifer Lambert. She is in B Wing. Take the lift to the second floor. Turn left and one of the nurses will show you to her.'

'Thank you,' I tilt my head slightly to read the name badge pinned to her uniform. 'Thank you, State Registered Nurse Helen Dudley.'

'You are most welcome.' Her face is already looking down at her book again.

As I wonder how it is that someone who looks like a New Age traveller knows people who can afford to have her transferred to a private hospital, I tap on the door marked Lambert, J. Hearing no answer, I enter, leaving the door open. Jennifer is lying on the bed still unconscious with one tube in her mouth and another, taped down, in her nose. She smells of bile and her skin looks pale and waxy.

I sit down and take her warm fingers in mine, being careful not to disturb the IV drip that is attached to her arm. Her face is yellow and lilac with bruising. The skin around her eyes is dark and puffy. I search her closed eyelids for a flicker of movement but there is none and the only sound in the room comes from her regular breathing and the bleeping of what looks like a radar screen, a menacing-looking machine that has the word 'defibrillator' on it.

'I'm sorry, Jennifer,' I say under my breath. 'I'm really really sorry. It was an accident.' I close my eyes and when I open them again they are filled with salty water. 'Jennifer? Jennifer? *You've got to wake up, Jennifer.*'

'Hello.'

I turn and take in a slightly built man, mid-fifties, framed in the doorway. His pallor is the same steel-grey as the three-piece suit he is wearing, his eyes are rheumy and opaque.

'Hello,' I say, blinking back a tear and dabbing my nose on my sleeve.

'I'm Jennifer's father.' Though refined, his voice is nasal and disconcertingly high in pitch. 'Andrew...' he adds, crossing the room without making a sound. 'And you are?'

'Michael,' I say, shaking his hand. It is dry and cold. His grip is firm.

'Michael Yates?' he says, levelling hooded eyes at me. 'You're the one who ran her over?'

A stocky man in a sports jacket and polo neck walks into the room, stands in the corner and folds his arms. We both look at him for a moment and then back at each other.

'I can't begin to tell you how sorry I am. I just didn't see her.' I look across to Jennifer and then back to her father. 'It was dark. There was mud on the road. What do the doctors reckon?'

'With any luck she will come out of the coma soon. The fact that she recovered temporarily after you hit her may be a good sign. Shows her spine is OK. It's brain damage they're worried about. There's a suspected clot. We're waiting for the latest scan results.'

'Christ, I hope she's...' I chew my lip.

We stand either side of Jennifer's bed, staring at her for about a minute. A mobile phone rings and I look at the polo-necked man. 'Hello?' he says into the phone. 'No, we're in the hospital.' He walks towards the door and, just as he closes it behind him, he says to Jennifer's father: 'Excuse me for a moment, sir.'

'My bodyguard.' Jennifer's father says this matter-of-factly. 'Special Branch. You're Tenant's son-in-law, aren't you?'

'You know him?'

'Doesn't everyone?'

There is a tap on the door. The Polo Neck pops his head round. 'Sir?'

'What is it?'

'The DG wants a word. Says it's urgent. There's a private office at the other end of the ward you can use.'

'Excuse me for a moment,' Jennifer's father says. The two men walk out closing the door behind them.

I sit on the chair next to Jennifer's bed, lower my face to my hands and rock backwards and forwards.

'Where am I?'

I look up. '*Jennifer!*'

Though groggy with sleep, her voice is well-manicured, low, smoky. 'Who are you?' she asks.

'Thank God! Thank God!' I gabble. 'I'm Michael. You're in hospital. In London. You've been in an accident. Thank God you're all right. How do you feel?'

'Like I've been run over by a bus. What happened?'

'You were run over by a car. You've been in a coma.'

'You're a doctor, right?'

'No. I . . .' I avoid her eye, 'I was driving the car. It was an accident. Didn't see you. I'm so very sorry. Really. Very very sorry.'

'Where's my bike?'

'I'm not sure, Jennifer. Do you live down there?'

'Everyone calls me Jenny. . . I was protesting.'

'What about?'

'A new town they want to build on a conservation area. Where's my bike?'

'I'll buy you a new one. Anything. I'll buy you a car.'

'Don't believe in cars.' She tries to raise her arm to her head. 'I've got a headache. Can you find a doctor?'

'Of course,' I kiss her hand. 'I'm so glad you're OK. I've been so worried. I thought you might be – '

'A doctor. Please.'

'Of course. Right.'

I find one in the next ward but as I'm walking back with him I see Jennifer's father and the man in the polo neck marching towards us from the opposite direction. 'I'll join you in a minute,' I say to the doctor. I check my watch. The back stairs are cold, concrete and littered with an astonishing number of cigarette butts. I go down them two at a time and, as I step outside and hail a taxi, I feel quite drunk with relief.

Six

The following morning is overcast – but this isn't why there's a pall of misery hanging over the small crowd gathered in Parliament Square. As my taxi crawls past them on the way to the airport I have a chance to study the faces: some wear expressions of anxious curiosity, others have tear-swollen, bloodshot eyes, many just look blank, pale and dazed as they cradle bunches of flowers they're not sure what to do with. One woman crossing the road in front of us drops her bag and just stares at it for a moment as if trying to work out what it is. A camera crew films her.

It is hard not to feel contempt for their predicable grief and their selfish attempts to stake their claim on a historical event. And it is a relief to reach the clear and calming blue air above the clouds a couple of hours later as I take off for Bucharest.

For the three-hour flight I manage to erase the moronic many-headed from my thoughts – but they return as the plane begins its bumpy descent into Otopeni Airport. A stewardess comes round selling single carnations wrapped in cellophane. I look out of the window to see the clouds below us grow dark again and, as we pass through them, I can see flurries of snow illuminated in the beam of the wing lights.

I turn the volume up on my Walkman. Elgar's Cello Concerto. I bought a recording of it while I was waiting to board. Unusual for me, this. When I stopped drinking I also stopped listening to classical music. The pleasure for me was in feeling maudlin. Nothing was too syrupy for my taste. Mozart, Ravel, Puccini. A log fire. A box of Kleenex. But even I found Elgar a little too sentimental to stomach. Now, though, as we judder around in the turbulence I find it a comfort. I have a vague idea that I might take Jennifer Lambert to a performance of it when I get back to London.

I read the sleeve notes as I listen. 'The Concerto for Cello and Orchestra in E minor, op. 85 was completed in 1919 and, following the death of Elgar's wife in 1920, was the last major work the composer completed before his own death in 1934. He began it in London during the winter of 1918 and finished it at the rented country cottage that he loved so much – Brinkwells near Fittleworth in Sussex.'

You never know when having information like that might impress someone. I picture myself slipping it into a conversation with Jennifer. Jenny? Jen? We would be staring out over the rolling hills near Fittleworth in Sussex, our backs against the knotty bark of an ancient oak, bathed in the glow of a lingering English sunset.

If I'd left the previous morning – as Bruce Tenant had suggested – I could've flown out with him on his Gulfstream jet. Thankfully I wasn't able to get my visa through until 5.45 and had to wait instead for the one flight a day which Tarom – 'the world's most friendly airline' – runs into Bucharest. I hate flying at the best of times. To fly in tandem with my father-in-law would have been gruesome.

Although an American citizen, Tenant has a European passport. No one is sure how. He also has more influence in more countries than do most heads of state. He is one of those men who is only ever known by his surname, even some of his wives called him Tenant rather than Bruce. I don't think I've ever seen him smile – although his secretary claims she has, once, just before he fired someone.

Everyone agrees: the man is cold blooded. He has, as the saying goes, something of the night about him. And the fear he engenders is not just psychological. Even at seventy-two he still manages to intimidate physically. He is almost completely bald, the remaining white hairs at the back and sides of his head always cropped close to the skin. He wears big square glasses that make his eyes look even smaller than they are. There is no kindness in these eyes, nothing you could reasonably identify as a soul. His features are saturnine: broad nose, cruel lips, skin so smooth and rubbery one newspaper profile described him as looking like a man on a stag night who has pulled a flesh-coloured condom over his head and now can't get it off.

His weight and height? Well. It's hard to decide which of the stupid, bossy rules that characterize the new spirit of England is the more infuriating. But a good contender is the law that everyone in the media has to use the metric system. And the willingness of editors to impose the letter of this repressive and foolish rule is truly depressing. I have tried to get into the habit of converting everything from imperial – but weights and heights still defeat me. Tenant weighs, I would guess, about fifteen stones and stands at a compact five foot four. Amanda, luckily, inherited her height genes from her estranged mother: a former Wonderbra model with Titian hair and legs so long Tenant had to stand on the tips of his toes to kiss her.

The thing is, everyone imagines Tenant to be much taller than he is – from seeing him on television, I suppose – and so they always look shocked when they meet him. They think his stature inconsistent with the aura of power that glows around him. Not me. I think it fitting. I see him as being the latest in a long line of diminutive megalomaniacs: Napoleon, Hitler, Stalin (five foot four, wore platform shoes to disguise it) and Tenant.

It's said that you can always tell when Tenant is about to pay a visit to the *English People's* offices because, mingling with the unleaded exhaust fumes pumping from the Bentley Continental he insists has to be kept running outside – and the aroma of Bolivar cigars which hangs around him like a nimbus – there will be a whiff of sulphur.

When I discover he has turned up unexpectedly to meet my plane at the airport, my gut tightens. Then, when I see the armed Romanian soldiers lining the arrivals lounge, waiting to shoot anyone who isn't prepared to pay a new airport tax they have probably just invented, I have a change of heart and feel grateful that the old sod has been able to drive right up to the steps of the plane, accompanied by two soldiers on motorbikes.

Tenant is in a large, chauffeur-driven jeep which has two small UN flags flapping on either side of its bonnet. Even these contrive to look intimidating in his presence, rather than reassuring. The idea that I should be flown out to cover the speech he is making at the UN peace summit occurred to him at the last minute, apparently. Even so, he has managed to square things with the authorities in anticipation of my arrival.

He greets me with a quick bear hug and a kiss on both cheeks, presumably for the benefit of the Romanian soldiers. I assume this is why he is also wearing a long, fur-collared trenchcoat and a Russian fur hat. I'm just starting to feel self-conscious about my old overcoat being too short for my arms when I feel his hand clamp on to the back of my head. He ushers me towards the jeep and ducks my head to get under the door, as policemen do with prisoners. 'Best not hang about,' he says in a gruff voice. 'Snipers.'

I nod at his bodyguard, David, a sinewy Welshman with dimples and a crew cut of sandy hair. He checks the wire that is permanently dangling from his ear, gathers his overcoat around himself and shuffles over. I like David, he lets me hold his Beretta pistol and once showed me how to open bottle tops with its trigger.

We drive past Royal Air Force One – England's Minister for European Affairs must be here, representing the PM. Behind this there is a giant tail fin painted with the cross of St George. An English Airways 787. 'I didn't know EA flew to Bucharest,' I say. Tenant ignores me. 'If I'd known . . .' I blow on my hands. 'Cold, isn't it?' There's a checkpoint to clear and more armed soldiers, this time wearing the pale blue helmets of the UN Security Forces. As they've been the ones to let Tenant into the airport, they wave him back out without stopping to check his passenger's passport and, inevitably, given the hassle it caused, his visa.

The sight of so many soldiers bristling with automatics is at once exhilarating and unnerving. There couldn't be a worse time to hold the three-day summit. It should have been cancelled. A number of heads of state – North America's, Israel's and India's among them – have already backed out because their security could not be guaranteed. Others intend to use the PM's funeral in

London as an excuse to leave the Bucharest summit early.

The place is a powder keg. After months of rioting, prompted by the collapse of a fraudulent savings company, Romania is about to hold an election to replace its prematurely dissolved parliament. Normal campaigning has so far proved impossible because of the likelihood that candidates will be shot at or kidnapped.

Combined with this, a four-month miners' strike has brought chaos to the streets of Bucharest. Tens of thousands of miners from the Jiu valley in the south-west of the country have descended on the capital protesting for more pay. And there are rumours that the Kosovar Albanians who settled here are now being ethnically cleansed. A UN Security Council resolution has authorized the dispatch of a European Army force whose task is to create a secure environment first for the summit, then for the election.

Inevitably, the Sino-Russian Alliance has taken a dim view of what it describes as this classic case of foreign powers intervening in the Balkans. Since the eastward expansion of Nato has taken in all but one of the former Warsaw Pact countries, the SRA has come to regard Romania as its only remaining ally in the region. The Romanians, of course, want to join NATO, too – they already have 'alliance' status – but are considered too backward economically and unstable politically for full membership. Unloved, in the cold and on the brink of anarchy, their country has become a no man's land between the old world order and the new. It's also ripe for exploitation by Western venture capitalists. And sitting next to me as we drive towards the centre of Bucharest is the man who was once voted 'Capitalist's Capitalist' by *Time* magazine.

As the chauffeur of his jeep swerves violently to avoid a pothole centimetres off being classified a crater, Tenant lurches sideways in his seat, checks with a liver-spotted hand the phantom hairs on his scalp, and buckles up his seat belt. He turns to me and gives an exasperated shrug. I shrug back ingratiatingly and peer ahead, as if to check that the motorbike escort is still doing its stuff. It is.

'Can you believe these fucking roads?' he drawls. 'It's like being in the Third World. I earn more in an afternoon than the annual GDP of this entire fucking country. What a toilet.'

'Quite.'

By Tenant's standards, this is a long conversation. The man is laconic, to say the least. He uses silence in the way that a terrorist uses the threat of a nail bomb. I'm sure he must know how uncomfortable it makes his interlocutor feel, but either he doesn't care or he does it deliberately. Then again, maybe he is just so socially awkward himself he doesn't pick up the signals. Borderline autistic, some reckon.

I remember once suggesting to him on the phone that I spend a week shadowing the Minister for European Affairs, in the run-up to the party conference. He fell silent for a full minute. I timed it on my watch – determined, for a change, not to buckle and speak first. I was squirming, of course. Finally he said: 'And you think that's a good idea, do you?' I remained silent. 'Well, so do I,' he said and hung up.

Not that I yearn to hear his voice. It's guttural and croaky, more like a distant, monotone rumble. But I prefer it to the silence.

We are speeding down a colourless, tree-lined boulevard. The jeep, a voluptuously upholstered Grand Cherokee, stands out among the drab-looking Ladas, stray mongrels, yellow trams and orange tractors. My father-in-law, I learn, had it flown out especially.

'Look at these bloody peasants,' Tenant mutters half to himself. 'So much potential in their country – oil, minerals, cheap labour for manufacturing – yet they haven't got the competence to boil a goddam egg.'

On the cement-and-iron balconies above us, washing lines are suspended between grimy satellite dishes. It's starting to snow heavily now and women who scurry out to gather in their washing stop to stare at the jeep as it passes below.

'Nice jeep,' I say lamely.

'Armour-plated, Michael,' Tenant says, not looking at me. He taps the window. 'Bullet-proof.'

'Just here is fine!' I joke, making as if to get out. I immediately wish I hadn't.

'What?' Tenant frowns. 'But I'm taking you to your hotel.'

'I know, it's just . . . the thought of . . . bullets . . . I . . .'

His phone rings. 'Tenant . . . Yeah, of course you should . . . Fuck them . . . Who told you that? . . .'

Tenant always does this. He could be having an audience with the Pope and he would still take calls on his mobile. There are only about twelve people in the world who know his private number yet he has it changed every three months for security reasons. I think he likes the thought that any of the men — always men — who run the various operations in his global empire can contact him day and night. As he only ever catnaps, he doesn't really have a sleeping pattern to break. His chief executives have to have a pretty good reason to call, of course, and that is why they always get through: rumours of a merger in Tokyo, a hostile takeover in Frankfurt, some new arms treaty in New York. The arrangement works both ways. He will call his people from whichever country he happens to be in, regardless of the time difference.

'Call me when you hear something... Sure. Bye. Now, Michael. I'm sorry I couldn't get you into the Diplomat tonight, it's full because of the summit... Hello? Yeah? Damn straight it is. Go as high as six if you have to. Call me when you get an answer...'

It's extremely difficult to keep track of who Tenant is talking to at any one point. Even when you can be sure it is you he is addressing, he will often have a distracted look in his eyes which means that someone is talking into his ear. Certainly I've never felt as if I've had his full attention since he started using one of those artificial sensory systems which don't require a mouthpiece. I'm not sure how they work — something to do with a silicon chip implant that picks up the voice patterns internally — but when Tenant gets an incoming call on his cellular earpiece he looks like a bad anchorman doing a live broadcast. He still needs a small handset for dialling out on and, despite the recent scares that these cause testicular cancer, he keeps his in his trouser pocket.

He ends his call and as he resumes his conversation with me he retrieves his handset from his pocket and presses the redial button. 'So I've arranged to have your bags moved over tomorrow night. You're staying at the Louis XVI. It's shit. You're gonna hate it.'

I'm about to say that I'm sure it will be fine when he interrupts again.

'And I'm sorry I couldn't give you a lift in my Gulfstream — but you can fly back with me after this is over. Heard you had some trouble with your visa.'

I look across at him to see if this is meant as a criticism — I don't suppose he's ever bothered with a visa in his life — an expression of sympathy is doing its best to play across his face. This is also part of the Bruce Tenant legend: he can be considerate in private, even to his worthless son-in-law, just so long as it doesn't undermine his reputation for being a ruthless, bigoted bastard in public. I nod and consider trying again to explain what I meant about getting out of the jeep. I change the subject instead. 'Shit.' I over-enunciate the word to show that I'm not intimidated by him. 'I think we've gone too far!' I point to the large arch we're approaching. 'This is Paris!'

'That, Michael, is the *Arcul de Triumf.*' Tenant says this without any outward sign of amusement.

Excellent, I think. He always loves showing off his general knowledge – and I'm not about to deny him the chance. 'Really? When was it built?'

'In 1922. To commemorate the Allied victory in WWI.'

'Cool,' I say, shifting in my seat to take a look at it as we drive past. I can't believe I've just said 'cool' and, for the benefit of the imaginary camera that follows me everywhere, I put my fist to my mouth, pretend to bite it and cross my eyes.

'Which side do you suppose will be commemorating victory in the next world war?'

'Who are we supposed to be fighting?' I say.

He gives a slow, velociraptor blink. 'The Gooks, of course.'

I look across to check if he's joking. His face is a mask of serious purpose. As one of the world's last repositories of sexism, racism and homophobia, Tenant has an image to protect. Even so, I haven't heard the expression 'gooks' since I was a schoolboy and, suddenly confronted with it again, I can't help thinking it quaint.

I've learned from interviewing celebrities that the best way to make someone like you is to listen to them in rapt fascination without interrupting. Also you should agree with them whenever the chance arises. 'I think you're right,' I say.

'I know I am, Michael. Those little Maoist bastards can't wait to goosestep their way into Europe.'

My mind returns to the pretty, almond eyes of Jenny, as I have now started referring to her in my imaginary relationship. (Jen is too abrupt. It will be Jennifer in front of her parents. Jenny in bed. When she is wearing my shirt. Exhausted and flushed after a playful pillow fight.)

43

As if from the far side of a foggy valley, I hear Tenant's voice droning on about the build-up of the People's Liberation Army.

'...I mean, for fuck's sake, why do you suppose the PLA now has five and a half million men? Peace keeping, my ass. We're down to twenty thousand. You know that? Twenty fucking thousand.' He transfers his weight onto one cheek and emits a short rasping fart, as if to emphasize the point.

I picture Jenny in a crisp, khaki PLA uniform, practising drill, charging with a bayonet.

'...And what the fuck do they need 380 submarines for?'

I point to my chest and raise my eyebrows to find out if he's addressing me. He nods. I shrug in answer to his question. 'I'll tell you what they need them for. Hello? Peter? Why the hell didn't you return my call? Where have you been? Hi, Phil, hold on a sec. Peter, I'll call you back. Phil, what's the Chinese chancellor said about the defence budget?...Jesus! That's $250 billion more than the Pentagon! Hear that?' Tenant is addressing me again. There is a great wreath of cigar smoke occupying the space between us. 'Are you trying to tell me they'll be happy just playing regional bully in Asia?'

'I...No.'

'Her billion and a half people have just 240 million acres of arable land compared to the 400 million America's 240 million people have. Phil? What's Washington's response?...Well, find out.' He presses a button. 'Peter, I want you to double our holding in those Chinese-built A-19s. Yeah, that's right. And better see if there's a chance now to buy into their ICBMs programme...You interested in defence, Michael?'

Couldn't care less. But I've heard the rumours about Tenant trying to set up some sort of arms deal with the Romanian government, before it is dissolved. It's one of the few countries which hasn't banned research into InfoWar. I presume that part of the reason he is here now is that he wants to help install a puppet government that will be sympathetic to his interests.

'Very.' What I mean is that on the plane I keyed in the words 'defence/NATO/Romania' on Profile, the Internet cuttings service. If all half-decent journalists have a gift in common it's an

44

ability to acquire superficial expertise on any subject at great speed, absorb it, regurgitate it and then forget it all the moment the article is published.

'The reason I wanted to catch you, Michael, is to brief you about my talk tomorrow. Here's what I want you to write.'

I rummage around for my tape recorder.

He looks me slowly up and down with cold eyes. 'This hasn't come from me.'

I put the tape recorder away and, as the jeep swerves for another pothole, Tenant tells me how important it is for English companies to win the defence contracts that a vulnerable Romania is clearly desperate to sign. New weapons technology being as sophisticated and perpetually evolving as it is, whoever supplies the weapons has effective control of the client country's defence system – because they also supply the training, the spare parts and the computer software that constantly needs to be updated. If we don't supply the arms they need, Tenant adds, China will. 'Look out there, Michael. What do you see?'

I lean up against the cold, bullet-proof glass. The snowlogged branches of the trees we were passing look like traceries for the tall dachas behind them. The walls of the buildings are pockmarked with bullet holes sprayed, presumably, during the Christmas revolution of 1989. At the end of the avenue of leafless trees are the silhouettes of two tanks.

'Tanks?'

'Chinese tanks,' Tenant corrects. 'The Romanians have been buying Chinese tanks.'

'Ah.' I narrow my eyes and nod thoughtfully. 'Not good?'

Tenant shakes his head emphatically and taps out a number on his handset. 'Very, very bad.'

My nervousness, the axle-wrenching potholes and the face-burning hair dryer that passes for the jeep's heater system make me feel nauseous. It isn't the most opportune moment for Tenant to ask if I've eaten. I have. On the plane.

'No,' I answer.

'Come round to my hotel once you've had a shit and a shave. We'll try the local caviar. Black Sea. Supposed to be excellent. You play poker?'

I don't. 'Yes.' I nod and try to remember the rules from the one and only time I have played.

'Good. Got some associates coming over after dinner. We need a fourth.'

The chauffeur stops outside the Diplomat, an opulent *belle époque* hotel, Tenant levers himself out, stops and turns. 'How's Amanda?'

'Fine.'

'Not still beating herself up about the kid?' He can never remember Emily's name.

'Well, you know. These things take time.'

'Sure. Sure...See you in a couple of hours.' He walks away, leaving a trace of cigar smoke behind him.

Seven

The Louis XVI is a shabby 13-storey block dating from the sixties. Slush has been carried into the lobby from the road outside and I stand in a black pool of it as I sign in. The concierge asks if he can keep what he refers to with rather suspicious emphasis as my *European* passport. As if. Without my Multicard I would be paralysed. I let him swipe it through his machine, however, keeping a careful eye on him and it as he does so. He has several goes before it works, pausing between each go to give me a significant stare.

The young porter who transports my bags up four floors in a rattly, wooden cage smiles, exposing a blackened front tooth, and says: 'You want girl?'

I try to avoid looking at him as I say: 'No, thank you. Married.'

'You married. I married. In Bucuresti no one he married.'

I smile again, more tightly this time, and shake my head. I'm just beginning to notice his pungent body odour when he asks: 'Drug?'

Now he's talking. 'Cocaine?'

He nods and the lift's concertina door cranks open. The door to my room has no handle on it so that all the porter has to do to open it is nudge it with my case. I give him a forty-euro tip, worth considerably more to him on the black market than its equivalent in lei, and inspect the room. At first I assume the lavatory has not been flushed from the last guest, but when I try flushing it I realize it's just that the water is brown. The minibar is the size of a wardrobe and is empty, apart from a tin of tuna and a green flannel. The TV is broken.

I unpack my laptop and, after making some notes on it about what Tenant said in the jeep, I play with its Simulated Voice Pattern. You can't exactly have a conversation with the new PowerBook G21 – it lets you issue verbal commands, allows you to dictate using the Via-voice option and, if you've got the time and energy, it can be programmed to receive electrochemical signals via your nervous system – but you can personalize it. You tell it the name you want it to call you, and you in turn can give it a name. You can also choose from a menu of voice types and languages, ranging from 'Wildwest Cowboy' to 'Yorkshire Farmer'. I have opted for a 'Baywatch Babe' – a sultry Californian drawl, and have called it, for reasons that only now strike me as mildly worrying, after my late mother, Kate. I now change the laptop's name to Jenny and give her a soothing 'Tokyo Rose' voice.

I ask 'Jenny' to call up the satellite television option, and I watch an item about the preparations being made for the state funeral. This is followed by tributes from the world of showbiz, including a quite impressively statesmanlike one from Lord Irons and another rather cheesy one from Sir George Michael. I carry on watching this through the bathroom mirror as I have a wash and a shave, but not, without hot water, a shower. An item comes on about the crowds of mourners in Parliament Square. A woman drops her bag in the middle of the road and stares at it. I realize this is the scene I drove past. Yet the handful of miseries I saw has now become a multitude. Someone at Millbank has been tampering with the news footage. Tut tut. I consider phoning our newsroom to tell them but suddenly feel too lethargic. It would be more newsworthy if the spin doctors hadn't got their computer paintbrushes out to swell the ranks of the bereaved.

As I'm putting on my new Huntsman three-piece – four-button cuffs, two that open, these things count – I ask 'Jenny' to dial the pre-programmed number of an old university friend in London, Gary Townsend, so that he can talk me through the rules of poker.

When Gary appears on the screen half his chin is covered with shaving foam, while on the other side is stuck a small, bloody scrap of tissue paper. He is just going out, he says, but he takes five minutes to remind me of the rudiments of the game on the pack of cards I know he, being a fastidious gambler, will have to hand.

The porter returns with the goods and I try a line before packing up my laptop. I wrap a scarf around my face and walk through the slush, past the domed national library and on to the Diplomat. Two UN soldiers in sky-blue berets and greatcoats are standing either side of the doorway. Machine guns, all the more sinister for being small, neat and matt black, are hanging from straps around their shoulders. I nod at the soldiers. They remain expressionless. And after checking in my laptop at reception for safekeeping, I join Tenant at his table. He has his mobile clamped to his ear.

During dinner – huge dollops of beluga on neat triangles of toast followed by a passable lobster thermidor – I drink mineral water while Tenant downs vodka. Tenant keeps asking for different flavours to be brought to our table – honey, lemon, blackcurrant, aniseed, banana, elderflower, there may have been more – and he tosses them down in one. As we're walking downstairs to the gaming rooms in the basement of the Diplomat, he stuffs a roll of notes into my jacket pocket, leans towards me and chuckles: 'I hope your friend in London is better at playing poker than he is at shaving.'

I stop in my tracks, trying to recall what else the old bugger might have eavesdropped on. When he walks on ahead I slip off to the lavatory and count the money: $35,000 in $500 bills.

I nod at David the bodyguard who is sitting at a table on his own a few metres away, cleaning his nails with a fish-knife. When Tenant introduces me to his other guests – an American congress-man and a walnut-faced Romanian businessman – it is with a hearty clap on the shoulder and an unnecessarily generous endorsement: 'This is my son-in-law, the brilliant Michael Yates. He's our star editor. Dammit, he's our star writer, too. Here to cover the summit.' The Romanian seems friendly enough but, at first, the American – late 60s, leathery, beaky nose – seems suspicious of me. He relaxes a little as the cigars are passed around, the whiskey sours knocked back and the cards dealt. He even tries to out-do Tenant in what is clearly a competition to pack the most expletives and expressions of prejudice into one sentence. He actually refers to 'pinkoes' at one point which makes me feel even more nostalgic than Tenant's reference to 'gooks'.

My blood chills, however, when Tenant starts talking in a whisper about the assassination. 'Never liked his politics,' he says, chewing on his cigar. 'All those focus groups. All that moral-courage-as-a-leader-at-war bullshit. So holier than thou. By the way, liked the piece you wrote about him in today's paper, Michael. The inner man. Yes, I liked that. Good joke...Hello? OK, put her on...' Tenant is talking at normal volume again now, showing off. '...Mrs President? Right, right...Martha's Vineyard. How's the weather? Good. That husband of yours behaving himself? Golf, eh? And you believe him?...Yeah, sure. Jiang Cheung isn't budging on this...I hear you, I hear you. I'd tell the Pentagon to hold off, though, at least until my speech tomorrow. Sure. And you. Sorry to hear that Buddy had to be put to sleep, by the way. OK, tomorrow. Bye.'

As I have lost nearly all my money at this point and am feeling so tired I'm beginning to suffer room spins, I thank him, excuse myself and walk with as much dignity as I can to the gents. I splash cold water on my face and Dyson up another line of Romanian laxative cut with washing powder. It clears my head in a vague, numbing sort of way; enough to notice that, when I sit back down, the mood at the table has changed. Having a break from the poker, the tycoon and his guests have pushed back their chairs. Talk is of the summit.

'Michael.' Tenant turns to me. 'What do you know about that contemptible puffball General Jiang Cheung?'

I know Jiang Cheung is the first man under the age of 150 to be made President of the People's Republic of China. I know that at first he drew ridicule from Western commentators for presenting himself as a war hero, despite never having fought in a war, and for his vanity in having portraits painted of himself in uniform: in a commanding pose, with chin held high and arms folded. I know that smiles were wiped off Western faces when troops under Jiang Cheung's command brutally suppressed the pro-democracy demonstrations in Hong Kong three years ago. I know that Jiang Cheung is a great one for military bravado: holding May Day parades of hundreds of his ICBM carriers outside the Great Hall of the People.

But I also know that, however much arms dealers such as Tenant might need him to be, Jiang Cheung poses no real threat to World peace. If anything, he is a force for stability. Since the Soviet Union collapsed and North America reverted to isolationism, the real power struggle is between the US of E and the Sino-Russian Alliance. Contrary to expectations, Russia fell into China's sphere of influence and signed up first to the Sino-Russian non-aggression pact then to the economic alliance, essentially a Chinese version of the Marshall Plan. Bilateral trade agreements between the two former enemies proved mutually beneficial: China needed power for its rapidly expanding economy and Russia had a surplus of energy. But with China's huge loan scheme, the SRA had in effect made Russia a Chinese protectorate. And by the time the million-strong PLA 'peace-keeping force' goosestepped across the Ural Mountains, the Russian army hadn't been paid for eighteen months. Mutinous, hungry, plagued by violence, suicides, alcoholism and disease, they welcomed the PLA as their saviours.

But Tenant has asked what I know about that contemptible puffball General Jiang Cheung – and the clue to the correct answer lies in the words 'contemptible' and 'puffball'.

'All I know is that he should be strung up from the nearest lamppost.' After a thoughtful pause I add: 'By his little Maoist testicles.'

'What did I tell you, gentlemen!' Tenant guffaws as he makes a benediction with his cigar. 'It's political insight such as this that makes Mr Yates here the best goddamn editor in the business.'

The others laugh and my brain is too fogged to work out whether I'm being mocked or not. Sometimes Tenant is being disingenuous when he flatters, other times he means it. I listen dumbly as they plan their speeches for the following day. Eventually I say goodnight as pleasantly as possible, collect my laptop and trudge back to the Louis XVI.

Half an hour later, I've barely settled my head on the pillow when I become aware of a faint knocking sound. Shivering and dressed only in my dog-motif boxer shorts, I open the door to see my drug-dealing porter grinning at me insanely. 'I bring you girls,' he says.

'What?' I adjust my eyes to the harsh strip lighting in the hall. I may say another 'what?'.

'They here.' He signals at two grumpy-looking women in furs standing over by the lift. 'Have look. Beautiful Russian girls.' There is a blur of movement as the two push past me and sit on my bed. The porter smiles at me, exposing his black tooth, and I signal for him to stay where he is as I go back into the room. The women are tossing between them the cuddly rabbit I found in Jenny's bag and which I had left out on the bed. One of them, although heavily made up, has the palest and shiniest face I have ever seen. She is also wearing a long wig of black hair and this complements the short red dress that can be seen under her half-opened fur coat.

She throws the rabbit at me when she sees me staring at her. This is followed by a snorting laugh. I hug the rabbit to me and rub my goosepimpled arms. The other woman is heavier and appears to have a light beard. I dare say they are both Russian – the one in the wig has Slavic cheekbones – but neither could reasonably be described as beautiful. Or girl.

Feeling shivery – and indignant about their mocking of Jenny's rabbit – I point to the door with a trembling finger. The bearded one waves a dismissive hand and says in a kind, husky voice '*Dos vidanya*'. The other points to my boxers, makes a 'woof-woof' noise and cups her hand over her mouth to suppress a giggle.

I close the door after them, breath rasping and blood pounding in my ears. Remembering that the latch does not lock, I sleep fitfully, shivering and expecting them to barge in again at any moment. At first I dream of Jenny lying unconscious by the roadside in the rain, then she turns into one of the prostitutes and I wake up feeling vaguely aroused but dehydrated – with no water safe enough to drink, I slip in and out of delirium, hallucinating about ranks of Chinese prostitutes in khaki uniforms goose-stepping towards me against a backdrop of a mushroom cloud.

The next morning, I wake myself up with a shout and look around my room in confusion. My sheets are damp from my sweating. The window is open a few centimetres – no wonder I was so cold in the night – and wisps of snow are finding their way into the room. I go over to shut it and, instead, open it wider to take in the scenery. From this height, four floors up, the freshly snow-muffled rooftops of Bucharest, the Little Paris of the East, look grand and dignified.

Tenant explained to me over dinner how the noble architecture disguises a brutish political function. Like Haussmann's great boulevards in Paris, their original purpose was to provide the widest field of fire for the artillery and the quickest access for the cavalry to charge anywhere the peasants might stage a rebellion. I can appreciate this now and my eye follows the narrowing perspective of the long boulevard below, all the way up to the vanishing point: a semicircle of tanks parked outside Ceauşescu's unfinished monolithic palace. I can see UN-flagged cars arriving and this prompts me to check my watch. It's 8.45 and the summit is due to start there at 9.30.

I instruct 'Jenny' to turn on its television function and, as I shave and dress, I listen to the news: the British Ambassador at the UN has approached the Security Council and requested a resolution ordering China to withdraw its forces from the Romanian border. As China is on the Council, this was a futile gesture, but it had the desired effect. The Chinese Ambassador removed his headset and marched out.

As I listen to the next item on the news, about the acres of floral tributes being piled up around Westminster, I hear a sullen thud. It sounds like a sandbag the size of a Ford Escort landing on a thick carpet. I look up to see the windows warping inwards a couple of centimetres. The air in the room is compressed and then sucked out of the window. The seconds of silence that follow the shock wave are broken by the whine of a burglar alarm. As I lean out of the window, I catch a whiff of something – nitro-glycerine, I guess, or cordite – and the association with fireworks on bonfire night makes me tingle with excitement. I see a cloud of smoke rising from an overturned lorry in the road below. As quickly as I can, I dress, zip my laptop into its case, slip the strap over my shoulder and half-run to the lift.

Eight

Major disasters I have covered: the great earthquake in LA, the slaughter of the tourists by Islamic fundamentalists in Casablanca, the IRA bombing of Gatwick Airport. At each I've noticed that people in fear tend to lose their shoes. Wandering around the aftermath you'll always find a scattering of plimsolls, sandals, boots, usually just a single one on its own. I've never worked out why this phenomenon occurs, but I suppose they are totems of panic.

The scene outside my hotel is a good example of it. Lying in the snow, in a nest of glass shards from the hotel lobby window, is a child's wellington – blue with a yellow top, tied with a yellow lace. It arrests my eye as I jog over to where the black-and-white lorry is lying on its side like a beached killer whale, oily-smelling smoke churning out from under its bonnet. I look around for the owner of the footwear but there doesn't appear to be a child among the people standing staring from a safe distance.

An ambulance is already on the scene. It must have been driving past when the explosion occurred. 'What happened?' someone behind me says with a tug on my sleeve. It is a UN soldier. An Italian, to judge by his accent.

'Didn't see. Just heard a bang.'

I follow him as he walks round to the other side of the truck and the snow creaks as it is compressed under our shoes. Someone who I assume must be the driver has been pulled free by two paramedics and is lying on a stretcher. He must be toast because there is a blanket covering his face. There is a strong smell of petrol in the air. A dazed-looking woman is sitting on the kerb ten metres away, nursing a lightly bleeding forehead in her hand. A mongrel is lying dead in the middle of the road just beyond her, dark crimson blood bubbling from its stomach on to the powdery snow.

Two Romanian paramilitaries arrive and brandish machine guns in an attempt to clear the area of onlookers. When one of them approaches me, I flash the conference press card I am wearing on a chain around my neck. I ask if he knows what happened. He mumbles in pidgin English that he thinks it could be terrorists. Maybe their bomb has gone off by mistake.

It must have been a small bomb as little else appears to be damaged: apart from the windscreen of a car across the road, the glass in the revolving door of the hotel, and a water main that is spraying over a shop awning. A traffic light a few metres away from the lorry is stuck on green. I ask the paramilitary if he knows who the driver is but he ignores me and starts signalling with big, self-important gestures at a fire engine that has just arrived.

The firemen soon have foam padding down on the truck and, the flames doused, they wrench the passenger side door open and examine the charred interior. One of the paramedics gives the man in the stretcher an injection. The paramilitary stands over the man, pointing his machine gun at him needlessly. The man still appears to be alive but his body is convulsing in shock. Whatever the injection is, it soon leaves him motionless.

The first paramedic runs back to the ambulance for an oxygen mask and when she returns I ask if she needs any help. She nods at me without smiling, takes hold of one end of the stretcher and indicates for her fellow paramedic to take the other. She then stops and looks at me again. 'Michael?' She says it hesitantly.

It's only now that I recognize her as someone I was at university with. I can't remember her name. She was attractive in an anonymous thin, blonde way. But now her hair is dark, tied in a pony tail. She has put on about 25 lb, I would say. Her face is pinched and without the heavy make-up she used to wear she looks plain.

'It's Sarah,' she says. 'Sarah Garnett.'

'Of course. Hi, Sarah. What you doing here?'

'What's it look like. You?'

I explain as they lift the stretcher and march it back to the ambulance with me holding on to one side, rather ineffectually.

'I didn't know you'd become a journalist.' She says.

She must have known. Everyone knows. Feeling mildly insulted, I check her face to see if she is having me on. Her expression is blank.

The woman with the bleeding head is manhandled into the back of the ambulance where she sits down and Sarah dabs at her face with a ball of cotton wool soaked in powerful-smelling disinfectant. When I climb in beside her, Sarah turns and looks me up and down and then gives a shrug which I take for an 'OK then'. The ambulance lurches off, its wheels spinning briefly before getting a purchase in the snow. I ask Sarah if she knows what has happened. She has been told by the *Securitate* that terrorists probably planted the bomb. Apparently, a group sympathetic to the striking miners has been threatening something like this.

The hospital, more like a neglected prison in appearance, is a five-minute drive away and, once the victims have been handed over, Sarah asks me to join her for a Turkish coffee. It seems an oddly normal thing to do after the frenetic activity of the past quarter of an hour and, realizing how dry my mouth has become, I accept readily. As we stand by the coffee machine sipping from paper cups – the coffee is almost undrinkably sweet – we reminisce about mutual friends from Bristol and she tells me how she came to work for Médecins sans frontières. It has meant her spending many years in remote trouble spots of the world.

'That's why I haven't been able to follow your career,' she says. 'It's good that we've both gone into professions which haven't compromised our youthful idealism, though, isn't it? Do you remember all those demonstrations we took part in? Anti-apartheid, veal crates, Poll Tax?'

I avoid her eyes. Within a year of moving to Fleet Street I had systematically reneged on every belief I had ever held. I wish there was a cause I could feel passionately about but there isn't. 'It seems such a long time ago,' I sniff.

'Being sent to all the trouble spots must be so rewarding. A chance to tell the truth. Take a moral stand.'

'Actually, I don't normally do this sort of thing.'

'Oh . . . Terrible about the assassination.'

'Yes. Poor bastard.'

'I was on a shift when I heard. Couldn't believe it. You?'

'Driving my car.'

'So did you get married?'

'Twice. You?'

'No.'

'Oh.' As I produce a photo of Amanda from my wallet my business card drops out. Sarah picks it up.

'Can I keep this, Michael? *Dekuji*. Thanks.'

I waft my hand at the card and say: 'It's good to see you again . . . You look tired.'

She shrugs. 'So what are you going to write about the UN summit?'

'Don't know yet.'

'The *English People*, that's Bruce Tenant's paper, isn't it?'

'Yes. He's here at the moment.'

'Has he told you what line you're supposed to take?'

'It doesn't work like that.'

'He's investing in InfoWar research, isn't he?'

'How do you know about that?'

'I thought everyone knew. Has he ever talked to you about it?'

'No. Well, yes. In a roundabout way.'

Sarah checks her watch. 'You doing anything for dinner tonight, Michael?'

I shake my head.

She purses her lips, tilts her head to one side and takes out a piece of paper from one of the zips in the arm of her jacket. On this she writes an address. 'We are,' she says, handing me the note. 'But you can join us.'

'Us?'

'My mother, she's staying with me at the moment.' As she says this she stands on tiptoes to kiss me on each cheek. Her breath is sour, and a robust smell of perfume mixed with sweat lingers for a moment as she turns and walks away down the corridor. She has a slow, hip-rolling gait, like a middle-aged model sashaying on a catwalk. 'Eight o'clock,' she adds without looking back. '*Na shledanou brzo.*'

When she disappears around the corner, I look her parting words up in my Romanian phrasebook – but I can't find them.

From the hospital it's a short walk to Ceauşescu's palace. And after being frisked by security men with cold fingers I enter the conference hall just in time to slip on the headphones and hear a translation of the last minute of a speech by the French foreign minister. A Spanish delegate is next and I use the twenty minutes of his speech to tap out an 800-word report about the bomb blast. I read it through in the coffee break that follows and then file it to London using, for the first time, my laptop's satellite modem system. Nervous that it won't really have gone through without being plugged into a phone socket, I ring the newsroom. Miss Monotone confirms that it is sitting in the news directory. She also says that a man from the *Evening Mirror* has been ringing for me – under my shirt I can feel a cool bead of sweat trickle down my back.

Tenant's speech, scheduled for that afternoon, is never delivered. A bomb alert during the lunch hour means that the whole, cavernous building has to be evacuated. As we are filing out, Tenant catches my arm. He is in an ugly mood and, dispensing with the usual unpleasantries, he hands me a copy of his speech, covers up the mouthpiece of the mobile he is talking into and tells me to write about it anyway. He adds that he'll be at the Diplomat if I need him.

I take a taxi back to the Louis XVI, pack my luggage, check out and walk over to the Diplomat. When I check in I'm handed a message from Tenant saying that the rest of the day's speeches have been cancelled and, as it looks as if the rest of the summit will also be cancelled, he is flying back to London at 9. If I want to fly with him, I should meet him at the airport at 8.30. It doesn't sound as if I have much choice, so I cancel my return flight and spend the afternoon writing a think piece for the op. ed. page on why we should be doing everything we can to increase our arms exports to countries like, well, like Romania.

I almost forget about dinner with Sarah – only when I'm

sorting through my receipts for expenses as I pack to leave do I come across her note. I quickly scribble an apology on a sheet of the hotel writing paper – explaining why I have to leave suddenly. In a moment of dangerous flirtation, I add that she should give me a call next time she's in London.

The taxi driver taking me to the airport says that Sarah's house is only a short detour *en route*. It isn't, of course, but the drive northwards along the Bulevardul Nicolae Balcescu and on through the sprawling backstreets of Bucharest proves edifying. We cross over the River Dimbovita and drive on past a partly demolished synagogue and four rusting cranes standing idle above unfinished towerblocks with colonnades and white marble frontages.

Sarah lives on the fifth floor of a derelict-looking block of flats. The lifts do not work and the stairs are a serious health hazard, littered as they are with used needles, empty cans, clothes, newspapers and dog shit. The paint has mostly blistered and flaked off the walls and has been replaced by graffiti, some of it so old it refers to Ceaușescu. There are no curtains in her flat and, from the balcony, you can see straight into the sitting room. The interior design of this, gloomily lit by one standard lamp with a hunting scene on its shade, seems to have been inspired by the stairs. The flock wallpaper is burgundy and has just one picture on it: a yellowing reproduction of a crucifixion scene, Renaissance by the look of it. In the far corner of the room, next to a gas fire, is an emaciated terrier, asleep. In the adjoining room, separated by a curtain of stringed beads tied back on one side, I can make out the shape of what appears to be a wizened babushka, wearing a black headscarf, sitting at a kitchen table.

The dog stands up, stares at me but does not bark. Tentatively, I slip the note through the letter box. It swallows it with a metallic clatter and I walk away.

Slightly out of breath after descending the stairs two at a time, I look blankly along the street for my taxi driver. It takes a few seconds for the light to dawn. I feel so stupid for having trusted the bastard to wait for me when he had my laptop and thousands of euros' worth of luggage begging to be stolen that my eyes water out of self-pity. I pace up and down. I look at my watch. I calculate the likelihood of my finding another taxi in this neighbourhood.

'*Dobry vecer*, Michael. Need a lift?' It is a woman's voice. I look up to see Sarah leaning over the balcony five floors up, fanning herself with my letter.

We don't speak much on the way to the airport but the silence is relaxed. When Sarah asks me to light a cigarette for her and put it to her lips, I do so flirtatiously. As she isn't allowed to take her black Trabant – which has only one working headlight – beyond the security gates, we say goodbye in the car, this time with a kiss on the lips. 'I know some people,' she says, winding the window down to call after me. 'I may be able to get your luggage back.' I stick my thumb up and turn the gesture into a wave goodbye. She stays in her car by the gate, watching me in the softening dusk. As a UN jeep arrives to transport me over to the sleek grey silhouette of the Gulfstream VII, I wave to her again and surreptitiously throw away the packet containing what is left of my drugs.

The seats of Tenant's jet are upholstered in embossed iguana suede, the floor carpeted in a deep, turquoise-and-white patterned pile. So are most of the walls, only these are interspersed with drinks cabinets – metal-bottomed decanters of amber liquid in moodily lit glass cases, held in place magnetically. There is a gym and shower compartment at one end of the aircraft and, at the other, a computer screen flashing stock market prices, a solid-looking chandelier, and a television covered in what is probably, knowing Tenant, real leopard skin. Above this, sealed behind thick glass, there is a dusty-looking preparatory drawing for an oil painting – it is of a limp hand and is outlined by pin pricks. On a discreet black and white plaque underneath is written: 'Detail. Descent from the Cross. Sir Peter Paul Rubens (1577–1640)'. I think of the crucifixion scene on Sarah's wall. The coincidence seems vague and unreal, like an hallucination. When I ask a passing co-pilot if the drawing is genuine he gives a tight-lipped smile and a nod.

I keep staring at the drawing as I sink into a squashy leather chair and pick up the first edition of the next day's *English People*. I try to read first my account of the bombing on the second page – it has been cut down to two paragraphs – and then my essay in the comment section. This has been rewritten.

I find it hard to concentrate, my eye returning to the drawing like the tip of the tongue to an annoying tooth cavity. I give up and rummage around in my one remaining piece of hand luggage for a Sony E-book. I switch it on, load *The Iron Chancellor*, an old biography of the new prime minister, and scroll down the first chapter. I feel it's only polite to try and read it.

Half an hour into the flight I take advantage of a neck massage being offered by one of the three remarkably friendly and prepossessing air stewardesses whose job, it seems, is to take it in turns to loosen Tenant's tie, sit in his lap and use their tongues to play with the ganglions on his leathery neck. He spends the flight in a cloud of cigar smoke, talking into his phone and ignoring the stewardesses. Even this does not distract me from staring at the drawing. It takes a shooting pain in my stomach to do that. I hobble to the washroom and sit out much of the remaining hour of the flight there, with my trousers around my ankles. I thought I'd been careful but somehow I'd picked up mild food poisoning, probably from the lobster.

Nine

At Heathrow, Tenant takes his helicopter on to his house in Wiltshire and arranges for his Bentley to run me back into London. I ask the chauffeur to pull over at the first service station we drive past so that I could get some Diocalm, and once I have crunched my way through twice the recommended dose of these I feel a bit better. My next request is to drive to the Cromwell Hospital. He says he doesn't mind and I promise I won't be long. The return of the toy rabbit seems a good pretext to visit Jennifer again. I'm told by the nurse on reception that Miss Lambert has been discharged by the consultant on duty, and collected by her parents.

Back in the car, I wonder out loud whether I will be pushing my luck to ask the driver to take me to a cash point in Battersea. Here I take out enough euros to pay for my fourth stop, for proper medicine.

Sally, I don't know her surname, nor do I want to, lives above a Japanese restaurant in Battersea Village. Her flat is full of antique knick-knacks and she, a middle-aged, unreconstructed flower child with dyed black hair, always seems to be sifting through them, wearing her dressing gown, whenever I call round. I dab some of the powder on my gums and am about to suggest a quick line with her (because she always uses her own supply for this) when I remember the chauffeur waiting outside. We have our usual elliptical conversation instead.

Me: 'Four grams of the ordinary' (she also does a 'special' cut with speed).

Sally: 'You're in luck, I think I've only got four left.'

If I asked for four hundred she would say: 'I've only got four hundred left.' Money changes hands, furtive glances are made while descending the metal fire escape at the back, and the ritual is over.

At 7.05 the following day, Saturday, the morning of my ritual lie-in, I come to regret my having bought four packets. I've stayed up all night with Amanda, taking line after line of the stuff and talking far too fast and too loud about the significance of the assassination and the Bucharest summit. My wife is normally in the country during the week but she has come up to our house in Pimlico to attend the state funeral.

I've just popped some diphenhydramine to help me sleep when the phone rings. It's Dysfunctional Alan, already at the newsdesk, telling me I'm to be part of the team covering the funeral that morning. I have to get myself to Westminster Abbey straight away to do some vox-pop with the Great Unwashed who have camped out there overnight.

I set my alarm clock for 9 – the funeral service isn't due to start until 11 – and try to get a couple of hours' sleep. I can't, just keep grinding my teeth and thinking about the events of the past few days. At 8.50, after three cups of espresso, I set off along Millbank to Westminster. All the roads are cordoned off to traffic and when I reach Parliament Square the crowds are so solid I have to shoulder my way through them, barking the word 'press' every few metres as I do so.

Feeling mildly hallucinatory from a combination of drug-taking and lack of sleep, I notice for the first time that the pavement outside Westminster Tube station is greyly polka-dotted with squashed chewing gum spat out lazily over many months by commuters – and this strikes me as being callous and disrespectful to the PM. To my right a vast video-board is advertising Smuggies biodegradable nappies and this, too, seems to hit the wrong note

– especially as the same screen was used for the PM's weekly broadcasts. The flags of St George on the rooftops around Whitehall are flying at half-mast. There is a long queue of people waiting to sign the books of condolence in the entrance to the House of Commons. Another queue is snaking towards Downing Street, its members waiting to add their cellophane-wrapped flowers to the fragrant mound already piled up there. At the Cenotaph, the band of the Coldstream Guards, dressed in grey trenchcoats, is playing Elgar's *Nimrod*. I cannot focus on them, though, as my eyes have clouded over. I find myself caught up in the sort of peasant hagiography you associate with Latin America. A very un-English carnival of grief. Eager to get some quotes down for my report, I approach a young man who begins talking calmly enough but, when I ask him why he has been crying, his mouth twists, his face creases and he bursts into convulsive, snotty sobs again.

The funeral has been arranged at an impressive speed. The shooting took place on Tuesday and it is now Saturday – the day chosen to avoid overlap with Remembrance Sunday. The cortège is to set off from the Palace of the People at 10.30, pass through Horse Guards Parade at 10.45 and reach Parliament Square at 10.55.

Outside the abbey, there is a muted cheer as Sir Mick Hucknall arrives. He has been asked to sing a rewritten version of 'Holding Back the Years' during the service and he looks pale and nervous. A large video screen erected outside the north transept of the abbey shows the departure of the specially converted Renault Espace that bears the coffin. The cross of St George flapping at half-mast on top of the Palace of the People provides a poignant backdrop for the five mounted policemen who lead the procession down the Mall. The black, open-top Espace is escorted on foot by twelve Grenadier Guards. Police, stationed every ten metres, are there to control the crowds – but they are not needed. Flowers are thrown, cameras flash, there is a smattering of applause and one woman shouts in a shrill voice: 'We love you!' But most of the onlookers are listening in silent contemplation to the crunch of the Guards' boots on the tarmac and the doleful toll of a bell – Big Ben – that marks every passing minute.

In a final masterstroke of presentation, a bouquet of white lilies and black tulips arranged in the shape of an electric guitar has been laid out on the coffin: the Fender Stratocaster the PM had played in private as a way of winding down at the end of a busy day. The First Lady, a picture of dignity in mourning black and sunglasses, walks slowly behind the coffin accompanied by her children and the PM's faithful Scottish press secretary.

If I had to choose between having a conversation about football and gnawing one of my own fingers off without an anaesthetic, I would get to work with my teeth every time. But if the choice was between talking about 'the footie' and listening to some bore tell me what he was doing when he heard the Prime Minister had been shot, I'd be straight in there with an opinion about Tottenham's chances against Arsenal.

Just because everyone can remember what they were up to – washing the car, doing the ironing, having joyless sex with ugly partner – doesn't mean they have the right to appear on television every night to tell the rest of us.

Already there's a programme devoted to this on Channel 294. It's called *A Million Moments*. The Great Lobotomized send in short videos of themselves reminiscing about where they were, how they felt, what ghastly item of clothing they were wearing at the exact moment they heard the news. The idea is that once the required number of videos have been collected they will be transferred on to CD-ROM and buried in a time capsule to be opened at the next millennium.

Supposedly, these glimpses into the sad lives of ordinary Englishmen will provide future historians with an invaluable snapshot of the nation as it was in the early years of the twenty-first century. According to the programme's producers, these clips will also explain how 'the assassination which shattered the dreams of a generation and changed the course of European history' could have come about.

Sickening.

There's only one memory of that leaden November afternoon which will be of any value to historians in the year 3000. Mine. And, back at Canary Wharf, it is with a mixture of gratification and panic that I see my 'moment' has made it into print. The first edition of the *English People on Sunday* put to bed, we browse through the early editions of our rival papers as they tick over the fax. I am just reading the *London Times on Sunday* coverage of the funeral when Gavin comes over with a page from the *Evening Mirror*.

'Seen this?' he says, folding it over to an item which takes up the whole of page 18. The headline reads: 'This Means War!' The story is about the daughter of the Vice Chief of the Defence Staff who has been run over by Bruce Tenant's son-in-law while cycling on a country road in Devon. 'Award-winning journalist Michael Yates, 39, knocked the cyclist down when he was distracted by the news coming through on his car radio about the assassination of the Premier.'

There is a photo of a severe-looking old duffer in a uniform above a caption which reads, 'Top brass: a furious Air Marshal Sir Andrew Lambert yesterday'. There is also a photo of Jenny lying in a bed with drips attached to her arms. And, below this, a grainy photo of me looking old and sickly with my eyes half closed emerging from the hospital. If you look closely, you can see I am picking my nose.

Ten

I don't recognize her at first. About a dozen protesters are standing around the remains of a campfire, prodding its embers with spindly branches, spitting to make a hiss. Jenny is on her haunches, talking into a mobile, her back to the group.

Three months have passed since the assassination. An ugly power struggle within the New Labour hierarchy has left the People's Party, and the country, in chaos. The police have not yet been able to identify the PM's killer.

Three months have also passed since the accident – and Jenny seems smaller and thinner than I remember. She is dressed in black jeans and an East German army surplus jacket several sizes too big for her, zipped to the neck. There is a badge on her sleeve which says: People Not Profits. Her hair is cropped short and dyed corn-yellow, dark roots showing. And although the early morning light is watery, she is wearing sunglasses.

Feeling self-conscious in my Aran sweater, waxed jacket and spotless green wellies, I drop a newspaper on the dewy grass beside her and sit down heavily. She finishes her conversation, snaps her phone shut and levels a questioning look at me over the top of the sunglasses.

'Jenny, isn't it?'

'And you are?' She takes her sunglasses off.

'You look different... You're not wearing glasses.'

'I'm wearing contacts. Do I know you?'

'Michael Yates.'

She studies me thoughtfully before asking in a neutral tone: 'Yes, I recognize you now. What do you want?'

'I wouldn't have had you down as the contact-lens-wearing type.'

'What do you mean?'

'Well, it's a bit, you know, for an eco-warrior, a bit – '

'Vain? I kept breaking my glasses. What do you want?'

'I've been writing to you.'

'I know,' she says, her tone softening. 'My parents sent the letters on.'

'Why didn't you write back?'

'Why do you think? You ran me over.'

'Yes, I can see why that would... Do you hate me?'

'I did.' She purses her lips. 'Your letters were quite sweet actually. Made me laugh.'

I feel relieved. I had put a lot of effort into them, must have written about a dozen. 'Were you happy with the compensation my insurance company paid out?'

'It was fine, I suppose.'

'Are you fully recovered now?'

'Still have to use this.' She holds up a knobbly walking stick which has been painted in bright tribal colours, as though it is some kind of talisman. 'And I still get the odd headache. And there were gaps in my memory for a while but I think I'm over that now. I hardly ever, like, think about the accident.'

She wanders off towards a large tent and I have to break into a jog to catch up.

'Jenny?'

As she turns, I catch her straightening her face. 'You still here?'

'So you're OK now?'

'Is that what you came down here to find out?'

I've driven down to this boggy wood by a river in Devon because, although my job title is senior executive editor, I write at least one feature a month (it's something I asked for in my contract, so that I can keep my hand in and my profile high). Even if Tenant hadn't for some reason requested that I cover this story, I would have volunteered to do it anyway. Not to keep up with my writing quota. Not for the pleasure of sticking to the new 55 kph speed limit for eight hours in a car capable of doing 300 kph. But for the off chance to bump into Jenny. We are just a few miles from where I drove into her.

'No,' I say. 'I'm covering the protest for the *English People*.'

She considers this. 'Where do your sympathies lie then?'

'Mine? I'm impartial. But I'd have thought any publicity you can get would be good publicity.'

She smiles. 'Let me show you round the camp.'

Talking over her shoulder as she leads the way, she explains that she had been doing a recce of this site at the time of the accident. She takes me inside what she describes as a Mongolian yurt, a circular tent about three metres in diameter with a hole in the middle to let smoke out. Through this we look up at 'benders', aerial bivouacs perched high in the branches overhead, linked by a network of suspended rope walkways. She points with her stick at where several treetops have been lashed together by metal hawsers. From these vantage points, Jenny adds, the protesters can monitor the movements of their enemies – police, bailiffs, private security teams. Woodpigeons are cooing gloomily in the branches overhead.

At the muddy entrance to a network of tunnels, Jenny draws my attention to a whirring sound. Compressed air is being pumped down a five-metre shaft to remove stale air and circulate fresh. The tunnel has wooden sides but rain has breached the planks and the floor is heavy clay.

'There's a labyrinth beneath our feet,' Jenny says, tugging her sleeves down self-consciously. 'Based on the principle of the Vietcong tunnel rat. It's like, "wow", down there. There are about eight of us who do it in shifts.' She gets to her knees and begins patting the ground.

'What are you looking for?'

'Newts. This site is home to a number of endangered species, of which the great crested newt is the most rare. Heavily protected under European environmental law. This is what we're basing our case upon.'

The land has belonged to the Ministry of Defence and Ethical Justice for years but, because it hasn't been needed for training, it's become something of a wildlife sanctuary. Ignoring its Special Area of Conservation status, the Government has decided to sell it off to property developers who want to build a new town on it.

'You know the real reason they're doing it?' Jenny asks.

'Go on.'

'The Government is running scared of the Tories. They're behind in the polls. They know they'll have to call an election in the next six months and the last thing they want is for the voters to think they're afraid of taking on the army.'

It's a hoary old theory that's been doing the rounds in London for weeks. Since the assassination there's been one of those seismic shifts in politics. The Tory Party elected as its leader a handsome Welsh woman with blonde hair and a first class degree. Galvanized, it has re-named itself the New Conservative Party and repositioned itself as a caring, pro-European, Centrist party – and established a fifteen-point lead in the polls. Compared to the dour Scotsman who has moved next door to Number 10, the New Tory leader seems dynamic, radical and, well, sexy. She has pledged to slash the defence budget, freeze debt repayments to the IMF, and channel the money saved into social welfare.

The bulldozers are due to arrive at dawn. I have to file a 1,000-word colour piece on the subject by three this afternoon, stay overnight in a hotel and then come back in the morning to do a follow-up.

'You do know you can't win, don't you?' I say as Jenny gives up looking for her newt and rolls a cigarette instead.

She blows the smoke in my face. 'Course. But they can't drive over us, can they? How would that look on the evening news?'

Over the next few hours the air of tension in the camp becomes palpable. Dirty-haired children, their faces painted with berry juice, shout and scream as they play with the emaciated mongrels that run free around the campsite. But the adults are pensive, as though on the eve of a medieval battle. Men with long, matted hair and beards spilling over their trenchcoats chant mantras and play bongos. Some daub slogans on to placards. Others discuss strategies over mobile phones. They are friendly enough. At lunch-time a group of them cook on a makeshift clay oven and share out their nettle soup and home-made bread. Afterwards they show me how to construct a twigloo from lorry tarpaulins stretched over hazel saplings. This they strap to a floor of pallets and winch ten metres up into the branches of a tree.

My brief is to find the most photogenic and least odorous female protester and tell the story through her. Jenny does not have much competition and when my photographer arrives I get her to pose for him, straddling the gnarled branch of an ancient oak and giving a clenched fist salute.

Afterwards, I ask how she has come to be involved in the protest. Her background – in constant rebellion against her privileged upbringing – suits my journalistic purpose well. She had a peripatetic childhood, her father being posted to six different countries in as many years. To give her some stability in her life she was sent to Bedales, the public school in Hampshire, and at the age of fourteen she became one of the few girls ever to be expelled from there: for stealing money from the headmistress. When her parents separated for a couple of years, she went to live with her mother and took her GCSEs and A levels at a local crammer. She also began seeing a therapist, she adds matter-of-factly, for something called 'behavioural dysfunction'. She went to Manchester to study for a degree in sociology but dropped out after one term.

Jenny won't tell me how old she is now – says that judging people by their age is a form of oppression – but she looks anywhere between fifteen and twenty, and I would guess she is nearer twenty-two. She does say, though, that for the past two years she has been moving from one protest camp to another, campaigning against the building of bypasses, supermarkets and airport runways. She has taken part in all the anti-capitalism riots organised by Reclaim the Streets as well as all the direct actions against GM crops. She has been arrested twice: once for affray, for which she was cautioned; the second time for defying a court injunction to stay away from a particular protest site. For that she was sentenced to two weeks in Holloway. She claims.

When I ask how she gets by financially a blush colours her pale cheeks. She mutters something about the Giro but, when pressed, she admits she has an allowance paid to her monthly by her parents. It gives her away: like the Pony Club accent she tries to disguise with her Americanisms. The first language of any English man or woman under the age of twenty-five is American. Television-sitcom American, to be precise. Jenny is no exception. Indeed, she even has that youthful habit of raising her intonation at the end of her speech. I loathe it normally. In her I am beginning to find it charming.

Later, as I sit in my car, the engine purring, writing up my report, Jenny taps on the window. As I lean over to press a button and lower it, she asks: 'Is it, like, really necessary to have this thing pumping out exhaust fumes?'

'Have to have the engine on. The heater would run the battery down.'

She pouts, rocks on her heel and gets in, leaving footprints on the Wilton carpet. The heavy door gives a satisfying clunk behind her. 'Couldn't you have used imitation leather?' she asks, running her hands over the shapely seats.

'That's Connolly hide,' I say without looking up from my replacement laptop, a G22. 'From cows that weren't allowed to come into contact with barbed wire. Hand-stitched.'

'You think your precious upholstery is worth the life of an animal, yeah?'

'Absolutely.' I turn to her.

'Have you ever campaigned for anything?'

'I once took part in a save the road protest.'

'That is so not funny,' she says. 'I mean, where do your loyalties lie?'

'Look, Jenny, I don't mean to be rude, but I'm on a deadline. Give me ten minutes and you can have my undivided attention.'

She runs a finger over the curves of the dashboard before noticing the leather-covered gear stick nestling in the centre console. It falls easily to her hand and she massages it suggestively. She finds a button which begins to lower the electric roof. I remove her hand and press it back up. She finds a lever that adjusts the seat. She moves fore, aft, up and down before tilting the seat with a pneumatic sigh to the horizontal position. 'How come you drive a car like this?' She is addressing the ceiling. 'Isn't it too expensive for a hack?'

'Not when he's married to the boss's daughter.' I hold up eight fingers and two thumbs. 'Now, please. Ten minutes.'

Jenny tucks her legs up in front of her, links her arms beneath her knees, and presses the rubber soles of her boots against the Italian suede-lined roof. They leave two muddy footprints. If anyone else did this I'd go apeshit, but I find her, well, amusing.

'My father drives a Rolls-Royce,' she says casually.

'Thought you disapproved of cars.'

'I do. I'm always telling him off about it.'

With the windows closed and the heater on I notice she smells of woodsmoke and BO. If she notices, too, she doesn't seem to mind, just carries on walking until her feet are over her head. She does a gentle backwards roll into the back seat. I can hear her shuffling around on to her knees, then I feel her warm breath on my neck. Her chin is resting on the rear of my seat. 'What are you saying about me?'

'That you're a pest.'

'Let me see.'

'No,' I say, unconvincingly. I am enjoying the attention. 'Please. I can't stand people reading over my shoulder.'

'Let me guess. Poor little rich girl. Became an eco-warrior to get back at the parents she felt hadn't given her enough attention.'

'Exactly. Now if you'll let me – '

'It's probably true, of course. Probably just a phase I'm going through. Wouldn't you say? Do you think me too posh to be doing this sort of thing? Do you think me a terrible fraud? How big do you think they'll run the photograph of me?'

My mobile rings. 'Hugh. Hi.'

'Hi, Hugh!' Jenny echoes from the back.

'Just sending it over now,' I say. 'Got some good stuff, I think. Call me when you get it. Bye.' Jenny starts humming and I adjust the rear-view mirror so that I can see her. She smiles and flutters her eyelids jokily. I turn back to my screen but my concentration is broken again after only ten seconds.

It has been calculated that when a cold sufferer sneezes, at least 100,000 million infected droplets are discharged into the surrounding air. And these can travel at 120 kilometres per hour. I feel the full force of this statistic against the back of my neck.

'Sorry,' Jenny says, nasally. When she sneezes again, I pluck a hanky from my pocket and wipe my screen and the back of my neck. 'Can I borrow that?' she says. 'I have to blow my nose.'

'You win,' I sigh, clicking the lid of my laptop shut and opening the car door. I find a quiet area under a tree about a hundred metres away, finish the article and try to locate a satellite signal to modem it in. Though I love my laptop dearly, especially when I watch it unfold its flexiscreen, it is, like all computers, designed to frustrate. It has a built-in obsolescence of six months. And even though mine has just been upgraded for Microsoft Satellite compatibility, it is already out of date. I give up and phone the copytakers. It is not a great piece but I know they will rewrite it anyway so I can't see the point in making more of an effort.

When I return to the clearing, the car has gone. Half running, I follow its muddy tracks out of the wood, hear it and run in the direction of the noise. It is in the middle of a field dusted with the lime-green shoots of some winter crop. And Jenny is driving it, in tight circles, churning up the soil. She has the window down and the sound of her whooping and singing along to a song on the radio carries above the throaty drone from the engine. I run towards her, nursing my laptop in one arm while waving with the other.

When she sees me, she unlocks the steering wheel, sends the pointer on the rev counter off the dial, and heads straight for me. I freeze. I turn. I zigzag back the way I have come, my shoes clogging with clay. I can hear her laughing as she mirrors my feints to left and right. Then I slip, drop the laptop, and lie face down, trying to catch my breath. The car speeds past, waltzes round gracefully in a spin and begins to sink. The more she revs, the more the rear wheels spin and fire mud pellets into the air. As the car submerges to its axles, blue smoke plumes from the exhaust pipe.

I struggle to my feet, flick soil off my jumper, and march over to the car. I lean over Jenny to pull the Multicard from the ignition and drop to my knees, my forearms resting on the frame of the lowered window. Our faces are about twenty centimetres apart.

'That was *great!*' she says breathlessly. 'I mean, like, really. The best.'

'You could have killed me,' I say flatly.

'You look like a wolf, you know.'

'You could have killed me,' I repeat.

'An addled wolf,' she qualifies.

'You look like – ' I can't think of anything. She looks like a pretty boy. Androgynous. But I can't say that.

She leans forward and kisses me on the nose. 'Of course I didn't try to kill you. I knew exactly what I was doing.'

I stand up, Jenny gets out of the car and, as we walk together to the boot, she grabs hold of my arm to steady herself. When she sees how far the car has sunk, she sucks in air through her teeth. 'Sorry,' she says shaking her head.

I blow my nose dolefully. One of the many and varied drawbacks to insufflation is that it makes you prone to nosebleeds. This is not a good time to get one but, as I stuff a ball of tissue paper into my left nostril and hold my head back, Jenny has the decency to give me some space.

'And sorry about this, too,' she shouts from a short distance away. She sucks my laptop from the mud and holds it up to show me the tyre mark running across it. When she places it down gently in the boot of the car I don't bother to switch it on to see if it still works.

It is dark when the headlights of the AA recovery truck finally sweep over the field. Jenny has kept me company in the car and our conversation hasn't flagged. We've been talking about the accident, about my wife, about her father. A keen wind has picked up and is now whistling around the car. Our faces are tinged green from the glow of the instrument panel. It feels cosy.

When Jenny suggests I stay the night, to find out what life is really like in a protest camp, I surprise myself by accepting.

Eleven

The Aston Martin is pulled free at the first attempt. I drive Jenny back to the clearing, drop her off and park by the side of the road. I phone Amanda to let her know I won't be staying in the hotel, remove my Multicard and set the anti-theft device to full charge. Any hairy troglodyte who tampers with the car in the night will receive the maximum electrical shock permitted under European law.

The evening air is laced with wood smoke. The orange glow of a bonfire can be seen in another clearing and, as we approach, its crackle can be heard. There must be about fifty people silhouetted against it, pagans warming their hands ritualistically, stamping their feet against the cold.

Whenever an empty tin of lager is crumpled up and thrown on the fire, it is followed by the hiss of a fresh can being opened. People are drinking whisky straight from the bottle. Others sip it from mugs. I am offered one with 'I shot the PM!' printed on the side. The temptation to drink has rarely been stronger, but I resist. I do have a few tokes on a spliff that is being passed around, though, and soon become mesmerized by the sight of sparks leaping from the bonfire. They describe arcs before turning to ash on the ground. I barely react when Jenny loops her arm through mine and presses herself against me. I take another toke, hold it down and pass it to her. 'Not the same now it's legal,' I say when I exhale.

'Everyone always says that. Such bollocks. I think it's better.'

I feel an immediate head rush. Skunk. How marvellous.

'Of course it isn't the same,' I continue. 'Think how much more enjoyable it's become to smoke cigarettes in public, now that there's a Euro directive banning us from doing it.'

'That's different.'

'Bet you didn't smoke until that rule came in.'

'Yes, I did.'

'All right then, tell me where you enjoy smoking most: in the privacy of your own home where it is allowed or in a public place?'

She shrugs.

Standing on the other side of me is a dull-eyed youth wearing a woollen Aztec-style hat, a 'No More Corporate Fascism' sticker on its dangling earflap. He introduces himself as Nettle. 'Everyone here is known by a nickname,' he explains. 'Because we believe that surnames are a form of oppression.'

'Everyone in my office has a nickname, too,' I say. 'Usually a woman's if you are a man.'

'Isn't that sexist?' he says.

'You tell me.'

'What's yours then?'

'Michelle. Because my real name is Michael. There's only one person in our office who doesn't have a nickname and that's Williams. He's too boring to inspire one. We've tried but nothing seems to work.'

'That's not fair,' Jenny joins in. 'I haven't got a nickname.'

'Yes, you have,' Nettle corrects with a broad grin.

'What is it?' Jenny sounds hurt.

'Williams.'

Ignoring Jenny's pursed lips, Nettle and I continue our laughing jag long after the comment ceases to be funny. I notice too late that he is wearing an 'I shot the PM!' badge on his lapel. In the months since the assassination, the title PM has come to refer to one PM only, and now it always will, whoever the premier happens to be. It's a bit like Elvis having a monopoly on the moniker 'King' – much to the irritation of the Palace of the People. Anyway, these badges are everywhere – along with 'I shot the PM!' T-shirts, mugs, bumper stickers, shoulder bags and keyrings – and they have become something of a warning sign. If Nettle finds out I'm a journalist I'll be stuck listening to his conspiracy theories all night. The websites dedicated to the assassination of the PM are still the most visited on the Internet. There are so many theories doing the rounds, the Conspiracy Channel is able to devote nearly all its broadcast time to discussing them.

'What line of work do you do in your office then?' Nettle asks.

Here we go. Before I have time to think of a lie Jenny answers: 'He's a journalist.'

'Oh right.' (Nettle to Jenny.) 'The one you were expecting, yeah?'

'What does he mean?' (Me to Jenny.) 'What do you mean?' (Me to Nettle.)

'Take no notice of him.' (Jenny to me.)

'So you must have heard the latest theory, then?' (Nettle to me.)

So far the police investigation that was launched a few hours after the shooting has cost tens of millions of euros and lasted three months. Some two thousand witnesses and suspects have been questioned. Yet no one has been charged. And the Dufflecoat still has no identity. No matches have been found for his fingerprints, dental records or DNA. No one has recognized him from his photograph. Without a name to go on, no bank account, Multi-card or school reports can be connected with him. The police haven't been able to find out where he was living – so they haven't even found the usual copy of *The Catcher in the Rye* on his bedside table.

Nettle is convinced that the identity of the assassin must have been known to the police marksman who shot him. He also thinks that the marksman was working for an extremist right-wing group funded by Bruce Tenant.

I try to inject some surprise into my voice. 'Now why would Tenant want to do that?'

'Because the UN Security Council was prepared to lift the

international ban on InfoWar development. And the only man stopping them was the PM,' Nettle looks over his shoulder and leans closer. '*On ethical grounds.*'

It's the sound of a dog barking somewhere on the ground below that wakes me. *Below?* At first I can't think where I am, then it comes back. Jenny persuaded me to sleep the night in a twigloo. Nettle helped her to winch me up. Blearily, I shuffle to the edge of the pallet, still in the sleeping bag I'd been given, look down and feel vertiginous. There is a heavy fog and the lower trunk of the tree is wreathed in it. I crawl back to the centre of the floor, sit up and discover that someone has clipped a safety harness around my waist. Jenny. I remember now.

I scratch the stubble on my chin and yawn. Surprisingly, I've had a good night's sleep; warm enough in an Arctic-condition sleeping bag. I only woke twice: when someone yelled out in shock after touching my car; and when Jenny snaked across the pallet in her sleeping bag, assumed the spoons position, wriggling her back against my front, and draped my arm around her waist as though it were a comfort blanket.

She is still asleep, snoring lightly, back on her side of the floor.

In the distance I can hear a muffled voice shouting through a megaphone, something like: 'By the powers vested in me...' But the wind carries the rest of it away. The fog is lifting and a convoy of a dozen minibuses now becomes visible. They trundle past my car and off the road into the clearing, forming a semi-circle about fifty metres from the campsite. I shake Jenny awake and we watch as the vans decant at least 150 men: half of them wearing hard hats and fluorescent green coats, the rest in full body armour, carrying batons and transparent shields. They space themselves five metres apart and stand in a line in front of the buses. It is getting light but the sun has yet to rise. I check my watch: 6.30 a.m.

'What happens, now?' I say. For some reason I am whispering.

'That's up to them,' Jenny sprinkles tobacco on to a cigarette paper and rolls it. 'Light?' I unbutton my thornproof jacket, arch my back and pat my trouser pocket. The lighter needs a shake before it will ignite and I have to hold my coat open to shield it from the wind. Jenny cups the flame and takes a deep drag.

The rest of the protesters have woken up now and are congregating around the circle of ash where the bonfire has been. Everyone is coughing and shivering, even those who still have blankets draped around their shoulders. One man pulls a black balaclava over his head. Another handcuffs himself to a 'lock-on', a metal spike set in concrete. A couple of men are urinating against trees. One middle-aged woman with windburnt cheeks and grey dreadlocks is squatting a few metres farther on. Plumes of steam are rising from the ground between her legs.

A man carrying a loud hailer makes his way to the front of the line. 'That's the Undersheriff of Devon,' Jenny whispers.

'Hiss. Boo,' I say, but she doesn't smile. There is a short whine as the Undersheriff turns his megaphone on and begins reading from a sheet of paper. 'By the powers vested in me...' His warning – that anyone who tries to interfere with the lawful work his men have come here to carry out will be arrested – is cut short when a clod of turf hits him on the shoulder. This provokes whistles and jeers from the protesters.

Two police vans arrive and these are followed by four bright yellow bulldozers which have orange lights flashing from their cabins. Even up in the tree we can feel the vibrations as their caterpillar tracks clatter over the ground. The tremors linger in the nerves for a moment after the engines have been silenced.

The entrance to the wood is now blocked with traffic and when a lorry carrying workmen turns up it has to park in the road. As they unload their chainsaws, another police van pulls on to the verge behind them. When the doors open, six Alsatians, straining on their leads, jump out with their handlers.

One of the protesters begins drumming: dull thuds with the flat of his hand on a bongo. In answer to this the security men begin striking their batons against their shields. The members of the TV crew edge past them and set up their cameras and lights on one side of the clearing between the two lines. Although the sun has now risen and the trees are casting long shadows, the crew rig up three powerful arc lights before they begin filming.

As if this is a pre-arranged signal, the security men begin marching in formation towards the protesters. They are immediately pelted with a volley of stones. When the security men charge, the protesters scatter: some shin up the trees and chain themselves to branches, others scramble down into the maze of tunnels. About fifteen disappear into the woods, pursued by barking police dogs. We can follow their progress as they double back on themselves only to be corralled into a semi-circle of waiting security men.

Two hours later all but a handful of the protesters have been arrested. One wiry youth thrashes and struggles so violently it takes six security men to lift him into the police van. A fire engine is called in to reach the protesters chained to the branches. Four men put up fierce resistance, kicking and punching, but once the cutters have bitten through the padlocks, most of them go quietly.

A yellow and white device resembling a lawnmower is brought in and this, Jenny explains to me, is to detect the tunnels. A transmitter mounted on the right side of it emits a ground-penetrating radar pulse every five centimetres. The reflective pulse is picked up by a receiver mounted on the left, which displays the results on a liquid-crystal screen. As it is pushed at walking speed, yellow lines are painted on the surface, to map the twists and forks of the subterranean network. Tear gas is used to flush out the tunnels and the wretches that emerge from them blinking and gagging in the light have to be taken away in ambulances. They are carrying gas masks which have been of little use.

Jenny and I are lying on our bellies unnoticed in the treetop bivouac. They haven't got round to checking our tree yet. *Our tree.* Melancholy laps over me at the thought that we will soon be evicted. A friendship has been forged between us and I feel like a child in a treehouse, untouched by the cold winds of the adult world.

I felt no sympathy for the protesters when I arrived and, to be honest, I still don't. But Jenny's optimism has stirred something long buried in me. Jealousy, perhaps, that she is still young enough to hold convictions without feeling embarrassed. I can't remember the last time I felt passionate about anything, let alone a point of principle. And yet here that feeling is, no more than an itch under the skin, but unmistakable.

A chainsaw screams to life and as its teeth tear into the bark of the first tree I look across at Jenny and see that tears are coursing down her cheeks. I squeeze her hand for a moment and we both get to our knees, my head touching the tarpaulin roof. I clear my throat softly. 'Shall we go down?'

Jenny sniffs. 'Not yet.' In a whisper, this. 'We can just stay hidden up here and when they chop our tree down we can go crashing down with it.' She wraps her arms around me, her face pressed against my chest, and begins rocking gently. 'It would be a fine way to die, wouldn't it, Mickey?'

I stroke her hair with my hand, smell it and kiss the crown of her head. I feel like crying, too.

'Don't call me Mickey.' I say. We remain like this for perhaps half an hour, deaf to the whine of chainsaws and the creaking of trees as they crash around us. It takes the Undersheriff with the loud hailer to shatter the spell. 'Anybody up there?' We stand apart from each other and something passes between us, a look of almost sexual intimacy.

I help Jenny into the seat harness and as I lower her down on the pulley I notice she has left a snailtrail of clear snot on the lapel of my wax jacket. Once she is on the ground I pull the harness back up again and lower myself down.

'Aren't you going to arrest me?' Jenny asks.

'I don't think there's any need for that, love. I can see you're not one of the troublemakers. You can just go and stand with the others over there.' The Undersheriff points to a huddle of protesters standing around looking miserable near the entrance of the wood. As we are walking towards them, we hear a chainsaw spark up and turn to see a cloud of sawdust being sprayed into the air. When the saw is only a third of the way through, our tree splits lengthways, twists and keels over.

I put a paternal arm around Jenny's shoulder. 'When a tree falls in a wood and there's no one to hear it...'

'This is, like, so sad.' There is a catch in her voice.

'I see my photographer has finally shown up.' I wave him over. He apologizes for being late and hands me a folded-up copy of the day's *English People*. I flick through it and see that my story has been cut to 200 words and run without a photograph at the bottom of page 5. I scrunch the paper up in disgust and turn to watch as one of the bulldozers starts up.

It raises its massive bucket off the ground. The three machines lined up behind it do the same. The clearing that had been about fifty metres in circumference has now doubled in size. The felled trees are dragged away by JCBs, leaving scars in the soil. All that remains of this section of the wood are twenty or so smooth stumps and the smell of fresh woodchippings. The lead bulldozer tips its bucket so that the teeth are pointing down, plunges it into the soil, and lurches forward. Five metres of mossy earth are scooped up in one go.

With terrible calmness, Jenny limps in front of the bulldozer, lowers her head and, resting both hands on her walking stick, stands quite still. She is dappled by shafts of weak sunlight filtering through the branches overhead. The great machine judders to a standstill.

'Christ!' my photographer shouts. 'Did you see that!' He raises one of the cameras dangling from his neck and begins clicking. Although the light has turned soft, Jenny casts a shadow which shimmers in the remaining wisps of fog. The bulldozer casts a bulkier one and the sight of this inspires the photographer to jump on to the trunk of a felled tree to get a more dramatic angle. As his shutter trips, two burly security men run towards Jenny. One gets her in a headlock while the other twists her arm behind her back.

I imagine it's something to do with my being six foot five, but I have always been passive and painfully self-conscious. No one has ever really picked a fight with me and even if they had I would have avoided fighting back for fear of looking ungainly. Probably. But now the sight of these two oafs trying to wrestle Jenny to the ground triggers some protective instinct in me. I run over and rugby tackle the nearest man, tipping him off balance and taking Jenny and the other man with him.

Jenny scrambles to her feet but is prevented from escaping when one of the men grabs her foot.

A time warp.

I'm trying to focus on a paramedic who is waving his hand in front of my face, asking how many fingers he is holding up. He tells me I've been headbutted and that I am suffering from concussion.

Groggily, I feel my nose. It is tender but there is no blood so I stand up and look around for Jenny. The paramedic makes me sit down again, drapes a blanket over my shoulders and hands me two Aspirin.

'Cool, Mickey.' It is Jenny standing beside me. 'I guess this means you've gone native, yeah?'

I shrug. 'Please don't call me Mickey.'

'Come on, you two.' We look round to see a policeman ushering us towards a van.

'You can't arrest me,' I say. 'I'm a journalist. Bruce Tenant is my father-in-law.'

'In,' he snaps. 'Now!'

On the drive to Exeter police station, I use my mobile to dictate an account of the morning's action to the copytakers. Normally I'm useless at this style of reporting: composing and ordering sentences in your head, unpolished, without seeing them written down. But on this occasion, the piece seems to write itself, effortlessly, as though I were in a trance. My descriptions are vivid and evocative, for once, the structure of the article natural and lucid. And all this without cocaine

Afterwards, I feel euphoric. I just sit grinning at Jenny who is sitting opposite me in the police van, grinning back.

The interview in the police station gets off to a bad start when Jenny gives my name as Mickey Mouse and hers as Minnie. But after four hours we are released with a caution. The police call a taxi for us and we drive back to Mowbray.

'What are you going to do now?' I ask as I check my Aston Martin for damage.

It is Jenny's turn to shrug. 'There's nothing to stay here for. That was my home they chopped down.'

'Can I give you a lift to London?'

'Can I stay with you?'

'Er, sure. We've got a spare room.'

Jenny thinks about it for a moment. 'It'll just be for tonight, Mickey. Thanks.'

We've been driving for no more than two minutes when she shouts for me to stop. She unclips her seat belt, jumps out of the car and, leaving the door open, runs in front. I lean forward in my seat, trying to make out why she is bent double running back and forth across the road. Eventually she pounces, cups her hands around something and holds them up in triumph. She is panting when she sits back down and asks me to lean over her to shut her door. She opens up her hands a fraction and I can see something dark and slithery. 'It's a great crested newt,' she says. 'You nearly ran over it.'

Twelve

Jenny holds the newt most of the way back to London, parting her hands slightly every so often to have a peep at it.

We talk for an hour or so until we come to a natural pause and I tune my radio into a music station. Dame Geri Halliwell's cover of 'Why Do You Have To Be A Heart Breaker?' is playing and Jenny begins singing along to it tunelessly. She even cajoles me to join in and, when I do, I feel light-headed. Neither of us knows the lyrics to the next song and Jenny soon falls asleep.

She doesn't wake up until we reach my house in Pimlico, and only does so then when I shake her. I tell her to be careful not to squash her newt which is sitting on the mat, having jumped from her hands when they went limp as she slept. Delicately, she scoops it up again. She looks disorientated as she walks out of the garage towards the house and she shivers when I swipe my Multicard in the front door. It rejects the card. I swipe again, there is a click and then there is the shrill electronic whine that precedes the security announcement. 'Your BMI has not been identified. Thought mode cannot be operated. You have twenty seconds to key in your manual override code.' I tap the numbers into the wall panel and the whining stops.

Jenny yawns.

'Amanda and I never got round to having our biomedical implants done,' I explain.

'You mean,' Jenny says sleepily. 'You have to actually switch on your own lights and open your own doors using your own hands?'

'No need for sarcasm.'

The automated voice says: 'Thank you. Welcome home.' Pause. 'Michael.' Pause. 'You have.' Pause. 'Voice-mail, e-mail and video-mail.'

I hold the door open for Jenny as she walks in with the newt cupped in her hands.

'What do you put them in?' I ask.

'A bath, I suppose.'

'There's one at the top of the stairs.'

'Won't your wife mind?'

'She's in the country. We have a second home.'

'Cool. I don't think I've ever met anyone as rich as you.'

'Your parents must know loads of rich people.'

She shrugs and walks upstairs. Once she has run some water and deposited her amphibian I give Jenny a quick tour of the house. It has five storeys and, being Georgian, has a marble fireplace in just about every room. The top floor is fairly self-contained, with a large guest room and bathroom and a door leading up to it. But I usher Jenny into the guestroom on the second floor, next to my study. I turn the light on in the bathroom that adjoins it. 'There's a toothbrush in the cabinet,' I say. 'Help yourself to one of the dressing gowns in the cupboard. If you leave your clothes on the landing I'll get our cleaner to wash them for you. Are you hungry? I could rustle something up.'

'I'm vegetarian, yeah?'

'So am I.' Well, I did consider it, once.

I have a bath, watch the evening news – Chinese massing tanks on the Romanian border – and look for the instructions for our Virtual Delia. When my wife is in town we have someone who comes in and cooks for us. When I'm on my own I usually order a takeaway. For Jenny's benefit I program our lifesize hologram of Delia Smith – it came with our kitchen – to talk me through celery baked in vinaigrette with polenta and shallots.

The Virtual Delia is voice activated and when she asks me if I've collected up a head of celery, six peeled shallots, two sprigs of thyme, one of rosemary, four leaves of sage, three slices of polenta and three tablespoons of virgin olive oil, I earn myself a rebuke by answering: 'Yes, Delia, but I'm afraid I'll have to go with onions instead of shallots.'

'Please answer yes or no.' Delia says it testily.

'Yes.'

'Now. Remove the tough outer layers of the celery, pare the outside of the root off, but leave it attached... Have you done that? Please answer yes or no.'

'Hang on, hang on.'

'Please answer yes or no.'

'No.'

'Good. Now cut across the celery about nine centimetres from the base, stand the lower half upright and – '

The microwave, where I have been defrosting the polenta, pings, breaking Delia's concentration.

'Please answer yes or no.'

'That was the microwave, Delia.' I ignore her and start browning the celery and the onions in a frying pan.

'Please answer yes or no.'

When I try to turn the Virtual Delia off, the hologram freezes but Delia's voice continues to harass me: 'Please answer yes or no.' The smoke detector begins to whine and Delia is triggered into a new recipe: 'First of all, place the venison and the pork into a large bowl and then place the bacon slices on a board stacked – '

'Shut the fuck up!' I shout at the hologram.

'That is not a recognized command. Please answer yes or no. I cannot help you if you will not answer yes or no.'

'For fuck's sake, Delia, will you give it a rest.' I pull the plug from the wall, open the windows to let the smoke out and make pasta for two.

When I call Jenny down for supper I get no answer. Her door is open. She has fallen asleep on the bed, wrapped in a towel. As I creep in and pull the duvet up around her I notice a small tattoo on her arm: the anarchist's circled A emblem. A frown mars the smoothness of her brow but when I kiss it gently it disappears. On my way out, as I flick off the light, she rolls over in her sleep and mumbles something which sounds like: 'Thanks, Mickey.'

The picture of Jenny standing head bowed in front of the

bulldozers has been run over three quarters of the front page. So powerful. It looks like that photograph of the lone student standing up against the Chinese tanks in Tiananmen Square in 1989. I read my copy with mounting excitement as I realize it has been run word for word. Jenny is rereading it for the third time when the phone rings.

'Where's the girl?' Hugh says.

'She's with me.'

'You sound terrible.'

'Think I'm coming down with a cold,' I stifle a sneeze as if to prove it. 'Caught it off her.'

'Get her on an exclusivity contract with us immediately. Offer her whatever she wants. She's not to talk to anyone else.'

'Who is it, Mickey?' Jenny asks.

'Hugh,' I say distractedly covering the mouthpiece as the sneeze comes out.

'Hi, Hugh!' Jenny shouts flopping down heavily on a sofa.

'Is that her?' Hugh is saying. 'They're all after her. Apparently the *Sun* wants her to pose topless. But everyone is going to have to run our photograph tomorrow. Good work. And a great piece by the way. Why can't you write like that all the time, Mike?'

Hate Mike. Hugh is the only one who calls me it.

Jenny is wearing a large cream-coloured dressing gown which I have never seen around the house before. I tell her her clothes should be back by lunch-time and that if she wants to get dressed before then she can help herself to anything in my wife's wardrobe that fits.

'This is her, right?' Jenny is holding up a silver-framed photograph of Amanda that she has just found on top of the Steinway. 'I recognize her from *Hello!* She's stunning, isn't she.' There is no question mark.

'Everyone seems to think so... You don't seem the *Hello!*-reading type.'

'You have to know the enemy.'

'Am I the enemy?'

'Don't know yet. Do you love her?'

I am momentarily thrown by her directness. 'That's a rather personal question. I'm not sure I want to answer it. What about you? Are you in love?'

89

'Haven't decided yet.'

A shiver of excitement at this. I'm out of practise in this area but I have the impression that I'm being flirted with.

'And who is this?' Jenny picks up a small round picture frame from the mantelpiece.

'That's my daughter.'

'I didn't know you had a daughter.'

'She died.' I take the picture frame from Jenny and place it back on the mantelpiece. 'Meningitis.'

'I'm sorry, Michael. I didn't know.'

'That's all right. Why should you have known.'

'She looks beautiful.'

'She was.'

'How old?'

'Four. Nearly five...' I check my watch. 'Now, I, er, help yourself to breakfast.' I point to the stairs. 'The kitchen's in the basement. I've just brewed some coffee. But I think we've got some herbal tea if you'd prefer. Milk in the fridge.'

While Jenny is downstairs there is a knock on the door. Instead of answering it, I look at the video monitor. There are two men: one in a suit is shifting his weight from one foot to the other impatiently, the other in jeans and a bomber jacket has two cameras around his neck. I remain motionless as the letter-box flap rises. 'Michael? Hello? I just want to ask you a few questions.' I hold my breath. 'It's Angus Spalding from the *Mail*, we met at the Tory Party Conference last year...'

After a few minutes he wanders out into the road, looks up at the house and returns to his car. The phone rings. I let the answering machine in the drawing room take it and have to crawl past the window to get close enough to hear the message. Whoever it is doesn't leave one. The phone rings again. I flick the machine on to automatic answer mode and use my mobile to ring Hugh.

'Everyone's got hold of my number,' I hiss. 'There are people outside. I think it would be best if Jenny goes into hiding for a few days. I thought maybe your place in Scotland. Do you still have it?'

'Let's keep things in proportion, Mike. This will blow over in a couple of days' time. Besides, the fashion pages want her for a shoot tomorrow.'

'I don't think she'll agree to that. She's a serious environ-mentalist, you know. She's not going to want to compromise herself.'

'What do you think, Mickey?' It is Jenny's voice. I turn around to see her standing with one hand on her hip, wearing a burgundy-coloured evening gown, a feathered hat and long satin gloves. Her mouth and the area of skin immediately surrounding it are smeared with bright red lipstick. She leans forward at the waist and wiggles her shoulders. 'Well?'

'You're quite the piss-taker, aren't you?' I whisper, cupping the mouthpiece.

'*Hello? Mike?*'

'Sorry, Hugh. I'd better go.'

'Persuade her to do the shoot. She's good for circulation. We sold an extra 84,000 copies this morning.'

'OK, bye.'

Jenny teeters towards me, shuffling in stilettos that are clearly several sizes too big for her.

'Oh, and Mike, I've just been passed a message which says that Sir Andrew Lambert called for you. Isn't that the girl's father?'

'Er, yeah.'

'I remember now. That business about you running her over last November. You should have mentioned that in your piece. And you should have played up the military man's daughter battling against the Ministry of Defence and Ethical Justice angle.'

'I think it's the Department of Environment she is protesting against.'

'Whatever. My secretary has his number if you want to call him back.'

I push down the aerial on my mobile, not taking my eyes off Jenny.

'Quite tall your wife.'

'Yes,' I mouth absently. 'Very. She used to model.'

'How did you meet?'

'She gatecrashed a book launch of mine.'

'Where did you say she is?'

'Gloucestershire. She doesn't get up to London much. I have a message to call your father. What do you suppose that's about?'

Jenny's face darkens and she wrenches her hat off. 'Don't tell him I'm here, OK?'

'I won't. Why don't you and he get on?'

'I don't want to talk about it. Can I put some music on?'

I show her the cupboard where the music centre is stored and then show her how to operate the CD carousel. 'Just tap in the number of the album you want to listen to and it will load it automatically. Here's the index.'

'Mickey?' She pulls a Courtney Pine CD out. 'Don't you have any records?'

When I tell her they are packed away in the attic she insists I bring them down. Scattering two hundred albums over the entire surface of the drawing-room floor is for her the work of a few seconds. I leave her to it and go in search of a packet of Lemsip. When I return with a steaming mug in my hand she is lining up a 12-inch single on the turntable. *12-inch single.* Until this moment I had forgotten that is what they used to be called. Thinking of a non-metric measurement makes me feel nostalgic. And when Frankie Goes To Hollywood begin singing 'Relax' the transport-ation back to my days as a student is complete.

I clear a space on the floor and join Jenny sitting cross-legged. There is the obligatory Beatles collection and a handful of albums from the seventies but most of these records are from the eighties: Heaven 17, Eurythmics, Simply Red. Suddenly, I want to hear them all.

Jenny picks out an early album by George Michael, released long before his knighthood. She positions the stylus by hand and, just missing the opening bar of 'Freedom', lifts it and tries again. There is an atmospheric crackling during which Jenny kicks off her shoes. When the song starts she grabs my hands and leads me tiptoeing around the scattered records and up on to the sofa. Very tall people cannot dance. It's a biological fact. Even if a very tall person has rhythm he still looks like a bewildered giraffe as soon as he wanders on to a dance floor. Yet when Jenny holds her hands in the air and undulates her hips in time to the thumping bass-line I find myself imitating her with all the cool and grace of a panther wearing sunglasses.

Thirteen

I walk rather than take a taxi to the Ministry of Defence and Ethical Justice, hoping that this will clear my head of the nagging anxieties I'm feeling about Jenny. I hadn't anticipated that my article about her would provoke the response it has. And I know that if my colleagues in Fleet Street get their inky hands on her they will turn her into a celebrity manqué. Within days she will have her own publicist and will be appearing on chat shows and in adverts. Already someone somewhere will be planning how best to approach her to make a charity single.

I can't allow this to happen. Not only have I not told her about the money other papers are prepared to offer her, I haven't even mentioned the fashion shoot which my own paper wants her to do. When I try to convince myself of the purity of my motives my conscience directs me back to an ugly truth: I fear that, if she becomes famous, she will have no more interest in me. I feel possessive. Jealous. What can I say?

We had danced on the sofa for about half an hour and it had left me feeling twenty years younger. I can't remember the last time I laughed so easily. Had Lambert not rung me on my private mobile, the one for which only my wife, agent and editor are supposed to know the number, we might have gone on dancing and listening to my old records all day.

Feeling nervous about leaving Jenny on her own in my house I considered locking her in. In the end I told her not to answer the door because my father-in-law had been receiving death threats. It was half true. He has been receiving them for years. And having grown up under conditions of high security herself, Jenny seemed to accept this explanation.

The main building of the Ministry of Defence and Ethical Justice is known as Main Building. And the grey, monolithic slabs from which it is constructed look out of place among the white, triumphalist architecture of Whitehall. Red Square is its natural home. Even the heroic statues that guard its entrance seem depressingly Stalinist and angular.

As I approach its steps I notice the translations under the sign: *Ministère de la Défense et la Justice Éthique* and *Ministerium für Verteidigung und Moralische Gerechtigkeit*. I also experience the feeling of intimidation that the slabs, statues and translations are intended to inspire – but perhaps this is as much to do with the prospect of meeting the Air Marshal. I try to imagine what the old Nazi wants to see me about. He had been vague on the phone, saying he enjoyed my piece about the protest camp and that he wondered if I would like to pop round for a coffee to discuss other matters which might interest me.

Once inside Main Building I report to Main Reception, explain I have an appointment to see the Vice Chief of the Defence Staff, and hand over my Multicard. The khaki-uniformed receptionist swipes it, curses under his breath, taps his machine, swipes the card again and stares at his screen. 'What was the purpose of your visit to Romania?' he asks coldly.

'That's on there? I was covering the UN summit.' I make a writing sign and give what I hope is an annoyingly patronizing smile. 'Journalist.'

'Fill in your name and the organization you represent and then sign and date it.' He hands me a pink form. Another soldier, standing on the far side of a row of Perspex tubes, gestures for me to approach him. I stand inside one that is open on my side, draw my shoulders in as it closes around me, and walk out the other side. Quite what it is supposed to have scanned me for I can't work out because the soldier then runs a metal detector around me, frisks me and searches through my briefcase. He leads me up some stairs, through a large double door which has the NATO symbol surrounded by the twenty-six euro stars engraved upon its frosted glass, and along a series of green corridors. When we reach a lift he tells me to go to the sixth floor where someone will meet me. I check my tie in the mirror as the lift judders upwards.

The walls on the sixth floor are painted yellow and lined with black and white photographs of whiskery, long-dead generals. I am shown into an office which has a wide mahogany desk at one end of it and told that the Air Marshal will be with me shortly. It is dimly lit: the shutters on the windows are down and the only light is coming from an Anglepoise lamp on the desk. Alongside this there is a model of a Spitfire and a shield which bears the eagle, anchor and crossed swords insignia of the MoDaEJ. On the wall behind the desk is a large, laminated map of Europe dotted with coloured pins. Along the wall facing the windows is a display cabinet which contains an old breech-loading rifle, several bayonets and an arrangement of cap badges.

I'm just trying to open this to have a play with the gun when Lambert walks in. 'Has anyone offered you a drink?' The thinness of his voice takes me by surprise again.

I am fine for the moment.

'How's Jennifer?' he says, sitting down at his desk and indicating for me to sit opposite. 'I understand she is staying with you.'

I shift in my seat, making the leather creak. Nothing you can teach these Lamberts about directness.

'She's fine,' I say.

'It was very kind of you to write her those letters after the accident.'

Don't like where this is going.

Lambert presses the tips of his fingers together, studies them and falls into a pensive silence. I am beginning to think he's forgotten I'm here when he says: 'As I mentioned on the phone, I was very impressed by your report on the protest camp. Of course, I am no more in favour of Ministry land being used for housing development than are the protesters. But that is not the point. It was an excellent piece. Powerful. Sensitively handled. As I said, I know your father-in-law – a good man – and he tells me you are one of the most respected journalists of your generation.'

'Stop it. You're making me blush.'

'Something has been brought to my attention and I think you might be the right person to follow it up. I can't go into detail here but suffice to say it will have massive implications for our national defence policy as well as for the European Army. Now, I'm not saying that things should never change, that we don't all have to tighten our belts from time to time.' He sighs as he searches for the right words. 'During the Cold War we had a very straightforward crisis management policy: if the Soviets did this, we did that. In Bosnia it all fell apart and the lines between peace keeping and peace enforcing became blurred. We had to adapt. And we did . . .'

I have read in the Air Marshal's *Who's Who* entry that he saw action in the Falklands, the Gulf and Kosovo and that he won medals for gallantry in every campaign. But sitting behind a desk in Whitehall, being evasive in his reedy voice, he seems to lack heroic poise . . .

'The thing is,' he continues, 'NATO is under great strain at the moment, with Europe and North America pulling in different directions. We must bring Washington back on side.'

'I think I'm missing something here, Air Marshal,' I interrupt. 'Why don't you just brief our defence correspondent about this? He could write a comment piece. Better still, you could write something yourself. It would have much more clout coming from you.'

'No. This can't come from me.'

He scrapes his chair back, plucks a key from his waistcoat pocket and turns it easily in the lock of a drawer. Using both hands, he removes a manila folder bound with a red ribbon and places it carefully on the desk in front of him. He stares at it as if expecting it to self-combust.

'Is it a letter bomb?' I ask.

He gives a wintry smile and pushes it towards me. 'In a manner of speaking.' I spin it around and read the block capitals that have been stamped across it: STRICTLY RESTRICTED CIRCULATION. Under this there is the portcullis motif of the House of Commons.

I'm about to mouth the word 'leak?' when Lambert points to the ceiling and puts a finger to his lips. 'We're swept for bugs once a week,' he whispers, 'but you never can tell. Perhaps I could get you a coffee now? Do you take milk?'

'Black, no sugar.'

I hear him lock the door on his way out.

The folder contains draft proposals for a Strategic Defence Review, the outline of which will be included in the New Conservative Party manifesto. As I flick through the sheaths of photocopied papers, I can feel the hairs on my arms begin to stand up under my shirt.

The document sets out the Opposition's plans to leave NATO, declare England a republic with neutrality status, reduce the RAF to one squadron, the Navy to two Trident submarines, half a dozen DD21 Land Attack Destroyers and one aircraft carrier, and all but disband the army in its present regimental form and replace it with a small, rapid-reaction, anti-terrorist force operating in conjunction with Apache attack helicopters. I begin making notes.

'... Heavy investment in English-made InfoWar software will ensure that the security of the nation is not compromised by these necessary and long overdue cuts ...'

'... The 316,000-acre estate of Army Training Lands will be sold to developers as part of our commitment to provide 5.4 million new homes over the next decade ...'

Ten minutes pass before the office door is unlocked. Lambert raises his eyebrows as he enters the room. 'See what I mean?'

'Pretty radical.'

Lambert produces a radio from his drawer and turns it on to a discussion programme on Radio 4. He leans forward and whispers: 'Absolute madness!'

'Where did it come from?' I mouth back.

'I could tell you,' he says under his breath, standing over me to close the folder. 'But I'd have to kill you afterwards.'

I laugh politely.

He walks around to his side of the desk, slides the folder back in the drawer, locks it again and resumes our whispered conversation. 'And I'm afraid it can't leave the building.'

'But my editor will ask to see some proof.'

'Yes, yes. Don't worry, they're not going to deny any of it. They can't.'

'How do we explain me seeing you today?'

'You had the story already and were gauging my reaction. Why don't you go away and put something together based on what I've shown you. It's up to you what spin you put on it.'

'Now we both know that isn't true, Air Marshal.'

He purses his lips briefly to keep a smile in check. 'Of course it is. But I could meet you for breakfast tomorrow morning if you like. Go over it with you. Any questions?'

'What happened to my coffee?'

I'm so excited about the leak I lock myself in my study as soon as I get home and do not emerge again until I've more or less finished writing the article, gone three in the morning. Jenny is still up, watching a DVD. She has made herself some scrambled egg but has left half of it uneaten on a plate on the floor. Realizing I've forgotten to eat, I make myself a sandwich from some cold beef in the fridge. The DVD has finished by the time I return to the drawing room. Jenny yawns and says she is going to bed. Only when she is half-way up the stairs does she remember to tell me that some people from *Hello!* magazine called round when I was out. They had told her they had an appointment to photograph the rooms but she hadn't let them in. They had wanted her to pose for them, she adds, which she thought a bit odd considering it isn't her house.

The foyer of the Prince Regent is empty as I sit furtively rereading the article. Even so, I feel paranoid that someone will try and read over my shoulder. It is explosive. A mother of a scoop.

I start guiltily when Lambert taps me on the shoulder. He has suggested this hotel near Marble Arch because, he says, it serves the best full English breakfast in London. But maybe it's because it overlooks the site of the Tyburn Tree where they used to execute traitors. There are three other diners in the restaurant, all sitting on their own, reading their newspapers in silence. We feel obliged to talk in subdued voices – but we probably would anyway, even if the restaurant was filled with chatter. Lambert orders bacon, sausage, two fried eggs, tomatoes, fried bread, kidneys and mushrooms. I ask for the same. As we wait for our food to arrive

Lambert asks if I have heard of Colonel Oleg Penkovsky. I haven't. The Air Marshal unfolds his napkin and leans towards me.

'He was an officer in the GRU, Soviet Military Intelligence. In 1961 he came over to this country with a Russian delegation and stayed at this very hotel.'

I twitch my eyebrows, unsure what sort of a reaction he expects this news to provoke.

'After saying goodnight to the others he made his way up the backstairs to room 360.'

'His room?'

'No, no. The room where two CIA officers and an agent from MI5 were waiting for him. They poured him a large vodka, turned on a tape recorder and listened as he talked about Soviet missile developments, nuclear plans, deployment tactics and the identities of other KGB and GRU officers working in London. It was a revelation. Much more important than the tittle-tattle Blake and Burgess had been feeding the Russians. It helped us realize that Khrushchev had been talking absolute bollocks about his missile superiority. It revealed that their missiles were in such bad condition they were unusable. Yet Washington refused to believe that boasts of Soviet missile superiority were untrue. The experts were unwilling to abandon their fear of the missile gap.'

'Is that why you like meeting people here? Because it reminds you of the good old days of the Cold War?'

Lambert gives a brittle laugh. At last. Evidence of a sense of humour. 'The world was a more stable place then, certainly. But I wanted you to hear that story for a reason. It shows how pointless information is – unless you know how to act upon it.'

There is a scraping sound of a knife on a plate. We both look in the direction of the noise: a pot-bellied man wearing T-shirt and jeans. A man wearing a pin-stripe suit on the table nearest us coughs, folds his paper loudly and stands up to leave. Another man, in a shiny, double-breasted suit, slurps his coffee, pushes back his chair and leaves, too. There is always an awkward moment in a business breakfast when you both know you have spent too long pretending it is not a business breakfast. That moment has now come.

With a sideways glance at the man in the T-shirt, I hand over the draft of my article. Lambert perches a pair of half-moon glasses on his nose and begins reading. When he gets to the second page he pulls a pen from his jacket, clicks the top down and makes some notes in the margin. He does this twice more, on pages 4 and 6, and then hands the article back to me.

Leaning forward, the Air Marshal says in a barely audible whisper: 'I think it hits exactly the right note. I've made one or two corrections which you'll see but otherwise it's exactly what is needed.'

I am pretty pleased with the tone myself: indignant, outraged, philosophical. Not that this is what I feel, of course. I don't feel anything much.

Lambert removes his spectacles. They have left two red pressure marks on the bridge of his nose. 'Will you be able to run it in tomorrow's edition?' he asks.

'Should think so. I'll need full corroboration and some quotes from big wigs at the Ministry. First reactions.'

'Yes, yes. I can give you some phone numbers. I don't think any serving officers will be able to comment but I know a handful of retired admirals and generals who should be happy to go on record.'

'I'll have to get a response from Downing Street. And Brussels. And I'll have to give a right of reply to the Tories. But I can wait until we are about to go to press before I get those. No need to let our rivals know what's going on until they see the second editions. You don't happen to know where Tenant stands on all this, do you?'

'Takes the same view as me. Thinks the Tories are being completely reckless. Irresponsible.'

'So he's seen the proposals?'

'He is aware of the contents.'

'But I thought he was all for investing in InfoWar technology?'

'Romanian IW technology. Not English. After New Labour denied him a licence to register his IW company in England, Bruce set up a plant in Romania. His scientists there have been working flat out.' Lambert conveys a forkful of egg and sausage to his mouth. As he chews, he points the empty fork at me. 'Personally, I find the notion of IW abhorrent,' he says, swallowing.

'I mean, worse than biological warfare in a way. They say a cyber war is a bloodless war but that is an oxymoron. When you target a stock exchange's central computer with one of these Trojan Horse viruses, or the networks that control a country's electricity supply, it affects everyone. And people die. What do you know about Tenant's research?'

'Only the rumours I've read in the papers.'

'Well, for the past five years, NATO has been working on a macro virus which ensures its own proliferation by adopting the characteristics of its host. Now we believe the Chinese have developed a far more virulent strain than anything we've come up with. Within just two generations it can infect twenty billion computers worldwide. And we have every reason to suspect they are planning an electronic Pearl Harbor.'

'And these things change characteristics each time they reproduce?'

'Exactly, exactly. So that they can't be discovered by virus detection software. Well, Bruce has come up with a new system that can tackle the polymorphic virus. He's calling it the Jennifer Vaccination.'

'Jennifer?'

Lambert laughs. 'I think he's sucking up to me because I've been pushing for it at the Ministry. I like it because it's humane. It can't be adapted for offensive use.'

'Like SDI.'

Lambert pushes his plate away. 'Not quite. *This* is going to work. And if the Chinese IW virus falls into the hands of a psychopathic dictator, we're going to need it to.'

A waiter brings a rack of fresh toast and the Air Marshal and I stare at it, lost in our own thoughts.

Fourteen

For an academic, even a semi-retired one, my father can be perversely dim, or at least deliberately forgetful. When he answers the door he just looks blank. 'Didn't know you were coming.'

'Yes you did,' I sigh with what I hope is enough good humour to avoid an argument. 'This is Jenny.'

He is six foot five, same as me, although he may have shrunk a little now he's pushing seventy-five. This height combined with his weight (about twenty stones, I would guess) and his straggly Rasputin beard (at least eight centimetres of ginger and silver nesting material) makes him a pretty imposing figure in the average domestic setting. He's also acquired wild starey eyes, sunk deep into his skull, which I'm sure he never used to have. Cultivated them for dramatic effect, I imagine.

'Hello, er, Jenny,' he says wheezily without offering his hand to shake. 'I'm in the middle of something. Help yourself to,' he wafts an arm in the direction of the kitchen, 'whatever.' The kitchen smells of frying bacon and this, for some reason, I find embarrassing. As he turns his back on us and shuffles in his tartan slippers across the hall into his study, I whisper: 'Don't take it personally, he's always in the middle of something.'

The something he is always in the middle of is a book. In the thirty-five years that he taught political science at York University

– working his way up from part-time tutor to assistant professor and eventually head of faculty – he wrote six of them, which was thought quite prolific. Since taking early retirement from lecturing, however, he has been publishing books at the rate of two a year – he'd produce more, I'm sure, if it weren't for the drink. The challenge he sets himself with each new one is to see if he can give it a title more off-putting than the last. He surpassed himself one year by writing a sequel to *Socialism in the Age of Dogma* called *Dogma in the Age of Socialism*. I have about 500 of his books on my shelf at home, or so it can sometimes seem. I have tried to read three. And this is three more than most people manage. His refusal to write commercial books has left him practically broke. Needless to say he despises what I do for a living. And he has never forgiven me for leaving my first wife in order to marry the daughter of Bruce Tenant.

For years I believed his claims that he'd never read any of my journalism. Then I discovered a pile of my cuttings under his bed. Now I can't rid myself of the suspicion that he regards his own turgid and inaccessible writing as a necessary balance in the world for my lucid and readable prose.

His style is so consistently arid, it must be crafted that way deliberately – even bad writers can't help stumbling across a colourful phrase from time to time. And when readers do manage to hack their way through one of his densely argued texts, the theories they uncover are so extreme and chilling they need trauma therapy afterwards. My father doesn't seem to mind if the position he takes is radical or reactionary, hard right or far left, so long as it is extreme. I confidently predict that a fanatical cult will be established one day which leans heavily on his obscure political teachings.

As I try to explain all this to Jenny, I come to the conclusion that my father's frustrations as an author may account for much of his battiness. That and his role as nominal head of our family. My mother died when I was fourteen, leaving my father to bring up two boys on his own. I have a younger brother, Philip. Unmarried. Works as an engineer with EA. When we were growing up we were both given a hard time by my father, especially when he'd been drinking, but Philip seems to have taken it more personally than me. Father and he don't get on. That doesn't stop him spending nearly all of his weekends and holidays at my father's house though.

In the car on the long journey up to Yorkshire, Jenny had laughed at my descriptions of my family and this took my mind off the dizzying maelstrom my article had caused. It had been run on the front page the day after my breakfast with her father. The Tory Party chairman had gone on the *Today* programme to deny it 'in the strongest possible terms' and to complain bitterly about the irresponsible journalism practised by the Tenant press. My editor was on the phone immediately to double check that my contact was unassailable. I reassured him. He asked me to appear on the midday news to defend my story and protest that I could not reveal my sources. The evening news and current affairs programmes were all extended to debate the issue. The next morning a Gallup poll revealed that 86 per cent of voters were in favour of the defence cuts outlined in the leaked manifesto. The New Conservative Party spin machine went into reverse. A smirking party chairman appeared on the midday news to accept that, upon reflection, he could see that, broadly speaking, the original story had been 'consistent with the truth'.

As my house in Pimlico was still under siege from photographers and reporters wanting to interview my celebrity protester, I had gone into the office that afternoon, taking Jenny with me. It was the first time I'd been in since my front-page lead about the protest camp. The one story following the other so closely did, I suppose, merit some respect. But I wasn't expecting to be greeted by a cheer. Having been resented by my colleagues on the *English People* for so long I had no idea how to react to their words of congratulation. The Boy Fielding even approached me, his eyes shining with admiration, and patted me on the back. The gesture unsettled me.

I didn't like the way The Boy was eyeing Jenny up and when I went to see Hugh and left her talking to him I felt even more uneasy. I told Hugh I needed to get out of London for a few days, that I was feeling claustrophobic and stressed out. He suggested I head up to Yorkshire to look into a dispute brewing between a prominent landowner and the Ramblers Association. Lord

Ingleton was threatening to shoot at any ramblers who crossed his grouse moor during the shooting season. As this was something they were entitled to do under the Government's Right to Roam policy, the ramblers were threatening a mass march across the land.

I know all about Lord Ingleton, as it happens. A charmless, pink-faced man. My father's cottage is rented from him. It's a funny old place with uneven floors and a thatched roof. I grew up there and, although I find it impossible to spend longer than a day or two in the company of my family, I always secretly enjoy going back.

When I came back out of the editor's office Jenny was sitting on The Boy Fielding's desk, flirting with him. I took her by the elbow and, as I led her towards the lift, I told her about the story in Yorkshire. She wrongfooted me by saying she wanted to come along. Trying to conceal my enthusiasm, I just shrugged and said: 'Why not.'

'When do I get to meet your brother?' Jenny asks as I show her to her room – my old room. I'm going to sleep on the sofa bed in the sitting room.

'You don't want to.'

'I do.'

'But he's so rude.'

I don't think she believes me until we sit down for the evening meal, a vegetarian dish that Jenny has prepared. Philip says hello to her and then sits down at the table and plays a video game called 'Assassinate the PM'.

'What do you do?' Jenny asks him.

'I make planes.'

'What sort of planes?'

'Aeroplanes.'

'You're looking middle aged,' my father says, turning his mottled face to me.

'I am nearly forty.'

Jenny tries to suppress a giggle.

Father pours himself a large glass of wine. Philip pushes a coil of pasta around his plate and says: 'What is this muck?'

'What does it look like?' my father growls.

'I'm sorry,' Jenny says. 'I'm a vegetarian and I thought as Michael is, too, I could – '

'He is not!' Philip snorts.

I grin sheepishly at Jenny. 'I'm afraid I told you a bit of a Jeffrey there.'

Father turns to Jenny and asks: 'Do you know any Greek?'

She shakes her head. 'I speak a little French.'

My father nods to himself, downs his glass, refills it and picks up his newspaper. For the rest of the meal he reads in silence and works his way through two bottles of claret.

The ordeal over, Jenny carries the glass of whisky and ice my father has insisted she have through into the drawing room and sits on a stone seat in the inglenook fireplace. I run upstairs, clean my teeth, gargle with mouthwash and spray under my arms with deodorant. Standing back from the mirror I shoot my cuffs and flatten my hair down – then tousle it again so that it doesn't look as if I've been trying to make myself look better. 'Did you get the impression my old man doesn't like me very much?' I say when I return.

'I rather liked him,' Jenny says. 'And your brother. Are they always like that?'

'God no. They were on their best behaviour.'

I know I now have about half an hour alone with Jenny: my brother will go to bed and my father will take his sheepdog for a walk. I settle down on the smooth stone next to her and, as we continue talking about my brother for a while, we both watch the amber liquid in her glass glow in the firelight. The conversation stops. She is breathing through her nose, quick, shallow breaths. Is she nervous? She yawns, stretches and smiles at me. My mouth is so dry I cannot speak; my heart is hammering with such force it is rocking my whole body. I want to put my arm around her but its heaviness prevents me. We listen to the ice crackling in her glass.

'That clock's ticking too quickly,' Jenny says standing up carefully and stepping outside the fireplace. In the corner of the room there is an eighteenth-century longcase clock. She stands next to it and I get up and move next to her. She taps the face of the clock and says: 'Perhaps someone has overwound it.'

I swallow. 'Perhaps.'

To my ears every word we exchange is charged with ulterior meaning. 'It was my grandfather's.'

'A grandfather clock.'

I smile. 'Not when he bought it.'

'Are these his books?' She plucks a mildewed volume of poetry from the shelf alongside the fireplace.

'No, I think my father bought them from an antique shop. We don't really have much in the way of family heirlooms.'

I have anticipated this. I take *Selections from Hardy* down and flick through its pages pretending to look for a poem, even though I had earlier turned down the corner of the page I wanted. The spine is frayed, the cardboard cover warped. I read from the first page: 'A good book is the precious life blood of a master spirit – Milton. And here it says "This book belongs to J. Tomlinson. School House. KHW. 1921." See? No one we know.' There is a loose page of folded sheet music inside, which I hadn't noticed earlier. 'Ferry me across the water by Christina Rossetti, Copyright, 1931 Walford Davies,' I read. 'The instructions are to sing it eagerly, as a dialogue song. First voice: "Fer-ry me a-cross the wa-ter, do, boat-man, do." Second: "If you've a pen-ny in your purse, I'll fer-ry you."'

I pretend to look up the first line of the poem I want in the index, find it and hand it to Jenny.

'You read it for me,' she says sitting down on the sofa. I pull up a chair next to her and clear my throat.

> *She wore a new 'terra-cotta' dress,*
> *And we stayed, because of the pelting storm,*
> *Within the hansom's dry recess,*
> *Though the horse had stopped; yea, motionless*
> *We sat on, snug and warm.*
>
> *Then the downpour ceased, to my sharp sad pain*
> *And the glass that had screened our forms before*
> *Flew up, and out she sprang to her door:*
> *I should have kissed her if the rain*
> *Had lasted a minute more.*

Jenny crosses the room to the window, holds back the curtain and peers out. 'No rain tonight.' She says it without looking at me, takes a sip from her whisky and offers me the glass.

'I can't,' I say. 'The thing I used to enjoy about whisky was dipping my fingertip in it and running it around my lips.'

'Why?'

'It tingles. I'll show you.' I take the glass from her, dip my fingertip and softly paint her lips. If she sucks my finger, I think, that will be my permission to kiss her. She doesn't. I wonder if she has noticed that my hand is trembling. We are in that zone, that moment of looking at each other for a second too long.

'That tickles!' she says, turning her head away and rubbing her lips with the back of her hand.

'You've got such small hands,' I whisper.

In the next room the radiator pings and then gurgles.

'No, I haven't. Let's see yours.'

When I hold my right hand up, fingers splayed, palm towards her, she presses hers against it. 'See?'

'Yes, but you're not measuring from the same starting point. We have to have our wrists level.'

'Yours feel hot, Mickey.'

Thank God they're not clammy, I think. 'Let me see yours.' I take her hand in mine and examine it. The nails are bitten, the fingers bony, the lines on her palm are as spare and subtle as a haiku. I raise her hand slowly, close my eyes and gently press my lips to it.

In my shock at hearing the front-door latch I drop Jenny's hand guiltily. My father lumbers in, lowers himself into an armchair and falls asleep almost immediately. My father has two dogs, the sheepdog and a Highland terrier called Attlee. Attlee now emerges from under the armchair, woken by the sound of his master snoring. 'It gets louder,' I say. 'The snoring. Give it a few minutes.'

Jenny smiles and gives my hand a squeeze. 'You don't have to sleep down here tonight if you don't want to. It *is* your old bedroom.'

Fifteen

My interviews – with the land agent for the Ingleton Estate and
the chairman of the local branch of the Ramblers – take up most
of the morning. By the time I get back to my father's cottage,
Jenny has had her lunch and is sitting out in the garden, wrapped
in a blanket, trying to read one of my father's books.

The weather is mild for February, the sky is cloudless and the
wind that had woken me just after six – by whipping the branches
outside the sitting-room window – has now dropped. I hadn't
been able to get back to sleep. Too long for the sofa bed, I'd had
to hang my feet over the end. And the more they froze the more
I lost the will to do something about it by getting up and putting
some socks on.

I had lain there for an hour, feeling sorry for myself, trying to
figure out why I hadn't taken up Jenny's offer to share my old bed
with her. Was it that I hadn't wanted to take advantage of her? No,
of course I had. Was it that I didn't want the first time to be in this
house, under the same roof as my preposterous family? More
likely.

Jenny doesn't notice me watching her. She is sitting on the edge
of the garden seat in a rhombus of sunlight, leaning her head back
to put her contact lenses in. This done, she tucks her legs up in
front. Huddled under the blanket, her hair ghosting in the

sunshine, she looks – and knows she looks – sublime.

She is frowning, trying to concentrate on the book she is holding through the material. Her hand emerges to play with her fringe and then returns to the folds of the blanket. It comes out again to scratch the tip of her nose. There is something about her childish profile, a fleeting play of light perhaps, that reminds me of Emily. With a pout of irritation, Jenny drops the book on the bench beside her.

In one liquid movement she shrugs off the blanket, stands up and places her hands on her narrow hips. She is wearing black leggings and a chunky grey polo neck which she must have found in my cupboard. It's far too big for her but as she closes her eyes and begins taking long, deep breaths I can nevertheless make out the rise and fall of her under-developed chest.

She puts one foot forward, places both hands on her knee and begins stretching. After a while she swaps to the other leg, does the same number of stretches and stands upright, feet apart. Now she raises her arms above her head and, bending at the waist, lowers them slowly until the palms of her hands are flat on the grass in front of her.

As she holds this position for about thirty seconds, the emotional atrophy that has defined me for years melts away. I feel light-headed with tenderness. My heart is palpitating and my mouth has gone dry. I long to run my hands over her thighs, to follow the curves that define her hips and ribs. I want to touch her mouth with my fingertips and kiss the closed lids of her eyes. I am mesmerized by her golden, blurred beauty.

I become aware of a grinding noise. It is my teeth.

I step backwards around the corner of the house, press myself against the wall and try to catch my breath.

That beguiling face. There was an experiment a few years ago in which a computer was used to generate an image of the ideal woman's face, as defined by thousands of people in dozens of countries. This perfect woman had a café-crème complexion and symmetrical features: large, dark eyes, full lips and a soft, heart-shaped face. I can't say Jenny conforms to that. Nothing about the size or shape of her features is exaggerated. Everything about her is average. Even the colour of her eyes seems to change according to the light: black one moment, dark green sometimes, cobalt blue. But her beauty is luminous, an objective fact. It is intoxicating and comforting, a signal to my brain to stop analysing, selecting, thinking.

'How did it go?' she asks when I cross the garden and announce myself with a cough.

'Fine.' I rub my hands. 'I don't think Lord Ingleton is serious about taking pot-shots at the ramblers. He's just pissed off because they got the start of the grouse shooting season moved back three months. Thinks having the Glorious Twelfth in November is a farce.'

'I think he should be grateful he's allowed to carry on shooting at all. It's barbaric, right?'

'You a rambler?'

'No, but I'm not dissing it either. It's, like, the principle of the thing.'

'I think my father once wrote a paper on the communist origins of the ramblers' movement. Mass trespass in the 1930s and all that. You should ask him about it. I'm going to take a drive over to the grouse moor this afternoon to have a look. Want to come?'

'Will it be boggy?'

'No idea. But we've probably got some wellies here you could wear.' I try to read upside down the title of her book. 'What did you make of it?'

'A riotous romp. Compelling and painful, heady yet every-day...' She breaks into a laugh, three descending notes.

'Good,' I say. 'The old man will be pleased.'

After the voluptuous, bracken-covered hills of Swaledale and the neat, dry-stone-walled geometry of the Ure valley, the purple moorland above Ingleton Hall seems flat and bleak. There isn't much to see – no militant ramblers – but I'm glad Jenny has come with me to see it. The horizon in London is rarely more than a few metres away and is made of concrete, glass and stone. Whenever I'm able to escape it and spend time in the Yorkshire dales I always feel vulnerable and exposed, at first, until I have adjusted my senses to its openness.

There is a red warning flag flying near where we park the car.

We ignore it and pick our way over the springy heather, holding hands to keep our balance. The grouse we startle fly off chattering but soon glide back to the ground. We reach a narrow sheep track and, though the going is now level, we continue to hold hands.

A row of shooting butts, made from wood and sunk into the ground, crosses the moor at its highest point. They are camouflaged by a layer of dried heather and moss and when Jenny lowers herself into one it looks like her lower half has sunk in quicksand. I join her and peel the cellophane off a packet of Marlboro Lights. She has one too and the smell of tobacco as it mingles with the moist and peaty moorland air is delicious.

My appreciation of this landscape has long been numbed by the anaesthetic of familiarity. But now, as I survey it, with my arm insinuated around Jenny's waist, its raw beauty fills me with awe.

Actually, what I'm thinking is: mustn't let on you love her.

'I think I'm in love,' I say quietly.

'Does she love you?'

'I don't know.' I want to add: *Do you?* But I hesitate too long and the moment passes.

Jenny grinds her cigarette stub underfoot, levers herself out of the butt and walks away without answering. When I catch up with her she holds out her hand without looking round. Her fingers are cold and, instinctively, I raise them to my mouth to blow on them. When I kiss the back of her hand she stops, turns on her heels and looks down at the ground. Her warm breath is visible as it hits the chilly air. I move a step closer, stoop slightly, and she raises herself up on the tips of her toes. Our noses, both cold, brush momentarily but our lips do not meet.

I think I've found happiness with her.

Can this be possible? We are close to consummation, and the trembling uncertainty of before is always better than the disappointed after. Could this be the happiest I will ever feel? The thought fills me with mortal panic. One day I shall die. It doesn't matter whether it happens tomorrow or in fifty years' time, one day my life will stop. And on my deathbed, when I recall the moment at which I was most happy, I know it will be this.

We stand back from each other and, to cover her embarrassment, Jenny says: 'My nose is runny.'

'Mine too,' I sniff, running my hands up her arms and squeezing her shoulders. Her eyes are watering in the wind.

'Should we go and see what that is?' Jenny points towards a small octagonal shooting lodge a short walk from the far end of the row of butts. It is made of stone, with leaded windows and a roof thatched with heather.

I try the door but it is locked.

Jenny presses her face against the glass: 'Just some tables and chairs.'

When she turns away from the window I pull her to me and run an icy hand under her jumper. As I touch her ribcage she flinches. I slide my other hand down the back of her leggings and feel for the elastic of her knickers. She isn't wearing any. Her skin feels as cold as marble.

'Look!' she says, pushing me off. 'Over there. A camera.' She runs to the corner of the lodge, picks up a camera and points it at me. It's an expensive one, a Canon covered in dials and buttons. Its long, telephoto lens has no cap on it and an LED display reveals that it is switched on.

'Cool. Someone must have been here today,' Jenny says.

'Haven't seen anyone. I suppose we should hand it in to the police.'

'There's half a film left in here. Should we use it up for them?' She points it at my feet and presses the shutter. When it trips three times in succession she nearly drops it in surprise.

'The speed motor is on. Pass it here.'

She hands it over and I adjust it to normal speed.

'Take some of me,' she says. 'Let's give them a surprise when they develop the film, yeah?' She turns round and pulls down her leggings. I click, try to focus and click again. The powerful lens has come in so close I can't really work out what the object being photographed is. I run back, retract the lens as far as it will go and use the autofocus. 'Hurry up!' Jenny laughs, her face hidden from view. 'My arse is freezing.'

She hitches her trousers up, turns to face me and lifts her jumper and sweatshirt so that they cover her face. 'Now take these,' she shouts in a voice muffled by wool. Her nipples are erect, the pale skin around them goosepimpled. I use up five frames before

113

she pulls the jumper down and goes into a mock pirouette, dancing on the balls of her feet, describing wings with long silky flaps of her arms. The camera comes to the end of the film and spools it back automatically to the beginning.

Jenny stays in the car when we stop outside the police station. I go inside to hand the camera in and, as soon as I'm out of Jenny's view, I remove the film and slip it in my pocket.

Sixteen

A pang of hunger and a tickling sensation on my bare foot rouses me. I roll over and tuck my legs up into the foetal position. I feel the tickling again and throw back the duvet. Jenny is fluttering a tiny white feather over my toes. 'Stop that!' I say with a laugh as I try and snatch it away from her. She moves her hand too quickly for me and plunges it into the lining of a pillow. She then produces a fistful of feathers and throws them in my face. I sneeze and feel for a half-smoked cigarette left the night before on my bedside table. Jenny yawns and scratches herself.

She's still wearing the sweatshirt she had on yesterday. The fresh moorland air had left us exhausted and when we got back to my father's cottage we collapsed into my bed without taking our clothes off. She fell asleep immediately. I, however, could not. As she lay in my arms, I cupped the area of material covering her breasts and tried to control my breathing.

As Jenny now swings her legs over the side of the bed, I see she has taken her leggings off during the night. Her thighs are firm and covered in a light, velvety down. She stands and whips away the sheet that is slewed around me. It parachutes open, snaps crisply and billows out again. She wraps it around herself and clumps downstairs to the kitchen.

I check my watch; it's 8.45. The eighteenth. It is my fortieth birthday and, as a present to myself, I take my old wicker-framed mirror down off the wall and empty a couple of fat lines on to it. As I haven't had any marching powder for several days the smell of ammonia and hydrochloric acid that wafts off it gives me an anticipation high.

I begin the ritual of chopping and shaping. I always feel it's important to have the lines symmetrical, I don't know why. I also consider it important to snort off a mirror because the self-disgust that comes with seeing your reflection in extreme close-up is an important part of the ceremony. Cocaine is an enigmatic friend. You hate its popularity. And the euphoric calm you feel at first is heightened by the knowledge that remorse will follow. And headaches. And irregular heartbeats. And sweating. And skin-picking. And confusion. And, sometimes, seizures. Invariably, you wish you'd never had your first line and, at the same time, you're grateful you did.

I run the straw along the line, toss back my head and massage the sides of my nose. As I dab at the crumbs with a licked fingertip, my lungs dilate, the capillaries in my nose constrict, and my central nervous system sighs with relief.

When Jenny comes back upstairs munching on a piece of toast I hide the mirror and ask: 'Is that my birthday breakfast?'

'*Mickey!* Why didn't you tell me?'

'I'm telling you now.'

'*How old?*'

'Don't want to talk about it.'

'How old?'

'Forty.'

She lets out a scream and circles round the room in mock panic. 'I can't believe I've just spent the night in the same bed as a forty-year-old!' she shouts. I pick up a towel and start flicking her with it. She grabs a pillow and brings it down on my shoulder. When we grow tired we flop back on the bed. Jenny wraps my arm around her waist and says: 'Let's go to the seaside. Birthday treat. Aren't we near Blackpool here?'

'I think Scarborough is closer.'

'No, let's go to Blackpool. I've always wanted to go.'

'It's a long drive.'

'We could take that motorbike in the garage.'

'That's Philip's. He'd kill us.'

'He won't mind.'

'Do you know how to ride one? Because I certainly don't.'

'Course.'

'You ask him then.'

When she goes off to find him I walk downstairs to answer the phone. It is Amanda in Gstaad. The snow is perfect, she says, and I should try to get out and join her. She wishes me a happy birthday and asks how I'm planning to celebrate. I tell her we're having a quiet family dinner.

I hear the revving of an engine and walk to the window. Jenny's feet hardly reach the foot rest as she sits back against the sissy bar of the Harley-Davidson. It's a chrome-plated 883 cc with chopper handlebars and she has to stretch her thin arms right out to rev the engine. When I wander out, she throws me a helmet and says: 'Get on.'

I tuck myself in behind her on the bucket seat and hold her hips.

'Fun, yes?' she shouts over her shoulder as we reach an open road. The vibration of the engine is exhilarating, leaving the skin sensitive. We stop off at Harrogate to fill the tank with petrol and buy some clothes more appropriate for biking. When I dismount I have to steady myself against a wall. Jenny leads me by the arm to a leather shop where we laugh as we try on several different sets of jackets and trousers before deciding on matching outfits of black trousers, knee-length biker boots, and long leather coats with fringes on the sleeves. Jenny offers to pay for them as a birthday present but when she sees the price she grimaces and I put them on my Multicard.

The sight of Blackpool, with its tower and Ferris wheel, makes my pulse quicken. In the thirties, couples came here from all over the north of England in search of sexual liberation under the pier. And you can see why. There is a whiff of decadence about the place. As we ride slowly along the Golden Kilometre, the exhaust spluttering musically, we take in the fish and chip shops and the billboards advertising matinée performances by has-been stars of nineties sitcoms. Stars such as Trevor 'where's-the-soap' Humphries whose catchphrase almost-but-never-quite entered the language of the English-sitcom-watching classes, but whose appearance has long since been forgotten.

A fine warm drizzle is blowing in off the sea, sending newspapers and sweet wrappers scurrying. The place has a faded appearance that no amount of neon illumination or signs to exotic sounding Winter Gardens and Sea Life Centres can dispel. It's off season and a sense of defeatism wafts out from the plastic flowers that line the windows of the half-empty B & Bs.

Jenny parks the bike outside one of several illegal salerooms that line the seafront. From the outside it is not obvious that they are salerooms at all – a curtain is drawn across the top half of the entrance. Attracted by the tinny sound of the auctioneer's voice over the microphone, we duck underneath the curtain and join the cluster of OAPs inside. After running up the bids on some shop-soiled toasters and microwaves we come away with a video camera small enough to fit in the palm of the hand. It costs 1400 euros.

Unsure of whether or not it is actually filming, I hold the camera up to my eye and record elderly women wandering aimlessly out of a bingo hall. I film Jenny going into an off-licence and buying a bottle of cider. I film her drinking from it without pausing for breath. Handing the bottle to me she mounts the Harley-Davidson, revs it aggressively and skids off towards Blackpool Tower.

I continue filming as she leans back and tugs on the handlebars, trying to make the front tyre bounce off the ground. I watch her leave the promenade and head down a ramp on to the beach. I run, still filming, as she disappears out of sight. Overhead, seagulls wheel and screech angrily before plunging into the sea like paper darts. I film them for a few seconds until Jenny reappears, skids the machine round and heads back towards the ramp, churning up sand as she goes. By now a sizeable crowd has gathered to see what all the fuss is about, but they soon ungather as the bike comes roaring up the ramp and back on to the promenade. With another wheel spin, Jenny turns the bike round a hundred and eighty degrees and rides up the pier. Grandfathers, teenagers and mothers with babies sealed in plastic-covered prams, stand back and watch as she shunts past. From where I'm standing it looks as though she's going to skid into the barrier at the end but instead she jumps off just before the bike, now on its side, bounces into the railings and stalls its engine.

Panting, I run the length of the pier and push my way through the crowd that has formed. 'I'm her boyfriend!' I shout. They open to let me through.

At first Jenny seems concussed then she focuses on my face and arches an eyebrow. 'Boyfriend?'

A voice in the crowd asks: 'She all right?'

I turn to see a barrel-chested man chewing on a mouthful of hot dog in soggy bun. 'She's fine now,' I say helping her to her feet.

'What about the bike?' she says with a hiccup.

I pick it up and begin wheeling it back along the pier. 'Come on, let's get out of here before the police arrive.'

Once we've managed to park the bike and lose ourselves in the streets behind the tower we get the giggles. Jenny points at a candy-floss stand and says with mock petulance: 'Want one.' In the distance, the whine of approaching police cars can be heard.

We buy two sticks of candy floss and a pair of kiss-me-quick hats. We then have our photo taken with our heads sticking through the holes in a cardboard scene of a fat woman in a stripy swimsuit riding a donkey being led by a skinny little man with his trousers rolled up and a knotted hankie on his head.

'You having a happy birthday, Mickey?' Jenny says, rolling up a cigarette.

'I'm not sure happy is exactly the word.'

As we stroll arm in arm, we take in the seafront hoardings, the faded advertising for the Shamrock Music and Laughter Show and elderly couples wrapped in overcoats, reclining gingerly in rented deckchairs. The penny arcades, faded pubs and fast-food kiosks all smell of stale chip oil. Two policemen walk towards us, hands on their gun holsters, CS gas canisters and handcuffs jangling.

'Hide your fag,' I hiss. Jenny holds it behind her back.

'I still can't get used to those battledress uniforms,' Jenny says once they are out of earshot.

'They should never have got rid of the pointy helmets,' I say. 'They looked so sweet in them. Do you think they were looking for us?'

Jenny talks through her laugh: 'They'll never catch us, Mickey. We're like Bonnie and Clyde . . . I'm Bonnie.'

Down an alley we find a square overshadowed by a crane. Around the base are half a dozen people looking up at a cage. A figure bungee-jumps from it. I'm not altogether surprised when Jenny says she wants to have a go. Twenty minutes later as I get into the cage, I still can't believe she's persuaded me to join her. She makes me go first and, as the supervisor ties the rubber harness around my waist and between my legs, I give a bewildered, nervous laugh. Everything is moving in slow motion. Reality is distorted.

I watch the lips of the supervisor but I cannot concentrate on his instructions, my mind too frozen with fear. Up until the moment I stand on the edge and look down stupidly at the crowd below, I remain in my dream state. Then I begin to hyperventilate. When I turn round to tell Jenny I can't go through with it she pushes me, using both hands. I grab for her, so does the supervisor, and I lose my footing. I am too shocked to scream as I fall. My legs and arms circle until the rubber rope reaches full stretch and I lurch back up. When I come to rest and am lowered down to the ground, I see the half-dozen spectators have wandered off.

It is at least five minutes before either of us can speak.

'Mickey?'

'Jenny.'

'Wow.'

'Wow.' I hold out my hand. It's trembling. 'Look.'

'Were you frightened?'

'You try it.'

'No thanks. Changed my mind.'

'I'll never trust you again.'

'If you say so.' She yawns. 'But you'll always remember this birthday.'

'Always.'

Jenny puts her hand to her mouth. 'I haven't bought you a present!'

'Jenny, I think we should go home now before one of us gets killed. Let me see that again.'

She hands me the Handycam, I open out its colour monitor and, for the fifth time, replay the footage she took of me falling. I shake my head.

'Mad!' she says. 'Aren't you enjoying yourself?'

There is an easy intimacy between us that wasn't there before. Not contrived. Not awkward. I study her face and feel aroused. And like a catatonic who has just woken up, blinking and excited, I feel consumed by an urge to procreate, to celebrate life while I can. Someone once said that becoming impotent is like being unchained from a maniac. I can feel the shackles being clanked on again.

'Mickey? Mickey? Why are you looking at me like that?'

I laugh. 'Yes, I am enjoying myself. Thank you. Thank you very much.'

'Let's go and find a present for you then.'

We stop at a novelty shop where I try on some bulging eyes-on-springs glasses. When I tap Jenny on the shoulder to turn round and look, she pretends not to notice the difference. We try a couple of clothes shops which Jenny dismisses as being 'too common'.

'You're roots are showing,' I say with a grin.

'What do you mean?'

'Well, what happened to Jenny the eco-warrior? Even your voice has reverted.'

'I don't know what you're talking about,' she says, punching my arm playfully.

We find a second-hand shop with a camp Lancastrian behind the till. He is wearing a staff label with the name 'Chris' on it. As I try on a linen suit and some black leather Oxfords which actually fit, Jenny tries on several large dresses which look like marquees on her. When she asks Chris if he has anything smaller he starts an anecdote about a customer he had in the other day.

'Get to the point,' Jenny says.

'Are you in a hurry?' Chris asks.

'No, I'm just impatient.'

We leave the shop without buying anything and our next stop

121

is a casino where Jenny asks me to kiss her hand for luck before she rolls the dice. She wins 250 euros only to lose it all on the roulette wheel. Afterwards, she buys some more cider from an off-licence and drinks it from the bottle as she watches me play the slot machines in an amusement arcade. She stands close enough for me to smell the cider on her breath.

Outside the Merrie England Cabaret Bar there is a billboard advertising *Austin Powers 6* and, next to this, a bandstand at which a Latin American band dressed in frilly orange shirts are playing a bossa nova. Without waiting to be asked, Jenny swings me around and I have to improvise as best I can. When the tune finishes, I sigh with relief and am just walking off when a tango strikes up. To cheers from a crowd of pensioners, Jenny turns the tango into a hip-grinding lambada then flips me around to start a conga line which the OAPs join in.

Feeling famished from the dancing, we look for a chip shop. All we can find is row upon row of unevocative boarding houses with evocative names such as Villa Rosa and Avondale, advertising late keys and one, with a stone-clad front, a chair lift. Realizing we must be heading away from the centre, we wander back towards the tower.

We eat with our fingers – blowing on the hot chips – and follow tram lines which run between little white pavilions with green onion domes. It's starting to turn cool and the sun is low in the sky. Feeling mellow and hungry again we look for somewhere to have dinner. We can't find a restaurant that doesn't look rat-infested, so we hail a cab and ask the driver if he can recommend anywhere. He knows a good restaurant, he says, about fifteen minutes out of town. It turns out to be a glorified pub – brothel red, fronds of palm everywhere – owned by the driver's cousin. But it is cosy and therefore ideal.

'Do you think they take credit cards,' Jenny says behind her hand.

'Not while you're looking,' I whisper back.

Throughout the meal – a bowl of spaghetti and tomato sauce which I only pick at – we reminisce about the events of the day, prompting each other's stories and laughing at our own jokes. There is a guttering candle between us and we take it in turns to play with the drips of wax. As the plates are cleared away we clink glasses and slip into a companionable silence.

A few minutes pass before Jenny lifts her chair back and the waiter asks her if she has brought a coat. 'Yes,' she says, looking at the coat stand by the door, 'that cream one.' She walks over to it and allows the waiter to help her into it. I don't know where to look. 'I'll bring the car round, darling,' she says jangling a set of keys she has just found in the coat pocket. She blows me a kiss and disappears out of the door.

I grin at the waiter and make an elaborate show of patting my pockets as I look for my wallet. I'm sure he is still staring at me as I walk out into the car park.

'Pssst!' Jenny is sitting in the driver's seat of an old Mercedes cabriolet. She finds the button that lowers the roof, leans over the passenger seat and opens the door. 'Mickey!'

I walk briskly over, trying not to crunch the gravel under my shoes too loudly. 'Don't you dare turn that engine on,' I say quietly, hoping the seriousness of my tone will shock her. 'Get out of that car right now.'

Her hand hovers over the key.

'I mean it, Jenny. This is so not funny. We'll go to prison for this.'

'*So not funny?* You've started talking like me, Mickey. How sweet.'

'Out!'

'Cool your boots. I'm not taking it far.'

'No, Jenny. Give me the keys.'

She pulls the keys from the ignition and throws them over her shoulder. 'Spoilsport,' she says.

Seventeen

Four days later, back in Pimlico, Jenny finds a polythene bag in my desk containing eight wraps of cocaine. She empties them all on to a plate, sits on the windowsill, holds the plate out of the open window and calls me in. As she tips it she says: 'You don't need this.'

I can't speak or move, at first. When my voice returns I'm shouting: 'What are you doing?'

'What does it look like I'm doing?'

I lunge at her, try to grab her shoulders but end up with my hands around her neck. She pushes me away and staggers back coughing and rubbing her throat. Her eyes are watering and, two seconds later, mine are as well. She kicks me in the groin.

Five minutes after she has slammed the door to my study behind her, I am still doubled up in pain, still feeling nauseous.

It's not really the sight of my drugs being thrown away that has provoked this situation. Since my birthday, an atmosphere of tension has been building up. We had argued after I had insisted on leaving the Mercedes – and the stolen coat – in the car park. Now, every time there is a knock at the door, I assume it is the police coming to arrest us. Our DNA prints were all over the car. And the waiter in the restaurant would have been able to give a good description of us. I think we both feel edgy and irritable.

Yet she shows no signs of wanting to leave, of wanting to return to her life of tree-hugging. Indeed she seems to have reverted to a life of bourgeois comfort with impressive ease. Her moods change constantly. She's the most mercurial person I've ever met. Sometimes I think she's flirting with me, others that she can't stand me. And I find my temperament has become as erratic as hers. I can shift from feeling confident to insecure and back to confident again in the same five-minute period. And yet I feel more alive with her than I have felt for years. She's good fun. She's dangerous. She's inscrutable.

I've made several attempts to continue where we left off on the moor, tried to press clumsy kisses on her neck, on her freckled shoulders, but each time she has straight-armed me: sometimes with good humour, half-teasing, half-protesting as she pushes me off, other times with a note of cold annoyance in her voice.

I keep writing letters to her but never let her have them. I wrote one that was full of crossings out, so I rewrote it neatly, then crossed a couple of words out anyway to make it look spontaneous. Sometimes I just write her name over and over, page after page.

I've made a list of every shred of information I know about her – favourite colour, favourite film, how many cousins, most embarrassing moment, what she would change about herself and so on. Sometimes she looks at me suspiciously when I recall a trivial detail, but she is flattered, I think.

I've tried being all the things you're supposed to be: cool, enigmatic, amused. I've reduced the friction between us by making her laugh. I've even given her space, accepting invitations to parties three nights running: the re-launch of the *Economist* at the Savoy (too crowded, wall-to-wall young men with sweating faces); the opening of the new Tracy Emin restaurant in Soho (full of beautiful but noisy young women); and a retirement party for the American ambassador (where I became so desperate for a glass of champagne I had to leave early). Actually, I asked Jenny to be my walker at all three parties, but she declined.

I can't stop thinking about her. I know when she's in the next room because I can feel her there. And when I'm in the same room as her I'm as tongue-tied and self-conscious as an infatuated schoolboy. Sometimes, when I look at her as she sits lolling in a chair with her legs over the arms, I can hardly breathe. When she leaves the house, I feel depressed, restless, eaten up with self-pity. Poor Michael Yates.

Buddhists believe that inner harmony comes from clarity of thought. It is clear to me that I can only be happy with Jenny. Love simplifies everything. Nothing else matters, especially integrity and dignity. I've started using a sunbed. I've even been to have my hair styled by Nicky Clarke.

It doesn't help that, knowing Amanda is away skiing, Jenny has taken to walking around the house first thing in the morning and last thing at night in just her T-shirt and knickers. Another distraction is the sight of her practising yoga barefoot every morning on the small garden terrace which my study overlooks. I've been watching her from behind the folds of my curtain. And I guess there have been times when she has looked up and noticed me. Am I wrong to do this? I don't know. No man is a villain to himself.

I wait until she finishes her exercises before I appear on the roof terrace carrying two glasses of lemonade. 'Hey, Jenny.'

'Hey, Mickey.'

'Thought you might need a drink.' I hand her one of the glasses. The light is grey and even. She is wearing a blue Nike tracksuit top and white tennis skirt and, as she sits down on the patch of lawn, with her back to the garden wall, she fans herself. And I am able to see her knickers. Amanda's wind chime, a memento from our honeymoon in Malaysia, ripples gently in the breeze.

'Thanks,' Jenny says, taking a sip and drawing her right leg in with her arms. This makes her skirt ride up. 'Why do you do so much of that stuff anyway?' She rests her chin on her knee.

'The dumb dust? It stops me drinking.' My voice has become thick and slurred with lust. I sit down to the left of her, trying not to stare too obviously at where her bare heel meets the material of her knickers.

'If you say so.'

'Do you have to say that all the time?'

'What?'

'If you say so.'

'Coke must do you more harm.'

126

'No, the drink is much worse. Definitely. But I'm going to give up cocaine anyway.' (Should never call it coke.)

'Of course you're not... The lemonade has made my fingers all sticky.' Jenny wipes them on my shirt. 'So how much do you get through?'

'As much as I can. It's like a drug to me.'

'Seriously.'

'Two or three grams a week. Sometimes less. Never more. Which means I've got it under control. Some people have to use up whatever supplies they've got in the house.'

'It makes you sound permanently bunged up with cold. Doesn't it damage your nose?'

'A bit.' A lot actually. 'It's the sleeping pills that mess you up.' I notice the bruising on her neck. 'Sorry about...'

'No, I shouldn't have...'

We fall silent.

I stare at her knickers.

'Are you staring at my knickers?' she says hotly.

'No.' I say it too quickly, not daring to look at her.

'Yes you were. Dirty bastard.' She seems to shock herself momentarily with the ferocity of these words, but continues anyway. 'Look at me when I'm talking to you.'

I level an agonized look at her and see the bruising around her neck. Her nostrils are flaring with anger and a wisp of hair is hanging dangerously over her temple. She is too pretty to look at and I have to turn my head away.

She begins to pluck at the hairs on the nape of my neck. When I don't respond she digs her fingernails into my skin, scoring four scratch marks.

'Well?' she demands.

I'm about to say that I don't mind being scratched when she interrupts: 'And don't tell me you don't mind.'

'I had no intention of.'

There is silence again.

'Was I hurting you?'

I nod, my face burning.

'If I was, it's because you're so easy to hurt. It's like you actually enjoy being hurt, don't you?'

I whisper: 'I don't enjoy it. I don't.'

'Then why don't you stand up for yourself? Why don't you fight back, yeah?' Slowly, as if in shocked recognition, she says: 'Oh, I get it. You're in love with me. Aren't you? Mickey? Well?'

I feel grateful for the sun as it dips behind a cloud. My clothes feel heavy and itchy. I'm confused. Head bowed, I mumble: 'No.'

'Of course, you are. Everyone is.'

'Well, I'm not.'

'Louder,' she demands. 'I didn't quite catch that.'

'I'm not.'

'Not what?'

'Not . . .' I rub my neck. 'I don't love you.'

'Why not?'

'*What?*'

'What's wrong with me? Don't you find me attractive.'

'Yes, of course I do.'

'So what are you going to do about it, then?'

'Jenny. Stop this. Please.'

'Are you going to kiss me or what?'

'Do you want me to?'

'Oh, for God's sake, you sap, just do it.'

I lean over and give her a light peck on the cheek.

'Be still my beating heart,' she says flatly.

I kiss her again, this time on the lips, holding the position for a few seconds. Her lips are cold and unresponsive. I edge closer, run an arm around her shoulders and give her a slight hug which turns into a pat. We sit like this for a short while, my hand feeling numb. From this close I notice the dried sweat on her tracksuit top and the garlic on her breath. I walk my fingers down her arm and, shifting position, sit upright so that, as if by accident, my right hand at first brushes, and then loosely cups, her right breast. It is small and firm.

Gradually I apply pressure and begin to circle with my thumb. She pushes me off and says: 'Don't touch me with those apologetic fingers.'

I shrink backwards, apologizing.

'And stop apologizing.' She makes a show of adjusting her sports bra and picks imaginary blades of grass off her sleeve. 'Look, if you want to grope me, just do it. Don't give me this pathetic seduction number. It insults my intelligence. Here, give me your hand.' She takes my left hand in hers and, with her other hand, unzips her top and holds open the material of her bra. She flinches as she presses my hand on to her warm breast. Roughly working my fingers for me, she says: 'There now, have a feel. Don't be shy. Get it out of your system ... Happy now?' She kneels level with me, smoothes down my hair and draws her hands around to frame my cheeks. 'Look at me,' she whispers, using her thumbs to wipe my face. We look at each other for perhaps a full minute before she smiles enigmatically and kisses me on the forehead. She reaches into her tracksuit pocket for a hanky and, putting it to my nose, asks me to blow. 'Sorry, Mickey,' she says. 'That was cruel.'

She stands up, walks back to the house and pauses at the french window. 'You're not a bad kisser,' she says turning round briefly to blow me a kiss before disappearing indoors.

I touch my mouth with my fingertips.

The photograph of Jenny sitting astride the branches of the tree at the protest camp is now on my desk, in a wooden frame, next to one of Emily on her fourth birthday. I take both photos down, kiss them and put them away in a drawer. I watch again the video we recorded in Blackpool and then put the Handycam in the drawer as well, on top of the photographs I've had developed from the camera we found on the moor. These unnerve me. After closing the drawer I open it again to flick through them for about the tenth time.

The ones of her mooning are here, although mostly out of focus. But the dozen or so frames before you get to them are of her as well, and me: the two of us walking like a couple of teenagers with our hands in each other's back pockets. Our near embrace in the shooting butt: grainy, from a distance. The two of us walking hand in hand towards the shooting lodge. We obviously disturbed whoever took them. He must still have been close by when we found the camera.

I suspect my wife is behind this surveillance.

I shall have an opportunity to ask her.

An invitation from Lord Ingleton has arrived. I examine the

postmark and the stamp. It has the PM's silhouette on it, where the sovereign's used to be. The writing on the envelope is elegant. Addressed to Mr and Mrs Michael Yates. I love this because my wife never changed her name from Amanda Tenant – and hates it when people assume she has. There is no letter of explanation accompanying the stiff white card. The pleasure of our company is requested for a shooting party the following weekend.

I e-mail Amanda and, while I'm waiting for her reply, my laptop tells me to stand by for a video conference call from Romania. It is Sarah.

'Is this working?' she says doubtfully, not looking at the camera.

'Yes, it's fine,' I say. 'Is that you, Sarah? You look different. How did you get my number?'

'It's programmed into your laptop. I found it. The laptop. I told you I knew the right people.'

'That was months ago,' I laugh. 'Has it only just turned up?'

'Well, I've had it for a couple of weeks but it's taken me this long to work out how to use it. How shall I get it back to you?'

'I wouldn't bother, Sarah. I've got a new one. In fact, I'm on my second replacement. My first got run over. I'd keep that if I were you. Sell it if you like, it's out of date now but it should still be worth quite a bit.'

'Thanks,' she sounds hesitant. 'Well, I might just hang on to it then.'

'You look different.' She looks older. There are dark patches under her mild eyes and her face looks gaunt.

'I've had my hair cropped,' she says after a slight time delay. 'Thanks for noticing. How's life in London? I'm afraid we don't get the *English People* here so I'm rather out of touch.'

'You can get it on the Net, you know. You'll find a bookmark on the laptop.'

'Can I? I must start reading it.'

After a few more minutes of stilted conversation we both relax a little and begin to talk properly. Sarah asks after Amanda. I tell her my wife and I have been invited to Lord Ingleton's for the weekend but that our marriage is as hopeless as ever. She laughs, says at least I'm *in* a relationship, and changes the subject to the victims of torture and mass rape she has been having to deal with and, without really paying attention to her stories, I tell her about my recent triumphs at work. About the Air Marshal. I'm not sure why, but I mention my feelings towards Jenny. Sometimes it is easier to tell the truth to a relative stranger.

When the call is interrupted by my laptop announcing I have mail, I say goodbye to Sarah and tell her to ring again soon. The message is from Amanda. I can't be bothered to read it at first. Amazing how you can lose all curiosity in someone you once loved, or believed you loved. There is no kindness left either. After a moment's hesitation I click the mouse.

'Darling M. Can't think of a single good reason why I should drop everything this weekend just to suit you. Then again can't think of reason not to. Skiing was fun but am so bored now that I'm back in Gloucestershire. The house seems so empty. I got such a sweet letter from one of Emily's schoolfriends. I cried for the rest of the day after reading it. Do you still cry? Do you think we shall ever stop crying? I hear you've adopted some waif from a protest camp. You haven't gone all environmental, have you? Nothing more toe-curling than a man who doesn't realize the menopause is upon him. Am I expected to shoot this weekend? Will Daddy be there? Sorry I missed your birthday. Did you get my present? Love A.'

Eighteen

Ever since I overheard Amanda refer with her usual freezing charm to 'the sort of person who wears a ready-tied at Glyndebourne' I've always tried to knot my own bow tie. The art, of course, is in not making it too neat – so everyone can tell you tied it yourself. As I try this and fail, twice, in front of the bathroom mirror, I avoid my wife's reproachful glances in the reflection.

She is sitting behind me at a dressing table, rolling the glass stopper from a scent bottle across her neck and on down towards her motionless cleavage. Her ritual hasn't changed. She dabs the stopper on one wrist and rubs it against the other. Concealer under her eyes. Blusher on her cheeks. The mascara is next, applied with mouth stretched open.

'Why do women wear make-up and perfume?' I ask over my shoulder.

'Because they're ugly and they smell.'

'You've heard it.'

'You told me.' Amanda has a muscular, chewy voice. 'A hundred times.'

'I did not.'

'Wasn't it Rita Rudner who said marriage is where you find that one special person that you want to annoy the rest of your life.'

'You always quote that.'

'No I don't.'

'Yes you do.'

Amanda sees me struggling with my bow tie and snaps: 'Give it to me.' Her whole face contorts with the effort and the tendons on her neck go rigid. She stands behind me to tie it. 'You've missed some patches of stubble,' she says, using the back of her hand to flick some apparent dandruff off the shoulders of my dinner jacket. 'Under your chin. Have you been on a sunbed?'

It's a pity couples never fall out of love as dramatically as they fall in it. The falling out is always such a slow and laborious process. Years of curdling and suffocation and losing the desire to please.

Amanda is wearing a halter-neck Grecian column dress, mushroom coloured, with a clinging corset strap at the back. The outlines of her nipples are visible through the material. On her feet she has strappy sandals. Her nails are varnished a dark claret, her auburn hair is coiled high above her head. I am shocked at how presentable she looks.

'You look unusually presentable,' I say.

'Don't try and flatter me. Do you think so?'

'No, I was just being polite.' I drop my razor into my wash bag and look around for something to buff my shoes with.

'You *do* like it, don't you,' Amanda says, standing up to smooth out the silk. 'Donatella designed it for me as a present. Says she's going to include something similar in her Paris collection.' She runs her hands over her hips and adds: 'Shit. I can't wear these. You can see the line.' She wriggles her hem up to her thighs and peels her knickers off, stepping out of one leg and kicking them off with the other. She has kept in better shape than me – but then she does have a personal trainer. I feel an unfamiliar urge to nuzzle her bare shoulders.

'You look . . .' I don't finish the sentence.

'I ought to. I cost a fortune. These alone,' she taps her shiny white front teeth, '18,000 euros each. These,' she points to the collagen-inflated lips that used to be so thin and sophisticated, '30,000. This,' a tap of her surgically straightened nose that used to be endearingly blobby. 'And this,' she pulls the skin taught on both cheeks, 'cost so much I'm embarrassed to say.'

'Worth it.'

'Did you know 95 per cent of plastic surgery is done on wives whose husbands have run off with a younger woman. I read it in *Tatler*.'

'What's that supposed to mean?'

'You tell me.'

'You tell me,' I repeat in a whiny voice.

'Why are you being so defensive, Michael?'

'What are you talking about?'

'You sound guilty.'

'I do not.'

'You do.'

'Well, who wouldn't sound guilty if they were just told they sound guilty. It's human nature. Like when you get stopped by the police, you automatically look guilty.' My heart is thumping. 'What is it I'm supposed to be feeling guilty about anyway?'

Amanda walks over to me presses her hand against my chest, holds it there for a moment then raises her eyebrow at me.

'Get off!' I say pushing her hand away. 'I refuse to have this argument with you. Is that why you've been paying someone to spy on me?'

She laughs witheringly. 'Don't flatter yourself.'

'I know we're all supposed to get used to being spied on twenty-four hours a day but I personally still find it a little creepy and, if it is you that's behind it, I'll thank you to desist.'

'"I'll thank you to desist?"' she imitates mockingly. 'Well, excuse me, your lordship.'

Neither of us want to hear the truth, whatever that might be. Like everyone else, I've heard the rumours about the woman who comes to stay at our home in Gloucestershire. Lola? Louisa? Lorna? She's Amanda's tennis coach or something. I've never met her and Amanda has never mentioned her, but then she doesn't need to.

Our exchange hangs in the air, poisoning it and Amanda continues preening herself: pulling a long face as she crimps her eyelashes and puckers her lips before kissing them on to the invitation we have been sent. Needing something to do to look more calm than I feel, I pick up my newspaper and watch her over the top of it. She is entering the final phase of her preparations:

strapping on the Cartier Tank Watch I bought her last year as a seventh wedding anniversary present, inserting her drop pearl earrings without taking her eyes off her reflection. I marvel at her unself-conscious narcissism as she dusts her face with a brush and picks an eyelash off her cheek.

'Do you think I should wear these?' she asks, fingering one earring. 'Or the diamond ones that Daddy gave me?'

I hate the way she refers to her father as Daddy. So affected. Like her saying 'what?' instead of 'pardon?' Although she was born in New York, she was educated at Benenden and Cambridge. Her manners are impeccable. Her King's English carries no hint of her American origins. And it embarrasses her considerably that 'Daddy' still talks with a gravelly Brooklyn drawl. I suppose I always make a point of referring to him as 'Dad' because I know it annoys her.

'Those ones your Dad gave you would be better.'

'What's wrong with the others?'

'Nothing.'

'Why do you prefer the ones Daddy gave me?'

'To be honest I couldn't care less.'

She splays her fingers to examine her nails and hisses: 'Piss off!'

The temperature in the room has dropped, the gap between us widened. It has taken us less than an hour to puncture the mood of reconciliation we felt when we arrived.

We'd been late. And a thoughtless comment I'd made about Emily – saying that if she'd been with us we could have dropped her off to stay at my father's, as it was so close by – made us both shiver. We were soon arguing about whose fault it was we were late. We had been left feeling tense by the farce of our not being able to work out that the vast eighteenth-century arch set in a wall of rough-hewn stone blocks – which dominated one side of the village green – was in fact the entrance to the hall. But after we'd followed the butler through the hall along a barrel-vaulted passage, down an absurd number of corridors, to a wing of the house which was a good five kilometres from where the other guests were staying, we'd got the giggles and flopped on our bed as soon as the butler had closed the door. We had felt like comrades. Allies in alien territory.

Now, feeling uncomfortable in our formal clothes, we don't

know what to say to each other. Ours is the sort of awkwardness that utter familiarity breeds. No observation we can think to make, no joke or gesture, will be original. I cut up a line on the bedside table, offer her some and, when she wrinkles her nose in disgust, I give a 'please yourself' shrug and take half of it. She then says, as I knew she would, 'I suppose it might make this grizzly evening more bearable' and finishes it off. We even fail to surprise each other with our drug-taking habits.

As we descend the cantilevered stairwell, trailing our fingers along the iron banisters, we stare up at the painted dome – a bucolic scene of nymphs and graces. We don't say anything but every click of Amanda's heels against the stone steps sounds like a reproach. There are hunting scenes depicted on the tapestries that hang from the walls and the floor, when we reach it, is slippery marble. The leather soles of my shoes creak loudly. As we approach the drawing room we can hear the chatter of the other guests: Ascot voices, scratchy and neurotic. The spot under my chin which I've just run over with a dry razor feels tender. I dab at it and inspect my fingertip. A smudge of blood. Great. Just what I need.

The butler is in the doorway holding a tray laden with flutes of champagne. When I ask for an orange juice he signals with one eyebrow at a liveried flunky standing in the corner and a glass is brought to me. Now I catch a glimpse of the twelve other guests. The men are wearing suits. It's too late to turn back and change and so I smile to cover my embarrassment. 'I thought you said this would be black tie,' I hiss at Amanda out of the corner of my mouth. Her lips twitch in barely concealed delight.

Lady Ingleton, a tall, silver-haired woman with a grousemoor complexion, comes over to greet us and pretends not to notice my clothes. She asks if we found our room all right, as if she'd half-expected the butler to leave us to find it on our own. We both yes-thank-you too quickly and compliment her on the arrangement of orchids that have been left on our dressing table. I think I may even ask if they have come from her greenhouse. I don't recall her reply; she probably blanks the question for fear that her brain might shut down from boredom if she dwells upon it.

Behind us a spark spits out of the fire and lands on a hearth rug, centimetres away from a sleeping Labrador. Lady Ingleton excuses herself and brushes between us to flick it back into the fire. As she is putting the guard up, we follow her, but by the time we reach the high marble fireplace she has bustled off across the room to greet another guest. Everyone is speaking too correctly and stiltedly, each acknowledging the other with false, ingratiating smiles. We stare at the fire and sip our drinks in silence. We have drained our glasses before my wife speaks. 'You've got blood on your collar.'

'*Shit!*'

'No. Blood.' Amanda plucks my handkerchief from my breast pocket, licks it and begins rubbing.

'Don't do that here,' I growl. 'What's wrong with you.' I can feel my cheeks burning, though I know this will not change their natural ashen hue. We have our backs to the rest of the guests, as people do when they're convinced no one will want to talk to them. It's as if we don't want to risk catching anyone's eye so that we can prove ourselves right. I feel a bead of sweat trickle down my neck and am just dabbing at it with the hanky when I hear Bruce Tenant's flat, deep monotone resonating across the room. 'Mandy, honey...Michael.' He signals us over. 'You know Air Marshal Lambert?'

'Hello again, Sir Andrew,' I say. 'This is my wife, Amanda.'

They shake hands and Lambert takes a step back to introduce his wife. Lady Lambert bows her head stiffly and offers me her satin-gloved fingers to shake. With her neat bun of raven-black hair and her clear skin she only looks about twenty-five. More like Jenny's elder sister than her mother. I make a mental note to avoid making this crass observation out loud.

'Jane,' she says. 'How do you do?'

'Pleased to meet you, Jane,' I say. I always like to use this non-U greeting in front of my wife because I know how much it makes her wince. Lady Lambert seems to sense this and gives me a searching look. It is almost flirtatious. I see Jenny in it.

'You could be Jenny's elder sister,' I say.

'How sweet of you. It's very good of you to put her up. It must be a terrible inconvenience.'

Yes, I think, a terrible inconvenience is exactly what it is. I can't sleep, I've lost my appetite and I spend every minute of the day fantasizing about her. 'Oh, not at all,' I say. 'She's a pleasant girl. Only too happy to help out until she finds somewhere of her own.'

'How is she?'

Fucking adorable.

'Fine. Fine. She sends her love.'

Lady Lambert – Jane – furrows her brow to say you and I know that's a lie. 'You have children?'

I look at Amanda. She avoids my eye. 'Had,' I say, almost inaudibly. 'A daughter. Emily. She would have been seven.'

'Eight,' corrects Amanda in an equally soft voice. For a moment cracks appear in the wall she has built up around herself. Then her face hardens. Through a smile that could twist metal she says: 'Your face looks familiar, Lady Lambert. Have we met?'

'Jane. Please,' Lady Lambert says, taking the hint about the change of subject. 'I don't recall.'

'Yes, I remember now, I saw a photograph in *Tatler*. Michael is always getting that, too. People thinking they've seen him somewhere before. Because of his byline picture.'

'I'd heard you were a journalist, Michael.' The way Lady Lambert says it makes my buttocks clench. She might as well have said: I'd heard there was going to be a man here who ate rat sandwiches. 'Andy enjoyed your piece on the Tory defence proposals.'

I bet he did. 'But what did *you* think of it, Jane?'

She smiles tightly and says: 'I haven't had time to read it yet. My husband says you must have been well briefed.'

'Michael is quite the little star again these days.' Amanda says, linking her arm through mine.

'He's our best,' grunts Tenant, slapping me on the back in that irritating way of his. I notice he's carrying a mobile which means that he hasn't got his cellular earpiece on. We might be able to get a relatively normal conversation out of him tonight.

'When he can stay off the sauce,' Amanda accompanies this with one of her false laughs. No one else joins in.

'Michael's story about the Tory manifesto is on the short list for Scoop of the Year at the English Press Awards,' Tenant says.

'I didn't know that,' I say.

'They're not announced until Monday,' Tenant adds. 'Congratulations.'

'Yes, congratulations,' the Air Marshal echoes. 'Bruce was just telling me about Cecil King.'

'Chairman of the Mirror Group,' Amanda says. 'Once tried to overthrow the Government.' This is another annoying habit of hers. Always has to prove she knows all there is to know about everything.

Tenant glowers at Amanda through a fug of cigar smoke. 'I must have told you about him already,' he rumbles.

It's tragic but Amanda actually swots up on current affairs before a meeting with her father. She tries to anticipate what he will want to discuss. She told me this once, in a moment of honesty. She is always desperate to impress him, to win his approval, yet in her heart she knows it is pointless. Tenant is incapable of feeling warmth for anyone. I don't imagine he's ever been in love. Or ever felt vulnerable. Certainly, Amanda has never seen him cry. I don't suppose Tenant has ever felt guilty either. It's said that as a young man growing up in Brooklyn, he pistol-whipped to death a shopkeeper who owed him money. Did it right in front of the man's wife and five-year-old daughter.

'King did indeed plan a coup,' Tenant continues, stubbing his cigar out in a vase. 'In May 1968. At Lord Mountbatten's flat in Kinnerton Street. He offered Mountbatten the post of titular head of Government in the event of Wilson being overthrown.'

'And your point is what exactly, Daddy?'

'The point is, we ought to be thinking of doing the same.'

'That's treason, Daddy. Very naughty.'

'I'll drink to that,' the Air Marshal says with a laugh. 'To treason.' We all clink our glasses.

'Yes,' Amanda says. 'But the point is, it didn't happen. Everyone just laughed at Mountbatten. We British – sorry, English – just don't do that sort of thing. Even the name *coup d'état* is foreign.'

'So is *putsch*,' Lady Lambert adds helpfully.

'But you're an American, Amanda darling,' I say. 'You wouldn't understand.'

Lord Ingleton has joined us, drawn by the sound of glasses clinking. 'What about William of Orange?' he barks. 'Stole the crown from James II in a coup.'

'Don't let's go down that road, dear,' Lady Ingleton says. 'You know that your doctor warned you about getting on to the subject of Roman Catholicism.'

General laughter at this. Lady Ingleton takes it as her cue to call everyone through for dinner.

The only light in the dining room comes from the fireplace and the four silver candelabras on the long table. The walls are painted dark burgundy and the sooty portraits which hang on them in gilded frames look spooky in the flickering candlelight. I am seated between Lady Ingleton on my right and Lady Lambert on my left. When I cover my glass as the red wine is being poured from a decanter, Lady Lambert asks me how long I have been a teetotaller.

'Five years?' she echoes, flapping her napkin open. 'I'm impressed. Then I shall have to drink for two.' And she does, catching the butler's eye whenever her glass is drained. After her fourth glass she is beginning to slur. 'You don't know what you're missing,' she says, holding the glass to my nose. 'Have a sniff at least. Lovely rotten bouquet.'

A mobile phone trills and Tenant answers it, making no attempt to soften his voice: 'Tenant . . . George, did that asshole go through with it? . . . Well, I wouldn't wait for it to fall much more . . . No . . . Hey, you listen to me, numb nuts, that's what I pay you for . . . No . . . Do they want a piece of me, huh? Do they? . . . right then . . .'

A French onion soup is followed by guinea fowl with a watery plum sauce. And when this arrives, as if by some pre-arranged signal, each woman begins talking to the man on her left.

Nineteen

Lady Ingleton is not the warmest person I've met, but her conversational skills have been well honed from years of practise. She tells me that her husband used to be something of a Tory grandee, the keeper of the party conscience, but since the voting rights of hereditary peers were abolished he has lost interest in politics. Indeed, since the party elected its new leader he has even considered defecting to New Labour. 'We've heard that she plans to introduce a supertax, you know,' Lady Ingleton says. 'Like we had in the seventies under Wilson. It'll be the end of estates like this.'

'Oh, I don't know,' I say ingratiatingly. 'The aristocracy always seems to muddle through. Just bobs its head down for a generation until it's safe to come out again.'

'I know, but it's a worry. This house has been in the same family since the 1750s. He built it.'

I follow her gaze to the oil painting hanging over the fireplace. It is of a middle-aged man in a blue velvet frock coat standing next to an elm tree and looking very pleased with himself. He is wearing a tricorn hat perched rakishly on a white wig. He carries a flintlock under his arm. 'Who is he?'

'The 2nd Baron Ingleton.'

'It's jolly good,' I don't normally use words like jolly but I feel sure that Lady Ingleton does and so can't help slipping into parody. 'Who's it by?'

'Gainsborough.'

I oh–really. Genuinely impressed.

'It's a rather sympathetic hanging, don't you think?'

'Sorry, I'm not with – '

'Above the fireplace there. Lends itself.'

'I'll say.'

I'll say? Where did *that* come from? I know I'm going too far with the mimicry but I'm enjoying myself too much to stop. I'm relieved when the pudding arrives, Lady Ingleton turns to her right, all the women follow and I'm able to talk to Lady Lambert again. She has become noticeably flirty now and says that she has been dying to ask me all night why I am wearing a dinner jacket. I blink, unable to think of a witty answer, and point out to her that the painting above the fireplace is by Gainsborough and that it is sympathetically hung. She squeezes my knee and says too loudly: 'I could tell you were a man who knew his old masters, Mr Yates. And I bet you have an eye for the ladies as well.'

Amanda, who is sitting opposite, hears this and says: 'That's about all he has for them these days.' The cheese knife she is holding upright between her forefinger and thumb is allowed to drop so that it is pointing down.

'I remember when I had my first drink, too.' I smile tightly at Amanda, raise a spoonful of bread and butter pudding and turn back to Lady Lambert.

'What was that you were saying about bringing back hanging?' she says, patting my arm. 'I'm a great believer in the power of the noose. Should never have abolished it in the first place.'

'I'm sorry about my husband's noisy eating, Jane,' Amanda says.

'Pardon, darling?' I say.

Amanda fixes me with a stare.

'There's a lot to be said for it,' Lady Lambert continues. 'It's like Dr Johnson said, knowing you're to be hanged in the morning concentrates the mind wonderfully.'

A young barrister who introduced himself to me earlier as Paul from Lincoln's Inn says in a fruity baritone: 'A majority in this country has always favoured the death penalty. If it were put to a vote tomorrow we would be hanging people again by next weekend.'

'That is the contradiction contained in the notion of liberal democracy,' Lady Ingleton says. 'You can either be a liberal or a democrat. You can't be both.'

'Americans can,' Tenant drawls, covering up the mouthpiece on his mobile in order to join in.

I lean towards Lady Lambert and whisper: 'What was Jenny like as a child?'

'Exactly as she is now. Never grew up.'

'She can be a bit immature. But I find it rather charming. She told me she used to see a psychiatrist.'

'She told you that?'

'Yes.'

Lady Lambert suddenly steadies herself, palms flat on the table. 'Excuse, me,' she says. 'I think I need a breath of fresh air.'

When Lady Ingleton hears Lady Lambert's chair go back she does the same and, moments later, everyone has stood up. The women file out and I am the first of the men to follow.

When Lord Ingleton coughs and says: 'Won't you join us, Michael?' I realize I am the only man leaving the room. 'Gentlemen,' he adds. 'Why don't we all move down to this end.'

Unbelievable.

The butler appears with a decanter of port as we shuffle down to occupy the chairs around Lord Ingleton. As the port is poured I whisper testily to Lord Ingleton that I hadn't realized this sort of thing still went on.

'My dear fellow, it depends where you go,' he says with a snuffling laugh. 'Not having any?'

'Don't touch it I'm afraid.' I sulkily flick his crystal with my finger nail to see if it rings.

'Cigar then?' He signals the butler over who proffers a box of them. 'Or something a little stronger.' He points to three smoothly wrapped joints at one end of the humidor. 'Since the stuff has been legalized we like to offer our guests a post-prandial puff.'

I widen my eyes. 'You surprise me. Don't mind if I do.'

A butler lights it for me and I take a deep lung-full, hold it down and nod in appreciation. I examine the spliff as if for a trademark. 'Which way is this meant to go round?'

'Opposite way to the port, old boy,' Lord Ingleton says with a waggle of his fingers. 'Opposite way to the port.'

I hand it to him.

'So, Michael,' Lord Ingleton continues after taking a drag and exhaling loudly, 'you're going to join us on the shoot tomorrow? See our side of the argument?'

'Rather,' I say, mentally pinching myself to stop the parody.

'Quis?' Lord Ingleton says holding up the spliff.

'Ego,' the Air Marshal says, taking it.

'It's the goddam Tories we should be shooting.' Tenant says this with what amounts, by his sullen standards, to a guffaw.

Paul clears his throat to speak: 'What are we going to do if they win the election?'

'I've told you,' Tenant says slapping his chubby hand down on the table. 'Send in the tanks. Surround Downing Street.'

'Tried something like that in '75' – Lambert in a clipped voice – 'said it was an anti-terrorist manoeuvre. Had jeeps mounted with machine guns driving round and round at Heathrow.'

'So what went wrong?' I ask.

'I'm not sure. Wilson must have promised to resign. Did, too. A year later.'

Everyone laughs at this. 'A military coup wouldn't work in this country,' Paul says, taking a toke from the joint. 'The MoD and EJ is a government department. That's why they wear civilian clothes when they work there.'

'But surely their first allegiance is to the Crown?' Lord Ingleton says. 'If our Welsh friend declares a republic, the military would be legally bound to act against her on behalf of the monarch.'

'I don't think it's that simple,' Lambert says good naturedly. 'Although I do think it would be a good idea to have a final march past of all the regiments she is planning to scrap. It would stir the viewing public up. Make everyone feel nostalgic. Have a few old tanks trundling past the Cenotaph followed by a handful of Chelsea pensioners.'

'Well, I think we should just string her up,' Tenant again, sounding drunk. 'Now. Before she can do any more damage to the public weal. You agree with me, don't you, Michael?'

All this talk of a coup has left me feeling detached. 'It would have to be a sympathetic hanging,' I hear myself say. 'After a fair trial.'

There is a long silence before the old sod grunts: 'What the hell is that supposed to mean?'

Lambert leans towards Tenant and says in a whisper loud enough for us all to hear: 'I think it's called gallows humour, Bruce.' There is another silence before everyone – except Tenant – has a fit of giggles.

Back in our room, just after midnight, Amanda and I laugh about how pissed Lady Lambert had been during dinner and how Lord Ingleton had become really competitive when we were playing charades: getting exasperated when his team couldn't guess the spanking mime he was doing for *Crime and Punishment*. I light up a spliff that I had slipped into my pocket after dinner.

A truce momentarily holding between us, Amanda pushes me on to the bed and falls on top of me, tugging my jacket off my shoulders and loosening my bow tie.

'So what's the Air Marshal's daughter like then?' she asks.

'Jealous?'

'Ha!'

When she takes the piss out of me for wearing a dinner jacket I find myself laughing too. She drunkenly tugs my trousers off, leaving my socks on. She can't undo the tie but manages to get my shirt off, leaving me looking like a Chippendale reject. I jump up on the bed and do a hip-thrusting dance and this gives us the giggles. She pulls my boxer shorts off and shrieks with laughter when she sees I have become aroused. 'Aggh! I'd forgotten what that looked like!' she says, swiping at it playfully with her hand. 'Keep it away from me!' The strap slips off her dress and, as she shakes her hair down, she hitches up her hem. I feel for the light switch, flick it off, close my eyes and imagine I'm with Jenny.

Afterwards, the usual post-coital tristesse. La petite mort. The loneliest feeling in the world.

The following morning we can't meet each other's eyes. After breakfast – smoked salmon and scrambled egg eaten in silence – I change into the shooting clothes Amanda has bought for me:

tweed jacket with concealed pockets and pleats in the back, and plus-two, knee-length breaks. I feel a complete arse.

I wander outside to check my mobile for messages. I have given the number to Jenny and have been hoping she will ring. I want to apologize properly for attacking her. And I am being driven insane wondering what she might be doing. Does she have a boyfriend? Will she still be at the house when I get back? There are no messages.

At the front of the hall there is a convoy of Range Rovers waiting, their engines running, exhaust visible in the cold atmosphere. Apparently, one of the gamekeepers is late – had a puncture – and everyone has to wait twenty minutes before we leave. Lord Ingleton is standing apart from the others, stroking the neck of a black Labrador. I walk over to him and the dog comes to meet me. It has a kind face. Patting it, I turn to take in the front of the hall. Lord Ingleton joins me.

'You're so lucky living here,' I say.

'It's a headache actually. The cost of running the place is astronomical.'

'It's Georgian, right?'

'It should be read as a standard Palladian quadrangle on to which the domestic pavilions have been grafted.'

'Oh,' I say, trying not to sound stupid. 'I see. Are those your sheep?' There is a packet of them grazing in the parkland next to the avenue of beech trees.

'Yes. Wensleydales. Very rare these days. Are you a sheep man?'

'Not really. They look very nice though.'

'I'd better go and see where that bloody gamekeeper has got to. Why don't you ask Andrew to show you the gardens?'

The Air Marshal is walking across a lawn lightly sugared with cobwebs and frost, leaving footprints. I catch up with him and we stroll towards some rusticated arcading, taking deep drags of the crisp morning air. We find ourselves in a pebbled kitchen garden, its paths lined with box hedges. A peacock is strutting about, honking raucously and half-displaying its feathers.

'You a gardener, Michael?'

'Yes and no, actually. Well. No. What's that?'

'A fruit cage. You should see it in the summer. Decorated with large finials in blue and gold.'

'Ingleton's a funny old stick, isn't he?'

'Known him years. A man you can trust.' Lambert drapes an arm around my shoulder. 'You recall that discussion after dinner last night?'

'Mm.'

'What did you make of it?'

'How do you mean?'

'About the defence cuts. We do have to do *something* about them, you know. The public has to be made aware of the implications.'

I purse my lips and nod thoughtfully.

'Take no notice of what Bruce was saying.' Lambert's nose has turned red with the cold and is beginning to run. 'He can be a pompous ass when he's had a drink. I'm thinking more about some kind of parade to mark the passing of an era.'

'A last hurrah?'

'Exactly,' Lambert sniffs. 'This country has had a standing army since 1640. We can't just allow such a huge chunk of our national heritage to be snuffed out without acknowledgement.'

'Quite.'

'And it may just change public opinion. We're still a very patriotic people, you know. At heart. Whatever the Tories would have us believe.'

'So when would you have this parade?'

'On the eve of the election, I should think.'

'And you want me to help?'

We walk back across the garden to where Lambert's Rolls-Royce is parked. He unlocks it and pulls out a pair of shotguns.

'Could you hold on to that for a moment?' he says, handing me one. 'We would need to give it maximum publicity. Put the right spin on it. Someone who knew how to manage the media would be very useful to us. If you're interested, we're having a meeting at my place the weekend after next. Will you come?'

'Who's we?'

'Some senior people across the board. Take the same view. Probably best if we don't name names at this stage. And best not to mention this to anyone else. Keep our powder dry.'

'I'm flattered to be asked, but there are people you could approach who are much better qualified at this sort of thing than me.'

'No. I think you're exactly the chap we're looking for.'

'What was it Lord Northcliffe said? A journalist's job is to explain to others what he personally doesn't understand?'

Lambert laughs. 'Now, there's no need for any false modesty with me, Michael.'

The moor we're taken to is the same one that Jenny and I visited. The sky is cloudless but the temperature is below freezing. Tenant has lent me one of his oily smelling Holland and Holland side-by-sides and I bring it up to my shoulder to draw a practise bead on a crow flapping lazily overhead. The beaters are standing around smoking and blowing on their hands. I feel self-conscious in my new tailored jacket – everyone else seems to be in deliberately tatty tweeds. It is loose enough to allow a cold updraught and so I tighten my cartridge belt. We draw numbers and I pick 'eight', the next butt along from Lambert. I notice him rocking back on his shooting stick taking nips from a silver hip flask. On the first drive, he proves to be something of a poacher: going for birds that fly over my head. I've been on plenty of pheasant shoots before but never grouse and being unsure of the etiquette I don't say anything. I feel slightly squeamish about shooting anyway. Not that I have any moral objection – these birds have a much better quality of life than factory-farmed poultry do – but I don't share the urge to kill things which most healthy males seem to have. Some hormonal imbalance on my part I suspect. That said, I rather regret not having had a go at fox-hunting before it was banned, if only because it was such an easy way of antagonizing the envious classes.

By lunchtime at least two hundred red grouse have been flushed out: heavy, dark cocks mostly, whirling over the brow of the moor, cackling excitedly – *go-back! go-back!* – as they glide down wind, round wings spread, moving from side to side at incredible speed. The air around them fills with sullen cracks and puffs of smoke and they describe perfect parabolas as they drop out of the sky. The eight guns bring down about seventy of them. I manage only four, much to the frustration of my loader, a bilious dalesman in a blood-stained cloth cap who keeps whispering instructions to me as he passes me a new gun. I feel unmoved as I examine the birds in the game wagon, blood on their open beaks, crops bulging.

A hot stew is served in the lodge with the leaded windows.

'Does you good to kill things,' Tenant grunts, warming his portly frame against the fire blazing in the stone fireplace.

'Exactly, exactly. But try telling my daughter that!' Lambert says.

'I can imagine she's not an enthusiast,' I say.

'She'll grow out of it.' Lambert shrugs. 'She thinks she despises all I stand for. Which is fair enough. At her age. I'd worry if she didn't.'

'Does she keep in touch?' Lord Ingleton asks. 'My youngest son hasn't set foot in our house for ten years. Don't know where he is at the moment.'

'Jennifer does tend to come and go as she pleases.'

'She can be quite difficult,' I say, enjoying the feeling of being paternal and somehow responsible for her. 'Do you suppose the accident had something to do with it?'

Lambert laughs. 'Yes, yes, her personality did change after she came out of the coma. She became more stable and rational!'

We all laugh at this. Conspiratorial. Chaps together. I love it.

A gamekeeper knocks on the door and sticks his head around. 'Think we've got company, sir,' he says, out of breath. 'Them bloody ramblers is back.'

We file out and scan the horizon. There are about eighty of them a kilometre away, walking towards us. The primary colours of their kagoules stand out garishly against the pastel shades of the heather. They are carrying placards but as yet we cannot read what is on them.

'Right, lads,' Lord Ingleton barks, his nostrils flaring in anger. 'Those bastards have been warned.' He breaks open his shotgun, slots two cartridges into the barrels and clicks it shut. 'Let's start the next drive. I don't think we'll need beaters this time.' The first birds fly over when the ramblers are roughly sixty metres ahead. Only Tenant and Ingleton fire. Four shots aimed up in the air. The ramblers scatter and dive for cover. Even though the light wind is blowing in their direction, a cry of pain is still carried on it. It is a man's voice.

Once they realize the shooting has stopped, the ramblers stand up and run back in the direction they came. Two men and a girl remain standing. One of the men raises his hands in the air, the other sinks to his knees clutching his chest. After a few seconds of each side facing the other, uncertain of what to do next, we emerge from our butts and walk towards them. When we are within about twenty metres the man with his hands raised shouts: 'Call an ambulance!'

The other man is now lying flat in the heather. We break into a half-run, Lambert tapping out a number on his mobile as he tries to keep up. The girl, no older than Emily would have been, runs towards me screaming what sounds like 'Dad, dad.' I realize as she gets nearer that the words are 'He's dead, he's dead'. The man is lying face down. I don't need to see him turned over to know that it's my father.

Twenty

I can't pass a mirror without checking my reflection in it —
surreptitiously, with a backward step, or a dip of the shoulder, or a
sidelong glance. I don't think it's narcissism. Insecurity, more like.
When I was in therapy five years ago — at my wife's insistence — my
therapist explained to me that for a healthy self to develop, to gain
balance and cohesion, the infant needs to feel affirmed, recognized
and appreciated, especially when he displays himself. If those needs
are unsatisfied, mirror-gazing in adulthood is a belated attempt to
obtain reassurance that you are really there, whole and in one piece.

So there you go. That's my excuse.

Jenny, I have noticed, does it nearly as much as I do. Since my
return from Yorkshire three days ago, our relations have improved.
She was upset when I told her about my father's heart attack, even
suggested we visit him in hospital. But she has gone back to being
flirtatious. She has also enrolled on a part-time art foundation
course in Notting Hill — her father is paying, I imagine. Four days
a week it takes up. Afternoons only. Just long enough for a builder
to install a two-way mirror in her bedroom.

He begins knocking the 50 cm x 30 cm rectangular hole in the
wall of my study at 2 p.m. By 5 p.m. he is Dysoning up the last
speck of plaster dust on Jenny's side of the wall — just 15 minutes
before she gets back.

I barely have time to put on Elgar's Second Symphony – with the volume turned up so that she can hear it and be impressed at my sensitivity. It's shameless, I know, but I must seduce her. It will be my salvation.

I'm not even sure I believe that. Part of me dreads finding out if it will or won't be. This is the whole point of infatuation, I suppose. When consumed with desire our brains produce the chemical dopamine. This is what makes us feel euphoric and breathless and what makes us unable to focus on anything other than the object of our love. Animals don't have the same chemical reaction – which is probably why they don't stalk their potential mates quite as much as we do.

An example. When I read in Jenny's diary that she is going to the Whistler exhibition at the English Academy on Friday, I leave work early on Thursday and race around the exhibits, mug up on the catalogue and listen to the audio guide. When she sets off, I follow her to Piccadilly Circus, nip up Regent's Street, cut back on to Piccadilly and make sure I'm walking towards her when she arrives at the entrance. I feign surprise, suggest we go around together and make informed observations about each painting. A small crowd even gathers to listen.

Under the influence of dopamine, then, installing a two-way mirror doesn't seem like such an immoral thing to do. The idea for it came from Jenny, actually. She wrote the words 'Keep out!' on the old mirror, using nail varnish.

True, I have been looking around her room. I need to satisfy my suspicion that she is seeing someone. I rummage through her Smartbin; I try to read a letter she has written on a notepad by shading in the pen indentations on the next page. Love excuses everything.

I have taped a note to Jenny's door, explaining that the cleaner broke her old mirror while trying to remove the varnish. A Fantin Latour still life covers the mirror on my study wall.

I always know, somehow, when she is near. Even though I do not hear the front door close I know she has come home. I give it a few minutes before taking the picture down.

Jenny is studying her reflection in extreme close-up, checking the ring in her eyebrow. She removes an eyelash. Her skin looks cappuccino-coloured through the smoky glass. It's eerie, being invisible. She looks straight through me. Who are you really, Jenny? I find myself wondering. What are you up to?

On her bed, next to where she has thrown her overcoat, there is a sketch pad and a cluster of charcoal sticks tied with an elastic band. She flops backwards on the bed, holds the pad at arm's length and flicks through it, pursing her lips and tilting her head first to one side then the other with each turn of the page. Still considering the drawings, she rolls on to her front and, using the toe of one foot to push against the heel of the other, she kicks off her shoes. I can see now that the page is open at a drawing of a man's torso and legs.

She disappears into the bathroom for a few minutes, the loo flushes and, when she reappears, she is tugging down the hem of her skirt. There is a blind spot in the corner of the room from which she now drags an armchair. She positions it in front of the mirror and, as she pulls her shirt off over her head, I see her armpits are unshaved. An attenuated web of black. She picks up her sketchpad, sits and begins to draw: bold, sweeping outlines that make her breasts quiver. As I stare at the nipple rings my heart dilates; my chest contracts.

The phone. As soon as I answer it, the caller rings off. I dial 1471. The Boy Fielding picks up. He says he has been trying to reach Jenny. I tell him she is out. Will I pass on the message that he rang? 'Sure,' I say. 'As if,' I think. I replace the handset without asking why he wanted to speak to her. Is he planning to ask her out? Just the thought of it makes my stomach convulse.

For the rest of the evening, I am unable to concentrate. Jenny goes out at about 7 and I stare blankly at my computer screen for half an hour, my mind wandering. I close it down, pick up my Sony E-book and tab to the page I've got to in the latest biography of the Minister of European Affairs. At about 8.45, the phone rings again. It is my brother Philip, sounding subdued. Dad still hasn't regained consciousness, he says, and is scheduled to have an operation in the morning. The doctors have confirmed that it was the shock of hearing the shotguns go off that brought on the heart attack. The police are investigating. I thank Philip, mumble something about trying to get up to see Dad in the next few days, and hang up.

The remoteness I feel to this news produces a stab of guilt. I go for a walk along Grosvenor Road and the cold slap of air on my face suspends my ennui for a moment. But then I recall the walks I used to take with Emily along here; her wanting to steer her own pushchair and then, getting too tired, wanting to be carried. The road is almost deserted now: a couple of joggers, a man walking his dog. It's a starless, moonless night and the only light reflected in the Thames is coming from the illuminations on Chelsea Bridge. A boat passes, the outline of lightbulbs dissipates for a minute and then swims back into focus like a shoal of fish. A gust of wind rakes the surface and shatters the outline again.

The cold makes my eyes ache and, when I narrow them, I am reminded of the river of gold you can see on a clear night from the top of the World Trade Center. The headlights on the cars driving down 5th Avenue are so far down they melt into a continual shimmering stream. And flowing in parallel to this are the red tail-lights of the cars heading up town. It's a fine sight, all the more heady for the sensation of vertigo it induces. When I first saw it, I wanted to leap off and swoop down over Manhattan, riding the air currents like Superman. Now, alongside the Thames, there is no sheet of glass to prevent me from flying. I straddle the wall and stand up. The blackness of the water lapping against the bank below is terrifying, yet, as I remove my clothes, I am transfixed by it.

It takes Jenny's voice to penetrate my reverie.

'Mickey? What the hell are you doing?'

My movements are so abrupt as I swing around I have to hold my arms out to steady myself. Jenny is leaning out of a stationary taxi. I look back at the water and feel as puzzled as an interrupted sleepwalker.

'Mickey?'

The hazard lights on the taxi are flashing.

'Where did you get the money for a taxi?' I say, jumping down and gathering up a handful of clothes to cover myself. 'I thought you were broke.'

Fifteen minutes later, Jenny is leaning back in a chair, her feet on my kitchen table, peeling an orange. A portable television is switched on, with the sound down. My lodger is frowning in concentration as she watches a documentary about Molly the cloned baby. 'So what were you doing on the wall?' she says without looking up. 'Were you going to jump?'

'I don't know. I don't think so. But I have been feeling rather odd lately.'

Jenny squares her shoulders, still not taking her eyes off the television. 'Why were you naked?'

'I don't know.'

'Sexual frustration?'

Why does she have to say things like that?

I look at her without answering. She looks up and throws a strip of orange peel at me. 'Stop staring at me like that. It gives me the creeps. You're always doing it. Why are you always doing it?'

'Sorry.'

'And don't keep apologizing all the time. Just be cool.'

Sorry sorry sorry.

'It's so hot in here.' She tugs her Argyle sweater off, revealing sweat patches under the arms of the coral pink T-shirt she is wearing. She fans herself with her hand. Her cheeks are flushed. The T-shirt does not meet her skirt and exposes her navel ring and a line of dark, downy hair.

Dare I just walk over and kiss you, Jenny?

'I forgot to tell you,' she says listlessly. 'Two men came round earlier asking about you. Wanted to know who your friends are, do you talk about politics, how long I've known you... I didn't tell them anything. Said I was just a lodger.'

'Did they say who they were?'

'No. Smartly dressed though. Suits. What's going on?'

'I don't know. Don't talk to them if they call again.'

'Something else odd I noticed. The bin men came yesterday, right, rather than today like they normally do. And they only took our bin. I watched them. You in trouble, Mickey?'

'No. I...maybe...Please don't underestimate me, Jenny. I know what's going on.'

She sucks noisily on a slice of orange and says: 'Is there a cause you would die for?'

I think about it for a moment. Perhaps I would die to save her life. 'No,' I say carefully. 'Yes. I think there is. I mean. Have you ever seen that film about, er – '

'Spit it out.'

'These games you play. I've never been any good at sexual politics.'

'Oh, give it a rest. *Please.*' She sinks bonelessly into her chair, her eyes fixed once more on the television. 'You always have to, like, analyse things. All this politics bollocks. You always make things more complicated than they are. There doesn't need to be a motive behind everything, you know.'

'But I can't seem to do anything right, Jenny. Tell me what you want me to do and I'll do it.'

She throws her hands in the air. 'There you go again! Always thinking of ways to please me. It's so claustrophobic. Lighten up. You're trying too hard.'

'No I'm not.'

'Now you're going to get all sulky on me. You always do that.'

'I don't.'

'And you always stand too close to me, yeah? I keep thinking you're waiting for the right moment to pounce.'

I fold my arms.

'What's Ed Fielding like?' she asks, apropos of nothing.

The Boy Fielding. Of course. My nemesis.

'Why?'

'Just making conversation.'

'Are you seeing him?'

She frowns. 'For God's sake. *No.* Chill out.'

'Why then?' I bite some rough skin at the side of a fingernail.

'Don't turn all scary on me, Mickey. I just want to know what he's like, that's all. I've been reading his column.'

'You promise you're not seeing him?'

'*Yes.* For God's sake! Just tell me what he's like.'

'Well, he's got halitosis, herpes and . . . he's a pervert.'

'I like perverts.'

'Meaning?'

'I had a boyfriend once who was into auto-erotic asphyxiation.'

I assume she is making some cryptic point about the throttling incident. 'I never really said sorry for doing that.'

'Eh? Oh. Forget it. I totally forgive you . . . You cool with that?'

I nod.

'You were provoked. Besides, it's been a while since I felt a man's fingers round my throat.'

'You are kidding me? Right?'

'Sometimes my boyfriend would do it to himself. While he watched me.'

'Isn't it a bit, you know, embarrassing?'

'You get such an endorphin rush you don't care. Haven't you read the Marquis de Sade?'

'Course.'

'Honestly?'

'No.'

Half an hour after Jenny has gone to bed, I return to my study and find my telecomp has been switched on. A website dedicated to auto-erotic asphyxiation has been called up on the Net. My eyes widen as I read how individuals achieve 'cerebral anoxia' by applying ligatures. The idea is to stop just before loss of consciousness. By interfering with the blood supply to the brain, it causes giddiness and exhilaration. The feeling of helplessness and the prospect of dying enhance the gratification. It also weakens the subject's self-control and judgement – which is why the practice often ends in accidental death. It was first documented in the early 1600s. The idea came from observers at public hangings.

Do I imagine it, or does Jenny cock her head slightly at the sound of me dragging my leather captain's chair across the floor of my study. I position it in front of the mirror, realize I'm too low and lift it on to the desk. From it I watch her pull her T-shirt off. The skirt she is wearing is actually a dress with shoulder straps. She unzips it at the back, kicks her shoes off, and hunches her shoulders forward to allow the straps to slip down. She pauses for a moment to check her reflection in the mirror, pushes her dress over her hips and lets it fall to the floor. Stepping out of it, she rolls down her woollen tights and sits on her bed to pull them off one foot at a time. She takes her contact lenses out and flicks them on the carpet.

Without averting my eyes from the mirror I unbuckle my belt

and slide it out of my waistband.

When I look up again Jenny is bending forward to pick up her tights. She rolls them into a ball and turns out the main light. The room goes black for a moment before she flicks a bedside light on. She stares straight into the mirror, uncouples her bra strap and shrugs her shoulders forward again. She hooks her thumbs under the elastic of her knickers, bends at the waist and steps out of them.

With blood hammering in my ears I say: 'Oh, Jenny.' She looks up. She has heard me. I notice the red light of a baby intercom plugged into my study wall. It is partly hidden under a chair. I recognize it as one Amanda and I had used when Emily was born. Jenny must have found it in a cupboard. I smile. Touché. Bugged in my own study. 'Jenny,' I say again, excited at the thought that she can hear me. 'I love you.'

Twenty-one

Silvery light is seeping into my study. It's morning. But for a few seconds I cannot tell where my dreaming state ends and consciousness begins. I can hear birds chattering on the branches outside the window. Dawn. I blink, try to focus on my watch – 5.45 – and sit up. My muscles fail me and I flop back on to the floor again. My telecomp is still on, making a gentle whirring sound. The Internet page about auto-erotic asphyxiation is still open on the screen. I sit up again and feel a mushrooming sensation in my throat. The belt. As I remove it I realize the knot in the end has come undone. This is what saved me. I rub my neck and succumb to a coughing fit.

I head upstairs to my bathroom and examine my neck in the mirror. Already there is bruising. I pop two Nurofen in my mouth but as I take a sip of water to wash them down I nearly choke. The liquid burns my throat and this is followed by a wave of nausea. I notice a sharp metallic smell but cannot identify it. Groggily, I crawl under my duvet and pass out.

When I wake again at noon I call the office to tell them I'm ill and sit nursing a black coffee for half an hour in the kitchen. Jenny phones.

'Hi, how are you?'

'Fine,' I say, feeling embarrassed.

'Just checking you're OK.'

'Why shouldn't I be OK?' It comes out in a more defensive tone than I intend.

'Oh, you know, last night.' She giggles.

'Why are you giggling?'

'I'm not.'

'Is that what you do with Ed behind my back? Have a good laugh at me?'

'For God's sake, Mickey.'

'This is just some game to you.'

She hangs up. Click. Dialling tone. I stare at the handset and say 'Sorry' out loud.

My throat is still sore and I have to apply foundation I find in Amanda's dressing table to cover up the bruising.

I stare out of the window at some scudding clouds, gaze down at my shoes and flick through the channels on television looking for something to lift my malaise. The BBC news, arts and lifestyle round-up – sponsored, sigh, by Starbucks – is showing the Leader of the Opposition working the crowds at a rally. The commentary is about the strapless Gucci dress she is wearing. I switch to a quiz show which depresses me even more. I watch it to the end before running a bath and reading the papers in it.

I'm about to go back to bed again at 3 p.m. when I get a call from Miss Monotone. 'The press officer at the Department of European Affairs has rung to ask if your interview with Lucifer can be moved back half an hour to 5 p.m.,' she says. 'Obviously he didn't refer to the Minister as Lucifer. That was me having a little joke.'

At first I can't think what Miss Monotone means, then I remember and flick through my diary. 'Christ! I'd forgotten all about it. Can't we move it to another day?'

'Think how many months it's taken to pin the evil one down to this date, Michael. I'd just go along if I were you.'

Although I'm half-way through *Lucy*, the latest biography of Lucifer, and though he is one of the few members of the cabinet I don't need to swot up on, I still panic about not having prepared any questions. I skim through his *Who's Who* entry, the dust jacket on the first volume of his autobiography, *More Spinned against than Spinning*, and his Website.

In the taxi that takes me to the City, I jot down about twenty questions. The driver pulls up outside the Deutsche Bank building, on the opposite side of the road from Lord Foster's experimental 'inside-out' Department of European Affairs. From the inside, the DoEA looks like a sort of pagoda but not, for some reason, from the outside. A security guard tries several times to swipe my Multicard, gives up and issues me with a visitor's pass. A smiling press officer is waiting for me inside, or outside, depending. She tells me the Minister is running ten minutes late and asks if I would like a coffee while I wait.

Exactly ten minutes later, a chauffeur-driven Mercedes sweeps into the lobby area. One of the Minister's gauleiters jumps out of the far side and runs around to open the near-side door. As the Minister steps out his trouser legs ride up and I notice his grey socks are pulled high up his calves. He emerges looking gaunt in a black felt cloak fastened by a chunky gold chain around his neck. He strides purposefully towards the revolving entrance door, not looking to left or right, and the temperature in the atrium drops. The gauleiter – young, Latin-looking, laden down with three red boxes – jogs to keep up.

I stand up but Lucy brushes past me, glowering straight ahead, too busy to waste time with small talk. Too busy, really, to waste time getting from his car to his desk. He reaches his private lift, which is being held open for him by a security guard, turns and points a black leather-gloved finger at me. He then curls the finger towards himself and I hurry over and join him in the lift. His gauleiter squeezes in behind me and all three of us stand facing the door.

'Hello, Minister,' I say. 'Busy day?'

'Hello, Mr Yates.' He says this without looking across at me. 'Of course it's a busy day. I do a proper job unlike members of your profession. What lies are you planning to print about me after this interview?'

'Oh, the usual.'

He gives me a measuring look. 'Remind me. I don't like you, do I?'

'You don't like anyone, Minister.'

He considers this and smiles crookedly. He seems to be in a good mood. With any luck he will be all snide witticisms and gossip. From this close I can smell his aftershave and see the orange powder blocking the pores in his skin. He must have just come from a television studio. His coal-black hair, clearly dyed, is slicked back. His eyebrows are plucked.

I'm quite surprised he's agreed to me doing the interview after our contretemps at the mayor's party last Christmas. I had written about Lucy's cronyism in finding a post for his Austrian boyfriend: head of focus groups and lateral communications at the Department of Animal Welfare. He had blanked me at first then hissed something about me being despicable. He had then harried my editor for a week afterwards with late-night phone calls. I presume the only reason he has agreed to this interview is that he is confident he can either intimidate or beguile me. You have to admire his chutzpah.

The lift doors open and Lucy glides towards an ornate double door which is being held open by a young man in a single breasted suit. I follow him and take in the largest government office I have ever seen. It must be at least fifty metres long by thirty wide, decorated with gilt columns, classic medallions and enormous mirrors. There are five sash windows and sumptuous thick folds of silk curtain gathered at the top of each. And, at the far end, there is a colossal wooden desk, four times the size of a normal one. While the gauleiter unhooks the cape and slips it from the ministerial shoulders, Lucy removes his leather gloves, peeling his fingers out one at a time. He is wearing a beautifully tailored suit with orange pin-stripes, a blue silk handkerchief and a dark red rose in his buttonhole. He gives it a surreptitious sniff.

'Nice office,' I say casting an eye along the portraits that line the oak-panelled wall opposite the windows. 'It's not really in keeping with the futuristic look of the building, though, is it?'

'The interiors had nothing to do with me,' Lucy snaps. 'It was Norman's idea. If only the press would bother to check their facts when they write their tittle-tattle.'

'Tradition in a modern setting, eh?'

'The size is perfectly justified. My office doubles up as a reception room. And the Pugin wallpaper is exactly the same as that used in the Lords, so there was no extra cost involved in designing it. The Persian carpets were a gift from the Iraqis. My only input was the choice of portraits: Tony Crosland, Clem Attlee, Hugh Gaitskell, Margaret Thatcher and Robespierre. Have a seat.'

He indicates an armchair. It is firmer than it looks and much lower than the leather chair which he himself sits in on the other side of the desk, underneath the portrait of Robespierre. He removes a pager from his belt and places it on the large pink blotter in front of him. On his desk, turned in my direction, is a signed photograph of Lord McCartney as well as three smaller, silver-framed photographs of children, his godchildren presumably. Also on the desk there is a glass case containing a bowl of what looks like guacamole preserved in formaldehyde. I stare at it for a second too long.

'Yes, it is a Damien Hirst,' Lucy says. 'And yes, it's supposed to be ironic. And no, we didn't pay for it. It was a gift. But I presume you didn't come here to talk about art.'

'Well, perhaps we can start with the rumours that you are planning a 4 May election.'

'You don't expect me to comment on rumours do you, Mr Yates?'

'In that case there's no point in asking if you're any closer to finding out who assassinated the PM.'

Silence. A long cold stare. 'You know, I cried for five whole days after I heard the news. Five. It was ghastly. Ghastly. Poor man.'

'I didn't know.'

He stares at me again before saying: 'We know who was behind the assassination.'

'You do?'

'Of course. But I don't suppose the American-owned media in this country will allow the truth to be printed.'

'Try us.'

'Off the record?'

I consider this for a moment and then lean forward and turn off the tape recorder on the desk – and leave the one in my pocket running.

'Your father-in-law.'

'Why did I guess you were going to say that?'

'The PM was blocking his InfoWar programme.'

'Everyone knows that. It doesn't make Tenant a murderer though. Anyway, if you are so sure, why not make a statement in the Commons? Use parliamentary privileges.'

'We will. After the election. For the time being we need Tenant on message.'

'What makes you think he'll come out for you?'

'He won't. But he will come out against the Tories. And that's just as good.'

Lucy leans forward and stares at the rope burns on my neck. I cover them with my hand and switch my tape recorder back on. 'I'm not afraid of Tenant, you know,' Lucy says, slowly drumming his fingertips on the desk. 'He's not as powerful as he thinks he is.'

'But you *are* afraid of MI5, are you not, Minister? It's the one institution your government hasn't managed to take complete control of. There is still a whiff of autonomy there. Isn't that why you're planning to scrap it?'

'Do you still live in Pimlico, Mr Yates?'

The question throws me for a second. I nod.

'And how's ... Jenny, isn't it?'

'She's fine.'

'Would you care for some tea?'

'Thanks. Milk, no sugar.'

Lucy leans forward and, without taking his eyes off me, speaks into an intercom. 'Terry. Tea for Mr Yates, please. Just boiled water for me.' He sits back. 'Where was I? Yes, in a stakeholder economy, in an open society, the intelligence services, like everything else, must learn to come out of the darkness and stand in the light; they must learn to survive on their own two feet.'

'Six feet. MI5, MI6 and GCHQ. Three sets of feet. And isn't that a mixed metaphor?'

'If you are going to be facetious, Mr Yates, we can terminate this interview here. Is that what you want?'

I hold up my hands in mock surrender.

'Good. Now both divisions must be modernized. They must be made more accountable, in line with European Directive 3543. They must also be rationalized. It is therefore right and proper that MI5 should be streamlined, to some degree. And we are keeping our options on the SIS open.'

'So you're going to scrap MI5?'

'The two branches will be merged into one.'

'To make a Third Way?'

He scowls at me.

'Is it true you're considering privatizing this new merged Service?'

'There will be a triple lock in place. First the cabinet must agree on the future of the Service. Then the European Commission. Then, in our annual referendum, the people of England. At the end of the day it is the duty of the security services to serve society, not the other way around.'

'But I thought you said there was no such thing as society?'

'As usual, Mr Yates, you have misquoted me. What I actually said was that Mrs Thatcher was misunderstood when she declared that there was no such thing as society. Whether there is or is not such a thing as society depends upon what you mean by society.'

'And what do you mean by it, Minister?'

'I mean a community of individuals who are free to choose how they want their children to be educated. Free to choose how they want to be treated when they are sick. Free to go about their business without being spied upon or bugged – '

'Unless it's one of your own private intelligence services which is doing the spying and bugging, eh, Minister?'

'My teams have always complied with the provisions of the Interception of Communications Act 1985.'

'Yes, but – '

'If you will just let me finish, Mr Yates. I am talking about a community of individuals who feel safe to go out at night without being mugged. Safe to own their own houses and cars without worrying about them being broken into. Safe to – '

'Are you taking your revenge on MI5 because they kept a file on you in the 1970s? Isn't all this chipping away at their power, first with the Freedom of Information Act then with the Tele-communications and Privacy Act, a vendetta on your part?'

'I would like to state categorically that my personal feelings have no bearing whatsoever on my decision-making process.'

'But that really irritated you, didn't it?'

He sighs. 'It was despicable. *Despicable.* Nasty.'

'And who will this new streamlined Service report to?'

He fixes me with a stare. 'The Prime Minister.'

'Will that be you?'

'The present leader of the New Labour Party has my full loyalty, support and backing.'

Lack of sleep has left me feeling irritable. My abrupt phone conversation with Jenny has left me agitated. My tolerance threshold for the prevarications of a politician is dangerously low. 'But if you lose the next election you *will* challenge him, right?'

'I have no plans at this time, or in the foreseeable future, to challenge the democratically elected leader of my party.'

'But you and he hate each other, don't you?'

Lucy's lips twist into a smile. 'Mr Yates, just because you and your colleagues in the American-owned media decide that there is a feud between the Premier and I, does not mean that there actually is one.'

'But isn't it true you can't even stand being in the same room together?'

'Mr Yates. The fact of the matter is that we in the New Labour Party have a job to do. Together. And that job is to get our party elected for another five-year term. As mature, civilized professionals the Premier and I will be co-operating with each other towards that end, in every particular.'

'So what you're saying is that he, like the rest of the New Labour party, has finally learned to love you?'

'I'm not going to dignify that ridiculous question with an answer.'

'Were you surprised by the speed at which the Premier assumed the leadership role after the assassination?'

Lucy slams the flat of his hand down on the blotter, making the pager bounce slightly. 'I expect a hostile interview from the Tenant press, Mr Yates. I wish my expectations would be confounded occasionally but I accept that for as long as the English media is owned by North Americans – '

'But – '

'For as long as the English media is owned by North Americans I am never going to get a fair press. And I have to accept that. I don't agree with it. But I believe in democracy and so I must accept it. I do not, however, see why I should sit here and submit myself to your puerile line of questioning. If you can't rise above the level of the playground, Mr Yates, then I suggest you – '

'With the greatest respect, Minister...'

Lucy looks surprised at being interrupted.

'With the greatest respect,' I repeat, 'go fuck yourself.'

Twenty-two

I expect Jenny to be back from college by the time I get home, but she isn't. I can't stop thinking about the Minister's face as he called for security to escort me out of the building. He will have been straight on the phone to old man Johnson – and Tenant – to complain about my lack of professionalism. But, frankly, I'm past caring.

I wait for Jenny in the kitchen until 7.30 p.m. then I try her mobile. It is switched off. I ring the art college to see if she's still there but the night watchman answers and says he doesn't know who she is. I try to convince myself that she's just having a drink with a friend from the course but my imagination keeps returning to the thought that she is seeing The Boy Fielding. At 8 p.m., I go for a drive along Millbank, on past the newly erected statue of Gerry Adams in Whitehall and back along the Mall towards the Palace of the People. At 8.45 I am parked outside The Boy Fielding's flat in Knightsbridge. I repeat to myself that she can't be seeing him, not after what she said, but I cannot shake off a nagging doubt. The light is not on and no one arrives or leaves in the half hour that I am there.

When I get back home I sit in my study playing Elgar too loudly, rubbing my temples. At about 12.30 a.m. I start pacing the room. I unlock the drawer in my desk where I keep a bottle of what used to be my favourite Cabernet Sauvignon. Amanda never found it when she was emptying the house of drink five years ago. I take it out and place it on the desk. I take a corkscrew out of another drawer and lay it alongside the bottle. I stare at the bottle for five minutes before grabbing it by the neck and pitching it against the wall. For some reason it doesn't smash.

I see the photograph of Jenny on my desk and slam that against the wall, too. It does shatter.

At 2 a.m. I hear the front door open quite clearly. I turn out the light in my study and feel relieved that Jenny has at least come home. Then I hear her shushing someone else as she creeps up the stairs. I hold my breath. There is suppressed giggling. The creak of a floorboard. A hiccup. 'He'll hear you' – said in a whisper. She opens the door to her bedroom and I can picture her feeling for the lightswitch. It goes on but, before I can see who she is with, she turns it off again, closes the door and flops on the bed. I press my face against the mirror to try and make out a shape in the blackness but I can see nothing. There is more whispering and then the sound of kissing. I press the palms of my hands hard against my ears. They are going at it like bastards in there.

Ringing. The phone. The sound of the answering machine clicking on. I prop myself up on one arm to check my watch. 11.30 a.m. As I walk towards the mirror, broken glass crunches under my shoes. Jenny's room is empty. The sheets are strewn around the bed. Her clothes from last night are in a knot on the floor.

I see Jenny in the hallway. She has her coat on ready to go out. I am half-way up the stairs gripping the banister. 'Who was he then?' I ask.

'Who was who?'

'The man you brought back last night.'

'I didn't bring anyone back last night.'

'I heard you.'

'Well, you shouldn't have been listening.' Jenny folds the belt on her coat into a double knot.

'There are surveillance cameras covering every street in London, you know. Was it Fielding? It's not going to be too difficult for me to find out who it was.'

'It was a friend, OK? He's been kicked out of his flat so I said he could sleep on my floor.'

'How generous.'

She opens the front door but hesitates before leaving. 'You look terrible.' She says it without looking back.

'I had a sleepless night.'

'See you later. I'm going to be late for college.'

'Did you have to sleep with him in my house?'

She swings round and stares at me, her nostrils flaring. 'You're disgusting!'

'Well, did you?'

'I didn't sleep with anyone last night. Not that it's any of your business if I did.'

I am still standing half-way up the stairs ten minutes after she has slammed the door behind her.

In the kitchen I empty a quarter of tomato juice into a jug, top it up with ice and swallow four Nurofen. My headache soon evaporates and I walk back upstairs unsteadily. As I enter Jenny's bedroom I trip over one of her rollerblades. I examine her sheets first, notice the Smartbin under her dressing table and empty its contents on to the bed: a banana skin, a yoghurt carton, crumpled up envelopes, balls of tissue paper. The evidence I am looking for isn't there. When I stuff the rubbish back in the bin it says: 'You have re-ordered... One banana. One yoghurt.' I am just about to leave the room when I see Jenny's newt in a jar on the table. I fish it out and, holding it by its tail, dash its head against a chair and flush it down the loo.

The rest of the afternoon is a blur. I walk around Hyde Park, walk around Soho, walk along the Embankment. By the time I get home I'm so tired I can't get the note Jenny has left me into focus. The handwriting is scratchy and I have to read it through twice before its meaning sinks in.

'Michael,' it begins. (Not Mickey.) 'You sick bastard! How dare you search my room? It's none of your business what I do. It's disgusting that you pace up and down outside my door and stare at me through your mirror. You are not my father. I can do what the fuck I want. Goodbye.'

The two-way mirror has been shattered.

★

170

When I wake next morning, Jenny has not returned. I know it even before I've checked. She has left some clothes in her room, however, and this gives me an idea. When she comes back to collect them she will find me about to hang from a rope tied to the banister. If I time it right she will think I'm just about to kick the chair away – and will come to my rescue, begging for forgiveness.

After five minutes of standing unsteadily on a chair in the hallway, I decide she probably isn't coming back. I remove the washing line tied around my neck, step down and phone Gavin.

Twenty-three

When I joined the Salisbury Club ten years ago I was told to regard it as my home. There are never more than a thousand members – Catholics, homosexuals, civil servants, barristers, journalists and spies, by tradition – and each considers himself to own one thousandth of the building. I like to think my thousandth is an area just in front of the fire in the Smoking Room. There is a horsehair armchair here which must be as old as the club. This is my sanctuary. My consolation. My cure for sorrows. From here you can see the area of dust that has collected over many years on the alabaster buttocks of Mercury. For some reason, perhaps according to some ancient club tradition, the cleaners always miss this bit and it fills me with a private delight whenever I notice it. Stretched out on this worn leather seat I can rest my feet on the fender. I can also just reach the iron bell-pull on the wall without having to get up.

I pull it and wait for the club servant to arrive. When he does, I order a black coffee and a Punch cigar, tuck my hands behind my head and contemplate the high ceiling. It is early evening, the fire is crackling and already the portrait of the 3rd Marquess of Salisbury which hangs above the fireplace is disappearing behind a thin vale of blue cigar smoke. An elderly gentleman with an imperial beard sits at the mahogany and leather reading chair opposite and picks up the *London Times* on a gripper rod. No one can remember what he used to do for a living and I should think even he has forgotten. I have a feeling he is a peer of the realm, one of the transitional hereditaries. We get quite a few of them drifting in here since they lost their dining rights at the Lords. I notice he has a soup stain on his waistcoat.

The sight of him makes me feel depressed. And my melancholia is not helped by a terrible urge I am feeling to have a drink. I study my hands as they shake. What non-drinkers don't appreciate is that withdrawal from alcohol is every bit as painful as from heroin. It only takes forty-eight hours to get the alcohol out of your system but the symptoms of withdrawal can go on for years. I am grateful to Gavin. He came straight round. Spent two days looking after me: checked I hadn't secreted any bottles anywhere, made me eat and take a bath. It was his idea that I move into the club for a couple of days. To get out of the house. If nothing else, he figured, having to put a suit and tie on would help order my thoughts.

All things considered, then, I can really do without bumping into the enemy. Two years ago, to my everlasting shame, I failed to notice that The Boy Fielding was up for membership of the Salisbury and so I was unable to blackball him. The smug little prick is dressed as fastidiously as you'd expect: linen suit, and – shudder – the club tie. The pianist in my head starts playing in a minor key as he walks over to me.

'Hi, Mike. Great to see you.'

Mike? He knows I hate that. The little maggot has picked it up from Hugh Johnson. At least I know he hates being called Ed.

'How are you, Ed?' I try to avert my eyes for fear that he will see they are bruised from crying.

'Fine. How are you?'

I think I'm going to throw up, that's how I am. 'Oh, you know.'

'Miss Monotone said you had flu. You feeling better?'

'Er, bit. Won't you join me?'

Hypocrite, Yates.

The servant arrives, pours my coffee, clips and lights my cigar. The Boy orders a gin and tonic, no lemon, no ice.

'I heard you gave Lucy a hard time. He's been on the phone to everyone complaining. He should have known better than to mess with our star writer, eh?' He says this with the sort of sycophantic smile you just want to punch.

I smile back and think: *Don't push it, sunshine. You haven't even started shaving yet and you reckon you can talk to me about journalism.*

'Flatterer.'

'I mean it,' he says. 'You've been on a roll lately.'

There is something almost Zen-like about my hatred for The Boy. Its purity makes me feel centred. It's hard for me to be objective about him, I know, but I'd say he has a certain floppy-eared charm and is reasonably handsome in an evil sort of way. To others, his wide mouth and strong nose might seem like attractive features. But when I look upon them I see the face of a gargoyle. I find myself smiling and nodding as I think this. How can Jenny prefer him to me? I wonder if anyone in the Smoking Room would react if I shot him right now, through the heart, with a silver bullet. There might be a rustle of a newspaper in the corner, and a disapproving cough from the monsignor by the window, but that would be about it. Legend has it that when a member dies *in situ*, as they do from time to time, other members actually applaud and raise their glasses as he is borne out on the stretcher.

'Fancy a game of chess?'

'Don't feel up to it, Ed. Backgammon?' I study his fingers as he clicks the counters down on the board and I imagine them groping Jenny.

'I can get you an interview with the marksman,' The Boy says without meeting my eye.

'Bullshit you can.'

'Seriously.'

'Now why would you want to do that for me, eh? Why wouldn't you want the glory for yourself?'

'You would do it better.'

'Credit me with some intelligence.'

'Because I couldn't be seen to be too closely connected to it.'

I roll my dice. 'Go on.'

'I have a friend who thinks he can set it up.'

'That's a friend with a capital F, I take it?'

'What do you mean?'

'I might have guessed you'd be a spook, Ed. When did they recruit you? Cambridge?'

The Boy takes one of my counters off the board. 'Not me. This friend.'

'You don't have to be coy. "From now on there will be no more culture of secrecy. Everything will be out in the open. To say you work for MI5 will be as unremarkable as saying you work for the NHS." Isn't that what the Minister said?'

'Yes, but, as I said, it's my friend.'

'Is it true they match your salary?'

'You'd have to ask my friend.'

I roll cigar smoke around my mouth, blow it in his direction and spit out a shred of tobacco leaf left on my tongue. 'I'd have thought a gent like you would have joined Six. Isn't Five a bit below stairs? I hear the *London Times* is crawling with Five.'

The Boy tries to suppress a smile at this.

'So, Ed, what's in it for your "friend"?' I make the annoying inverted commas sign with my fingers and so wish I hadn't.

'He wants a favour in return.'

I scratch my chin.

'There's a meeting being held this weekend. At Air Marshal Sir Andrew Lambert's house in Hampshire. My friend believes you have been invited.'

'Well, I haven't.'

'Yes, you have.'

I let out a low whistle. 'And you want me to sniff around for you? Out of the question. Tenant would skin me alive.'

'He need never know. My friend could put wires on you.'

'Wires? Bit crude, aren't they? I thought you spooks used transmitters the size of a match head.'

'Deniability, I guess. Wires are commercially available.'

'And why is your friend so interested in this meeting?'

The servant arrives with The Boy's drink. 'Because his job is to counter covertly organized threats to the security of the nation.'

'Meaning?'

'He thinks there's a coup being planned.'

I pull a scornful face. 'Grow up, Ed. Anyway, I'm not risking my arse for an interview with some poncing half-wit who goes around shooting chief suspects.'

The Boy edges closer to me and lowers his voice. 'What if my friend could give you some information about the assassination.'

I have to laugh at this. 'Bollocks he could. What sort of information?'

'There's a phone tap, apparently. A rather interesting conversation which took place a couple of weeks before.' He makes a gun sign with his finger. 'It reveals who was funding the – '

'Why has no one been arrested then?'

'Maybe some people are too big to arrest.'

'You're talking about Tenant, right?'

'Among others.'

I shift uneasily in my seat, try to diffuse the conversation. 'The most extreme form of censorship, assassination. Do you know who said that?'

'Shaw?'

'Well, anyway. You know why he was assassinated, don't you?'

'Because he kept saying "Look, you know, guys, trust me"?'

I laugh at the impersonation. 'Not bad, but no.'

'Why then?'

'No moustache.'

'Eh?'

'All great dictators have to have a moustache. So they can use doubles for public engagements. Hitler, Stalin, Saddam. The PM forgot that golden rule: let your double take the bullet.'

The Boy looks at his hands. 'My friend needs to know how far up it goes before he makes a move. He knows that something else is being planned.'

'You're pushing your luck a bit, aren't you? Why should you trust me?'

'Because I think you are a man of principle.'

Right. Of course you do. 'Did you know Guy Burgess was a member of this club?'

'I thought he was the Reform.'

'Was he? Still. Makes you think, doesn't it?' I study The Boy's face. 'Aren't you forgetting who pays your salary, Ed?'

'Can I confide in you?'

I mime zipping my lip.

'I've had an offer from the *London Times*.'

'Political editor?'

'Editor.'

This shocks me. I try to look unimpressed. For a moment after rolling my dice I'm too flustered to count my moves. I've been working up to the subject of Jenny but now I can't bring myself to mention it. Cowardice perhaps. Fear of confrontation. Feeling jumpy about making a soon-to-be-powerful enemy. But I don't really want to know the truth, anyway. I need to cling to the grain of doubt I have left. I know I'm being manipulated by Ed, but I'm not sure how. 'And do you suppose they would have a job for me too – after I've shopped my father-in-law?'

'I'd see to it personally.'

'And where exactly would I be living after my wife has thrown me out of her house?'

'My friend would be very grateful.'

'He'd give me a house!'

'And pay off your overdraft.'

'Aren't you supposed to positive vet me or something first?'

The Boy smiles.

'And how do you know about my overdraft, Ed?'

'My friend has seen your file. Close to 1.5 million euros, isn't it? That must be quite a headache.'

'And you've been authorized to offer me this?'

He nods.

No more overdraft. No more waking up in the middle of the night in a cold sweat. Financial independence...I try to sound nonchalant. 'Well, it *would* mean not having to sell my Aston... What else does it say in my file?'

'I haven't seen it.'

'Could your friend get me a copy?'

'Would it help persuade you?'

'It might. I'd have to see it first.'

'He'll expect more in return.'

'Like what?'

'Well, to start with we need you to hack into Lambert's computer.'

'You said "we".'

My coffee arrives. The Boy Fielding shifts in his seat.

'I love her, you know.'

'Who?'

'I feel hollow without her.' I blink back a tear. 'How is she?'

'Lambert's daughter? I've no idea. She never returned my call that night when you answered.'

I search his face and realize I have underestimated him. He's even better at lying than I am.

'Why did you want to speak to her?'

'To see if she could help us get to her father.'

'You said "us".'

The Boy eyes me thoughtfully. 'I know I've only met her once, but...' He taps the table. 'How can I put this? From what I've heard she is petulant, childish and spoilt.'

'And contrary. And capricious. And...what's the word?'

'Scary?'

'Scary.'

'So what do you see in her?'

'I have no choice in the matter, Ed. Love makes fools of us all.'

'Did you know that it was Tenant himself who requested you be sent to cover that protest story in Devon?'

'Yes, I did know, actually.'

'And what conclusions do you draw from that?'

'The same as you I imagine.'

The Boy smiles. 'I just wondered.'

I think I see Jenny, her back towards me, standing in a shop doorway in Victoria. I don't recognize the lime-green coat she is wearing but it is her figure and her short blonde hair caught in the glow of a street lamp. I indicate, slow down and shout at her out of the window: 'Jenny?'

The young woman who looks up is not Jenny. Attractive though. As she walks slowly across the road towards me she straightens her skirt by tugging its hem. 'You can call me whatever you like,' she says with a harsh Mancunian burr.

'Sorry, I thought you were someone else.'

'You called me Jenny, right?'

My heart is pounding. 'Will you come home with me?'

She glances from side to side. 'I normally work from here. Is it going to be worth my while?'

'Money is not a problem.'

'How far is home?'

'Pimlico.'

'It's 950 for an hour?'

'Euros?'

'Or 350 if you're paying in dollars.'

'Fine.'

She gets in, fastens her seat belt and rummages around in her handbag. She produces what looks like a Walkman. 'See this? It's a transmitter which pinpoints where I am. Get rough with me and I press it. Two very large men will come and find me. And you.'

'I think I follow.'

'Nice car.' She unwraps a stick of chewing gum, folds it in half and pops it in her mouth. 'What is it?'

'An Aston Martin. What's your name?'

'Want some?' She holds out the packet of gum.

'No, thanks.'

'What do you want it to be?'

'People in your profession really say that?'

She rests her thigh-length boots on the dashboard and gives me a peeved look.

'I'll call you Jenny then. You look like her.' I half-cover my mouth with the back of my hand. 'This may sound like an odd request but I don't want to...you know. I just want...I just wondered, would you mind dressing up in her clothes?'

'Whatever. The hair's not real you know,' she takes her wig off to reveal closely cropped brown hair. 'You going to show me a picture of your wife and burst into tears then?'

'Is that what usually happens?'

'No. Men usually show me a picture of their wife and then beat me up.' She falls silent for a minute before she adds: 'You married?'

'Not very.'

'What's your name?'

I hesitate. 'Ed Fielding.'

'Got any music, Ed?'

I switch the radio on. The Golden Oldies station. Take That are singing 'Want You Back for Good'. I recall singing along to the radio with Jenny on the drive back from Devon. 'Got anything else?' says 'Jenny', breaking into my melancholic trance with her ugly accent.

'Jenny,' I say. 'When we get to the house, would you mind not talking.'

The first thing I notice is that the front door is ajar, the latch broken. The second thing is that a cyclone has passed through the drawing room. My CD collection is scattered the length of the carpet, Amanda's collection of first editions has been pulled from the shelves, the crystal in my drinks cabinet has been smashed. Pictures are hanging crooked on their hooks. Plant pots have been overturned. Cushions have been ripped apart, scattering foam and feathers everywhere. The words 'Fuck the rich' have been spray-painted on the wall.

'Ever thought of employing a cleaner?' says 'Jenny'.

I ignore her and walk through to my kitchen, instant coffee granules crunching underfoot. All the cupboards and drawers have been tipped out, all the jars emptied.

'Is this Jenny?' 'Jenny' is holding up a photograph.

Not really concentrating, I nod.

'Does she live here then?'

'Huh?' I say, confused for a moment about why this strange woman is here. 'She was staying in our spare room. Upstairs.'

I phone the police and inspect the burglar alarm in the cupboard under the stairs. It has been tampered with. My study has been ransacked as well. Jenny's bedroom looks relatively un-disturbed. I sit on her bed, feeling dazed.

'The door was open.' It is the real Jenny's voice. I look up to see her standing in the doorway of the bedroom.

'I came back for my stuff.'

'I . . .'

'Are these her clothes then?' 'Jenny' emerges from the bathroom holding Jenny's East German combat jacket and her 16-hole DMs.

'Those are mine!' Jenny says with a frown.

I turn to 'Jenny'. 'Could you leave us, please.'

'Don't worry, Ed, I'm out of here. But, er . . .' 'Jenny' holds out her right hand and rubs her finger and thumb together. 'Can we settle up first please.'

'Can you just bear with me for one second,' I whisper to Jenny as I brush past her on my way to the study. As I'm rummaging around in my desk for some money I can hear Jenny emptying drawers next door and slamming them shut. 'Can I have my jacket back please?' I hear her say. 'Did he want you to wear it?'

'Jenny,' I call after her as she marches back down the stairs. 'It's not... I can explain.'

'You sad bastard,' she says with a cold, incredulous laugh.

'Jenny!'

When she slams the door it swings open again.

I have been sitting on the stairs staring at the door for about a minute when I become aware of 'Jenny' sitting on the stair behind me. 'Call it a straight 200,' she says holding out her hand. She is shivering. I finally find the wad of money I was looking for and as I'm counting it out into 'Jenny's' hand I notice blue light revolving on the ceiling, I follow it to where the front door is open and a woman police officer is standing in the doorway.

'We had a report of a burglary,' she says. 'Hello, Sophie. Straying from your usual patch, aren't you?'

I pinch the bridge of my nose and close my eyes.

'Are you Mr Yates?'

I nod.

'How long ago did the burglary occur?'

'I don't know. It was like this when I got back half an hour ago.'

A second police woman steps into the hall. 'Is there anything in particular missing?' she asks.

'I haven't had a chance to look round.'

'Mind if we do?'

I open my arms and I wait on the stairs feeling sick.

Five minutes later, the first WPC appears on the landing holding a clear plastic bag containing about half an ounce of cocaine.

She raises her eyebrows at me.

'Not just now,' I say. 'But do help yourself.'

'Thanks for finding the bail, Ed,' I say as The Boy Fielding drives me from the police station next morning.

'You have to return in six weeks. Did they tell you?'

'Yeah. I couldn't sleep last night. Some arsehole in the cell

181

opposite. Completely shit-faced. Singing and weeping all night.'

'My friend says he can get both charges dropped.'

'Can we keep it out of the papers?'

'That shouldn't be a problem.'

I light up a Marlboro and wind the window down. 'Who burgled my house?'

'We don't know. Not us. But we'll find out. Can you think of anything they might have been looking for?'

'No. I'll think about it . . . You mentioned clearing my debts . . .'

'Already taken care of.' The Boy Fielding leans towards me, opens the glove compartment with one hand and pulls out a bulging blue file tied with string. As he drops it in my lap I see that it has my name across it.

The detail is staggering. School reports and university exam results on sheets of microfilm. Dental and medical records including my various treatments for alcohol abuse. Inland Revenue. Bank statements. Cuttings dating back to my first job in journalism on the *Yorkshire Post*. My CV. Every address I've ever had. Details of my parents, wife and daughter. Statements taken from friends. Transcripts from my phone calls. Pages of e-mail intercepts. A dossier of photographs taken of me over the years. Even the shoot that was supposedly for *Hello!* – and which Jenny had told me she hadn't posed for – is here.

'What's this?' I say holding up a grainy black and white photograph of a man leaning over a body on a road.

'That was taken when you ran over Jenny.'

'How?'

'Surveillance camera.'

'In a country lane!'

'I think it was some experiment the Devonshire County Police were doing to monitor every centimetre of road in the county. What are you doing to her in that photo?'

'Nothing.'

'You didn't try it on while she was lying there unconscious did you?'

'No!'

'Hope for your sake she never sees that.'

'Are you blackmailing me?'

'Course not.' The Boy checks his rear-view mirror. 'You'll see they have a surveillance camera picture of your attempted theft of that Mercedes in Blackpool, too.'

'That was Jenny!'

He looks at me.

'Don't worry, my friend has seen to it that no charges will be pressed.'

I flick my cigarette butt out of the window. 'So I guess this means we have a deal.'

'I'll send someone round to show you how to hack into Lambert's computer if you can get near it. He'll also help you tape the wires on. I'm afraid it will mean shaving off an area of your chest hair.'

'I'm confused, Ed. Five is there to protect national security, yes? So if this cabal at Lambert's house is about what I think it's about, shouldn't you be supporting them?'

'What *do* you think it's about?'

'Preventing the Tories from scrapping the Armed Forces. Convincing the Chinese we can defend ourselves. Protecting national security.'

'When there are grounds to believe that an organization intends to undermine parliamentary democracy by political, industrial or violent means, the Service investigates them. And that's as far as they are permitted to go.'

'Is that a yes or a no?'

'It's not MI5's job to defend the country against attack from foreign powers.'

'It's the Army's job?'

'Exactly.'

'So who defends the Army?'

The Boy shakes his head and grins.

'Call me when you get back from Lambert's.' He gives me a card and writes his home number on the back. 'This is a secure line. And Mike...'

Please God, don't let him say 'good luck'. Please don't.

'Be careful.'

I pick my teeth with the business card and shrug.

At home I start tidying up the wreckage and find the process therapeutic. In Jenny's room the smartbin is tipped on its side. I notice a crumpled up sheet of writing paper and smooth it out. It is a letter that Jenny has started but not finished. Odd words are crossed out.

'Dear Mickey,' it begins. 'I've just been next door to check you are all right. You'd gone quiet. Just as well I did. I liked it when you said you loved me.'

Twenty-four

In a damp, wooded valley on the border between Hampshire and Dorset there is a greystone manor which I would give my best friend's right arm for. You see the big-hipped roof of the house and the bricks of its six chimney stacks as soon as you drive over the brow of the hill – but the prettiness of its mullioned windows, lichened pilasters and gabled wings doesn't really hit you until you reach its large iron gates.

I'm met by two soldiers in plain clothes, one of them carrying a clipboard. I suppose they might be Special Branch officers but I've already been through one checkpoint, about two kilometres back, on a bridge over a smoking river. I'd been waved down, asked for my name, middle name, address, phone number and date of birth. They wanted to see my ID card; asked if I owned the car; made me open the boot. I was then made to wait five minutes in the car while one of them talked into a radio. They then asked me to get out again and stand alongside the car while they took a photograph of me. As I had driven away the security officers had given me a tight-muscled salute. And Special Branch don't do that.

One of the soldiers at the gate asks me to step out of my car again while the other, an Alsatian by his side, asks me to open the boot. Satisfied that it is empty, he runs a rod under the engine, gets down on his knees and feels for something with his hand. 'Did you know you had this, sir?' He holds up a metal object the size of a matchbox.

'Oh yeah, obviously. What is it? A tracking device?'

'A bug. Government issue. I'd get your car swept more often if I were you, sir.' He peers into the back seat.

My pulse goes off the scale as the first soldier runs a metal detector over me – it doesn't pick up my transmitter but it does give me a guilty urge to scratch the area of chest where the wires are taped. I'd quite warmed to the man – an Intelligence officer, I assumed – who'd come round to attach them earlier that morning. He was Asian, stockily built and wearing a suit that was buttoned up even though it was too tight for him. His hair was shoulder-length, his eyes bulging, his accent Thames Estuary and his grin, which he deployed at the slightest provocation, toothy. He introduced himself as Haresh Makara and as he snipped away a square of chest hair about the size of a CD box and applied shaving foam he asked if I wanted it squared or tapered. When he finished he held up a mirror and said: 'Little more off the side?'

He then demonstrated how to hack into Lambert's computer using what looks like a mini-laptop. It is half the size of a normal one and much lighter, but with its flashing green standby light and its infra-red eye it looks more sinister. GCHQ records show that Lambert bought a state of the art Apple Mac from a shop in Guildford five months ago. Haresh asked me what computer I normally used and when I showed him the eight-month-old Apple Mac in my study he explained that there had been three new models since then but the basic functions hadn't changed much between the eight-month and the five-month versions; you turned it on in the same way and used more or less the same software on the hard disk.

Haresh showed me where to position the infra-red panel on the front of the mini-laptop so that it could talk to the panel on the front of Lambert's desktop. He took me through the procedure for pulling down the edit window, highlighting the Appletalk option, clicking on the 'transfer all data?' section, and pressing return again when it asked if I wanted to include the wastebasket. 'Very important that,' Haresh said. 'People always think they have thrown documents away for good when they press "empty wastebasket" but it's still all there if you have the tools to get at it. You usually come across some interesting porn, too.'

Haresh explained how to override the request for a password: seven numbers that can be tapped in and which only a handful of Apple Mac programmers know – as well, of course, as all three branches of the Security Service. These numbers unscramble the code. Once they have been keyed in, Haresh said, I should get a message informing me that 'the transfer of 500,000 gigabytes of data will take approximately two minutes'.

Haresh had written all these instructions down for me and, as the second soldier now notices the mini-laptop device on the back seat, I nervously finger the piece of paper he had written on.

'What's this?' the second soldier asks.

'A laptop.'

'Can you turn it on please, sir.'

I press a button, the screen lights up, the soldier nods and I click the lid of the laptop shut again.

I now notice the black police helicopter circling overhead.

A closed-circuit camera mounted on the gatepost follows me as I get back in the car. The first soldier talks into an intercom grille built into the gatepost and there is a whirring sound as the gates part electronically.

I drive along a short avenue of pleached limes and park by a yew hedge. In an effort not to bump into any of the cars already parked here – two Range Rovers, three BMWs, Lambert's Rolls-Royce, a Jaguar with diplomatic plates, Tenant's Bentley, its engine running, his chauffeur sitting inside – I almost back into a sundial which is partially hidden in an overgrown alcove. There is a large red helicopter standing in a field behind the house. It has a royal crest on its cabin door. I see it as I cut across a terraced lawn to get to the round, sandstone arch of the porch – and I see that this, creeping with leafless ivy and wisteria, has the date 1696 carved into it. I'm letting out a whistle of appreciation at this fact when Jenny's mother opens the door.

'Hello again, Lady Lambert.'

'Jane, please.'

We shake hands and, when she holds on to mine for a few

seconds longer than is normal, I lean forward and rather awkwardly kiss her on each cheek.

'Lovely place this.'

'I grew up here. It was so nice to be able to move back after all those years being posted abroad. Mind your head.'

I duck to get inside and, when I straighten up, my head is almost touching the beams on the low ceiling. The walls in the hallway are panelled in a nut-brown oak and hung with sepia watercolours, a framed needlework map of Hampshire, and a Flemish tapestry.

'It belongs to your family then?'

'My great grandfather bought it.'

'Looks like you've got quite a gathering here today. The cars.'

'Yes, they've already been at it for an hour or so.'

I furrow my brow at this. 'But I was told to be here for 10.'

'I think they had some other issues they wanted to get out of the way first.'

Oh fine. Don't mind me, gentlemen. I'll be the paranoid one pacing up and down outside if you need me.

'Who's here?'

'I think you'll recognize everyone. They shouldn't be long. I was asked to have some coffee ready for a break at 10.30.'

Lady Lambert takes my coat, drapes it over a large Armada chest and leads me along a corridor, past a door at which a man in a double-breasted suit is standing guard and through to a drawing room.

'Can I get you anything?'

'Oh, I'll wait for the others I think. Who's this?' I point to a bust of a man in an RAF cap.

'Bomber Harris.'

Above the fireplace there is a painting of a Battle of Britain dog-fight. I study it briefly before my attention is caught by a silver model of a Harrier Jump Jet on a shelf alongside it. I leave a fingerprint on it which I try and wipe off surreptitiously with my sleeve. Below this there is an occasional table caught in a shaft of sunlight. Dust motes are swirling around a yucca plant and three framed photographs: the Air Marshal being presented to the King, Jenny as a baby and Jenny as a teenager clearing a jump on a pony. 'I never had her figured as a Pony Club type,' I say, picking it up to examine it more closely.

Lady Lambert sits down on a Knole sofa and invites me with a discreet pat to join her. 'She used to be mad about horses. Rather lost interest when she discovered boys.'

A large Burmese cat appears and jumps on her lap. As she starts stroking its neck it begins to purr and pricks its tail up vertically in the air.

A miserable thought comes to me: my life is withering without Jenny. 'Do you know where she is at the moment?' I say, not meeting my host's eye. 'She and I had a bit of a misunderstanding.'

'You're asking the wrong person, Michael. Jennifer never lets me know where she is staying.' She says this with a vague sigh that makes me feel sorry for her. I put a sympathetic hand on her knee. We both stare at it.

'Are there any old friends of hers you know who she might be staying with?' I remove my hand.

'It might be worth visiting that new eco-village they've set up in Streatham.'

'I heard something about that on the news. They're squatting on some derelict land that belongs to Safeway, aren't they?'

Lady Lambert nods. 'I know she's very interested in that sort of thing. There might be someone there who knows where she is, even if she isn't there herself.'

'Thanks.'

'You know, Michael, sometimes I think she has it right about this direct action...' She trails off and stares out of the window.

Down the passageway I can hear a scraping back of chairs followed by a door opening and the Air Marshal's voice: 'Darling?'

'Excuse me, Michael.'

She returns with her husband.

'Michael,' he says. 'Glad you made it here safely. Directions OK? 'Fine.'

'There are some people I would like you to meet.' He holds the door open into a dining room that is dominated by a walnut draw-leaf table. It has thick legs that seem out of proportion to its top, as if whoever made it was delirious. These are carved with Ionic capitals which seem far too small. It is such an oddity, I don't notice, at first, the dozen or so people seated around it.

'This is Thomas Hardwick, Permanent Under-Secretary of State for Defence, Joseph Boyd, Minister for Defence Procurement, Bruce, of course, you know.' Tenant nods at me and taps the redial button on his mobile. 'And Lord Ingleton . . .'

'How's your father doing?' Lord Ingleton asks with an embarrassed cough. I shock myself with the realization that I haven't checked how the old man is in days. 'Fine, I think. He's a tough old sod.'

'. . . Prof. Robert Sutton of the Adam Smith Institute, Sir Nicholas Wright, Deputy Commissioner of the Metropolitan Police, Assistant Private Secretary to the Foreign Minister, Tim Cooper, foreign policy advisor to the American Ambassador, the Bishop of Worcester, General Sir David Gainsford, his Aide-de-camp Peter Fellowes . . .' I go round each in turn trying to consign their names to memory and applying a pressure of the hand. The bishop has a surprisingly firm grip. Her hand is dry. How weak and clammy she must think mine.

'Sir, may I introduce Michael Yates, senior executive editor of the *English People* and, er, Bruce's son-in-law?'

The young man smiles shyly and rises to offer his hand. It is hot and soft. The grip is light. I can't remember whether I'm supposed to call him Your Majesty or Your Highness so I smile tightly and say nothing. I take the only empty seat, between Tenant and the Under-Secretary. Lambert resumes his place at the head of the table. 'Now, Michael, just to fill you in. We will carry the imprimatur of a committee but we're not keeping any minutes and, needless to say, with the existing uncertainties, what we are discussing must not go beyond this room.'

I feel a prickle of heat on my cheeks. 'Don't I need to sign the Official Secrets Act or something?' I ask.

Lambert's lips twitch. 'No, no. That won't be necessary. This meeting is, to say the least, unofficial. We can, I am sure, rely on your discretion.'

'You must be mad, I'm a journalist!'

A few people chuckle at this. I glance around the room. Everyone seems self-conscious, as though aware they are playing a role in a real-time historical drama. In the discussion that follows, the word 'coup' is never mentioned. But there are elliptical references. And there seems to be an understanding that we are all talking about the same thing. Lambert sets out his proposals for the parade on the eve of the election, which must be called, he says, on one of two Thursdays: 13 April or 4 May. A thousand soldiers from the Royal Marines, Paratroop Regiment and the Blues and Royals will lead the march, followed by half a dozen Challenger IV tanks, a dozen Scimitar and Warrior armoured vehicles and a fly-past of a dozen Apache attack helicopters. It will be a show of strength to inspire the voters and remind them of the constant threat to national security posed by the Chinese. They will remain in London at the Knightsbridge barracks until the day after the election. If Labour wins they will be dispersed. If the Conservatives win there will be a second march past for which the roads around Whitehall will be sealed off.

I try to concentrate on all this but the room is hot and I keep breaking out into a sweat. When I dab my forehead with a knotted piece of loo paper I find in my pocket, I realize my hands are shaking. Stomach cramps follow. I excuse myself, find a bathroom and splash cold water on my face. The pain melts away. When I sit back down, I still can't focus my thoughts.

Knowing that I don't have to pay attention because I'm taping the proceedings doesn't help. Nor does the presence of the King. I try to make it seem as if I'm not staring, but I can't keep my eyes off him. How fascinating he is. More handsome in person than he looks in photographs. Almost androgynous. Foppish yellow hair. Slightly flushed cheeks. Dapper in navy blue blazer and twills. I recognize the pattern of his Turnbull and Asser tie. He listens intently, pursing his ample lips and cocking his head to one side. He doesn't contribute.

Occasional words drift into my consciousness – like I'm listening to someone speaking into a faulty mike which keeps cutting out. The general is reading out a list of regiments that are to be scrapped '... The Royal Armoured Corps, the Guards Division, the King's Division, Royal Artillery, Light Division, Prince of Wales Division...' Now Lambert is answering questions about the march past. '... Yes, yes. Ideally we would start at 11. The King's Troop in St James's Park would fire their gun as the signal and the first phase should take us to noon...'

The Permanent Under-Secretary of State for Defence, a tall

man in a blue pin-stripe suit, checks his side parting, rakes back his chair and collects a brown leather briefcase from a cabinet in the corner of the room. He sets it down on the table, pops the latches and takes out a pile of documents. He hands them round and, when he comes to me, exchanges a quick glance with Lambert. It is four sheets of paper stapled together: tables, graphs, pie-charts showing a breakdown of NATO's military capability compared with that of the PLA. 'As you can see, we have sold off all our old tanks – '

'We always do that,' Peter Fellowes rasps. 'When the Second World War started we had to use weapons from the First World War because we weren't prepared.'

Two people try to speak at once and then Tenant's low drawl silences them both: 'China has been doing deals with Russia to have access to advanced radar and navigational systems, as well as smart bombs, simulators and electronic missile guidance systems...' he trails off and takes a puff from his cigar. 'Not to mention their InfoWar programme. According to our cyber spooks they are years ahead of us. We have to act now because the public do not know what is best for them. What we really need is for the Chinese to shoot down one of our planes...'

'Do we still have an arms embargo following the killings in Hong Kong?' This from the Bishop.

Professor Sutton sighs and says he thinks we should address 'the constitutional implications'. 'Cromwell had the New Model Army, the first standing army not directly controlled by the monarch,' he says. 'But even with this behind him he turned down the kingship when it was offered. It's one thing offering a referendum, but if martial law is declared – '

It's the Air Marshal's turn to interrupt: 'If we intervene, professor, our legal experts can always rustle up a justification under international law. But I think we are straying from the point. We all understand the implications of our gathering today. Bishop, you asked me earlier if I was prepared to go through with it. Well, I've been thinking this over and my answer is yes, I am of a mind to. But I've only one bullet in my gun. I can't afford to miss. Can I count on the support of everyone here?'

There are murmurs of assent. I want to tap my glass with a

spoon and say: *Hello? hello? Could someone please explain, what the fuck are you all talking about?* But at this point Lambert turns to me and says: 'Michael?'

'Hello?' I realize everyone has been staring at me because I haven't been murmuring my support.

'Is there anything you would like to add?'

'What about a group photo?'

Silence.

'To commemorate today's historic meeting.' I produce a slim Leica from my pocket, grin and make a clicking motion.

Lambert looks shocked. 'No, no. I really don't think – ' he begins.

'Strictly for the archives,' I grin, standing back from the table. I bring the camera to my eye, press the shutter and a flash leaves the gathering blinking in bewilderment. I return to my seat.

The King is the first to break the awkward silence that follows. 'I'm a bit worried about the way the media is going to handle this. What do you suggest, Mr Yates?'

'I think we should make a video, Sir. To be broadcast the day after the election.' I'm floundering, of course, hoping people won't realize that I haven't been paying attention. 'A documentary reporting on the true situation with the Chinese build-up of weapons. The threats to our security. If the defence cuts go ahead how...defenceless we will be. There would have to be a press statement. To avoid panic. Explain the situation. Explain that this is a temporary measure. A press conference. I could write a leader. Thing is, I'm not really clear about all this.'

'Michael,' Lambert smiles patronizingly. 'The last thing we want is clarity. If you could get on and organize the documentary, that would be splendid. We can liaise on content. Try to compartment-alize it. Keep things as vague as possible so that no one on your production team gets wind of it. Now, I think it is time for lunch.'

As everyone drifts through into the drawing room, I find myself shuffling alongside the King. 'Have you travelled far?' he asks. Can you imagine being a royal? A lifetime of having to ask moronic questions. 'Pimlico, Sir. Did you come by helicopter?' What a tactless subject to bring up. That's what happens when you know there is a subject you are supposed to avoid.

'Yes, I'm having lessons.' He smiles toothily.

'Sorry about your father,' I say, digging myself deeper.

'It's how he would have wanted to go. What was that about *your* father? Is he ill?'

'Lord Ingleton shot at him, Sir. Well, over his head. Grouse shooting. He had a heart attack.'

'I'm sorry to hear that . . . Have you been with the *English People* long?'

'Five years.'

We have reached a table which is covered in plates of sandwiches, salad and coronation chicken.

'Excuse me, Sir,' I say, 'I just need to get something from my car.'

No one seems to notice me as I come back in, trampling mud from the lawn. Holding the mini-laptop under my arm, I creep past the door to the drawing room and head upstairs. 'First door on your left,' Lady Lambert says, appearing from nowhere. I turn round and thank her. She winks at me. I smile back.

The first door on the right is Lambert's study. I look over my shoulder and try the doorknob. It's locked. I rummage around in my pocket for Haresh's instructions. The sheet of paper has his number on it. He should be in a surveillance van a few kilometres away, recording everything. As I tap his numbers into my mobile I mutter: 'What do I do now? The bastard is – '

'What kind of a lock is it?' Haresh says. I'd forgotten he was listening in to everything I was saying.

'How should I know?' I whisper.

'What does it look like?'

'It looks like a normal door lock. Hang on, there's something written on it. Banham.'

'Can you take a photo of it?'

I take several just to be safe and then, treading as lightly as I can, I go back out into the corridor and walk along until I come to what I assume is Jenny's old bedroom. You can tell she hasn't lived here since she was about fifteen: the walls are covered with rosettes, postcards and pop stars I don't recognize. There is a half-burnt joss stick on her bedside table and a wooden statue of Buddha.

The Burmese cat slinks past me, rubbing itself against my leg and I follow it into the next room along. It looks like the master bedroom. I put my laptop down on the bed, sit next to it and stroke the head of the cat.

I notice a walk-in wardrobe. Its open doors have full-length mirrors attached to them. There is a powerful smell of mothballs coming from inside. Lady Lambert's dresses and shoe racks are on one wall, grey military uniforms on the other. I push these aside and see a safe bolted to the wall. It has a combination lock. Three numbers. I knead my thumb and forefinger together and get to my knees.

It will be birthdays. Backwards. Bound to be. Jenny's maybe. But I don't know what hers is. I take hold of the dial anyway and the heavy safe door swings open towards me. Someone has been careless. There are jewellery boxes inside, a pile of letters tied with white string and a grey canvas holster. I take this out and remove the pistol. It's a Browning 9 mm semi-automatic. Standard RAF issue. I remember firing one when I was in the cadets at school. I hold the blue-grey barrel up to the light, sight it and swing around to see my reflection. Instead I see Lady Lambert framed in the entrance to the cupboard.

I lower the gun. Give an embarrassed grin. 'Er, hello, Jane.'

'Hello, Michael. Was there anything in particular you were looking for?'

'I thought there would be a loo in here.'

'As I said, it's first door on the left.'

I place the gun on top of the safe. 'I saw the cat come in here. I thought it might not be allowed.'

'Were you planning to shoot it?' Her tone is friendly.

'Well, I – ' Another grin. 'You have to be strict about these things.' Pause. 'The safe was open. I don't normally...I was just curious – '

'I think we both know why you came up here, Michael.'

I pull a guilty face and shrug playfully. Now I'm really confused.

'Don't think I'm not flattered. You're a handsome man.'

'Thank you. And you're a very attractive woman.'

She takes a step forward. 'Michael?'

'Yes?'

The Air Marshal's voice carries up the stairs: 'Jane, darling?'

Lady Lambert doesn't move; she looks me straight in the eye. 'I'm in the bedroom, dear.'

We listen to him walk to the top of the stairs and stop. 'Have you seen Michael Yates?' he says. 'Bruce wants a word with him before he leaves.'

Lady Lambert stares at me impassively for a couple of seconds and then puts a finger to her lips. 'I think I saw him walking around the garden.'

'Right. Don't be too long, darling. People are leaving.'

We listen to his footfalls as he hurries back downstairs.

'Thanks,' I say.

She gives a tight, neutral smile and stands to one side to let me squeeze past. I pick the laptop up off the bed as I'm leaving.

Five minutes later, as I'm walking towards the car park with Tenant, I look up at the bedroom window and see Lady Lambert standing there like a ghostly apparition. I wave. She hesitates, raises her hand for a brief moment and then turns away.

Twenty-five

I shiver. I sniff. I turn up the black velvet collar on my overcoat. So chilly, churches, even when they're heated. The air is damp and heavy with the smell of flowers, wood polish and mildew. There is a smell of fear and death here also. Everyone can sense it. We all seem spooked, like horses who can smell the blood on the knacker's van when it pulls into the farmyard. I have a knot in my stomach, the sort of sick dread you feel on Sunday evenings, that nameless apprehension about leaving the comfort of home and going back to school.

Typical of my father, I think, to issue instructions that he should be buried in a church that has been deconsecrated for ten years. If he had believed in angels, it would have been fair enough – but he was on the side of the apes; his only belief, as far as I can recall, was in Darwin. My mother is buried here, which is why an exception is being made. It was his wish to have his coffin laid on top of hers. As she died twenty-six years ago, I don't suppose there is much left of her coffin.

The local vicar suggested that we have the service at the modern prefabricated church which replaced this one, and afterwards drive on to this graveyard. But he was persuaded to re-open the church because, apparently, and I have no recollection of this, my father used to play the organ here. It seems unlikely, but maybe he put in just enough time to swing this funeral one day. It's the sort of joke that would have amused him. He played the organ badly and would have ruined the hymns. I smile at this thought. It's the first time I've smiled in days.

The church is unexpectedly crowded, at least 150 mourners, and I am having to stand at the back in the vestibule. Who are these people? I don't recognize anyone. Surely they aren't devotees of his books? No, they don't look psychotic enough. More likely they are ramblers, making his funeral a protest thing. He'd have liked that. He found religion embarrassing and primitive, which is probably why I do as well. *Found*. The past tense shocks me.

Now I look around I can see why this place would appeal to him. Like all Norman churches it is dark and depressing and my father never liked to pass up the opportunity of making people feel miserable. There is an ancient flag of St George which is tattered and dusty, a plaque bearing names of parishioners who died in the Great War, the faintest outline of a fresco showing the stages of the cross. The whitewash on the walls has long since flaked off and the stones exposed beneath are green with lichen.

The interior is intended to remind everyone of their place in the feudal system. One of Lord Ingleton's forebears, in the seventeenth century, I think, had been obsessed with opera and he'd had an opera box built in this church for his family to sit in, high above the peasants on their warped and creaky pews. The opera box has plush velvet seating and a curtain that can be closed during a boring sermon. It's a way of showing that, contrary to the message in the Bible, we're not all equal in the eyes of God. The current Lord Ingleton is in there now. Asleep probably.

The day is becoming more blustery and, as the wind picks up, the leaded windows rattle and I hunch my shoulders. My father has even managed to lay on funeral weather. It's almost as dark outside as in. The electricity must have been cut off long ago – which is why the place is lit with candles. I shuffle forward and see, for the first time, the coffin in front of the altar. It is huge. I was supposed to help carry it in but I arrived too late.

Now I can see that a place has been reserved for me on the front pew. My brother is there, with his arm around my aunt. What hypocrites grief makes of us. When he phoned to tell me the news of father's death he was in tears. I cried, too, on the drive up to Yorkshire. I kept thinking how much I wanted to tell my father about the meeting at Lambert's house. He'd have had some good advice on the subject. He'd have had views. In the row behind I can see Amanda's hair. She is checking her lipstick in a compact mirror. She clicks it shut and turns round to see who is in the congregation behind her. As I'm trying to work out why she has decided to turn up I think I catch a glimpse of Emily next to her. No, it's someone else. I nod to myself. A trick of the light.

My hands have turned blue. I rub them and then stuff them in my pockets. I touch the sheet of folded paper on which my reading is typed. My father has specified that I should read it and, I suppose, I should feel flattered. I take it out but see that what I have hold of is the crumpled note from Jenny. I reread the last line '. . . I liked it when you said you loved me'.

I sniff again and feel distracted. My thoughts are like a wasp in a jam jar and I can't articulate any of them. It is so cold my nose has begun to run. I hope people won't think I'm crying.

A hymn is sung – 'I vow to thee my country' – and I nudge my way through the mourners to get to the front. Philip hands me an order of service sheet and I see my reading is next. The hymn finishes, I unfold the paper and walk to the lectern. The words float in front of me. I clear my throat and try to concentrate. I can hear someone in the congregation coughing. 'This is a quote from *The Lion and the Unicorn* by George Orwell.' I clear my throat again and begin reading too quickly. 'When you come back to England from any foreign country, you have immediately the sensation of breathing a different air. However much you hate it or laugh at it, you will never be happy away from it for any length of time. The suet pudding and the red pillar-box have entered into your soul.'

Someone sniggers. I march briskly back to my pew unable to look at the congregation. Trust Dad to choose something eccentric like that as his reading. He wasn't even patriotic. Dad hated patriotism. Dad. I hadn't called him that since I was a child. We used to have a game where if I wanted something I would keep saying 'Dad' over and over again in an annoyingly whining voice, stretching out the vowel, until he burst out laughing and gave in. I'd forgotten that he used to laugh. I'd forgotten I called him Dad. I recall the day he told us we were too old to go on calling him Daddy and that Dad would be more appropriate. Now I no longer have a dad to protect me. I'm no longer someone's child. I feel the panic of knowing that I too must one day die. The only certainty. I look at the coffin and imagine his cold body inside. How does that creepy message on the gravestone go? 'As I am now, so will you be.'

I never really knew him. Never made the effort. Didn't even make the effort to say goodbye. It can't be that I miss him. But the world seems a colder and lonelier place. And I feel sorry for him and for myself.

The vicar, a young man with sideburns and gelled black hair, steps up to the pulpit and delivers an impersonal homily. He confesses that he never actually knew my father and that he will leave it to Philip to say a few words of remembrance. I stand up to let my brother past. He does not read from notes as he describes Dad's eccentricities, his extreme political views, his unreadable books. Those of us who knew him laugh fondly, the ramblers look slightly appalled. Philip says he can imagine Dad looking down on us and chuckling that his funeral will have inconvenienced so many of us today. He wanted a church service, he said, because he believed people don't cry enough at crematoriums. He was not a religious man and used to quote Nietzsche's line that if there is a God he'll have to forgive us because that's his job. I look across at the vicar who shifts uncomfortably in his seat.

'There was one belief which he held throughout his life, however, and that was in liberal democracy.' Philip pauses. 'Going through his study I found a quote he had cut out of the *Spectator* and stuck to his typewriter. I'll read it: "For every Elizabeth I there is a Charles I; for every philosopher king, a motley fool. Demos, for all its failings, is godlike because it makes no attempt to throw up gods." I think he would have liked to go in the way that he did, fighting for the democratic rights of the people.'

There is a smattering of applause at this from the ramblers at the back. Philip nods at them and returns to our pew. As I pat my brother on the back I realize how little I know him. The service over, I file with him and two wardens to the coffin. We each stand at a corner and one of the church wardens mouths that we should lift and shoulder it on his signal. It is heavier than I expect. I am at the back with Philip and when I see one of the wardens in front extending his arm underneath the coffin so that he can lock his hand on to the other's shoulder, I do the same with Philip. We cannot seem to keep in step as we walk out of the church and it is a squeeze to get through the crowd.

The church, with its squat, greystone tower, is in an appropriately desolate place: on a high ridge overlooking the North Yorkshire moors. There are three leafless trees in the graveyard and their branches are bending in the raw easterly wind. The ground where we have to leave the path is muddy and Philip slips but steadies himself and stays on his feet. Cold rain is lashing our faces, umbrellas go up and women with hats have to cling on to them with one hand while keeping their skirts down with the other.

We shuffle to the side of the open grave, lower the coffin on to two blocks of wood and stand back. My mother's headstone is still in place and the marble edges of the grave are still here, too. The green crystal pebbles that lay on top of it have been scooped off and left in a neat pile to one side. There is a JCB standing in one corner of the cemetery but I can't believe they used it to dig this hole. How could they know how far down my mother's coffin was? Besides, the pile of dark clay a few yards away has two spades stuck in it. The two wardens step forward and thread two ropes under the coffin and then they, too, stand back. The ends of the rope are bound in blue electrical tape. The vicar, his cassock flapping, reads the funeral rites.

I hear a child sobbing and look across at Emily. It isn't Emily. It's a girl from the village who used to go for piano lessons with my father. Her cheeks are windburnt, her eyes red, her hair, in a tight plait, drenched. For a moment, I forget she knew Dad and I wonder, with slight irritation, why she is crying. Normally I'm too selfish to cope with other people's grief but when I see Amanda squeeze the girl's hand and position the umbrella she is holding in her other hand over the girl's head, I edge sideways and take her free hand. I peer into the hole but cannot see mother's coffin, presumably they leave a discreet layer of soil between the two. It seems too cold and dark a place to leave a body. Some half-remembered lines by Betjeman drift into my head. Maggots in his eyes. His mouth open wide to let the Yorkshire clay come in.

The two wardens are joined by two more and each takes hold of an end of rope. They lift the coffin over the hole and, at a signal from the vicar, feed the ropes slowly through their hands. The coffin is lowered half a metre before it founders. The narrow end fits in the hole but the wide end has wedged against the marble edges of the grave. Everyone looks at the vicar. The vicar looks at one of the wardens. The warden shakes his head. Dad would have loved this.

It occurs to me in an abstract thought that if they turned the coffin on its side it would fit, or at least half of it would. But the wardens lift it again and lay it back down on the blocks of wood. The vicar concludes the burial rites and, turning to me, says that the marble slates will have to be taken up and the coffin lowered later. My face is wet with rain, but not tears. I nod and, letting go of the girl's hand so that her mother can take hold of it, I lead the mourners away. Lord Ingleton comes over, his complexion florid, and pats me on the shoulder. 'Terrible business,' he mutters, avoiding my eye. 'If there's anything I can do . . .' I smile with cool politeness and say: 'You weren't to know he had a dodgy ticker.'

I look around for Amanda. She is talking to Gavin Sennett whom I hadn't noticed was here until now. He is holding her at arm's length, his hands on her shoulders, nodding gravely as he listens. He looks across at me and must see the look of puzzlement on my face because he drops his arms and walks towards me.

'Hello, Gavin,' I say to him (Gabby seems too frivolous for the occasion). 'I didn't know you knew my father.'

'Yeah, I, er. Well, I didn't actually. I came to keep Amanda company.'

'I didn't know you knew Amanda.'

He looks at his shoes and laughs uneasily. 'She was worried about you. Thought you might be about to hit the bottle again.'

'Oh.'

'My condolences, by the way. Your father.'

Condolences? The word sounds odd coming from Gavin: too formal, too serious, as if he is acting the role of a mourner. 'God, Gabby. Don't you get all heavy on me as well.'

'Sorry.'

'Anyway, it gives contours to the soul.'

'Eh?'

'Gives you depth. Something a shallow person like you wouldn't understand. I tell you, mate, my soul looks like an Ordnance Survey map of the Lake District... Yours is more like the Utah desert.'

He doesn't rise to the bait.

Amanda has caught up with us. 'I got in touch with Gavin,' she says. 'You're lucky to have a friend like him.' She turns to Gavin. 'I need to talk to Michael alone.'

We watch in silence as Gavin walks towards the car park and then Amanda says: 'There's something I have to tell you.'

I widen my eyes.

'I'm pregnant.'

I blink.

'Did you hear me?'

'Yes, Mand.' I exhale loudly. 'That's great. It *is* great, isn't it?'

'That depends.'

At first I'm confused. I remember the night at Ingleton Hall. A smile stretches across my face. 'Well, as far as I'm concerned it's great. I know things have been difficult between us but maybe this is what we need. You know, to bring us together.' I kiss her on the cheek and think to myself that maybe this is what I need to get over Jenny. And Emily. After all, happiness is not so much having what you want as wanting what you have. Who knows, maybe I could even fall in love again with Amanda. Because I think I did love her when we got married. I thought I did. I wanted to. Maybe this is what it will take to make me realize I love her still. As a husband and father I can feel safe and secure and normal again. 'No,' I add. 'I think it's great news, Mand. Great. I can't believe it.'

'Michael.'

'What?'

'You're not the father.'

I blink again. 'I'm not?'

'It's Gavin.'

An invisible fist punches me in the solar plexus. '*What?*'

'He and I have been seeing each other.'

'You have?'

'Well?'

'Well, I didn't see that one coming, Mand. I thought you were with what's-her-name? Lola? Lorna?' It's the first time I've dared mention the subject.

'Louisa. I still am. Look, it's complicated. And now's not the time. Let's meet up and talk about this when we get back to London.' She pats my arm. The warmth of her gesture makes me realize how tense my neck feels. I swivel it around and rub it with my hand.

'You OK?' she asks. 'You look tired.'

I nod uncertainly and watch her pick her way back across the muddy grass, holding her umbrella up against the wind and trying to keep it from snapping inside out. She flaps it open and closed a couple of times to shake the rain off it before getting into the passenger seat of her car. Gavin is in the driver's seat. She says something to him, he looks over his shoulder at me and then gets out of the car. He shields his eyes from the rain with his hand as he runs towards me.

'Michael,' he shouts breathlessly as he gets close.

'Yeah.'

'I'm sorry.' He bends double trying to catch his breath, straightens and looks me in the eye. 'I love her.'

I don't feel angry with him. I had told him all about Jenny. And I'd told him how I thought my marriage was over. But I feel... jealous. Frightened. Hurt. I always had Amanda as a fall-back position, a safety net. I don't want to grow old on my own. 'What do you want me to say, Gav?'

'I don't know.' He looks across at the coffin. I follow his gaze. Two men are levering the marble stones out with a crowbar. 'Sorry about your old man.'

I shrug. 'You've already said that... So what are your plans?'

'I'll make sure the divorce is fair,' he says.

'*Divorce!*'

'She didn't tell you?'

'No, Gav, she fucking well did not.'

'We're planning to get married.'

I shrug again, turn and walk over to the gravediggers. I know I shouldn't look back but I do. Gavin is watching me. I raise my

204

hand. He runs his hands through his wet hair, smiles sadly and gives me a small wave back. The rain is pelting down savagely now, stinging my face. Gavin turns and runs back to the car, wrapping his coat tightly around himself.

There's just the gravediggers and me left. I watch them stack the marble slabs up and start digging another half metre of turf from one side of the hole. The rain begins to ease and I listen entranced to its gentle patter on the lid of the coffin. Other sounds add to the percussion: the spades cutting into the soil and hitting stones; the grunts of the diggers; the low whistle of the wind in the branches.

Another noise. The dull throbbing of helicopter blades. It gets louder and I search the sky in the direction it's coming from. The white helicopter looks fluorescent against the pewter clouds. It circles twice, hovers down and lands in the field next to the cemetery. A young man in a charcoal grey suit jumps out, and runs in a crouching position towards me. I don't recognize him. He shouts above the noise of the blades: 'Is this the funeral for Dr Yates?'

'Yes,' I shout back. 'But you've missed it.' I can make out Tenant sitting in the cockpit, chewing on a Bolivar and talking into a phone. 'Is that Bruce?'

'We got held up because of the weather.'

'I'm Michael.' I hold out my hand.

'Peter Doyle. I'm Mr Tenant's new assistant.'

'Well, thank him for making the effort anyway. I wasn't expecting him.'

The young man runs back to the helicopter, has a brief conversation with Tenant and then runs back over to me.

'Mr Tenant wants to know if he can give you a lift back to London.'

'I've got my car here. But thank him anyway.'

The helicopter hovers a few metres off the ground, turns 180 degrees, dips its nose and is gone.

One of the gravediggers tries to make the hole wider with a spade while his colleague jumps on to the JCB and starts it up.

Twenty-six

The cross hairs on the sights dip below the black helmet and then rise up again as I hold my breath. I take my finger off the trigger, lower the rifle – a PM L98B2, apparently, 7.62 millimetre – and turn to the marksman.

'You forgot to breathe,' he says with a twitch of his thick moustache.

'I know.'

'Have another go and this time, once you've sighted your target, allow the rifle to rise naturally as you breathe in, then lower it as you exhale. It's all about using the rhythm of your body. Think of the gun as an extension of your arm. Feel the energy in the bullet. Once the hairs are over your target, visualize the mechanism turning as you squeeze the trigger. Don't pull.'

I loop my arm through the sling once more, using its tension to support the gun with one hand. I then pivot on both elbows, take a deep breath and squeeze. There is a pressure on my shoulder, a smell of cordite and a hole appears in the chest of the target – a lifesize cut-out of a charging soldier, 500 metres away.

'Much better. There's no cross wind today, which helps.'

I roll on to my back, slip my ear protectors off and lever myself up. 'Thanks for letting me have a go at that. Now,' I hand him the rifle and reach for my tape recorder, 'we'd better get down to business.'

The marksman gestures with his fingers and thumbs, avoids my eye. I produce the four thick, clear plastic wallets I've been asked to bring: $400,000, in thousand-dollar bills. Trying to persuade the jobsworths in bought ledger to come up with this amount in cash had been predictably tedious. We didn't want to get Tenant involved and luckily, once old man Johnson got on the phone to them, we didn't have to. I hand the cash over and the marksman flicks one of the wads of notes with his thumb and nods to himself.

We are the only people using this range – on the South Downs, hidden behind bosomy hills – and it has fallen eerily silent after the sharp report of the bullet. I'd never have found the place on my own – it's not signposted from the road – but luckily I didn't have to. Haresh collected me from my home and drove me here. He is now waiting for me in his surveillance van, parked in the lane.

The marksman suggested this as a venue precisely because no one can ever find it. He likes to come here to practise, he says. It makes him feel safe. It had been his idea for me to have a go at firing the rifle before we started the interview, so that I could get a better understanding of what his job entails.

'I don't even know your name,' I say.

'Call me Dave.'

'As in Michelangelo's Dave?'

'As in Dave. It's not my real name.'

'Dave' won't tell me much about himself for 'security reasons'. When I ask his age he says 'let's say about 30'. Whether he has a family or not is, he says, unimportant. He is similarly reticent about the details of his career. What he will say is that, contrary to what the news reports have said, he's not with special Branch but with the SAS. I make a note of this and, as I'm writing, I size him up: slightly below average height, body hardened by exercise, skinny legs. Slight northern accent. Raspy. He is wearing jeans and a lumberjack shirt with the back untucked. On his right arm – hairy – he has a tattoo of a dragon. His sandy-coloured hair is cropped very short, military style. He is wearing sunglasses even though the sky is marbled with cloud.

As we walk down the range to collect my target I slip my own shades on as it arrives on a pulley-rope and ask him the one question everyone is desperate to know the answer to: why did he shoot the Dufflecoat, even though he had dropped his gun and was running away?

'I was told to.'

'You knew there was going to be an attempt made on the PM's life before it happened?'

'Nope. An order came through.'

'On the radio plugged into your ear?'

'That is correct.'

'What did it say?'

'"Drop him".'

'And who issued that order?'

'My commanding officer.'

'What's his name?'

'Can't tell you that.'

'Was he SAS?'

He folds his arms. 'Can't tell you that either.'

'Didn't you think it was odd that you were being ordered to shoot an unarmed man in the back?'

'I didn't know he was unarmed.'

'But you must have seen him drop his gun?'

'I saw him drop *a* gun.' 'Dave' makes a hard, chopping motion, one hand against the other. 'I wasn't to know he didn't have another. I had a split second to assess the situation.'

'To decide whether to fire or not?'

'Nope, that wasn't my decision. I'd been given an order.'

'You must have heard the theories – that you are part of a conspiracy.'

'Dave' pulls the paper target off the plywood cut-out it was attached to and hands it to me. He pins a new target back up, tugs at his moustache and levels his eyes at me. 'You know what scientists are taught? All things being equal, the simplest explanation has to be the right one.'

'So?'

'So, the gunman was just some crank acting on his own. I wasn't working with him. I didn't double-cross him. I was just doing my job.'

'And I'm just doing my job – '

'Look. I did not receive any extra money for doing what I was paid to do.'

'I hadn't said anything about money.'

'But you were going to.'

'How do you feel about shooting the only man who could have shed any light on the assassination?'

'Dave' sighs heavily. He makes no attempt to hide the irritation in his voice. 'How would *you* feel?'

'Haven't you ever wondered who the assassin was? Whether he really was a crank acting on his own or a professional killer hired by some foreign power?'

'Of course.'

'Dave.'

'Yep?'

'Has anyone ever told you you're a bit of a cold fish?'

'A cold fish?'

'A cold fish.'

'Nope.'

Ten minutes later I'm in the passenger seat of the surveillance van, being jostled back along the lane.

'Well, Haresh, that was a complete waste of 400,000 bucks.'

'Couldn't get nothing off of him?'

'He wouldn't even pose for a photograph.'

'You can't really blame him.'

'It would have been in silhouette.'

'I'm sure you can get something out of the interview.' He nods at a suitcase between us on the seat. 'I've got that transcript of your recording if you want it.'

I take it out. It's thirty pages long. 'God, there's enough of it.'

'It was very difficult to tell who was talking. You'll have to go through it for us and try to remember.'

I scan a few lines from page 10. 'I don't remember any of this being said. Can I have a copy of the tape? Then it'll be easier for me to identify the voices.'

'I'll see what I can do, mate.' He examines his nails. 'I suppose it would be easier for you off of a tape. But we don't want too many copies of it knocking around, do we? Here, there's something else in the briefcase which might interest you. In that brown envelope.'

It is a statement from a personal bank account, off shore. The name of the account holder has been blanked out with liquid paper. I cast an eye over the transactions. There are regular monthly deposits of 1600 euros and then one, dated 1 November, for 1,600,000 euros. 'What is it,' I ask. 'Computer error?'

'No.'

'Whose account?'

'Guess.'

'Dave's?'

'He's not that stupid.' Haresh grins toothily. 'It's one of his friend's.'

As we reach the outskirts of London the traffic drains to a halt. We are stuck in between two supermarket lorries, Sainsbury's and Tesco. 'Did you know,' I say to Haresh, 'that supermarket delivery vans account for 83 per cent of all London traffic?'

'How do you figure that then?'

'There was a report out recently. It's since everyone switched to home deliveries.'

'I never use the Net for that,' Haresh says, jutting his lower lip out. 'I prefer the experience of going round a supermarket myself. All those colours and smells and things you never knew you wanted until you walk past them. My local Safeway's is always empty these days. They have one of those machines which can read your whole trolley in one go. Takes about five minutes from parking to loading up your car... Hello? Michael?'

I've been distracted by a news-stand billboard with the splash: 'GENERAL CHEUNG SAYS WEST RISKS WORLD WAR.'

'Look at that.' I point at it.

'What? Oh yeah. A bookshop. Don't see many of those these days.'

'Not that. The newsagent's next to it.'

Haresh squints and reads: 'West risks war. Think he's bluffing?'

'I feel sorry for Cheung. NATO is doing the sabre rattling and he's the one getting the blame. The whole Chinese threat is being talked up.'

'By Tenant, you mean.' Haresh checks his rear-view mirror. 'Do you think he suspects anything?'

'About me? Dunno. Lambert was on the phone last night asking what progress I'm making with the documentary. I told him I'd been preoccupied with my father's funeral. But I reassured him it would be ready on time for election day.'

After we have sat in silence for half a minute, Haresh switches the radio on. We catch the end of a report about Cheung's speech and this is followed by an item about the assassin's pistol. New evidence shows that the PM's killer left a signature on the bullets – five tiny, evenly spaced indentations on the Remington cartridge case – and these may be his trademark. Police say the marks do not match anything seen before in England or on forensic laboratory databases around the world. The headlines close with a story about an auction of prime ministerial relics at Christie's: these include old school reports, a rare recording of him playing guitar in his band at university and a fragment of front tooth chipped away when the PM was playing cricket at school. His old headmaster used to collect things like that in a curiosity box; apparently, he'd kept the tooth fragment for years.

When we reach Notting Hill, Haresh checks his rear-view mirror, indicates right and parks the van in a quiet, residential road.

'Why have we stopped?'

'Want to show you something.' He directs a thumb over his shoulder. 'In the back.'

As we walk to the back of the surveillance van I check my reflection in its darkened windows. Haresh closes the back door behind us and shows me a panel of wood to which is attached a cross-section of a lock, its cover removed, its mechanism showing.

'This is a cylinder lock, same as the one on Lambert's study door,' Haresh says. 'It's a piece of piss to open.' He inserts a wrench into the keyhole and exerts pressure on the lock bolt. He then uses the side of his finger to guide a metal pick into the hole alongside it. 'Basically you've got a cylinder inside which has to be turned to retract the bolt. You do that . . .' he trails off and sticks his tongue out of the corner of his mouth in concentration '. . . there . . . You do that by jiggling the pick around until you raise the spring-loaded pins inside. There are five of them and you hold the others using the sprung-metal tension wrench. Here we go. Two. Three. Four. Five.' The bolt springs back. 'You have a go.'

I try it but it takes several attempts before I hear the bolt go back.

'Now, do it again with your eyes shut.'

'Haresh, to be honest with you, I'm not that keen to go back to the Lamberts' house. I think they think I'm a bit weird.'

'It'll be fine. Say you've come back to apologize for snooping round their bedroom. Take them some flowers.'

'And what do I say if they ask me *why* I was snooping around their bedroom?'

'Tell them the truth.'

'Which is?'

He rolls his eyes. 'That you followed the cat in. Say you thought he wasn't allowed in there.'

'I already did. Lady Lambert thought I was going to shoot it.'

'It probably wasn't his first offence.'

'Speaking of guns . . .' I hesitate and study his face. 'Haresh. We're mates, right?'

He eyes me cautiously.

'I got a phone call last night. A man who wouldn't tell me his name. He threatened me.'

'What did he say?'

'He said "Be careful, Yates. We're on to you. You're playing with the big boys now." Then hung up. I tried dialling 1471 but the number was ex-directory.'

'And?'

I crack the joints in my fingers. 'And I'm crapping myself.'

'What do you want me to do about it?'

'Give me a gun.'

He laughs. 'Just like that?'

'Well . . .' I nod.

'Where am I supposed to get hold of a gun?'

'You could give me yours. I've noticed the bulge under your jacket.'

He snorts at this and undoes the button on his jacket and holds open one side to reveal a leather holster strapped around his shoulder and under his arm. 'Right. And when my governor asks me why I no longer have a gun I tell him what exactly?'

'That you lost it?'

He laughs again and then weighs me up through narrowed eyes. After five seconds he shakes his head. 'I must be mad,' he says and removes the cover from a spare tyre clamped to the inside wall of the van. Taped to the inner rim of the tyre is a small black pistol. 'Lucky for you I have a spare for my own use. Unregistered. You ever used a .38 calibre before?'

I shake my head.

He removes the magazine and checks the mechanism. 'This is the safety catch, right?' He flicks a lever on and off. 'Red means it's ready. Very important.' He hands it to me, butt first. 'Polyamide grip. Get a feel for it. If you're going to carry this thing let me show you how to use it. There's a firing range down in Wandsworth I go to. Half an hour there should be enough to stop you shooting yourself. Tomorrow night?'

I run my finger over the name Walther engraved in the side, hold it in both hands and sight it with one eye closed. I love handguns. Show me a man who says he doesn't fantasize about owning one and I'll show you a liar. 'Can I keep hold of it until then?'

'OK but I'm not giving you any ammo until we've been on the range.'

I sight it again, out of the back window of the van.

'Shit!' I clamp a hand on Haresh's knee.

Haresh ducks down instinctively. '*What is it?*'

'Jenny! Coming straight towards us.'

He follows my gaze and sees the young woman approaching, holding a wrapped bunch of lilies in one hand, while swinging a black handbag covered in rubber spikes in the other.

'Get down,' I hiss.

'It's OK. She can't see us.'

As Jenny walks past, she stops to check her nose stud in the mirrored window. She tucks a few stray strands of hair behind her ears and stares straight at me. I get frostbite. She walks on twenty metres and stops outside a large, white Regency house with a columned entrance and dips her hand into the rubber bag. She produces a set of keys, takes the steps two at a time, and lets herself in.

I give Haresh a sideways glance. 'You knew she was living here, didn't you?'

'Don't know what you're talking about, mate. Never seen her before in my life.'

I put an arm around his shoulder. 'You know, Haresh, when I wake in the night the thought of her is immediately in my brain.'

'Like I say, never seen her before.'

'So you just decided to park here for no particular reason?'

'I needed to show you the lock.' He flashes his toothy grin at me again. 'Now. Close your eyes and let's go through it one more time.'

I'm on my second glass of orange juice when the waiter minces over and says: 'You are Michael Yates?'

'Why?'

'Your guest just rang to say he's running late but he'll be with you in 15 minutes if you hang on.'

I have suggested the Vine, Damian Carlton's new wine bar on the Brompton Road as a place to meet Simon De Jong, the urbane deputy editor of the *London Times*, because it is always quiet this early in the evening and always dimly lit. I hold my finger under a drip of hot wax running down the candle on my table. The wax reminds me of my dinner with Jenny in Blackpool – and, consequently, makes me feel maudlin. I upend my box of matches and let it fall down again. I take a match out, light it and lick my fingers so that I can hold the still-hot end and allow the stick to burn down to the other end without breaking. I check my watch, have another look at the front page of the *London Times* and tap a Marlboro Light out of my packet. I am just stubbing it out when my guest arrives.

'Hi, Michael. Sorry I'm late.'

He looks flustered. I've known Simon since we worked together on *Newsnight* years ago and in recent years he's lost most of his hair and become jowly. His brow is damp with sweat.

'Breaking news?'

'They've just called the election day. It's 4 May.'

'Next three weeks are going to be pretty manic for you then.'

'Actually, it was Romania I was tied up with,' he says, loosening his tie. 'We're getting reports that a NATO F1–22 has been shot down in Romanian airspace. Or at least that it has crashed. A Pentagon briefing is expected within the hour.'

'A virus?'

'That's what everyone's assuming. Washington is talking about a computer failure.'

'PLA?'

'Who knows. Anyway, I'm not going to be able to stay long.'

'Of course. Thanks for taking the time.'

'Sorry to hear about your father. You bearing up?'

'I'm fine. Thanks.'

Simon glances at his watch. 'This about Ed?'

'Yeah. How much has he told you?'

'I know he's joining us. But the editor doesn't.' He gives me a significant look over his glasses.

'How many people *do* know?'

'Just the MD, you and me, as far as I can tell.'

'And how much do you know about my exclusive?'

'Ed wouldn't give me any details beyond saying that it concerns the assassination. He called it "the scoop of the century".'

'Well, it is.'

'And I guess the fact that you don't want to give it to the *English People* means it has something to do with a certain grizzled autocrat we know. Am I right?'

'It might do.' I light up another cigarette. 'I'm still working on the story. There are some loose ends to tie up. But I should have something for you by polling day. That would be the ideal time to run it. What I want to know – and Ed said you were the man to ask – is what kind of deal you can offer.'

'What did you have in mind?'

'A million for the exclusive. Dollars. A book deal with Campbell and Courtney's for twice that amount. And,' I study my nails, 'the post of Washington correspondent.'

Simon whistles. 'I couldn't agree to any of that until I know more about the story. And Campbell and Courtney's may be in the same stable as the *London Times* but we can't go around making deals on their behalf.'

'See what you can do. I'll need it in writing. I promise you won't be disappointed.'

'Between you and me, Michael, if Ed is going to be our new editor and he wants this story as badly as he seems to, then who am I to pour cold water on it? I'll see what I can do.'

'We'll need to make special arrangements for the production side of things. High security at the printers. A bogus first edition. We'll have to design and sub the story ourselves. You, Ed and me. The fewer people who know about it the better.'

'Michael?'

'Yeah.'

'You are *sure* about this?'

I stub my fag out and give him a reassuring wink.

As I'm walking back to my car I tap out Lambert's number on my mobile. I listen to the answering machine message and say: 'Hello, Air Marshal. It's Michael. Look, I don't know how to say this quite but, um, I'm afraid I'm going to have to pull out of the documentary. So, er, sorry about that. Hope all goes well. Bye.'

I click the mobile shut, quicken my pace and whistle a couple of bars of Colonel Bogey.

Twenty-seven

An Aston Martin Volante is not the most inconspicuous car in which to do a stakeout, but it is the most comfortable. I check my watch. Four hours have passed since I parked outside the house in Notting Hill that I'd seen Jenny enter, and no one has come and no one has gone. I've moved my car twice. Once because I was blocking someone's garage, another time when a traffic warden approached – I had tried to swipe my Multicard through the parking meter but the useless piece of junk wouldn't read. I'm now twenty metres down the road from the house, in a space reserved for disabled drivers. And I'm probably drawing attention to myself because the engine is running – it's raining and I have to have the windscreen wipers on. The windows keep steaming up, I've listened to the same Annie Lennox CD three times, I've rung Simon to find out if he's heard any news about the book deal, I've read my interview with Lucifer in the *English People*, twice, and I've run out of cigarettes.

I have to walk past the house to get to the newsagent's at the end of the road. I buy a copy of the *London Times* and a packet of Marlboro Lights. As I don't have any euros on me, the newsagent lets me pay in dollars. I'm back in the car, reading an interview with the PM's widow, when the front door of the house opens. I raise my binoculars. A middle-aged man wearing a Burberry steps out, looks up at the sky and goes back indoors. He reappears wearing a fedora and carrying an umbrella which he opens before stepping out from under the entrance. He's in his fifties, I would say, sallow skin, paunch, curly grey hair that is almost collar length at the back. He walks with a slight stoop and takes short, awkward steps as if movement causes him discomfort. He crosses the road, walks off in the opposite direction to me and stops outside a blue garage door. A biometric key, the door slides open and he disappears inside, emerging a minute later in a yellow Saab.

I follow him, always trying to keep one car between us. I nearly lose him at Marble Arch but see him again turning off Park Lane. He parks at the bottom of an underground car park on Savile Row and I park near the top. Half running, I head back out on to the street and wait in the doorway of a café opposite for him to emerge. I follow fifteen metres behind as he walks down to Cork Street and into a private gallery that has three large abstract paintings displayed in its window. I watch him hang up his coat, hat and umbrella, sit down at a large oak desk in the corner and pick up a phone. Cradling the phone in his shoulder, he signals a young woman over and covers the mouthpiece with his hand as he says something to her. I stand back from the gallery window and look up at the sign: R.M. Galbraith. Fine Art. Established 1973.

In the office I key in 'Galbraith/Art' on Profile: several catalogues as well as a photograph of the man I have seen. He owns the gallery. He also lectures on the history of art at the same art college Jenny attends. Apparently he's something of a legend in the art world. He has to get an anonymous agent to bid for him at auctions for fear that, if his rivals see that he is interested in a particular English portrait (his area of expertise), they'll assume he has found a 'sleeper', a valuable Old Master that has passed through the auction houses miscatalogued as something worthless.

I check his entry in *Who's Who*. Harrow. Christ Church. Doctorate at the Courtauld. Curator Wallace Collection. Married with two children. Publications: *Portraiture in the eighteenth century*. Clubs: Athenaeum, Travellers' and White's. Recreations: choral singing, walking, military history. There is a phone number for the gallery at the end. I ring it. He answers.

'Roddy Galbraith.' The voice is dark, oaky, well modulated.

'Hi, this is Michael Yates from the *English People*.'

'Oh, hello.' Interested.

'I've been thinking for some time now that you would be a fascinating subject for a profile. I was wondering if you had anything coming up that we could peg one to.'

'What did you have in mind?' Flattered. 'I don't normally give interviews.'

Come off it, I think. This is the first time you've been asked. 'Oh, the usual four-page feature in the weekend magazine. Possible cover. I thought maybe one of your sleepers might be coming up for auction or something.'

'As it happens, there is one. At Sotheby's next month. The only known portrait of Philippa of Hainault, wife of Edward III, saved from seven hundred years stored in dark cupboards.'

'Sounds perfect. The interview shouldn't take more than an hour and we could do photographs on a separate occasion. I always find it easier that way. Perhaps I could give your number to our picture editor?'

'Sure. So when would you want to do this?'

'Soon as possible really. Tomorrow?'

'Let me check my diary... I've got meetings all tomorrow afternoon. How about in the evening at my house?'

'Seven?'

'That should be fine.'

Roddy Galbraith is wearing blue docksiders, blue cords, a tattersall check shirt and a chunky blue woollen cardigan when he greets me at his front door with a smug smile and a damp handshake. Dangling on a chain around his neck are tortoise-shell glasses, half-moon. At close range I notice that he is wearing fake tan and that his eyes are the sort of cornflower blue you only get from wearing coloured contact lenses. He leads me through into a large drawing room which has half a dozen portraits hanging on the walls and a fire crackling in the grate. He offers me a drink, I ask for mineral water and, when he leaves the room to pour it, I have a sniff around. The pink marble fireplace is full of invitations to weddings and private viewings. There are some family photographs, an antique magnifying glass and a collection of porcelain thimbles on a side table. A vase of fresh tulips on a wooden plinth. The bookshelves are stacked with leather-bound volumes, titles in Latin.

'I bought them as a set,' Galbraith says as he returns and sees me inspecting the spines of the books. He hands me a glass of fizzing water and takes a sip from the large glass of white wine he has poured for himself. 'I secured this from an auction in Vienna last year,' he says pointing to a large portrait behind his sofa. 'It's of James II. This is not for printing but I'm negotiating at the moment to sell it privately to the King. The Palace of the People is where it rightfully belongs.' He plays with a cornelian intaglio ring on his little finger.

'Do you live here alone?' I ask.

His face darkens at the directness of my question. 'I have a lodger actually. My wife stays in our house in the country. I join her at weekends.'

'Is she here now?'

'Who?'

'Your lodger.'

'How did you know my lodger is female?'

Good question. How do I know? Because I've been staking out your house, fat boy.

'I didn't... May I turn this on?' I produce a tape recorder from the shoulder bag I am carrying.

He wafts his hand superciliously. 'Be my guest.'

'So what's the appeal with portraits then?'

He puckers his lips. 'I like them because they reflect the vanities of society more than any other form of art. They put across things that the sitters want to say about themselves, as well as what the artists want to say. In subsequent generations, portraits were often adapted to conform with the taste of the time, the equivalent of plastic surgery. Faces were prettified, cleavages prudishly covered up, eyes moved closer together or wider apart, hair colour changed and double chins removed.'

'And how can you tell whether a portrait is a fake or the genuine article?'

'Well, it's interesting you should ask that because thanks to my discoveries, everyone, professional and amateur art dealer alike, wants to find a sleeper...'

Already he is beginning to irritate me. Pompous arse.

'...More to the point, everyone wants to sell one – even if it means faking it. There are a number of techniques for giving a painting the patina of age, for making it look scruffy and abandoned. A battered old frame. Dark varnish. Lots of old gallery labels on the back. You have to develop a heightened sense of self-protection against these things. You have to learn to almost literally smell the fakes. Let me show you some.'

He leads the way upstairs, puffing at the exertion, to his workshop-cum-study. It smells of turpentine. There is a threadbare chintz sofa in one corner and a Formica table in the other. This is scattered with photographs, velum-bound inventories and catalogues. Stacked against the walls are dozens of canvases. Galbraith shows me an X-ray of a painting he has just bought. 'The paint on this one, for instance, can't be from the sixteenth century because it has ICI chemicals in it.' He slips his glasses on and tilts his head back to read from a sheet of paper before handing it to me. 'Carbon dating and pigment analysis.'

He seems to be wallowing in the attention, bustling around the room, holding up canvases to the light. I notice the mirror on the wall. The design is similar to the two-way mirror I had installed in my study. There, facing it, is an old leather armchair and an easel with a canvas on it. There is only the barest outline of a nude sketched on it in pencil, but it is recognizable as Jenny.

'Who is she?' I nod in the direction of the canvas.

Galbraith shifts his weight guiltily from one foot to the other. 'No one in particular.'

'Your lodger?' I light a cigarette. 'Do you mind?'

He avoids my eye and pretends not to have heard. 'There is always a tendency to credit one with mystical powers when discovering pictures. But it is actually as simple as this: you have to have an absorbent memory for essential idiosyncrasies. And if you get to know an artist's style well, it's like being able to recognize a voice, that of your wife, say. So even if the voice is halting with passion or putting on a fake foreign accent, its core will still be recognizable.'

'Or like your lodger's voice?'

'The Duke of Marlborough sold the Lady Hamilton portrait

over there before the Second World War.' Pause. 'Well, during it. Let's just say he sold it in the first half of the twentieth century.'

'You're obsessed with accuracy, aren't you?' There is a tone of menace in my voice which I cannot disguise.

'You have to be, in my profession.' He can't disguise the mounting panic in his. 'So. We have discussed so far conservation and restoration and have been side-tracked on to fakes – '

'Fakes,' I repeat.

He gives a tight, nervous smile. 'When you know that some-where there is a family portrait that could fill the space above the fireplace, you just have to find it. It's that achingly missing piece of jigsaw. You have to make things fit.'

'There's something which doesn't quite fit here, Galbraith.'

My using his surname unnerves him. 'What do you mean?' He runs a hand through his thinning hair, his face, in the chiaroscuro lighting of the room, half in shadow. 'Really it's just a matter of translating a cheap hunch into reality. No. That's too pretentious sounding. A hunch into a fact.'

'I've got a hunch about you, Galbraith.' I light another cigarette with the butt of the last one and blow smoke in his direction.

He has edged towards the door now and is standing with his back to me. He looks like he might make a run for it at any moment. 'The thing you have to appreciate, Mr Yates, is that finding sleepers becomes completely addictive. There is a feeling of elation when a problematic painting proves to be a beautiful object. When you reveal something that has been covered for two hundred years – reveal the artist's original strokes – you experience a numinous feeling bordering on the spiritual.'

'What have you done with her?'

He turns around slowly, sees the gun in my hand and swallows. 'Who are you?' he says in a barely audible voice.

'Let's just say we have a mutual interest. Is that her bedroom next door?'

He nods. I give two flicks of the barrel to indicate that he should lead the way. He opens the door, turns on the light and walks over to the bed. It is made. There are no signs of Jenny's clothing anywhere.

'Tut tut.' I look from him to the mirror and then back to him again. 'Get an eyeful do you?'

He scratches his neck and says nothing. Keeping the gun pointed at him I open and close the drawers on her bedside table. They are empty. I stare at Galbraith, breathing heavily but feeling calm. It is almost as if he is resigned to his punishment. I cross the room silently, pass the pistol from my right to my left hand, and swing at him back-handed. There is a flat, dull noise. His legs buckle and he collapses heavily to the floor without a cry. He appears to feel embarrassment more than pain. I don't blame him, it's an awkward act. Staged and clumsy. I stand over him feeling divorced from my action. A trickle of blood has appeared at the corner of his mouth. He dabs it with his fingers.

'Up.' I try to control the emotion in my voice.

Like a man in a trance, Galbraith levers himself up on the bed.

'Back into the other room.' I dig the muzzle into his kidneys as he walks past. 'Now drop your trousers and sit on that chair.' With slow movements he obeys. I produce a thick roll of electrical tape from my bag and throw it across to him. He misses it and I pick it up. 'Now begin wrapping that around your legs.' His hands shake as he draws his hairless calves together and presses the tape to his skin. The roll makes a squeaking noise as it is pulled out. Galbraith has wrapped it seven times around his legs when I tell him to stop. 'Now put these on.' I pass him a pair of handcuffs. 'Behind your back.' He can only get one side on and so I help him with the other. I carry on wrapping his body in tape until I've used up the whole roll.

I turn my back on him and pick up the canvas of Jenny, holding it at arm's length. 'It's a good likeness. You've definitely caught her.' I look through the mirror, with the light now on in the bedroom I can see the bed clearly. 'If you have harmed her in any way, you know, I shall kill you.' I don't look at him as I say this. 'When are you expecting her back?'

He can't find his voice at first, then he whispers: 'I don't think she's coming back.'

'Why not?'

'Are you her father?'

'You poor sod,' I say with a laugh. 'You don't know anything about her do you? ... Did you and she ever – '

'No. Never.'

'Did you want to?'

He closes his eyes. 'Naturally.'

I feel a sudden pang of sympathy for him. Only now does it occur to me that he and I are more alike than different. I tug open his shirt and lift his fleshy chin. There are rope burns on his neck. 'She suggest that did she?'

'Yes. Not directly. But yes.'

'Did she say she wasn't coming back?' I pull the back of his hair to raise his face.

'Yes. Sort of. We had an argument. She left.'

'What was your argument about?'

'I told her I loved her.'

It is my turn to lose my voice.

'What are you going to do to me, Michael? Your name is Michael, isn't it?'

'Do you honestly think I would give you my real name?'

'Suppose not.'

'I haven't decided what I'm going to do with you yet.'

'I won't tell anyone. I can't, can I? How would I explain the mirror.'

'Are you expecting anyone else? Your wife?'

'Our cleaner will be here in the morning.'

'Good. Well, that gives you a few hours to contemplate your sins...I'll just...' I stuff a handkerchief in his mouth and tear off a strip of tape which I stretch across his lips. '...There. Have a comfortable night.'

I collect the papers I've touched and wipe the doorknobs down with a cloth. I then drop the keys for the handcuffs into a vase on his desk, so that Galbraith can direct his rescuer to them. As I go back down the stairs I run the cloth along the banister and, when I reach the front door, I use it again to turn the knob. Here I pause. The glass of water. Back in the drawing room, I drain the glass in one and drop it into my shoulder bag.

Twenty-eight

It's more of a feeling than an actual sighting but as I walk out on to the street I do sense a malevolent presence — something palpable moving in the shadows. I check my watch and feel for the unloaded pistol in my pocket. It's 3.40 in the morning. Who knocks on your door at 3.40 in the morning and then disappears without giving you time to get dressed properly? My encounter with Galbraith earlier in the evening has left me jumpy. I'm tucking my shirt tails into my trousers when the first baseball bat makes contact with my back. I slump to my knees as a second blow is delivered to the shoulders almost simultaneously. A series of strikes follows in such quick succession I can't even work out where I'm being hit.

I somehow get on to all fours and stumble for a short distance before another blow to the side of my face brings me down again. I try to shout for help but a boot to my windpipe silences me.

I roll into the foetal position, covering the back of my head with my hands. Now I double up in pain, winded, as I'm kicked repeatedly in the ribs and stomach.

In the semi-darkness I can't work out how many attackers there are — three or four. Their movements are blurred. But I do see they are wearing donkey jackets and balaclavas — and wielding baseball bats. They go about their task in silence, not a curse or a gasp for breath, unemotional.

There is a balled fist raining down on the side of my face and neck. After the first blow I become numbed to the pummelling. I can hear the tearing of cartilage in my nose and taste iron in my mouth. Blood. My face is wet with it.

Aware of someone plumping up my pillow, I try to open my eyes. They are glued. I shift my position so that I'm lying on my side. My limbs grow heavy and I feel the spin of sleep.

When I next awake I am able to open my eyes but they sting under the harsh strip lighting and I can't focus on anything. My stomach heaves and I taste bile in my throat. This is followed by a searing headache. I close my eyes again and retreat back into unconsciousness.

A sharp metallic smell pricks the air. Resinous. Is someone offering me a cigarette? I blindly feel for it with my swollen lips.

Several hours – possibly days – pass before I open my eyes again, blink to adjust to the light, and see a luminous shape. A nurse. She is repeating my name, towering over me, her chin creasing into chins. I watch her out-of-focus lips move and hear a voice that seems remote: 'You've been in a fight, Michael. But you're OK now.'

The voice sounds familiar and reassuring. I try to speak but cannot. My teeth feel loose and chalky. My intestines feel at once bloated and shrunken. I have a stomach cramp. When I try to move my head I realize I have a neck brace on. The nurse squeezes my hand and I discover there is a cast on my wrist.

The ward is dark when I next come round. It's easier on my eyes. Groggily, I try to call out for a nurse and this time my voice works, though my lips are so numb and my tongue so swollen my words are almost unintelligible.

'How long?'

'Six days,' the nurse says crisply.

'What's the date?'

'Tuesday, 16 April.'

The words and figures mean nothing to me. I see that there is a pulley above my bed. 'Traction?'

'No. You were lucky. No bones broken.' The nurse makes me flinch as she dabs my cheeks with cotton wool.

'Not the face! Not the face!'

The nurse laughs. 'How are you feeling?'

'Like I've been tenderized. How do I look? Do you have a mirror?'

She holds one up and I don't recognize myself. My eyes are puffy and bruised, my nostrils have splints up them and the bridge of my nose is taped. There is a bandage around my head and a thin tube taped to my jaw. My lips are blistered. I cannot lift my arms to touch them. There is a line of black stitching across my cheek. 'I always wanted a duelling scar,' I manage to say before I pass out again.

The following day I am able to sit up and talk properly. I'm in a private room, it turns out, at the Cromwell Hospital. 'Someone out walking his dog spotted you on the road near your house and called an ambulance,' the nurse tells me. 'We were able to get you into hospital just in time. You'd lost a lot of blood.'

'Sarah?'

'I wondered when you'd recognize me.'

'What are you doing here?'

'All English citizens have been told to evacuate Romania.' Pause. 'It was terrible out there. They've been finding mass graves. Kosovar refugees they reckon. I wanted to stay but then I heard that anyone with a European or American passport was being taken hostage. To be used as human shields.' She looks at the floor. 'I wouldn't work in a private hospital out of preference. This is the only job I could find.'

She looks better than she did the last time we made a video conference call. Her face seems less lined, the crows' feet not so noticeable; her hair, in an Alice band, less lank.

'I thought you worked for Médecins sans frontières.'

She gives me an uncertain smile. 'I expect I'll go back to them eventually but I wanted to come home for a while. See my family... I tried to reach your wife but she is on a fishing holiday in Quebec and is uncontactable. Is there anyone else you'd like me to contact? Your brother came to see you.'

'He did?'

'Yes. He brought you those.' She nods at a bunch of wilting carnations in a vase.

'How long will I be in here?'

'A few more days. Just so we can keep an eye on you. We need to do some more tests and scans. And you'll be seeing a physio.'

'Have they caught the men who did it?'

'The police need to talk to you about that. They didn't have much to go on until you came round. There were no witnesses.'

'Lucky about the dog walker passing. And lucky for me that you should be working here, Sarah. Nice to see a friendly face, especially one without a balaclava on.'

'Bit of a coincidence, really.'

'Indeed.'

Long pause.

'I'm really interested in all that.' Sarah picks up the chart hooked on the end of my bed. 'Strange phenomena. I've just been reading an article in the *Fortean Times* about research they're doing at the Koestler Institute in Edinburgh . . . It says here you've been passing blood. Has it cleared up?'

'You tell me,' I nod at the catheter snaking out from under my blanket.

'Anyway, the remarkable thing is not how often coincidences occur but how often they just fail to. Long-lost friends are just failing to bump into each other as they turn round corners all the time.'

'Never thought of it like that. Funny we bumped into each other in Bucharest then, really.'

'The article gave this amazing example of the coincidences surrounding the assassinations of Lincoln and Kennedy. Let me see if I can get this right.' She drums her fingers against her lips. 'Lincoln was elected president in 1860, Kennedy 1960. Both were assassinated on a Friday in the presence of their wives. Both were shot from behind and in the head. Their successors, OK, both named Johnson, were Southern Democrats: Andrew Johnson was born in 1808 and Lyndon in 1908. Their assassins were born in, I think, 1839 and 1939 respectively. Lincoln's secretary whose name was Kennedy, advised him not to go to the theatre. Kennedy's secretary whose name was Lincoln, advised him not to go to Dallas. Oswald shot Kennedy from a warehouse and ran to a theatre. Booth shot Lincoln in a theatre and ran to a warehouse.

Lincoln was shot in the Ford Theater. Kennedy was shot in a Ford Lincoln. Both assassins were killed before being brought to trial.'

'Sarah?'

'Yes?'

'I'm feeling a little tired.'

'Sorry.'

'That's all right... Incredible about Kennedy.'

'Isn't it.'

'I think I know who the Premier's assassin was.'

'What do you mean?'

'What I said. I think that's what the attack was about. It was a warning.'

'You were going to write about it?'

'Going to.'

'You're not now?'

'I don't know. There are things I'm tied up in. At the moment I don't want anything more to do with any of it. I just want to disappear.'

Sarah considers this for a moment. 'I'm going to my parents' cottage in Wales for a few days' break; why don't you come with me? You'll be safe there. You need to convalesce. I can look after you.'

I blink. 'Thanks. I might just take you up on that. You mustn't tell a soul though. No one can know I'm there.'

'No problem.'

'Aren't you going to ask me who did it, then?'

'Would there be any point?'

'Suppose not, won't be much of an exclusive if I go around telling everyone.'

'Michael? Michael?'

It is Haresh's voice. I open my eyes.

'How are you feeling?'

'Bit better thanks.'

'Maybe I should have given you some bullets for that gun.'

'I don't think it would have made much difference, Haresh. They came at me from behind.'

'Well, I'll give you some now, just in case.' He takes a clip from his pocket and tucks it under my mattress. 'Don't forget they're there . . . We'll soon catch the bastards who did this to you. We've got our best men on to it. We look after our own.'

'I'm one of you?'

'Course you are, mate.' He blows his nose. 'You're an "intelligence consultant" now. It's official.'

'I'd prefer "agent of influence".'

He smiles. 'Whatever.'

'Can I have a rank?'

'What would you like to be?'

'A brigadier general.'

'Brigadier general it is, then. You know we promised you some more material?'

I blink.

'Here it is.' He lays an envelope on my bed, takes a felt tip from his jacket pocket and writes the word 'confidential' on it in capital letters. He thinks for a moment, grins and adds underneath it: 'For the eyes of Brigadier General Yates only.'

'I don't think I'm going to be writing the story any more, Haresh.'

'Wait till you see what we've got for you. The transcript from a phone conversation between Tenant and Lambert. It took place one week before the assassination.'

'If it's that good, why haven't you acted on it?'

'Illegal tap, Brigadier General, sir. Inadmissible.'

'And you want it to appear in the *London Times* so that you can panic them, right?'

'Exactly.'

'And you won't be implicated because I have a legal right to protect my sources.'

'Bingo.'

I pick the envelope up and weigh it without opening it. It is still warm from his hands. 'Can't do it. You'll have to find yourself another journalist.'

'It has to be you.'

'Why?'

He taps his teeth with a pen. 'You write with a voice of authority. You have independence. You're an award winner.'

'Don't patronize me.'

'All right, then, if we use anyone else it will be assumed we are behind it. You're seen as being in the Tenant camp. It'll make your report more credible. We'll write a draft of it if you like. You can just stick your name on it.'

'Oh please. I haven't sunk that low yet. I just don't know. I don't know what I'm doing here. I don't know whose side I'm supposed to be on. I don't know why I'm talking to you. Why *am* I talking to you?'

'Because, Brigadier General, sir, you want to do what is best for your country.'

'Let me get this straight, then. You, sorry, we want to shaft Tenant because Tenant wants to shaft the Tories?'

'Something like that. And we want the Tories to win because Labour wants to shaft us.'

I try to lift my arm. 'So who tried to shaft me?'

'That would be Tenant.'

'Oh, I don't know, Haresh. I'm confused. Let me think about it.'

'Don't take too long, the election's only a couple of weeks away.' He puts his felt tip back in his jacket. 'Incidentally, there's no need to go back to Lambert's house. We sent someone else in to do it.'

'Haresh, mate?'

'Brigadier General?'

'How did you know I was here?'

He smiles, walks over to the door, turns and says: 'I'll call you tomorrow.'

I've just finished reading the transcript of the conversation between Lambert and Tenant – highly incriminating, if true – when Jenny knocks on the door and ghosts in without waiting for an answer. She is wearing the glasses she wore when I first saw her, as well as gold hooped earrings – but no stud in her nose, or rings in her eyebrows. Her cheesecloth dress is white, her skin is as pale as a mushroom, her hair is now black. I want to smooth my hair down but I cannot lift my hands – muscles still too weak. Jenny stops half-way across the room and flutters her fingers in greeting. 'Hiya,' she says. 'How have you been?'

The sound of her voice makes me want to cry with gratitude. Sometimes it takes the offer of a glass of water to make you realize you're dying of thirst. 'Better,' I say when I find my voice. 'I mean, I've felt better.'

Jenny fidgets in her seat. 'You look shit.'

'Thanks.' I cannot turn my head to see her properly so she moves her chair forward. 'How have you been?'

'Fine. Fine. Sorry to hear about your dad.'

'Thanks.'

'How do you feel?'

'About the old man? Bit depressed. It takes a while for it to sink in. He was a good man. Honest. Moral . . . I missed you.'

'Don't say that.'

'When I got home the other night my television announced it had recorded part two of a drama that I had supposedly watched part one of. I couldn't think what it meant at first. Then I figured it must have been you.'

'Yeah? I think I did start watching something.'

This is becoming one of our usual desultory conversations. I wait for her to add something. She wants me to apologize for what happened between us. I won't. 'What have you been up to?' I ask.

She scratches her nose. 'You know. This and that.'

'I'm sorry about – '

'Forget it. I was as much to blame. I shouldn't have left that note.'

We fall silent, each avoiding the other's eye.

'I found your other note.'

'What other note?'

'You liked hearing me say I love you.'

'Oh that. You went through my bin?'

I try to shrug but a shooting pain in my chest turns the gesture into a wince.

She laughs. 'It's OK. I would have done the same. Can I help? You don't look very comfortable.' She edges her chair closer still to the bed and holds a glass of water to my mouth. I take a sip but nearly choke on it and end up dribbling it back down my chin. She picks up a towel and dabs my mouth.

'My head is throbbing,' I say.

She massages my temples with her finger-tips and I flinch again when she runs the back of her hand over the welt on my cheek. When she squeezes the fingers on my bruised hand, I cry out in pain.

'Sorry,' she says, matter-of-factly.

'I meant it you know,' I say.

'Meant what?'

'That I love you.'

Pause.

'I know.'

'That night,' I say. 'It wasn't Ed, was it?'

'No.'

'Galbraith?'

She shakes her head and laughs again. 'No. You don't know him. Anyway, that's, like, *so* over now.' She looks around the room and flicks through the channels on the telly using the remote on my bed. She stops at a party political broadcast by the PM's widow. 'Don't you think she's laying it on a bit thick, still wearing mourning black after all this time?'

Before I can comment, Jenny flicks through six channels and stops for a moment on the Shoe Channel, she then flicks on to a head-to-head debate between the leader of the New Conservative Party (big white smile, fine blonde hair, diamond euro-sign pendant around her long, slim neck) and the leader of New Labour (five o'clock shadow, furtive eyes, sweaty brow). Sir Jeremy Paxman is in the chair, barely concealing his contempt as he says: 'So let me get this right, Prime Minister, you expect us to believe that you had *no idea* your own wife was buying BBC shares on your behalf just two days before *your own* Government announced that the BBC was to be floated? Is *that* what you are saying?'

'What I am saying, Sir Jeremy, is that there was no way we could have – '

'Just answer the question, yes or no.'

'I am trying to. If you will just let me finish.' The Prime Minister does that strange gulping thing he does. 'When the government first put forward the green paper on privatizing the – '

'What do you think?' Still slouching, Paxman swivels in his chair to face the leader of the New Tories. She smiles flirtatiously and says: 'Well, I think it would help if the Premier and the First Lady communicated with each other a little more. But I suppose that is difficult if the only time you meet your wife is when she is summoned for a photo call on the steps of Number 10.'

There is a big cheer from the studio audience at this.

'Yes,' Paxman says. 'The Conservatives have a 70 per cent lead in the polls. Feeling confident?'

Another smile. 'Yes, Jeremy, we are.'

Jenny flicks channels again and stops at one of those televised executions they do live from China. 'That's disgusting,' she says and flicks the set off. 'I called in on Roddy by the way, just after you left him. He was very pleased to see me. It took me about an hour to untangle him. He'd soiled himself.' She giggles at this.

'Has he been to the police?'

'He said he wasn't planning to. Doesn't want his wife to know about me.' Her golden giggle again.

'I think I might have over-reacted.'

'I know who was behind the attack on you.'

'Who? Galbraith?'

She takes hold of my hand, gently at first and then starts to twist it. I scream out in pain.

'Me,' she says.

I miss a beat. Speechless. She couldn't have. '*You?*'

'Joke. Joke. When I first heard about you being beaten up I wondered whether Roddy might have been behind it.' She trails off, removes her glasses and rubs them on her skirt. There is a ladder in the knee of her tights, a roach burn on her skirt. 'Who do you think did it?'

'I've no idea.'

'It was my father, wasn't it.' It is a statement rather than a question. I search her face. Her eyes look pink and sore. She is expressionless.

'Would you care to elaborate?'

'I know all about the coup he's planning.'

'How?'

'So there is one then?'

'No. I mean . . . Yes. How do you know?'

'I overheard you talking about it to Sarah. On your computer.'

Sarah and I have made a few video calls now, but I don't recall ever mentioning that.

'You know Sarah?'

'Are you going to stiff them then?'

'Sarah told you that?'

234

A twitch of a smile. 'You're planning to go over to the *London Times*?'

'I don't know. I wish I'd never got involved. I think I'm just going to disappear for a while. At least until the election is over.'

'You can't.'

'Why not?'

'You have a duty to help them.'

'Help your father?'

'Yeah.'

I snort. 'I know you like to think of yourself as an extremist, Jenny. But I've never had you figured as a crypto-fascist.' I start to laugh but it hurts my chest and I end up coughing. 'I suppose it makes sense. Anarcho-communism and crypto-fascism are pretty interchangeable really.'

'Of course I'm not a fascist. It's just I believe that what the Tories are planning is irresponsible. Did you know they're planning to sell off all the Army Training Lands to property developers? You of all people should understand. You remember that night you stayed at our camp in Devon? You were on our side then, weren't you?'

'I don't want to sound patronizing, Jenny, but what your father is planning is undemocratic. Simple as that.'

'You've got to have a cause, Mickey.'

'But your father and my father-in-law think they can ignore the will of the people just because the people don't happen to share their views. They think they can just dispose of whoever they want to, to get their own way. Me. The PM. Anyone. They don't have a single moral fibre between them. Not one.'

'And you do, Mickey? Who are you trying to kid?'

I think about it. Feel indignant that she thinks she knows me better than I know myself. 'It's true, I've never been troubled by a conscience much in the past, but recent events have... My father ... Why do you hate me?'

'I don't hate you, right.' She twists a strand of her hair.

'But you don't love me either?'

She doesn't answer.

'Jenny?'

'I don't think I've ever been in love.'

'Sometimes you have to allow yourself to be.'

'If you love me, Mickey, help my father.'

Long pause.

'I have to think about it.'

'You mustn't write that story for the *London Times*.' She laughs softly. 'I'd be grateful.'

'What do you mean?'

'We could pick up where we left off.'

'And where was that, exactly? Me feeling suicidal? Jealousy corroding through me like acid?'

'Things wouldn't have to be the same as before,' she says standing up to rearrange the pillow under my head. 'Why are you looking at me like that?'

'Whatever happens, I was planning to go to America.' I close my eyes as a waft of her perfume reaches my nostrils. 'On the first plane out after...'

'After what?'

My teeth begin to chatter. 'You could – '

'I could fly out with you? That pillow doesn't look very comfortable. Do you want me to come with you?'

I open my eyes.

'You would do that if I didn't write the story?'

'I'm sure she would.' Amanda's voice. Jenny and I look towards the door.

'I thought you were in Quebec,' I say.

Amanda saunters in, wearing a black, cashmere overcoat and large sapphire earrings. Her russet hair is cut into a Louise Brooks bob. 'You must be Jenny,' she says holding out a leather-gloved hand.

Jenny stands up, shakes Amanda's hand and says: 'And you must be Amanda. Hello. I was just leaving.'

'Please don't on my account,' Amanda says.

'No, really.' At the door Jenny turns and adds: 'Mickey, I'll call you. I'm serious about America. Buy me a ticket.'

'Mickey?' Amanda repeats after Jenny has gone. 'She's not as pretty as I'd imagined she would be. More posh, though. That voice. Is she posh?'

'Her father drives a Rolls-Royce.'

236

'No, then.'

'I thought you were in Quebec.'

'I came back when I heard.'

'Who told you I was here?'

'Daddy... I've brought you a present.' Amanda rummages in her handbag and produces a couple of grams of cocaine. She slips them in the top drawer of my side table. 'Pain relief. And I've taken care of your hospital bills.'

'Thanks, Mand. When did you get your hair cut like that?'

'Oh, last week. Poor Michael. Are you suffering terribly?'

'Not as much as I was. How are you feeling? Everything OK with the baby?'

Amanda pats her midriff. 'Fine, fine. I've been feeling a bit nauseous in the evenings but no worse than last time. The doctors want me to test for some gruesome things called placental insufficiency and fallopian malfunction, because of my age, but I'm not going to. What will be will be.'

'Thought of any names?'

'Emily, if it's a girl... Would you mind?'

'I'd rather you didn't. How's Gavin?'

'Fine.' Amanda takes my hand. 'I've been worried about you,' she says. 'When they worked you over, that was just a warning. You know that, don't you?'

'Some warning. Did "Daddy" sanction it then?'

'I'm serious, Michael. Don't fuck with these people. Just do what they want you to do and keep your head down.' She lets go of my hand and starts rearranging my pillows. 'And don't trust the spooks. They're using you. They're the ones who broke into our house.'

'How do you know?'

'I just do. And they buggd everything: your shoes, watches, pens. I had the whole house swept... Look, you mustn't write that story, OK... If you won't listen to me, listen to Jenny.'

'Did "Daddy" send you?'

'I'm sure what Daddy is doing is for the best. You can see that. Just don't mess things up for him. You know what he's like.'

'Did you tell him that you wanted a divorce?'

'Not yet. But knowing him he's probably found out

already... Since you mentioned it, I've brought some papers for you to sign. To start proceedings.' She searches through her handbag again, produces an envelope and places it on the bed.

'So that's that then.'

'I'm sorry, Michael. I wish things could have worked out differently.' She leans forward and kisses me on the forehead.

Twenty-nine

Sarah's parents live in a remote area on the Powys–Shropshire border. Their granite bungalow is ugly and overgrown with ivy. The lane that leads up to it is potholed and the paddock in front of the bungalow is full of rank, tussocky grass.

It is unseasonably hot. The sky is a cloudless, cadmium blue, and Sarah has invited me to go riding with her. I protest at first because any movement makes me ache, but she insists that it will be good therapy and that, anyway, her parents ride old cobs which are so docile you could let a hand grenade off next to them and they wouldn't be spooked.

The stables are a ten-minute walk away. We cross through an orchard and take a short cut through a neighbour's garden. Sarah shows me a moss-covered statue of a woodland nymph almost lost in their neighbour's topiary hedge. This was her favourite place as a child, she says. Her secret place. Her initials are scratched in its base.

I wait by the mounting block on the stable yard while Sarah leads out two thoroughbred horses that couldn't look less like cobs. One is chestnut, one grey, both, at seventeen hands, are huge. I laugh when I see them. 'You don't expect me to get on one of those monsters, do you?'

'They're quite friendly,' Sarah says calmly. 'This is Sterling and

this is Nelson. He's yours. Does Daddy's jockey cap fit all right?'
While Sarah disappears into the tack room for the saddles, I hold
the horses, nervously, watching their breath plume from their
huge, velvety nostrils. As Sarah slips his saddle on and tightens up
the girth, Nelson twitches his ears lazily and swishes his tail.

I used to ride when Amanda and I first got married but I'm out
of practice now and Sarah has to remind me to take a shorter hold
of my reins and to keep my heels down in the stirrups. To my
relief, Nelson does no more than amble along, while Sarah on
Sterling trots on ahead, circling back over every now and again for
me to catch up. As I plod across the open pastureland I drink in
the colours of the landscape – the late April blossom, the
thickening hedgerows, the lime-green leaves – and I feel like a
submariner getting his first taste of natural light and non-recycled
air after a four-month tour of duty. In the distance I can hear
church bells pealing and, closer, a skylark warbling loudly as it
circles overhead before swooping back to earth in silence.
Although this is clearly a worked landscape, with evidence of the
modern age all around – pylons, a wind turbine, a giant red tractor
pulling a twenty-share plough – it's also the sort of timeless,
Arcadian countryside Constable would have wanted to paint. And
I soon find myself falling in love with it.

There is a condition called lateral inhibition which occurs
when your eye surveys a featureless environment – the cells in the
retina close down to create the contrasts of light and dark you
need in order to see. But when your ear becomes habituated to a
constant sound at a single pitch you become deaf – unless the tone
is varied. As I now appreciate, the need for contrast applies to our
relationship with the natural world, too: the vivid colours of the
countryside can only be appreciated after the greyness of a city, the
muggy mildness of a Welsh spring after the chill bite of a London
winter.

We hack along a riverbank, following its course as it snakes
through a valley bottom, and we come to a halt on the outskirts
of a spinney. Sarah dismounts and tethers Sterling to a branch. She
walks over to me and holds Nelson while I dismount. As she ties
the second horse next to the first I walk around bow-leggedly,
trying to get the circulation back to my legs.

We stand with our backs to the bark of an oak and shield our eyes with our hands as we take in the scenery. Sarah entwines her fingers with mine and smiles kindly when I do not flinch. She has an easy, attractive, unself-conscious smile which makes me feel safe.

'I like it when you smile,' I say. 'You're like my guardian angel, aren't you?' She takes hold of my whole hand now and, turning her back to me, wraps my arms around her waist. I look down at the crown of her head and smell her hair. The wildflower meadow before us takes on a warm glow in the afternoon sun. There is a blue haze over it and the smell of garlic and elderflower. I inhale deeply.

I imagine everyone who has had a near-death experience feels a little hormonal afterwards. But when your experience happens in springtime you're especially vulnerable. I feel I could burst with gratitude for being alive. I love the stickiness of the countryside around me, its texture, its aching beauty. The grass seems impossibly green. The sound of Nelson, snorting and hoofing the ground seems unfeasibly clear. I can feel every knot and grain in the bark of the tree.

'Sarah? You know that bomb in Bucharest? Was it real?'

'Depends what you mean by real. Why?'

'I was just thinking about it ... You know, you don't need drugs in a place like this, do you?'

'Definitely not.'

'I think when I get to Washington I'm going to check myself into a rehab clinic.'

'Good idea.'

I think of Dad. Such a principled old sod. What would he do about the Tenant and Lambert cabal? Would he blow the whistle? I think I know. He used to tell me that it doesn't really matter what you believe as long as you honestly believe it. 'For every Elizabeth I there is a Charles I,' I say under my breath. 'For every philosopher king, a motley fool. Demos, for all its failings, is godlike because it makes no attempt to throw up gods.'

'What's that from?' Sarah asks.

'It was a reading at my father's funeral ... Sarah?'

'Yeah?'

'I don't want to be a moral cripple any more.' I squeeze her and once more breathe deep the smell of her hair. It is as if I've never smelt another person's hair before. I look down at the fairy wisps and my eyes fill with tears.

'You've gone very quiet, Michael,' Sarah says, her voice distant. 'You all right?'

'Let's go back.'

I almost fall asleep in the bath, my muscles still stiff from the ride. When I get out of it too suddenly I feel dizzy. There is a dressing gown hanging on the door and I slip this on and inspect my face in the bathroom mirror. My lips are still scabby, my skin still yellow from bruising, but the swelling on my face has gone down and the haircut the doctors have given me – almost all shaved off – quite suits me. I sit down on the bed, aching and out of breath.

Sarah has been having a bath at the same time and she now wanders through into my bedroom. With her back to me she opens and refolds more tightly the towel she is wrapped in. 'Can you dry my hair?' she says, sitting on the floor between my legs. She hands me a towel. The drying causes the towel to fall slightly and Sarah makes no attempt to adjust it. 'You're very gentle,' she says. 'Can you brush it?' She sits forward and crawls across the floor to the dressing table. The sight of her still-damp calves and the cellulite on her thighs is unexpectedly arousing. She picks up a hairbrush and hands it to me. 'That's lovely,' she says as I run the bristles through her hair.

I stare at the freckled skin of her shoulders and fight an urge to touch it with my lips. Sarah leans back in the crook of my legs, closes her eyes and draws up her knees so that the towel stretches tight. As I brush and stroke I notice the white hairs on her head and will the towel to slip a fraction more to reveal her breasts. It does, and another fraction, before falling to her waist.

'That's lovely,' she repeats. 'What are you thinking about?'

'Nothing.'

'You *are* going to write your report, aren't you?'

'I haven't brought my laptop.'

'I've brought that one you gave me.'

I laugh silently and kiss her head. At least I now know who she is. 'You people think of everything,' I whisper.

She turns her head to nuzzle my knee. 'What do you mean?'

'Does my young friend Fielding know I'm here then?'

Sarah playfully bites my calf but says nothing. As I remove my dressing gown our lips brush and her towel falls off completely. She presses a nipple to my mouth. It is wrinkled and hard like a raisin. We are unable to look at each other as I slide off the bed to join her on the floor. I kiss her neck. She smells of flour, tastes watery. When I feel the mallowy softness of her thighs against my hips, I hold my breath.

'Are you thinking of Jenny?' she asks.

I smile and shake my head.

Thirty

'What about "Coup attempt foiled"?' Simon turns to Ed.

'Bit pompous. Who says foiled?'

'"Fucked" then?' Simon looks over his glasses at me, deadpan.
'"Coup attempt fucked."'

All three of us laugh.

Under the desk my right leg has started to judder as though a
nerve is trapped. I lick my lips. I feel focused. Excited. Centred. I
am sitting in front of a large Mac screen that has been set up for
us in the production editor's L-shaped corner office. Ed and
Simon are sitting either side and I think we are all feeling the same
rush of adrenaline.

It is 3 a.m. on polling day. The first edition, with its attic about
nurses planning to demonstrate outside polling stations, is already
spooling off the presses. My story is being kept for the second
edition – which goes to bed in an hour – so that our rivals cannot
see it in time to run spoilers.

My leg is making the computer vibrate.

The copy on the front page fits, we have subbed it ourselves, and
the full-bleed photograph – the one I took of the conspirators at
Lambert's house – takes up the top half of the page. But we cannot
agree on the banner. Simon thinks that naming Tenant and Lambert
as the men behind the Premier's assassination is the stronger story.

Ed is wearing a hairy tweed jacket with patches on the elbows. He takes this off and, finding nowhere to hang it, lays it under the desk. He clears his throat softly and says that he thinks the coup attempt should lead.

I suggest a compromise. Headline: 'Conspiracy.' The standfirst should read: 'Exclusive: Press baron and military chief plotted PM's murder. Now they plan coup.' I key it in to show them how it will look.

Simon takes a sip of gin and tonic, pursing his lips before the glass reaches them. '"Conspiracy" is a bit weak,' he says. 'What about "Treachery" exclamation mark.' I look at Ed who nods and says: 'But we don't need the exclamation mark. Too tabloid.' I key it in. It fits.

Simon again: 'I think it would be better if we changed the second sentence in the stand to: 'If the Tories win today, plotters will stage coup.'

I key this in and ask: 'What about mentioning the King?'

Ed and Simon exchange glances. 'That comes in the first par,' Ed says.

Me: 'And what about plugging my interview with "Marksman Dave"?'

Ed: 'We've got that in the puff at the top.'

Simon taps the screen with his finger. 'How about "Exclusive: Press baron and military chief plotted PM's murder. If Tories win today, they will join forces with King in *coup d'état*."'

'Yeah, that's tighter,' I say. 'I'm not sure about the headline now though. How about "Enemies of democracy"?'

'Bit dull for a splash,' Ed says. 'You could have that in the picture caption.'

Me: 'How about "Enemies of the People" as the head and start the picture caption with "Conspirators".'

Ed: 'Sounds too much like the *English People*.'

Me: 'Well, that would be good, wouldn't it? Readers would make the association with Tenant's paper.'

Simon: 'Yeah, but it would be the wrong association. As if the conspirators were the enemy of his paper.'

Me: 'True.'

A plastic water dispenser in the corner bubbles to itself.

Ed: 'Got it. One word "Bastards!" With exclamation mark. You remember that quote from the Chancellor, "I'll hunt down the bastards who did this to the ends of the earth...?"'

Simon: 'Brilliant!'

I key it in, save it and think of Amanda. The divorce papers I signed for her should have arrived in this morning's post.

'OK,' Ed says. 'We just need to do the pull quotes and then this page can go. I can do them. Simon, you give the printers a call and tell them it's on its way.' Simon stands up, his trouser pockets bulging. I remember this about him from the last time we worked together. We all used to speculate about what he stuffed them with: books of matches, marbles, peardrops. 'Mike,' Ed says turning to me and interrupting my thoughts, 'well done. This is the best thing you've ever written. Pulitzer-prize-winning material. You must be pleased.'

'I suppose I am, yes.'

'And I hear you've got your book deal all sorted for when you get to Washington.'

'Yes.'

'You looking forward to starting your new life?'

'I think so. I should be the one thanking you, Ed.'

'Well, we're not quite there yet. You'd better make those calls.'

I have been dreading this. The story runs over five pages on the inside, followed by my interview with Marksman Dave, and we have left space for a quote from Lambert and Tenant. Right of reply. It will be too late for them to file an injunction or to slap a D-notice on us and they may just be confused enough to make a confession.

I return to the desk I have been using and find a small package with my name on it and the words 'deliver by bike'. It is Jenny's handwriting. I rip it open and read the note inside: 'Dear Mickey, I've been thinking about our conversation. You must do whatever you think is right. Either way, I will come to Washington with you. Did you get my ticket? Give me a call tonight. I'm staying at Roddy's house. I've enclosed something for you. To make up for when I threw yours away. Love you always, Jenny.'

What? 'Love you always'? Where's that coming from? I pick up the package again and tip it upside down. A small white wrap lands on the desk. Just what I need. But after the calls. I slip it in my pocket and turn the tape recorder on. Tenant is engaged. I count to ten and press the redial button. He answers after two rings.

'Bruce?'

'Who's that?'

'It's Michael.'

'Who?'

'Michael Yates... Your, er, son-in-law?'

'I'll take this on video-con.'

I turn on the office long-screen and position myself in front of the camera. A life-size image of Tenant comes into focus. He is standing up, smoking a cigar, wearing a tracksuit with a towel around his neck. There is a halo of cigar smoke above his bald head. 'What do you want, Michael?'

I take a deep breath. My heart is pounding like a jack hammer. 'The *London Times* is running a story about your involvement in the assassination of the Premier.' I swallow. My mouth has gone dry. 'And the military coup you are – ' I can't find the right words. I can't look at him. 'Do you have any comments?'

His silence cuts right through to the bone. I can hear him breathing heavily. After a minute he crooks his hands rheumatically and speaks in his terrifyingly calm monotone as though conserving energy for a more important interlocutor. 'Look at me, Michael.' The voice is so deep it distorts the bass on the speaker. I raise my head and flinch as he gives me a sulphurous look. Talking slowly and deliberately, enunciating every word in a sarcastic singsong, he growls: 'What are you talking about, Michael? Huh?'

I repeat the question.

'Are you crazy? Are you out of your fucking mind? Look at me.'

He is staring at me with contempt.

'Do you have a comment, Bruce?'

'Yes, I have a comment, you worthless piece of horseshit. I'm gonna kill you. That's my comment.' His expression does not change as he says this. His lips barely move. His voice remains flat and toneless.

'Are you threatening me, Bruce?'

'You got that straight, freakshow. I'm gonna ruin you. I'm gonna crucify you.'

'Too late, Bruce.'

'We'll see who's too late.' Pause. 'You wanna piece of me? Huh? Do you, Michael?' He actually squares up to the camera as he says this. He narrows his eyes and looks past me. 'Are you recording this?' Pause. His chubby finger rises up in front of him. It is foreshortened as it looms up towards the camera and flicks it off.

The phone rings about eight times before Lady Lambert answers groggily. 'Hello?'

'Hello, Jane.'

'Michael? Is that you? We were asleep.'

'I need to speak to Sir Andrew. It's urgent.' I can hear her repeating the words 'says it's urgent' as she hands over the phone. The sound of a man coughing. 'Michael? It's 3.30. What's going on?'

A long silence follows my explanation.

'Michael.' His voice is calm. 'Stay on the line, I'm just going to another phone. I'll put this one down.'

The minute or so it takes for him to pick up the other phone seems like ten. I look at my reflection in a glass partition and see a faint moustache of sweat on my top lip. I am trembling.

'Michael. Stop and think what you are doing.'

'I've thought it through.' I hold my hand up to my face. 'Do you have a comment?'

Silence.

'Sir Andrew?'

Silence.

'So you neither confirm nor deny that you and Bruce Tenant hired an assassin to shoot the Premier?'

He laughs coldly. 'Off the record?'

'On.'

'Yes, I deny it. Yes.'

'And off the record?'

'You're making a complete arse of yourself, Michael.'

'And you deny that you were motivated by the PM's decision to ban research into Infowar?'

'Absolutely.'

'You cannot deny that you're planning a military coup?'

248

'Yes, yes. I can. I do.'

'I was there.'

'Then you should know we are planning no... That nothing of the kind is being planned.'

'What do you mean?'

'I mean that today there will be peaceful march past of some of the regiments that are to be disbanded, should the New Conservatives win the election. That is all. It's a demonstration. I think you've been set up, Michael. Who told you this?'

'I have proof.'

'What sort of proof?'

'Transcripts of conversations between you and Tenant.'

'Did you hear them yourself?'

'I – '

'And who gave you them?'

'I can't say.' I try to hide the uncertainty in my voice.

'It was MI5, wasn't it? Don't you see? They're not interested in the defence of the realm. They just want the Tories in because New Labour has threatened to scrap them. They're using you.'

'I'm not being used.'

'They knew you would use the tape without checking it because they knew you were a typical journalist – vain, corrupt and lazy. That was why I asked you to do the Tory manifesto story for me.'

'That was – '

'You've been staying with that Sarah woman, haven't you? Who do you think she works for? Do you suppose it was an accident she bumped into you in Bucharest?'

I rub the bridge of my nose. 'No. I mean, of course. I'm not stupid. But so what? It doesn't change the fact that you are planning to overthrow the democratically elected government of this country.'

The cold laugh again.

'Michael, I think you'd better read out to me what you are planning to print.'

'I can't do that.'

'How can I give you a quote unless I know the context?'

I stare across at Ed as he sits at the computer in the glass-walled office. The screen is reflected in his glasses. He is frowning in concentration. There are dark sweat patches on his shirt.

'OK, Sir Andrew.' I hold up a proof. 'Here's a paragraph that appears about half-way through the piece. "The group intends to declare martial law and appoint the King as the titular head of the interim government. This will be a temporary measure until an e-referendum can be called. Before the electorate vote on whether or not to downsize England's armed forces, they will be subjected to a ruthless propaganda campaign by the coup leaders. This will play up the supposed threats posed to national security by the Chinese and will attempt to reassure voters that in staging the coup the military is acting within the constitution. The armed forces swear allegiance to the Crown, not to the Government, they will argue. And as it is the Tory leader's intention to abolish the Monarchy, the armed forces have a patriotic duty to oppose her."'

Sir Andrew snorts derisively. 'Go ahead and publish if you want to humiliate yourself. Your story is laughable. And libellous. And you're pathetic.'

'And you . . .' My hand is now shaking with anger. 'Randolph Hearst said that journalism is what someone, somewhere doesn't want us to know. The rest is advertising.'

'It's also what someone, somewhere wants you to think . . . The Service is using you, Michael.'

'How can you talk to me about using people. You even used your own daughter to get to me.'

'Is that what she told you?'

'Well, it didn't work. She doesn't care anymore. And she doesn't mind if you end up in jail. She's coming away with me.'

Lambert gives a short laugh. 'Poor Michael.'

'What do you mean?'

'She went through a period of hating me, too. When Jane and I had our trial separation. Do you think you're the first father figure she's tried to punish . . . Hello? Michael?'

I hang up.

Ed is tapping on the glass of his window. He mimes someone typing. I shake my head and mouth the words: 'Denied everything.' Ed sticks his thumb up and returns to his screen.

Agitated by the phone calls, I head to the loo for a line from the packet Jenny sent. But when I sprinkle the white powder on to the seat cover it gives off an unexpected smell. Pungent. Chemical. Dizzying. My stomach tightens and I back out of the cubicle.

I have a memory of this smell. A vague one. Difficult to place at first. Damp woodland in autumn. Soft peaty air. A teenage visit to a friend's farm. Everyone is standing back as the boy's father pumps 'gas' into the rabbit warren. We all wait to see which holes the white powder will float up from. Then we get to work with the shovels, filling them in.

Cyanide.

My stomach plunges and floats up again as I stare at the white powder on the seat cover. I stand like this for perhaps a full minute before I pull two paper towels from the dispenser, make a pouch with one and, holding my breath, use the other to brush the powder into it. I flush them both and spend a further minute washing and rewashing my hands.

I return to my desk and tap out the number for Jenny's mobile. 'Jenny?'

'Where are you, Michael?'

She never calls me Michael.

'In the office.'

'Did you − ?'

'I got your package, yeah.' Silence. 'That was very thoughtful, Jenny. I haven't tried it yet. Thought I'd save it for the airport.'

'Right.' Her voice is unsteady.

'So you coming with me?'

'Yeah. Sure.'

'I bought you a ticket just in case. You packed?'

'Yeah.'

'Passport?'

'Multicard, yeah.'

'It's good to hear your voice.'

'Likewise.'

'I needed to hear it.'

'Michael.' Her tone is falsely casual. 'I think I'll drive to the airport.'

'Why? My taxi will go right past Galbraith's house.'

'I just want to. I can come and pick you up if you like. Wapping right?'

'You haven't got a car.'

'I'll borrow Roddy's. He won't mind. Three quarters of an hour, yeah? Outside your building?'

'If you really want to. But I think it would be a lot easier to go by taxi.'

'I fancy driving.'

'OK, do you know East Smithfield? You turn right off Tower Bridge and it becomes the Highway? Wapping is just off that. You can't miss the high fences. There's a cobbled alley that runs between the warehouses, Pennington Street. That's where the side entrance is. Wait for me there.'

'Five o'clock.'

'Jenny?'

'Yeah?'

'Can I ask you something?'

'Go on.'

'I need to know if you did love me. For a while.' Silence. 'Tell the truth.'

'You don't want to hear it.'

I don't. 'Lie then.'

She laughs. 'See you at 5.'

Ed walks over and sits on my desk. 'Who was that?'

I press the disconnect button. 'Jenny... Has the edition gone then?'

He yawns and runs a hand through his hair. 'Five minutes ago. I feel shattered.'

'Me too.'

'It's all right for you, Mike. You can get your head down on the plane. I'm going to be sweating it out in front of the TV cameras all day, I imagine.'

'I should think so, too. You've got a lot of explaining to do. I hope they give you a hard time... What if we're wrong, Ed?'

'Don't. We're not.' He eyes me quizzically. 'You do know we've had Jenny under surveillance for the past three years, don't you?'

I try to look nonchalant. 'I didn't know actually.'

Ed is still chuckling as he reaches into the office fridge and pulls out a bottle of vintage Bollinger. He pops the cork with a deft twist and fills a flute so badly he has to put his mouth to the glass to stop it bubbling over.

Sarah rings on my mobile. 'Hi, it's me,' she says. 'Everything OK?'

'I think so. Everything still OK with you?'

'Yes. I'm already at the airport. I thought I'd check in early.'

I feel under my desk for my bag. I've packed the gun Haresh gave me and I feel jumpy about it being there. 'We've just finished here, Sarah. I should be with you in about an hour.'

'Be careful. We've just heard that Tenant has asked for his jet to be on standby. The pilot has been told to prepare a flight plan for Mexico.'

'That figures. Tenant has an island just off the coast there. He could do with a vacation...I wonder if he's planning to take Lambert?'

'Well, anyway. Take care love.'

Ed has drained his glass, refilled it and is pouring a glass for me. As he hands it over, he says: 'I think we deserve this.'

I lick my lips and take the glass gently, as if it were a lover's hand. 'I can't.'

'One glass won't harm you.'

'Jenny tried to kill me. Why would she want to kill me, Ed?'

'Because she was bored?'

'That's good. I might have to steal it.' I clink with him, put the glass to my lips and hesitate before taking a sip, my first in five years.

'Know what, Mike...?'

I close my eyes and savour the sting. The devil in velvet trousers is back.

'...I've always admired you.'

'You have?'

'Course.'

I drain my glass, pour and drink another and pat him on the shoulder. His eyes, I notice for the first time, are a luminous blue. 'Thanks. It's a funny thing, Ed. But I used to hate you. Now you're probably the only real friend I have.'

Ed puts his glass down, opens his arms and hugs me. I can smell the sweat mingled with aftershave on his neck. When it becomes clear he intends to sustain the embrace for some time I raise my arms and link them around his waist. The awkwardness is unbearable. 'Ed,' I whisper.

'Yeah?'

'I can't breathe.'

'Sorry.' He releases his grip, refills our glasses and dabs his eyes surreptitiously with his sleeve.

Thirty-one

There are no streetlamps in the alley. No sounds either. As I wait in the shadows, one leg either side of my suitcase, I try to imagine what deafness is like. There must be cars on the roads somewhere – alarm clocks going off, arguments starting, babies crying – but I don't hear them. The silence is as thick as glue.

I check my watch. It's 5.

Vibrations disturb the molecules of air around me. My eardrums move in and out under waves of changing pressure. Gradually, they focus on London's permanent background noise: car alarms going off. And now I hear the dawn chorus, a sound so familiar it never wakes you, yet makes you paranoid when you cannot sleep. Those three tiny bones – hammer, anvil and stirrup – connect to a miniature harp in my ear and I decipher the individual songs: a chaffinch, a blackbird, a starling. How sweet they sound.

The night sky is violet-edged now. The air cold and damp. I detect a barky smell, early morning moisture on the trees. I clap, stamp my heels against the cobbles, check my watch again.

An RAF fighter screams over the London skyline, shattering the silence. I duck instinctively as it is followed by two more. I check my watch again and wonder what is going on. Are they on patrol? My heart is in fibrillation, my head still slightly buzzing from the champagne.

A huddle of blankets stirs and coughs. I start guiltily as a hand extends from them and a man's voice asks me for change. I pat my pockets, hear the jingle of coins and hand them over. The man lurches to his feet, stretches and shuffles off into the velvet gloom without saying thank you. As I return to my suitcase I try to recall what car Galbraith drives. A Saab, I think.

I see its headlights before I hear its engine. They cast an arc of yellow on the warehouse wall at the far end of the avenue. Jenny must have missed the first turning off the main road and found the second. I see the fleeting silhouette of the man in the blanket before Jenny passes him. I straighten my back. It is time she and I confronted a few truths. Her headlights are on full beam and though she must see me shielding my eyes against their glare she does not dip them. Nor does she slow down. Thinking she can't have seen me I wave both arms. But the rhythmic padding of the tyres over the cobbles gets faster.

I pick my suitcase up and run, making it to the corner before her. She has to decelerate to take it. The main road is about thirty metres away and I've covered half the distance by the time Jenny catches up with me. Realizing the suitcase is slowing me down, I throw it in her path. She swerves to avoid it and scrapes along the wall of the warehouse for a few metres before braking. Looking back over my shoulder, I see her reverse and lurch forward again.

On the main road, approaching from the left, are some headlights. As I sprint towards them I take in the grey hulk of a lorry. It has the *London Times* crest on its side. A stitch is searing my stomach and my lungs feel like they're being scalded. I've almost reached the road when Jenny catches up with me again. This time I have no choice but to dive to the side – and my momentum keeps me rolling until I reach the safety of the fence. My face is so close to the tyres as they crunch past, I feel a spray of grit on my cheeks.

I look up in time to see the Saab plunge into the side of the lorry and bounce back like a pin ball. The scream of buckling metal, braking tyres and shattering glass is sickening. The lorry jack-knifes, whips the Saab with its tailgate and drags it twenty metres down the road before coming to rest in the forecourt of a Texaco garage.

For a few seconds I just stare at the wreckage, trying to catch my breath. The silence tightens around me again, even thicker than before. When I lever myself up, using the fence for support, the movement makes me gasp in pain. The whole of my right side feels bruised and my hip-bone feels like it might actually be chipped. I gag, stay doubled up for a moment and then limp in the direction of the lorry. The tarmac feels soft underfoot.

When I'm about ten metres from the garage I stop. The Saab has been crushed. Jenny couldn't have survived the impact. Did the airbag inflate? What if she is paralysed? I blink but do not move any closer.

I could look after her . . . I could feed her, read her stories, brush her hair.

No. The car is compressed almost beyond recognition. I put my hands to my ears to block out the chatter of my thoughts, the lorry makes a hissing sound and I notice liquid, coloured orange by the street lamps, snaking across the road towards me. Petrol. Circulating in my head now, fragmented questions and answers. Why didn't Jenny stop when she saw me? The accelerator must have been jammed. But she stopped and started again. How pathetic a man in denial can be. I know why I can't bear to think she is dead. Is she? Is she dying? I could hold her as she dies. No one should die on their own.

I shiver. Feeling winded and empty, I take a step backwards. I take another step, turn and run. I don't look over my shoulder once as I run down the Highway towards Tower Bridge, my legs and arms pumping hard, my bruised hip forgotten. It can't take me more than ten minutes to reach the north side of the bridge and when I do I double up again, holding my sides. The lining of my throat has turned to sandpaper. I fumble in my jacket for a cigarette, light up with trembling fingers and hold the smoke down until I feel dizzy.

My suitcase. The gun.

I can't go back for it. I check my watch. Seeing the yellow light of a black cab approaching the south side of the bridge I wave both arms.

'Heathrow,' I pant at the silver-haired driver before opening the door and collapsing on to the back seat. I'm drenched in sweat and

I can see the driver eyeing me suspiciously through his rear-view mirror. Is he judging me for leaving the scene of an accident? No. No one can connect me to it, yet.

'You look terrible, mate,' the driver says, his neck wobbling as he turns in his seat.

I take my jacket off, roll up my sleeves and check my jacket pocket for my plane ticket, my Multicard and my photograph of Emily. I have Jenny's ticket with me as well. How do I explain that? She was supposed to come with me, I will say if the police stop me. I waited for her but she never showed up so I assumed she was making her own way to the airport. Thankfully, Sarah has arranged her own ticket. Having two on me would have been overly suspicious.

'You all right, mate?'

I try to focus on the driver but my thoughts are blurred. I feel giggly, breathless, hysterical. I lower the window, press my face to the doorframe and feel revived a little by the cool, rushing air. I look across the Thames to the red neon of the OXO Tower but I can't really make sense of it. The lights along the Embankment are with us. There is no other traffic on the road. Except the flashing blue light ahead. An ambulance hurtles past in the direction of the crash. It is followed thirty seconds later by a fire engine. Neither has its siren on.

The driver is narrowing his eyes at me again through the mirror. 'Here,' he says. 'You're that bloke in the paper, aren't you?' He holds up a copy of the English People. My byline photograph covers the top half of the front page. The headline says: 'TOP JOURNALIST IN MI5 PLOT.' I have to reread the headline several times before its meaning registers. I smile vaguely. At least they used a photograph of me that I like.

'You want to read it?'

I shake my head.

The cabby balances his spectacles on his nose without opening the arms and reads: 'Says here "Michael Yates, 40, was employed by MI5 to fabricate a story about an attempted coup."' He mutters as he reads on to himself and then looks up. 'Says here you're a drug addict...'

I stare at the bald patch on the crown of his head.

'Talkative, aren't you.' This is said under his breath.

'They're just trying to discredit me,' I say eventually.

'What's it all about, then?'

'Have you got a copy of the *London Times* there?'

He perks up at this. 'No, mate. That's what I normally read. For some reason it hadn't arrived at the newsagent's I usually go to. So I got the *People* instead. Funny thing that. You being on the front page. Is it true, then?'

I can't answer. I don't know the answer. And shock has dulled my responses. In a trance I tap out seventeen numbers on my mobile. 'Ed? What's the hold up?'

'Christ, Mike. It's been a nightmare. The computers crashed at the printers. They think they've got it sorted out now but it looks like someone virused us . . . Hello? Mike? Are you there? . . .'

'Yes, I'm here.'

'It was Tenant. Have you seen the front page of the *People*?'

'Yes. Can't we virus him?'

'We've tried. He's got some virus block in operation.'

'The Jennifer Vaccination.'

'The what?'

'It doesn't matter.'

'Anyway, Mike, don't worry. Our friends are about to close down Tenant's plant. Security alert. It'll be mid-morning before his presses are running again.'

'Jenny's dead . . . I think she's dead.'

'What?'

'I'll call you from the airport.' The mobile slips out of my hand and lands on the floor.

'Who did you say was dead?' the cab driver asks. I ignore him.

Before we turn towards Trafalgar Square, I see for an instant the asymmetrical skyline of the Palace of Westminster. Its neo-Gothic façade is floodlit and mellow – frozen music as someone once described it. The driver's lips are still moving but I can no longer hear what he is saying. I look up at Lord Nelson. The reason his head and shoulders are always free from pigeon shit, I've heard, is that a weak electrical current runs up the full length of the column. Birds are not similarly discouraged from perching on the new bronze of the PM which now occupies a plinth in the square.

His Caesar fringe is almost white.

A London Times van pulls up alongside a news-stand in the square. I ask my cab driver to stop for a minute. The van's hazard lights come on. A man jumps out, opens the back and drags a bundle of newspapers on to the ground. I lean forward in my seat to try and see the headline on the top copy: BASTARDS!

As we turn down into Whitehall I see there are three monolithic shadows parked in front of the Ministry of Defence and Ethical Justice building: Challenger IV tanks delivered early for today's parade. They are shrouded in green and black canvas, only their gun turrets exposed.

We drive past the Cenotaph and I take in the plaque which marks the spot where the PM fell. It, too, is covered in pigeon shit. My thoughts get louder. Pigeons exist in the moment alone. Chatter, chatter, chatter. We, self-conscious beings, are bound by time, the before and after a constant consideration.

'Why do you reckon the Dufflecoat did it, then?' the cabby asks, nodding at the plaque.

'I thought I knew _ Maybe he was just bored.'

'Eh?'

Jenny. I try to analyse my feelings. Revulsion at the randomness of her fate. Pity. But no regret. The beauty of her face dims as I try to picture it – like the giant spider that is said to shrink in front of the patient being cured of arachnophobia.

'Not much traffic,' the cabby says. 'Should only take us half an hour to the airport from here.'

Half an hour before I'm with Sarah. What I feel most is relief. My bones ache with tiredness, but the trembling in my arms and legs has stopped. I weigh Jenny's ticket in my hand. It's too heavy. As I tear it down the middle, my thoughts fall silent. I tear the two halves into four, the four into eight and the ticket feels lighter. I hold my hand out of the window, close my eyes and let the pieces slip from my fingers.